THE TINY CRAWLWAY
WAS AS WIDE AS A KING'S HALL

Had they kept going straight from the hole by the river, they would have found the next door. But they were moving to the right, and she did not know how far they had gone in the pitch black. In fact, she was not even sure which way they were currently heading. The horrible noises behind them had seemed to change direction.

Jiana began to feel the oppression of millions of tons of rock pressing down on her. She had terrifying visions of being buried alive in the blackness by a sudden cave-in caused by the movements of whatever was behind them. With every beat of her heart it got closer, and the shaking grew worse. She could clearly hear a sound like a baby sucking on its fist.

She surged and lunged forward, not letting go of Dida, though he was like a wet sack of cornmeal. And then, there was a rocky wall in front of her. There was nowhere left to crawl.

Dafydd ab Hugh

Or,
How He Wound Down
the World

*For Joan Jett and Amy Madigan,
and other Real-Life Jianas.*

HEROING

Copyright © 1987 by Dafydd ab Hugh

"Questflowers" © 1987 by Vani Bustamante

A Baen Books Original

Baen Publishing Enterprises
260 Fifth Avenue
New York, N.Y. 10001

First printing, October 1987

ISBN: 0-671-65344-X

Cover art by Larry Elmore

Printed in the United States of America

Distributed by
SIMON & SCHUSTER
1230 Avenue of the Americas
New York, N.Y. 10020

Questflowers

a face conceals itself
from itself
a mask is the truest guise.
I went on swordquest and discovered
only flowers of the mind

I bloom and know myself
I bloom and lose myself
dead blooms litter my path

a mirror brings me
almost home
there is no winter of the mind

I bloom
again, again

—Vani Bustamante

Chapter 1

A Prince Returns; a Warrior is Rebuffed; Great Journeys Begin with a Single Cup

-1-

Jiana fished another dirty coin out of her pouch and paid the tea-master; her comrade seemed not to notice the man's outstretched hand and imperious throat-clearing.

"So fish—sho finish your shtory," she slurred, impatient. The other listeners grunted and poked at Dilai until he set his cup down and continued.

"Right. So Alanai returns to Bay Bay, having slain the vicious grybbyn, with its claws like onyx poinards and its teeth like alabaster daggers.

"The crowds gather—they sprout faster than spring-weeds! They stare at the great prince as he rides into the city, victory-proud, dripping blood and casting favors like they were rose petals."

Dilai, you must be destitute, Jiana reasoned. *Thus you are now the storyteller of the Severed Ear.* He flipped his long, silky, perfumed hair from his eyes with a practiced grace. Jiana watched him dispassionately; she felt no desire for him anymore.

Suddenly he leaned over and emptied the last two pitch-

ers of strongtea he had drunk into the bronze pot at the
end of the bench. His audience edged toward the other
end of the table, and grumbled impatiently.

A Lord of the City, Jiana thought, curling her lip in
disgust. But she poured him another cup, for Dilai's tongue
tended to loosen as he drank—as Jiana well knew from the
month of nights they had spent together. He sipped the
tea and waited, requiring more than just wet lips and a
burning throat this time. Finally, she sighed and found
another coin for him; it was her last. He smiled and
resumed his tale.

"The children run along the roads and alleys like ivy,
creeping over walls and entwining trees and lampposts.
Soldiers swagger and boast in the streets: 'I was there! I
saw the great beast fall! I struck a blow when His
Serpentinity lost his footing and stumbled!' Ho! So many
claim a blow in the bloodletting that one would think
Prince Alanai was accompanied by half the royal guard of
Bay Bay, rather than a mere seven stalwart companions, as
advertised."

To the others at the table, the news was old; they had
been there, and had seen for themselves. But Jiana had
been in jail at the time, and had missed the glorious
return of His Avian Majesty to Bay Bay, the Floating City,
the prince's eyrie. She had killed again, this time a City
Lord; and though the court had agreed with her that it was
self-defense, still they had sentenced her to two less-
moons in prison (that being the going rate for innocence in
Bay Bay).

Jiana swallowed another cup of strong-tea and brooded.
The man had been her employer; with his death she was
out of a job. Few men in the city would hire a woman for
her sword—most especially a woman who had slain her
master, however unwanted his advances.

But at least the incident had brought her momentarily
closer to Dilai: it was his father she had killed, and as soon
as the palace accountants figured out the death tax, he
would inherit both his father's lands and his titles.

"Ah, it is indeed a grand sight!" said a shipwright, across
the charred oak table from Jiana. She blinked and shook

her head. What was Dilai saying? She had no idea. He continued his story.

"Net fishers arrive, breathless from the docks; their sandals flap wet and their hair reeks of brine. Eighty lantern bearers and two hundred torch-lighters caper and illumine the streets and canals, though it is nearer noon than night! It seems as clear in my mind as if it were only yesterday."

"Dilai, it *wash* only yeshterday." Jiana refilled his tea-cup, killing off the last pot. She shook her head as he sipped it. *How do you do it, my erstwhile lover? How do you drink so much without staggering and slurring, my little swine? More reasons for me to feel inferior.* But she said nothing, not trusting her own drunken tongue or grizzled temper. She assumed she was the drunkest one at the table, Dilai included. *So what? So what the hell are you all looking at? Haven't you ever seen someone on a tear before?* But it embarrassed her anyway.

"Ah, of course. Only yesterday—but tomorrow and next year it shan't be, and I shall still tell this same tale! I remember, I recall: even the bleary-eyed drunks in the tearooms and alehouses stagger out into the streets, and actually refrain from vomiting or falling off the floats into the ocean until the prince is well past and out of sight!

"The crowd mobs Alanai's flanks, catching his pennies and serpents and striving for a brush of his garments, a thread from his robe. They certainly agree there is no prince princelier. The ministers and the gentry, they grin numbly and agree, for they remember betrayals discovered and families taken hostage. Sacrifice is offered, he to his Eagle, we to our Serpent.

"Aye, truly the prince is back. He is victorious; he is loved; he is feared! There's to be a grand parade tomorrow."

Jiana let her head fall onto her arms, just for a moment. Thoughts whirled in her stomach—thoughts of princes, kings, queens, knights, ladies, heroes, pirates, highwaymen, rebels, magicians, witches, monster-hunters . . . and of the slate grey life led by out-of-work mercenaries and unremembered adventurers. Just for a moment!

When she opened her eyes, years had passed. It was dark, and she was alone. Dilai and her four former comrades in arms had left her in the Severed Ear Tavern and Teahouse, with the bill. When the tea-master returned, she could not settle the charge, of course; instead, she doubled him over with a fist in his gut, apologized softly, and fled the tavern. *Another room where I can never show my face*, she thought; but it could not be helped. Jiana was now as broke as Dilai.

The night was cloudy and black, and in her condition, she almost fell into the water four times on the way home.

Once, it was told, the Floating City had been built entirely on land. Centuries of expansion and an uninhabitable desert on its shore-side had driven Bay Bay into the sea.

To Jiana, from far to the east, it was a dream and a nightmare. The blocks were great, wooden floats upon which buildings were built, and the streets were pontoon bridges connecting them. Thin boards lay between the smaller blocks, where a street was considered unnecessary; these were the alleys. A thief could float in the oily, freezing sea, nearly all underwater, waiting to seize the feet of a passing merchant. But only at a price, for sharks and venomous skeeniks prowled the shallows under the city, waiting for just such a treat as an unwary footgrab.

The clouds were heavy and black, and in the absence of starlight and moonshine, the city's ten thousand lanterns reflected fire red in the water, transforming Bay Bay into a jumble of islands in an ocean of lava. The seas were choppy, despite the great breakwater, and the streets and buildings surged beneath Jiana's feet, making her stumble like she had the palsy pox. People scurried out of her way as she staggered, swore, and raged like a maddened pirate.

She burst through the door of the Dog's Tongue Tavern, her temporary home, and bolted up the stairs two at a time, just to show she could do it. She stumbled on the last step, then wrenched open the door to her room.

Tawn lay diagonally on the bed, reeking of ale and snoring as loudly as the grybbyn that Alanai had allegedly slain.

For a time she looked down at him, vainly trying to find the tenderness that had once dwelt in her heart for Lucky Tawn. He was rough and tall, and his blond hair was cropped close. He spoke like a thrown spear, thought as deeply as a warhorse, and was reasonably straight with most friends.

"Get up," she ordered, kicking him awake.

"Wha—why? Where're you? Out boozhing, I . . ." He fell back, muttering incoherently. Now it was she who was sober in comparison, and her bile rose at the scene she must have caused in the Severed Ear.

"Get up. A stinking grybbyn. A goddamn stinking lousy bloody grybbyn! Tha's all he did, jus' kill a freaking grybbyn! With jus' a little, tiny, eensy-peensy bit of destruction of the s'rounding countryside . . . jus' a tad!"

"Who? Wa'sh happenig? Wha's up?"'

"Tawn, I don't know what's up. It ain't me, though. I gotta quit this lousy, stinking business, being a hero. I mean, who cares? No one wants the real thing anymore. No one wants heroism for the shake—for the sake of action, for jus' *doing* something, for Serpent's sake! It's all so damn mercenary and ulittle—*utilitarian* now." Jiana stared at her pitiful pile of possessions, the cumulative total of ten years of adventures, wars, and duels to the death.

"Look at me. I've scaled snowy mountains five miles high, fleeing the fearful Flower Emperor himself! Demon-goats in the terrible Tarn, they said. . . . I tramped for weeks through burned, sun-bleached, blasted lands, hearing the trumpets of the dead by day and the cries of the damned by night—and I caught them! I killed two, and drove the others from the land! And the bastards laughed, and said they were only hill goats whose bodies had been burned in a brushfire."

She sat down heavily on the floor beside Tawn and cracked her knuckles, distracted by her broken yesterdays.

"I buried a certain mad little girl once. I thought she was dead. I thought these hunts and adventures were for joy and boldness alone. But I want something more; she still drives me, I'm sure of it. Maybe she's risen anew, like a barrow wight, and seized control of—"

Tawn struggled up to a sitting position, and began pawing at her limply.

"Hey, Ji—ya wanna you-know-what?"

"Get your hands off me," she said. "I wandered from the point. Look, deed for deed, between me and that bastard bird-prince, *I* am the stronger, *I* am the bolder! But I'm no one, and everyone remembers Alanai.

"Who knows me? Who sings for me? Who lights lanterns and torches, and capers?" Jiana let her head fall, suddenly dizzy. She ground her hands against her tightly shut eyes until she saw sparks.

"I hate this place. I hate you. I don't have any money."

There was no response. When she looked at Tawn, she discovered he had passed out again.

"I broke out of the impress—the impurge—how do you say it? The im-preg-na-ble fortress of Bay Din once, years ago. Far underground, I felt something monstrous pass by me, but I guess I was too tiny for it to notice. At that very moment, a voice I thought long stilled whispered in my stomach. It whispered a song—a horrid song I never thought to hear again." Tawn snored faintly.

"Do you wanna you-know-what? Okay, it goes like this:

"Sing a song of syrup,
Sing a Lifeless horse;
A hangman lost his stirrup . . ."

She stopped, thoughts tumbling around and around in her stomach so quickly she could not follow them herself.

"All right, Tawn, you win. Tomorrow I'll get us some food, even if I have to steal it." She rolled him off the bed and fell asleep.

In the morning, Jiana fled the room before Tawn awoke. She sought the distraction of the prince's great parade, following it by the blaring trumpets and howling populace.

She walked the rolling streetwalks with one hand over her mouth and nose, for a horrible odor had moved into Bay Bay during the night and set up a bivouac. It was as if the Nameless Slithering One Himself had turned up for the triumph of the Feather Prince.

"What the hell is this stink?" she demanded of a netfisher, who swaggered drunken along the heaving wooden board with an ease that made Jiana jealous.

"Yaal, it bay the shoretonies," he drawled. "Once't or

twace a yar t'ey swum in t't'e Bay in sach numbers t'ot t'ey ate up awl t'e food, or samet'ing, and t'ey awl die in t'e waiter. T'an, t'ey sot to stank up t'e place like bay! Ain't she a lavely odour, t'ough?"

Jiana gagged and marched on, timing her footsteps to the motions of the float with fair success. No one else seemed to mind the odor very much, though they joked about it. Shoretonies, they all agreed. Jiana hated the slimy little fish, though she had never even eaten one.

The great royal army rode its horses along the same path taken by the House of the Eagle, Alanai's line, every coronation day for four hundred years. In the taverns and teahouses, the thieves of Bay Bay called it the Golden Trail, and for a month after it was used, they could all live like Eagles themselves, owing to the generosity of unwary spectators.

The parade wound snakelike across the tops of the waves toward the King's Causeway, strutting gingerly along those streets and squares that could bear the weight of so much horse and human flesh. At times, the five hundred men were insects crawling down the middle of a vast road of shops and mansions. Then, on turning a corner and stepping onto another floating pier, they were only a hoof's width away from the green, clutching sea, choked with the bodies of a million dead shoretonies.

Jiana guessed the route they would take, and scurried across a dozen narrow alleys to beat them to the causeway.

The parade rounded a corner, marching in broken-step. There was none of the precision marching that they practiced so diligently on the prince's training fields on solid ground; the combined force of a single step of five hundred horses might splinter the street and plunge the entire government into the shoretonie burial waters.

The din was great, but Jiana could still hear her pulse pounding in her ears. Fires, flares, rockets, banners, silks, gilt and silver, jewels, mirrors, and brilliantly dyed clothes filled the street and exploded through the Slaughtering Square.

Black-haired, black-clad, Jiana sidled up close to the stall of the black-hearted butcher, while the fat, gouty old man hollered and screamed. "Long live His Royal Majesty! The Feathered One bless Prince Alanai!" *That tears it,* she thought. *The pig of a butcher is an Eagle.* Her feelings of guilt vanished like smoke in the wind.

The prince waved condescendingly at the butcher, so it seemed. While the old man worked himself into a frenzy of patriotism, Jiana reached across his counter and seized the biggest roast she could see. She hid it behind her, and backed nonchalantly out of the stall's enclosure.

Jiana, the great warrior! sneered the voice of the Tormentor, within her stomach. *Savagely braving capture and death in the face of overwhelming odds.* For a moment, she considered throwing the beef into the sea to feed the skeeniks, but hunger won out over pride. She stuffed it into her bag, slung it over her shoulder, and slipped away unseen to the Dog's Tongue.

Tawn had just awakened.

"Well, well, the mighty provider!" He smiled a crooked grin, his teeth biting his lower lip. Once she had found it breathtaking, but now it just reminded her of a dead shoretonie.

"Here. Eat and choke on it." Jiana dropped the carcass on the floor in front of Tawn. "Appreciate it. I had to fight two devils and a feathered demon-prince to get it."

"Two what? Are you on about that still?"

"Shame and Guilt, and their flighty liege-lord, Prince Pity himself. But I roused the fortunate alliance of the Lizard King, Desperation, and liberated the leg of cow anyway."

Tawn just scratched his head, and fell to on the cold roast like a prince devouring an unlucky grybbyn . . . *which, after all, had only been doing its job by ravaging the countryside,* she thought.

Children still starve, and battles still rage. Men slay their wives for suspected adulteries, and the scales and feathers strike the great down in their prime. Ministers and princes still sell their offices for a coin, except for Lord Stupidity, who reigns with an iron foot stuck in a mouth of filth.

"What change?" sneered Jiana, as Tawn wolfed his portion of the meat and some of hers. "Just a slight diminution in the grybbyn population. You know what I heard, o weak-stomached one? The forest of the erstwhile grybbyn is still deserted, for now the foolish farmers have convinced themselves it's haunted by a grybbyn ghost! And for this, *he* gets a parade." Tawn grunted in reply, oblivious to all but his meat.

Suddenly, Jiana had to burst out the door and flee down the stairs, skipping every other step in her haste to get somewhere, anywhere, without Tawn. She wanted no one to see her like that, with her stomach filled by a greedy, gory godling she thought she had slain in her little days.

Eight weeks passed, and grybbynmania slowly waned, along with the stink of the swiftly decaying shoretonies. Jiana adjusted, as she had to the other wild ways of these strange people on the western coast. A hundred days' ride to the east was White Falls, New River, where she had been born. The tiny town had its own share of the strange and surreal, she supposed, though it was a familiar surreality. In Bay Bay, the fog days had begun, and every day was shrouded until noon. Jiana remained anonymous, and still returned to Tawn at night. She advertised as a sword instructor and cut her hair, casting the strands into the blood-black waters at midnight, just to see if a shambling thing could be summoned.

"Who wants to be taught by a woman?" snapped once-carefree Dilai, his black silk hair already turning grey as he tried to manage his father's estate. He was right. Jiana and Tawn had to move from their inn to a cheaper one, jutting out against the cruel ocean like the stubborn, last tooth in an ancient grandmother's mouth.

That very day riders arrived, breathless, from Bay Din principality. They rode straight to the palace, on the mainland, without even stopping to water their horses or announce their business in the tearooms. They spoke privately with the Eagle, claimed the rumors, and then fled back to Bay Din without raveling the mystery.

Temple attendance doubled. "What's it be? What comes?" cried the societies of waves and sand. Feeling the tension and fear in the briny air, Jiana began to walk with a lighter step and wider eyes—excitement! opportunity! She was told of eerie possibilities, all bearing the verification of a friend of a friend: An entire county of sea-sorcerers in the South! A kingdom razed and a goddess imprisoned in the East! A land-ship of lost souls, plying the hills and deserts and seizing citizenry in the North! Merchants laughed, but mystics warned, and only the courtesans saw real profit from the frustrations and anxieties of the leading citizens.

At high noon on the last day of the ninth week since the grybbyn-kill, the boards and bills sprang up like summer flowers in the market maze:

WANTED!
Heroes! Paladins! Myrmidons!
wanted by H.A.M. Prince Alanai!
Willing to Travel a MUST!
Fame! Fortune!
Blessings of Eagle and Serpent Both!
Apply Swine and Cheese Tavern tomorrow morn,
to be interviewed by the Prince.

Jiana shook her empty purse, visions of carnage swimming through her mind's eye. Yet still she was undecided . . . keeping on was so easy.

"Yo! Jiana!" yelled Dilai from across the square. "How fine to see you. And how are you and Tawn this while?"

At once she made up her mind.

-2-

Jiana screened the sun with her hand and tried to guess how long she had been standing in line, rocking slowly up and down like the pendulum on the Great Clock. She had been there ever since sunup, and it seemed nearly noon, though she couldn't be sure in the middle of winter, when the sun passed so far south. Taking an odd turn, as was customary for Bay Bay, the clouds had lifted and the air begun to swelter. *Of course, if it were summer*, she thought, *there would be rain and chilly winds*.

Again she stepped out of line and leaned against the flimsy sea railing, straining to see a terminus—a door, a building, *anything* marking an end to the waiting. The line had not moved from the last time she had looked, nearly twenty heartbeats ago; but then, neither had it moved all morning.

She turned back, and the crowd had closed up behind her again.

"Damn you!" she barked. "You did it again!"

"Into the ocean wit' you!" yelled a swaggering young "soldier" who reeked of smoked meats and tanning fluid. "You tryin' to cut line, skirt?"

Jiana looked him over. His clothes were new, and his sword was unscarred. He was surely a tanner's boy who had run off to join the adventure.

She put her hand on her knife, looking as dangerous as she could.

"I shall gladly cut line. I'll cut *your* line so short you'll have to stick your hands down your throat to piss! Now move *back!*"

"Awwww, fat'er told me never ta hit a woman." He backed up, his face whiter by a shade than before. A little knot of people in front and behind grumbled, but they reluctantly made room for her to get back in.

There had been no wars in the Water Kingdom in a score of months. Jiana counted on her fingers, and arrived at the grim conclusion that every soldier, adventurer, or sellsword in Bay Bay would be in as bad a fiscal situation as was she, no matter how frugal he was or how great his severance pay.

And it seemed that every one of them and his brother and cousin had materialized for the recruitment.

And like a fool, she thought, *I spent my night in a teahouse, thinking that sunup would be early enough to arrive!*

Another group of palace guards suddenly rowed up to the street in a little boat, as they had thrice before that morning.

"Again?" Jiana howled, incredulous. "*Again?*" The Eagles began pushing her part of the line down an alternate street, over a rickety board of an alley, and into the end of another line a block away. Jiana and the rest of the line began hooting and spitting at the royals, but they paid her no mind. They trotted off back to their boat with the air of busy carpenters who had already fallen far behind.

"The hell with it!" Jiana said out loud. She turned to the young tanner behind her: "Hey, snakeskin, I'm popping out for a drink. Save my place, hunh?"

For a moment he was nonplussed, and then a crafty look seized his eye.

"Certes, skirt. I mean, lady. Take as lang as you like! Be here I will, certes!" He smiled, ineffectively trying to charm her.

"Thanks, o ravisher of porcine beauties." His brow lowered as he tried to assimilate what she had said, but she left without waiting for a reply.

Jiana stepped to the edge of the wooden street and climbed onto the railing, which creaked and complained ominously. She stretched and leapt outward, barely catching hold of a spar that supported the nearby building. She looked down into oily ocean, and then back at the crowd still in the useless line. They were all watching her, expectantly.

"That's entertainment," she muttered, then climbed hand over hand up the slanted board until she reached the wall of the Curdled Lobster, a bed & board whose height dominated the northwest section of the Floating City, past the Garrison Bridge. The Lobster rose a full four stories above the sea, with the lodging rooms in the top half. Jiana had heard that in the winter, when the waves broke as rough as the prince's horse dragoons, the inn economized greatly on food. Everyone was too sick to eat.

The side of the building presented a challenge, but by planting her feet against a wooden trim and lying back against the rain gutter, she scaled her way to the roof. The final two stories had windows, which made excellent ladders.

The crisp salt wind at the top refreshed her. She studied the city, floating far below. Like a bear climbed high in a tree studying a river, she tracked the course of the line up and down the streets and across the pontoon alleys, over the surging blocks and under the bridges whose foundations were driven deep into the subaqueous silt. At last, it wound back by devious ways to join itself again, like a headless serpent.

Jiana grinned, in spite of her anger at the trick.

"I make it a point," she said, "to never do as the rest. And now that I think, it makes sense. Is there an Eagle in Bay Bay who would deign to interview ten thousand Serpents and foreigners to fill a mere handful of slots? But where . . ."

She searched carefully, trying to make sense of the unfamiliar aerial view of the city to deduce where the real recruitment took place. At last she saw a likely candidate: the Dancing Bull Tea Emporium. It was the most expensive establishment in the Garrison Bridge quarter, surrounded by cheap and decent alehouses and fleshrooms— thus, ordinary mercs and knifemen avoided it like worms or ring-eye. And Jiana could see it was almost at the heart of the great knot of people the guards had tied.

"But now," she wondered, "how am I to arrive?" Bay Bay was not built as an ordinary city. She could not simply walk across to the Dancing Bull, unless she could stand like a peering-fish on the top of the water. And naturally, the streets themselves were impassable, for they were clogged with so many angry, frustrated, starving, armed bid-blades that the floats had nearly sunk under the sheer weight of organized violence. There were many sopping wet feet, and every now and then a barely audible scream as someone lost his footing and fell to feed the skeeniks.

But a mere fifteen feet from her, there stuck up out of the next building a grand flagpole, strung with many fish kites and a line leading down to the lower roof. From there, a strong and lucky woman could leap from roof to roof and land finally on the Dancing Bull itself.

For many long heartbeats she eyed the first jump.

"Damn me," Jiana finally whispered. "Why couldn't I have been taller? Lithe, graceful . . . My *mother* was thin, my *brother*—" She snarled and shook her head, dismissing the woulds and wishes. "Hell, I'm a bear, a fat, black bear. I'd better aim for the pole, not try like a flying monkey to snag the line." She stepped back and, with a running start, her heart in her throat, powered off the roof, aiming toward the thick wooden pole itself.

She aimed well, and it punched her like a Flower-rider's lance, smashing her nose and bruising her ribs. She managed to wrap all four limbs around it, and slowly, painfully slide to the ground, taking the flags with her. Only a few splinters managed to penetrate her thick, black-leather jerkin. She rejoiced that her willpower had held and she had worn it, despite the heat. Jiana sneezed violently a dozen times before she was able to continue, and her nose still throbbed. The rest of the route seemed tame by comparison, though a single short jump would have plunged her into waters still icy despite the heat of the land.

Finally, she leaned far out over a roof and stretched out one gauntleted hand. It caught on an ornamental pig head, and she swung across the gap to the other roof. Jiana was on top of the Dancing Bull.

She pressed her palms against the sloping, oaken roof, and crawled into the shade near a smoke vent. She sat still, panting with the unaccustomed exertion.

You're fat, Jiana-Bear, her inner voice whispered.

"Non . . . nonsense . . . always . . . always been stocky."

That isn't muscle, silly. It's fat! When did you last step on board of a scales? She shook her head and ignored the voice.

Suddenly, she heard a voice—a living voice. It was far away and metallic. She finally realized it came from the vent above her head. She cocked her head to listen.

"Why have you come? What want you of me?"

The voice was cold and imperious, like beaten gold. Jiana wondered whose it was—Alanai himself, or just another royal relative?

The second voice sent a shiver of fear through her body. She stiffened involuntarily, as if she had heard the pad of an assassin's feet. The voice was death.

"I knew you could not be ahead in the line, Your Grace. There was no other place you could be, Sire." The honorifics were uttered with exaggerated sincerity, and Jiana heard them as mockeries. But Alanai—it had to be him—heard only acknowledgment of his sovereignty.

"So you realized that was not the true line! Splendid, sir knight. You passed the test of cleverness."

What cleverness to figure that? Jiana thought. *Sure, the Prince of the Floating City himself, personally interview-*

ing five thousand scruffy warriors! The only trick was where to find him. Who knows how many aleshops this voice searched before coming to the Dancing Bull? But then she remembered that she herself had spent the whole morning in that same line . . .

She slipped a bit suddenly, and grabbed for the vent to hold herself up. It creaked ominously, but held her weight.

"Tell me your name, if you will, sir. How are you called?"

"Hraga si Traga," answered the dead voice through the vent. "I hide my face from none, and my name is open to all."

"Sir Hraga, I like you! I like a man such as you, and can see you being a great asset to my quest. Never has my farsight led me astray."

Hraga si Traga said something quietly that Jiana could not hear. She leaned farther into the vent, balancing ever more precariously.

"Nobly spoken. But perhaps you will think again, when you hear what it is we shall stand against. We seek nothing less than the Last Dream of the Sleepers, the First Men. We quest for the World's Dream of the Ti-Ji Tul. And against us shall stand every army of chaos, destruction, and evil left in the world!"

Without warning, Jiana's feet slipped on the oak. For a moment, she teetered on the edge of a nasty plunge to the street or the sea. Then, by sheer luck, she seized the lip of the vent and steadied herself, but she made much more noise than she should have.

"It has been a long-moon since I returned from slaying the grybbyn, called Kagali; yet this tale stretches back much farther than that. Its roots lie in the mists of the days before Bay Bay, before the principalities, in the time of the Ti-Ji Tul, the First Men. As for myself, not a day has passed since, as a boy, I first crept unbidden into my father's sanctuary and studied his lead-bound grimoires, that I have not thought about this First Tale, and pondered how best I might finally complete it."

Jiana suddenly realized that this was too important to be left to her own lackluster memory. She balanced forward and fished around with her free hand to pull out some parchment, on which she had written the beginnings of a poem, and some charcoal. She began to take notes.

"Many ages ago, the World's Dream was lost. In that time, dreams were common, and each man was a Sleeper. Every man knew the value of his own. He cherished and nurtured it, and made it the identity around which his being could anchor, as he helped to carve the first great empire from the wilderness. With these dreams, he established civilization, and wrested mankind from a wandering barbarism, little different from that of beasts."

Jiana smirked, and bit her lip to avoid actually laughing.

"What dreams do men have, beyond the dream of wealth and position?" asked Hraga si Traga.

"Now, that is true. But it was not always so. In Ruiy Ouidn—of which Bay Din is a modern corruption, built on the very ashes of Ruiy Ouidn—there was a great scholar. Like many of that time, he concerned himself with dreaming. His name was O-onakai Tonaronakai, and he dreamed of the stars. He thought the lights to be far-off cities of the spirits they worshiped—and who knows? Perhaps he was right . . . stranger things have been found true. Men of science say the earth is but a ball that circles the sun, much as long and short moon circle the land."

On the roof, Jiana rolled her eyes. Such philosophies were as cheap as market-day vegetables. On the back of the parchment she scribbled furiously, as the prince continued the fey-tale.

"O-onakai Tonaronakai was no fool; he knew the stars were farther than the farthest corner of the Earth. They could only be reached by the combined dreams of all of the First Men.

"For many years, he labored to convince them of the worth of his own vision and, at last, his silver tongue swayed enough minds. All men came together on a great island, where now stands Oort, and they lent their dreams to his great task. He hammered them all together into a great sorcery—the World's Dream."

Hraga muttered something too soft for Jiana to hear through the vent. She squirmed closer, and again the slippery, greased roof betrayed her. The vent squealed in protest, but supported her.

"O, such arrogance—and such danger," Hraga si Traga mused. Again Jiana shivered, though she did not know why. Something indefinable in his voice made her feel the bony coils of death rustle about her breast. "For what if they were to lose it?" More and more, it seemed to Jiana as if Hraga was leading the prince on.

Alanai answered with a great sadness, almost as if he had been there himself when it had happened, but Jiana could feel nothing. It was a children's story, fit for a campfire on a picnic in White Falls.

"Indeed," Alanai continued, "lost it became. I know not how, yet. But since that day, all our dreams have been small and cold, unworthy of our promise as men.

"This, then, is my quest: I must find that Last Dream, and restore to us our visions!"

Silence reigned for several moments, except for the various armed men tramping about the room, rattling their armor. Finally, Hraga spoke, sounding as sincere as false dawn.

"It is good. I know little of such matters, but I know where I shall ever stand: at your side, Highness. Should you ask, I would follow you to the gates of the hell moon!" Jiana shook her head. For a moment, she was sure he said "allow you to the gates." But that made no sense.

"I knew you would, you are a good man, Master Hraga . . . perhaps better than you think yourself. But there will be others involved in this quest. Not all of them shall be mortals, nor every one an ally. Planets are aligning, as they have not since the very days of which I spoke. Now is the time for the final assault, for the World's Dream, once lost, is now located." His voice quieted.

Jiana leaned forward carefully, charcoal poised over the paper.

"So? then you have it!" Hraga seemed suddenly very eager.

"I said located, Master Hraga, not recovered! 'Twas done before I was even born, though none realized it at the time. It was only another entry in an already massive tome.

"Its corporeal form lies buried or drowned in mythic Door, far to the south of the lifeless Tarn, and even of the barbarous satrapy of Noon. The songs that tell how to control it are now in Bay Din, I believe.

"But now a curious tale has just come to my attention. Perhaps you took some note of the delegation from Bay Din that took audience with me?" Jiana snorted. Nothing else had been discussed in Bay Bay for days.

"Bay Din, as you may know, is currently held in despotic tyranny by a band of bandits who usurped the rightful less-prince of my own house, and seized control by villainy, treachery, and foulest murder. Long have been the cries and lamentations of the people, begging for deliverance!

"But always, it seemed the brigands led a charmed rule. Every scheme was discovered, every plot thwarted, and thus they remained in blasphemous possession of that most ancient and holy city . . . which was odd in itself."

"Ah, shall we ride then to liberate her?" Hraga had said nothing untoward, but the thirst for blood cried out from every word. Jiana swallowed, fearing the worst.

"Nothing so simple. This delegation represented those priests of that snake god who are still loyal to the true royal blood. They brought news that was at once disturbing and heartening. It seems they have discovered the source of the pretenders' power: Somehow, the Toradoras have a means of drawing upon the magick of the fabled World's Dream itself, distant though it lies. They must have the songs of its control, and by these it may be found."

Jiana shivered as the prince's voice took on a sudden tone of menace.

"These villains shall indeed have a pretty tale to tell."

A wave shook the creaking pilings supporting the Dancing Bull, and Jiana suddenly felt herself slipping, falling. She yanked on the vent, and with a horrible wrenching sound, it ripped from the roof, taking a score of shingles with it. She slid along the slanted roof and barely managed to grab the gutter, checking her fall.

"Like a cat, Ji!" she muttered. Realizing her compromising position, she hung on with one hand and jammed the parchment into her leather jerkin. She was barely in time, for the door of the Dancing Bull opened, and a soldier yelled, "ho, the roof! Down on the ground, yer bloody assassin!"

Wildly Jiana looked about her, wondering if she could pull herself up and flee across the rooftops. But then it occurred to her that so far, the only damage was to her pride as a silent, master warrior.

What the hell, she thought. *You wanted to get in to see the old fart anyway, didn't you?* Feeling a flush spreading over her face, she swung out and dropped in, landing on all fours on the street. It rocked violently, but she held on and did not fall, like a wallowing bear, into the frigid ocean. She stood and approached the main door.

A second royal bodyguard came out of the tearoom and stared at her.

"I'll be sheep-dipped," one of them said. "It's jus' a little boy! Yer father know yer—?"

He stopped and leaned forward to stare. His companion reached out and pulled Jiana's floppy, black hat from her head; she did not stop him. They both began to laugh and nudge each other. The first soldier took hold of her elbow and led her into the tavern.

"Yer Highness," he called. "Lookit the next *man* in line!" He shoved her roughly into the smoky, blistering interior, lit by the fire of a score of fuming torches. She continued to cough and choke for a few minutes, wondering how Prince Alanai could stand the smoke and the heat.

Jiana had never seen the prince before, yet as she blinked and the dimness gradually brightened, she knew it was he. He looked like a prince—regal, from boots to bonnet. His face had a grace about it that would have looked silly on a commoner.

For a moment, before she could see him clearly, she got the impression of an enormous, golden bird, but soon she saw it was only his cloth-of-gold shirt, with sleeves so wide they brushed the floor at his sides. Everything about him suggested nobility and imperial breeding. Even his boots were of imported southern leather. He smiled tolerantly at her.

"My, it seems we are discovered! What is the name of this pretty young thing?"

Jiana choked down her first response; one had to make allowances for certain people.

"Jiana of Bay Bay. Once of White Falls, New River." She took a deep breath. "I'd like to join your expedition, Your Highness."

The prince laughed, a hand on his stomach.

Suddenly, her attention was seized by a dark lump in the corner. It was a pale man, wearing black and grey. As she stared at him, she felt a tremor brush her heart. She knew immediately that he was Hraga si Traga.

If Death walked, She would look like you, Jiana thought. But strangely, there was nothing she could point at and say it was fearful. By pieces, he was a man, nothing more. In the whole, he reeked of the grave.

"By the Nameless Serpentine!" said Alanai, as he finished laughing. "I should call you 'Spunky'!" Jiana turned back to him, and her mouth dropped.

"Oh, Jiono, I should dearly like to take you along, if only to add some beauty to what will otherwise be a dreary crew! But it is too dangerous for a woman. We travel lightly, with great speed, and we shan't have time for a cooked meal or mended clothes!"

For a long time she looked at him. Then she smiled a predatory grin, and explained quietly and carefully.

"Highness, I care nothing for cooking or mending; I am a warrior." She touched her sword, Wave, wrapped around her waist. Alanai stared at it, then his face clouded.

"Is that a belt?" He leaned closer, squinting.

Jiana drew Wave partway, letting him see the whiplike, flexible steel with an edge sharp enough to sever a young tree with a single stroke.

"I think," said the prince sternly, "that that is far too dangerous a toy for you to play with. Perhaps you'd better give that to me and go home." He stepped forward, reaching for the sword.

Jiana jumped back, evading his grasp, but the prince persisted, lunging forward and grabbing wildly for the handle.

It was too much. With a moment to think, she might have reacted differently, but he moved on her too fast. Acting purely from instinct, she stepped in and drove her

fist upward from her hip into Alanai's solar plexus. His
face whitened in shock, and he crumbled to the ground,
trying to breathe.

The tavern was suddenly silent. The soldiers drew their
weapons. The captain of the guard looked especially grim
as he advanced on Jiana, sword toward her chest.

"Striking His Serpentine Majesty is treason," remarked
Hraga si Traga, conversationally. "It seems somebody made
a rather serious mistake." He looked pointedly at the
guard-captain, and smiled in anticipation.

"It was a mistake you will never forget, my lady," said
the soldier, without a trace of mercy in his voice.

-3-

Jiana twisted out of the way of the captain's first thrust,
dodged the second, and dived for the ground to avoid the
third, then rolled out under their feet and across the
room. She snapped Wave from her belt-sheath, and tried
to still her mind while the soldiers advanced.

"Better drop those weapons, you heathens, or prepare
to eat a yard of steel!"

The guards continued their attack unfazed. *Aw, hell,
Ji—always worth a shot, ain't it?* They advanced on her
and she gave ground, preparing a defense. Jiana calmed
her breath; her heart and stomach followed.

For many years, drifting around the world after leaving
White Falls, New River, Jiana had picked up fighting
styles haphazardly. When she finally studied in earnest,
across the ocean in the army of the Flower Emperor, she
had to unlearn everything, and offer her first master what
he called an 'empty cup,' into which he poured his ancient,
venerable, traditional wisdom.

She whirled Wave about her head like a riding whip. It
sang as the grass in a high wind, words the death-poet Ta
had captured: Joy-ee! Joy-ee! Die in steel, die in fire;
donate bile to the brothers of the hearth! In the Flower
tongue, the words sounded exactly like the wind-ringing of
a reed sword, such as Wave.

First step, she thought. *Check their weapons.*

The soldiers advanced cautiously, clutching their dull, bludgeonlike blades with two hands. Only the captain's sword respected delicacy. He used a thin fencing blade. It would be useless in a war, but he knew its efficacy against a lightly armed, unarmored woman. One man held a spear, but his stance branded him as a novice.

Hraga si Traga stood apart, without a weapon.

"Where's your sword, Hraga?" Jiana called out to him. "Did you let these men take it for your interview?"

"You got more than him to worry about, woman!" snarled the captain.

"I never carry one," said Hraga quietly. "It has never been necessary."

The prince still rolled on the ground gasping; barely thirty heartbeats had passed since her temper had erupted through her fist.

At once, the captain led with three successive stop-thrusts, and moved her back toward the wall. He would have driven her farther, but she took advantage of the youngest guard, moving behind him so that he and the captain tangled on his spear. She flicked her blade, and it bent into a graceful arc around the younger man to nick the captain, who leaped backwards in surprise. He withdrew, holding his cheek and staring at Wave.

"Is that a sword or a whip?" he asked. "Your blade's as flexible as a horsehair rope, yet it stings like a firebrand!" His accent was more like his prince's than like that of the common sergeant-at-arms. He was an officer, most likely a noble second or third son.

Jiana smiled—dangerously, she hoped.

"She's a wave, flowing over my enemies. She's a gift from a great god from across the ocean. Her birthplace was a house of the holy. And she's thirsty!" The boast was mostly true. Jiana had stolen Wave from an abandoned, black-and-yellow temple that was rightly rumored to be haunted. But who would care to hear the story in that form?

In the second assault, two of the men attacked together. It was a stupid mistake, as Jiana made sure they got in each other's way, and both withdrew blooded. Jiana finished with a showy swing about her head, and tried to snap the blade straight and rigid, as did the great blade-masters of the Flower Empire. But it wobbled noticeably . . . it was the most difficult basic maneuver to learn, and she had fled the land before mastering it, and thus the first sword set.

After two years, Jiana had left her first teacher. She relearned all of her dirty tricks from a real master, who did not believe in empty cups or tradition.

"A cup's for its contents," he roared. "I'm not so over-flowing with excess spirit-breath that I can keep filling up students like a Tjing Zao wine merchant!"

His great teaching was 'mutual kill': total commitment.

"Kaiiiii!" she screamed, and unexpectedly charged the guards. It would have worked against the younger men, but the seasoned captain retreated diagonally and kicked a stool in her path. She fell, and instantly the others were upon her.

The youngest royal bodyguard reversed his spear, and tried to thump her with the butt end. She rolled, then grabbed it and pulled him down next to her. She kicked him in the head and he fell back, groaning.

"Afraid to kill me?" she taunted, and used the young one as cover to rise to her knees, holding now the spear in her left hand and Wave in her right.

"Master Hraga!" gasped out Prince Alanai, still doubled over from her fist. "Join thee the fray and show us what thou'rt made of!"

Jiana wasted a moment noticing that when hard-pressed, the prince reverted to a more aristocratic mode of speech. Then she realized her mind was wandering.

The captain took her right flank, and another took her left. The youngest, now weaponless and half-unconscious, crawled as fast as he could to a demilitarized zone.

"My," said Jiana through clenched teeth, "how chivalrous you are! Such flowers of knighthood and nobility!" The verbal thrust was calculated; her second Teacher had always taught her to use every weapon she had, both physical and emotional. But the captain said nothing, and the other guard only laughed; honor was not taken as seriously in Bay Bay as in the Flower Empire. But where had Hraga si Traga gone? He had vanished from his corner.

The left flank struck, and she parried with the spear. Seeing this, the captain tried a lunge, but he was too late. Had they attacked in concert, she would have been skewered by one or the other. She parried and riposted, and the captain avoided injury only by an ungraceful backwards stumble. Left flank swung again, but she ducked his sword and stepped inside its range.

Suddenly, something as light as the wind encircled her throat and squeezed as tight as the jaws of a skeenik. It was a wire loop, thrown from behind her back. She clenched her neck, but it cut off her air nonetheless.

Hraga, she raged, *as surely as dogs howl!*

She whirled Wave about her head, and the blow which had been mere ornament two previous times severed the wire behind her. Then something struck her left elbow, numbing her hand; she dropped the spear.

"She's mine!" yelled another of the captain's men. He rushed in to finish her off, but she sidekicked him in the solar plexus and he dropped like a slaughtered bull, joining the youngest on the floor.

The kick had turned her, and she could see Hraga grinning, a silver-tipped baton in his hand. Her left hand still refused to work.

"You fight well," admitted the captain, "for a woman."

She charged him recklessly, crying the death song of the Tarn nomads, but before she had covered half the distance, something swept her feet out from under her and she fell again. This time, no one got in the captain's way, and he disarmed her with a vicious kick to her wrist. Too late, she realized she had fallen prey to the same sort of verbal attack she had tried on him.

She staggered up to her knees, holding her throbbing wrist with her still-numb left hand, and saw what had happened: The youngest guard was stunned, and could not stand . . . but he could pick up her dropped spear, and had used it to send her sprawling.

The remaining royal bodyguard grabbed her and stood her up before the white-faced prince, who still strained to breathe normally. He looked as though he had regained some of his charm and equanimity, though.

The captain gripped her midnight hair and yanked her

head back; the two others struggled up and pinioned her arms. Hraga si Traga sidled up beside her, but he was in the periphery of her vision, and she could not read his expression.

"Um, this might not be the best time to ask," Jiana said, "but could I possibly sign up for your quest now?" The youngest guard dropped her arm with a gasp. When she did not struggle further, the prince nodded at the others and they, too, let her go.

"You are young," said the prince, gasping out his words, "and as I said, you have spirit. I will not hold that to your disfavor today, for I praised that very quality earlier. Go home, Jiono of White River; go home to your family and heal your anger."

"Anger?" asked Jiana, ignoring the continued mangling of her name. "What are you *talking* about? You attacked me!"

"There is no shame in having been born a woman! There is no reason to be bitter and resentful, for we men need you. Without the fair sex, what beauty would there be in the world?"

Jiana sputtered, but caught herself in time. Seven armed people was too many to face while weaponless.

Go ahead, mocked a little girl's voice inside her. *Show us the great Jiana hero!*

The prince and his men let her stand and think for a few moments. Slowly, a plan began to form in her mind, a scheme for joining Alanai's quest . . . later. But the first step, she realized, was to leave the Dancing Bull without getting anything important sliced off.

"Go home to your husband," ordered the captain, "or to your mother."

"Yes, sir. I will, sir. That's a good idea sir . . . and I'll think very hard about what you said, Your Highness, Sir." She tried out her sincerest and most earnest look. Since it was what the prince expected, he accepted her groveling as genuine.

She held out her hand for Wave, but the captain shook his head, his lips pressed grimly together.

"Like His Highness said, that's too dangerous a toy for you to play with."

No deal, Jiana thought. True, she was no longer in danger of arrest and execution, if she left immediately. But she doubted she would ever pick up such a wonderful blade again, and she would fight with no other. The common weapon of the Water Kingdom was a knight's sword and shield, but they required more strength than even Jiana owned to wield effectively. It simply was not the weapon for a woman—even a strong, stocky one like herself.

I can dodge like smoke in the breeze, and strike as suddenly as the Nameless Serpentine Itself! Should I lug about a hunk of metal as heavy as a tree?

But on the other hand, which would I—my sword, or my life?

The answer came fleetly, on the wings of certainty.

Why not both? What the hell. I was getting tired of this city anyway.

The prince was too well guarded, but the youngest guard, who was nearly a boy, stood by himself between her and the door, holding his head where she had kicked him. She walked dejectedly, as if leaving, but as she passed him, she grabbed his arm and twisted it behind his back. With a flash of steel, she pulled her boot dagger and held it against his throat, against the great artery next to the windpipe. Instantly, all swords and spears were leveled at her breast again.

"I need that sword," she said, trying hard for a tone of quiet authority, though the knife-edge of fear pressed against her own throat.

"He is a soldier," said the captain grimly. "He is prepared to die." The boy swallowed but did not say anything as the man advanced.

"Who is he?" whispered the prince, as if seeing the boy for the first time. "He is so young for a guard!"

"He is Driga," said the captain, "first son of Master Driga, who distinguished himself in service in the far South. What matters it? He's a soldier!"

"I only want my sword," Jiana repeated.

"Give it to her," said Alanai. "She asks little. It is not worth young Driga's life."

Reluctantly, the captain put Wave on the floor and kicked it across to her.

"Pick it up, Driga," she said, and bent with him as he slowly retrieved it and handed it to her.

"But," continued the prince softly, "know that you shall *not* be forgotten." Jiana smiled, and raised her sword in mock-salute. Then she shoved Driga into the room, into the other guards, and bolted out the door.

She slammed the door shut, and looked around frantically. With a cry of anger and frustration, and icy terror, she slid off the street into the freezing blackness.

Gods, no skeeniks! she thought, before her mind was washed by the blackness that covered her head. She grabbed at the pylons that sank through the waves into the ground, supporting the Dancing Bull.

Jiana pulled herself under the building. It was one of the few in Bay Bay City that actually rose a few feet above the waterline, even during the high tides. Her head broke the surface, and she gasped air. Jiana fumbled Wave back into her sheath, still treading water.

The guards tramped up and down the street, and looked into the adjacent buildings. Jiana took a deep breath, and swam under water past several streets and under another floater. Then she grabbed an alleyway board.

Suddenly, she felt something massive and alive brush past her in the murky ocean. It was at least fifteen feet long, and seemed like a hundred. Panicked, she heaved herself up onto the sagging board, just as something broke the surface water and dove again. An ugly, jagged, vertical tail fin flipped up and then was gone beneath the choppy waves.

Jiana shivered and trembled for several minutes, hearing the noise of the prince's guards recede. Then she crawled to the street, and stood unsteadily on the rolling dock.

She cursed, and smashed the side of her fist into a wall, but she missed and hit a window instead, slicing up her hand. She stared at the red line that slowly widened and began to bleed heavily . . . it was her first wound that day.

"The perfect denouement to a fine day's catastrophe," she grumbled. *Oh, come on, it's not that bad. You've got a plan, don't you?*

"Sure, with just one tiny, little setback: I've just started a blood feud with the leaders of the very expedition I intend to join!"

She needed a drink and a pipe. She knew of another tavern, in the market maze of Bay Bay . . . a cheap one, unknown to princes or decent folk. She started walking, winding her hand with chewed leaves and pieces of cloth from her surgery bag.

"I *will* go," she muttered. "It's my destiny. That's it!" She sounded unconvincing, even to herself.

"I'll just find a way to *make* them take me."

The billboards disappeared from the Market Maze. Alanai had selected his eleven men, including the foul Hraga si Traga. They would leave on the morrow: it was the Day of Equal Moons, when greater Fear and lesser Hope rose at the same instant, presaging twenty days of Hope rising higher in the sky.

Equal fear and hope described Jiana perfectly. Somehow, broke though she was, she had to get the money for a rig. She needed food and supplies, maps, better clothing— and a battlehorse.

But first, she needed money.

"I am *not* going to turn thief again," she said, gritting her teeth. For a few minutes she pondered; then she grinned, and set off to locate a certain miserable sot.

The tea-master at the Dog's Tongue would not come out from his strongroom, but he directed her to the Steaming Pig Tea Emporium. From there, she was sent to the Tinker's Hang, the Severed Ear— where she could not enter, of course, but only accost passers-by—and finally was directed to the Excited Mule. In a corner, dead drunk, she found Tawn.

A horse's trough and some children's tea, without alcohol, sobered him enough to stand and listen. A leather-gloved hand idly fingering Wave persuaded him to cooperate. And, of course, there would be something left over for him.

"Now, all I gotta do is pretend to rob this aleshop? Then you'll . . . what'd you say?"

"Then I'll chase you out, and the alemaster will reward me out of gratitude. What could be simpler?"

"How much?"

"Not much. So we do it to four or five places."

The first place went down easily. First Jiana cased it. She offered her services as a bouncer, and when refused, hung around for a drink.

Then Tawn sauntered in and grabbed the alemaster, sticking a dagger up against his throat.

"Gimme everything you got!" he snarled. The few customers all watched with interest; no one intervened. The shops had been carefully chosen for their vulnerability. They had no guards, like a teahouse would.

Jiana crept slowly up behind Tawn, with such amazing grace that he did not even see her. She suddenly slugged him with the side of her hand across the back of his neck, and he collapsed unconscious.

"Such a fighter!" breathed the shaking alemaster. "Why, it seemed you barely touched him! Yet, there he lies, impotent."

"It's a gift," she explained. "And, speaking of gifts . . ."

"Here," he said, pushing three silver scales at her, "you deserve it. I'm lucky to be alive! Let me call the garrison, to take care of the—"

"Oh, no, please. I'd be happy to handle it for you. I'll take him over to the prison, and you come by later and swear out a complaint. Come on, you!" She nudged Tawn with her foot, and he made a miraculous recovery. She marched him out with his arm in a come-along.

"Gimme everything you got!" he screamed in the next alehouse. It went pretty much as before, with Jiana's great battle-prowess knocking Tawn sprawling, and his own remarkable constitution allowing his speedy recovery. The largess this time was seventy-two serpents, and Jiana began to gloat.

"Hey, Ji, if I'd known you was so good at spotting aleshops to hit, I'd have . . ."

"What'd you say, Tawn?"

He was silent for a few moments. Then he spoke, sounding a bit subdued.

"Can we take a breather? Say, an hour? I've got an errand to run."

"Sure. Back at the Prince's Nostrils by five, okay?"

"Check." Tawn threaded his way across the square, and then disappeared along a creaking side street.

Jiana spent a few copper serpents sipping carrot and yellowroot juice, and watching the banners and bunting being tacked up for Prince Alanai's departure in the morning. *Another dumb excuse to celebrate*, she thought. She watched the shadows, and finally, it was time to meet Tawn. She trotted along the loose street, making it rock and bob in the water, and entered the Prince's Nostrils.

"No, sorry," said the master, a burly man too fat to offer much resistance. "I don't need no guards. What you think this be, anyways? A teahouse? You think I gots moneys to toss after wimmins what don't cook? I got a guard—he jus' off today!"

"All right, lard-belly. So just give me a drink, okay?"

"You got moneys? What color? Copper, silver, blood red?"

"Here! All right? Now give me a damn drink!" She slapped a handful of change on the counter, and he brought her a cup.

The door burst open.

"Nobody move!" It was Tawn. Jiana was about to stand up when she noticed the two other men with him. They all had crossbows, including Tawn. He looked right at Jiana.

"That means *nobody*," he added.

She nodded slowly. One of the other men ran behind the counter and backed the toadlike alemaster away from the bar. The thief began scooping coins out of the strongbox on the floor into a bag.

Jiana glared at Tawn, tasting hatred in her mouth. *Betrayer!* her eyes accused. He merely smiled at her; it was an ugly smile.

His partner finished cleaning out the loot, and they all backed toward the door. Jiana rose from her seat and walked toward Tawn.

"I'm warning you, Ji . . . stand back! Don't try to follow us."

"I'm not afraid of you, Tawn. I never was. Boy with a bow!"

They were out on the street now. Jiana stopped, and let

Tawn and his two triggers get a few steps away. They still covered her with their crossbows.

"So what're you gonna do about it, hunh? Jiana of White Falls?" He looked at the alemaster behind her, making sure he had heard her name. As soon as his eyes left Jiana, she dropped to a crouch and grabbed the street. It was narrow enough that she could grip both edges with her hands.

"Tooqa!" Tawn swore, his eyes widening; "you wouldn't—"

With a scream of rage, Jiana threw her entire weight to her left, wrenching with her right hand and jamming down with her left. The street twisted, staggering the thieves. Then, with the sound of rotting timbers, it cracked right in the middle, spilling them all into the sea.

The two swam across the narrow channel to the opposite street. But Tawn had the moneybag; he would not let it go.

"Drop it!" Jiana yelled. He just looked at her, pleading with his face. "Drop the damn bag! You're going to drown!"

He sank beneath the waves, still clutching the bag to his chest.

"Tawn! You can't even swim! Tawn, drop the bag—Tawn!" She stared at the place where his head had been a moment before. A few bubbles rose and popped.

Jiana stood up again. Her own piece of street had not sunk, but it had drifted away from the front of the alehouse. She paddled it over to the door again.

"He's dead."

"You think I'm stupid, no? You think I cannot see?"

"He's at the bottom. With your money."

"So what do I care? You think I'm stupid, that I not fight for my moneys? I got insurance! Who cares where he sinks to! But thanks, lady. Thanks for nothing! Now I gotta fix street, too!" He led her by the arm into his shop, and pushed her out the side door. "Now, just you go home, hokay? Don't do me no more favors!" He slammed the door in her face.

She stared at it for a few moments, trying to feel something.

"Funny thing, Tawn," Jiana whispered. "I just can't seem to care much. I'm sorry."

She fished around in her purse, and pulled out the six silver scales and change.

"Well, this should be enough for one. Bye, Tawn. Hope you fit better in the Scaly One's coils than you ever did up here."

She walked off briskly toward the Drive Shop in the Maze, but her legs were still shaking.

-4-

The glory prince of the Floating City left at sunup on the Day of the Equal Moons. He and his men galloped across the King's Causeway onto the mainland, through the main gates of Bay Bay City, and across the wheat, corn, and bean fields that fed the rolling city. They rode with great care along the irrigation roads, for the prince was great and wished no harm to his subjects' livelihood.

They were followed by three thousand cheering merchants, net-fishers, street repairers, peasants, farmers, craftsmen, chidren, and wives, all laughing and throwing paper favors as they ran indiscriminately through the crops.

Jiana followed an hour or so later, walking her new horse at an easy pace. She was accompanied by Lord Dilai, riding double, who told her Rat Tail was in jail again. Jiana frowned at the devastated fields surrounding them.

"Fly, Jiana! Run him faster, faster! See how the tracks of the prince—those not obliterated by his zealous apologists—show a gallop. They shall far outdistance you!"

"Don't be so poetic, Dilai. Haven't you ever hunted? How far can you gallop a horse, especially bogged down with armor, spears, and weapons? He'll pull up, soon as he's out of sight of the spectators. Look! They're already straggling back."

Jiana walked the horse along the middle of the road, forcing the exhausted citizens to detour, either into the trampled bean field to her right to trip over the collapsed wooden trellises holding up the vines, or into the muddied irrigation ditch on her left to drown. They were too tired to curse her.

"Besides, this is as fast as this horse-thing can go. What a deal! A mere four scales, the bastard said! Well, now we know why."

"What's her name?"

"His name . . . I must have misheard it. But I'd swear the horse thief said his name was Running Spots, on account of the dapple in his otherwise grey coat."

"Sounds like something you would catch in Tool, were you a bit too licentious." Jiana merelly grunted in reply and reigned in her horse.

"Okay, off you go."

"Was it something I said?"

"No. This is just where I begin to venture alone. You didn't want to chase after Alanai with me, did you?"

"Mm-mm," Dilai said, shaking his head. "Again we'll meet—here or there. You know?"

Dilai looked so sad. In one month he had grown a pot belly and a stoop, grey hairs and nag lines. Success did not suit him.

"Off!" She pushed him off the horse, and they saluted one another. Then she rode off down the road, without looking back. She found herself blinking back tiny tears in her eyes, but whether it was for Dilai, Tawn, or the fairly easy life of Bay Bay, she did not know.

She identified a splay hoof on one of the horses, by which she should be able to pick Alanai's band of questors out of a crowd. But there was little need. They made no attempt to conceal their route, and rode with a shocking carelessness. They tramped along the Road of Yellow Marshes, the most crowded, most sterotypically "royal road" in all Bay Bay Principality. It led straight southeast, without a curve—directly toward Bay Din.

"Along the road!" Jiana marveled. "Doesn't the bastard know there's a grybbyn in every bog and trools behind the trees?"

Perhaps the great prince considers himself above such mundanities as the beasts and the hellborn, sneered her other self.

"Death is death, even if your eyes look over the tops of the clouds." It was an unfortunate thought, and Jiana shivered in the heat as she glanced left and right at the

dense vegetation that pressed in against the road. The air
was breezeless and quiet, except for the buzzing and clicking of insects she had never heard before.

Away from the Floating City, the fog had lifted, but now
it was overcast, and the grey ceiling made the countryside
look dead. Crowded though the Road of Yellow Marshes
was, there were still lonely stretches, and Jiana hated
being alone.

She pulled out her notes, uncertain of her memory.
"Songs of control in Bay Din," she read, "Help usurp.
Rule." Alanai was as predictable as golden autumn in
White Falls. He would have to start some nastiness to
steal whatever controlled the World's Dream, for he be-
lieved that only with such songs could it be found.

"He'll be overconfident," she said aloud. She felt better
hearing a voice, even her own. "He believes the grybbyn
he slew was the meanest, most dangerous creature in the
world. Bay Din ought to be no trouble." Jiana grinned.

By bitter experience, she knew he was wrong; human
beings are much more dangerous enemies. There was an
excellent chance that, by strength or guile, the prince and
his fellowship would be captured. They would not be
killed out of hand; a prince is a valuable captive.

"And that's my chance," she laughed. Jiana knew many
secret ways in and out of Bay Din; she had spied there two
years with the New River Area People's Organization,
before fleeing to Bay Bay. "I've broken out of so many Bay
Din cells that surely I can break into a few!"

And then, she knew, they would *have* to accept her.
Just like her game with the aleshops.

"After I break them out of Bay Din, we'll ride south,
beyond the Valley at the Center of the World . . ." She
paused to look at the cheap map she had bought. "Mulla
. . . or Caela, or Taela, depending on whose map, to the
Tarn desert. Once past that, we'll be in either Noon on
the west or Tool in the interior, depending on whether we
seek coastline or more desert. Door is immediately south
of either."

She stared at the map a few moments. Something did
not jibe. Abruptly, she realized its makers had exagger-

ated the size of Bay Bay at the expense of the other principalities of the Water Kingdom.

"Step one in Bay Din," she appended, "is to get a better map. Maybe one of Onan Tondai's, that won't have these silly dragons tramping around New River, and the edge of the world clearly marked before you even get to the Flower Empire."

The day passed uneventfully. There were few travelers along the yellow marshes, and those she saw were mostly afoot and arguing. Jiana snarled and swung her horsewhip menacingly, forcing them all into the crumbly bracken on either side of the road.

She spent the time trying to get used to her horse, and to think up a better name than Running Spots; however, nothing she could think of fit her specifications of being both glorious and bearing some slight resemblance to the animal. She rode for hours muttering, "Stormcloud Snail-walker? Clover Demon? Amblequest? Tardystalker? Move, you bastard! Want to become a gelding?" She kicked it in the flank, and the horse sped up to a trot for several yards, then slowly wound down again.

"You run like a Norther clock," she told him, but he did not respond.

Finally, at dusk, she climbed a big hill and saw a town a mile distant. The map gave it no name, but called it twenty miles from Bay Bay City.

About as far as if you had gotten off the horse as it passed through the old gate and walked the rest of the way, she thought. The town pushed up against the banks of a tiny river, running through the valley below her.

Jiana scanned it carefully, from end to end. It consisted of about fifty buildings in all, none higher than one story. Most were brownish and made of wood or mud; some were grey-white—possibly piled stone. Her attention was drawn to an enclosure near the largest building. There, she saw corralled a small group of twelve or thirteen horses, among them several the same color as those that she remembered from Alanai's party. They grazed contentedly.

The warrior bit her lip in consternation. She had started out the day only an hour behind Alanai's quest, but unless the stable boasted a dozen hands, it would have taken much longer than that for so many horses to be watered, unsaddled, and brushed. They had gained quite a bit of time on her. Tomorrow she would have to pick up the pace, perhaps by taking a shortcut.

She pitched camp where she was. The town was small enough to contain but a single hostel, where Alanai and his hired heroes were surely staying. For a moment, she considered slipping into town to spy on them, but before her common sense could unlimber itself, she said, "No, no, don't say it—you're right. I've no death wish today!"

She unslung her food bag. It felt too light. She pawed through it and saw, to her disgust, that she had eaten nearly three days' worth of the food she had brought, just munching along the road.

"Hm. I have to become serpent now, hey? Catch my food from now on." The plan sounded wonderful.

Jiana hunted around and found a stream, but there were no fish that she could see. She thrashed through the underbrush and missed a rabbit with her bow, and finally had to content herself with three careless squirrels.

It was dark by the time she caught them, and cold when they were cooked. The sky was overcast, so she couldn't see any stars. The light of her fire was feeble, barely enough to be able to read.

Hesitantly, Jiana reached inside her jerkin and pulled out an old, yellowed piece of parchment. The ink was faded from the sun, and smeared by years of handling, but the words of the poem were still visible. It would not have mattered if they were not, since she remembered every word. She had written it.

There had been a time in her life, years before . . . *Yes!* urged the temptress, *bring me back. Remember!* Argumentatively, she folded up the parchment and tucked it away. She blinked her eyes rapidly. "The pain is gone," Jiana insisted.

She began to shiver. Though the days were panting-hot, the nights were freezing, for it was indeed winter. It was not as cold as she remembered in White Falls, New River, but she had grown soft and unused to the old life. She crawled under her blankets and curled up for warmth.

Best sleep now, she thought. *You'll have to rise with the sun to catch his trail.* Alanai seemed like the type who would spring up at dawn and suck in the air with a great breath, beating his hairy chest and chanting, "Up and at 'em! Rise and shine!" With this thought in mind, she drifted off into the demented, half-dreaming state between sleep and wake.

But she could not fall all the way asleep. Every few moments, she would wake up enough to think, *Here I lie, still awake.* The problem was obvious: in Bay Bay, she had never gone to bed before the second bell, and rarely before dawn. There were too many distractions and diversions during the night. With nothing to do but sleep, she fidgeted with boredom.

Strange noises conspired with the ennui—faint calls on the wind, which brought to her mind the disturbing memory of bloodletting, screams of the battle-fallen, the far-off rattle of spear on shield, sword on helm.

Spirits abroad to suck dry my soul! She rolled the blankets tighter around her, shivering. Strange thoughts grabbed at her mind, resurrected from her childhood. *You can't let a single foot stick out from under the blanket, for if an iron-cold hand were to GRAB IT . . .* She gasped and curled tighter, further than ever from sleep.

The cries still sounded, carried on the wind, and terrible scenes flashed through her mind. She remembered the doomed rebellion of the Monks of the Black Left Hand. She had fought to suppress it in the horse army of General To of the Flower Empire; he was the only high commander who did not mind a Captain-of-Twenty being a woman, and worse, a foreigner. Jiana was allowed lead of an entire lancer company, and rode into battle with a grand red banner strapped to her back and eight steel lances sheathed at her saddle.

But the Hand army had deserted, and eight hundred monks, seeking heaven, threw themselves empty-handed and bare-chested upon To's leaf-bladed spears.

The butchery that followed had so sickened Jiana that she fled the field before the sun had set, leaving behind her horse, her lances, and her name. Her first command! She swam across the narrow Sea of Memories, clad only in her feelings of guilt, to the White Island, where she met her second master.

All this Jiana remembered, lying on the ground under the black and starless sky, hearing death cries on the wind, and she tried again to understand her feelings. Of course, she lay sleepless still.

Her eyes opened, and she noticed a red glow coloring the sky in the south. She fearfully rolled face-down and buried her eyes in her arm. Fires from hell! For a moment, the blankets pulled away from her foot, and she was panicked until she squirmed it under again. *Damn, whose cold touch is that?! Blast it, only a rock. Sleep, sleep, sleep!*

The longer Jiana lay awake upon the ground, the madder she got. She knew that above her head, the invisible stars were turning in their courses, and the moons were setting. The hours sped by, and she began to grow anxious as she thought of the ever-shrinking time before she had to get up—which, of course, made sleep even more difficult.

Since the rebellion of the Black Left Hand, hissed the accuser in her head, *surely you still flee the world of the warrior!*

No! No! I fight, I conquer!

You scavenge. What are you doing now, but picking at the prince's leavings, making water in his wind? You shuffle along the ground, dear Jiana, grubbing roots and berries, and wait for the eagle to fall at your feet from the sky! Her throat tightened, and she held her breath, trying to let the thoughts and emotions pass, as she had been taught.

When dawn finally came, she was tired and haggard. *Dawn is here*, she thought. *Have to get up*. At last the spirit-screams were silent, no longer tainting the air with their vengeful hatred for their living slayers—many hating her in particular, she knew, for she had slain many. *Time to get up*, she told herself. Only then did she fall into a deep, dream-forgetting sleep.

Jiana suddenly woke. The sun was high in the sky, but the air was still cold from the night. For a time she lay still, convincing herself that she ought to get up and do something. She remembered the prince, but somehow the chase did not have the urgency of the night before. After a time she rolled over, still under her blankets, and looked down on the tiny town in the valley below.

It had been obliterated. What few buildings still stood were black and sagging, and smoke darkened the sky above. Isolated spots still flickered red and yellow.

She threw off her blankets and bounded to her feet. She staggered and almost fell from standing too fast, but shook the dizziness off. "Gone . . ." she whispered. "But it was just—"

After staring for an eon in numb rapture, she shook herself, pulled on her clothes, saddled her horse, and spurred him down into the smoking remains.

The sun was high overhead by then. What was left of the wooden homes stood black and crumbly in the stark noon light. Even the buildings built of stone were gutted and lifeless, while those of mud had baked brittle and crumbled into the street. The town was a dead campfire, smelling of ash and blood.

Jiana slowly walked the horse along the town road, staring at the devastation. Everywhere she looked she saw death and blood. People wandered aimlessly through the rubble, calling for friends and relatives, and sobbing helplessly. Jiana heard cries on the wind, and they made her shudder. She recognized them from her nightmares.

"I heard you," she whispered. "I heard you and did not know . . ." She swallowed, tasting bile.

She looked carefully around her, suddenly struck by a curious anomaly. There were many, many bodies—young women in homemade armor, or half-dressed; men and boys with cudgels and sickles; the aged, hewn from behind. Even the children had not been spared, and they died clutching tiny knives and toy swords. But nowhere were there any bodies that did not look as if they belonged in the town—no obvious "attackers," though there were many bodiless black cloaks lying scattered among the ashes.

Some people were trying to aid the wounded, or put out the fires with buckets of water. Jiana watched as a young woman finished dousing a fire. The woman then stood and stared at the gutted building in shock, confused as to what to do next. Jiana stopped her horse nearby, and waited until she was noticed.

The woman screamed and staggered back, drawing her sword. When Jiana did not react, the woman slowly lowered her weapon and watched her warily, but she never sheathed it.

"Lady," said Jiana, "I have seen many campaigns, and won and lost a share. My horses have overrun poorly armed sergeants-at-arms who were starving and plague-ridden, and fell with the minorest wounds." This last was more nearly true than what she had told her general at the time, as he decorated her bravery.

"But in my years, I have never seen a perfect operation. I don't think such a thing can exist—a battle without a single casualty among the winners. Where the hell are the bodies of your enemies?"

"You speak truth," the woman responded bitterly. She seemed to be barely twenty years old, yet her face was lined and hardened from toil and responsibility. "This all they left, whilst their corporate selves fled to yan Hell back." She kicked at a black cloak, unsinged though it lay among the still-glowing embers.

The cloak landed near Jiana's horse, but she made no move to pick it up. The cloth was the exact midnight color of Jiana's hair and tunic, which might have accounted for why the woman had stared at her with such terror.

She looked up suspiciously at Jiana. "Who are you? What do you want here?"

"Who attacked you?" Jiana asked. The woman stared at her in silence; finally, she seemed to come to a decision about Jiana. Her eyes fell, and she began to talk.

"Hellions banged in air in our black, swarmed and attacked His Highness, Prince Alanai. Devils! But he fought valiant, against evil odds, and drove them yan town from."

She closed her eyes, and crouched down to rock back on her heels, as if in the steam of a Purifier, telling tales of hurt and pain. She still held her blooded sword bare.

"You fought by his side?"

"Nearly . . . he were twice in sight, each time engaging two or three of yan fell fiends, back a burning wall

against—by the Nameless, a warrior true . . ." She stared
into space. Gently, Jiana queried her further.

"When killed, these demons left only their cloaks?"

"Nought but what you see." She glanced toward the
crumbled garment, still lying untouched on the street.
"The citylord bravely drove yan hell-creatures our town
from, at great risk." She glared at Jiana as she said the
words, daring her to contradict.

Under normal circumstances, Jiana would have held her
tongue. But she already felt guilt at having heard the cries
and not known what they were. Without meaning to, she
hurled the gauntlet right back.

"But who do you think lured them here in the first
place?"

"How can I answer? I know nought of demons, magick,
princes! They might have been sent by some foul magus,
or evil spirit, perhaps!"

"Sent for you, or for Alanai? Were he not here, would
they have come?"

The woman glared at Jiana coldly. "His Highness cain't
be blamed for war's destruction. You look soldiery yourself. Do you take yourself upon every death of your campaigns?" Her voice had a touch of frenzy in it. *Leave her
be!* warned Jiana's common sense.

"I begin to." Jiana closed her eyes, and for a second she
clearly saw how the town must have looked a few hours
earlier. It linked inextricably in her mind's eye with carnage and destruction she had seen in her own past, with
eyes wide open and steel dripping crimson. "They clutch
at me now, every one; weigh me down like armor in the
sea. I see them leering, in my wine cup and my looking
glass . . . don't you? Doesn't Alanai?"

She opened her eyes and stared directly down at the
young woman.

"Couldn't the bastard have at least stayed and helped
clean up his holocaust?" She had not meant to yell.

The woman leaped to her feet, furious; she brandished
her blade for an answer. Instinctively, Jiana whipped Wave
from its sheath around her waist.

"Fall yan horse off and face me, coward and traitor you!
Prince Alanai is a great hero! I saw him fight and slay

many times his number, of the foulest bogles hell from!
Say it, or I'll cut your tongue out, and your heart soon
after!"

"I don't want to fight you. Disengage, woman!" But the
girl pulled at Jiana's legs, waving her sword wildly at the
same time. Jiana feared her untrained mount would bolt,
so she kicked the woman in the face, and leapt off her
horse while her opponent regained her feet.

"I am Jiana of Bay Bay. Tell me your name that I might
know whose life I deprive." She tried to frighten her, still
hoping for a nonviolent end to the duel. Jiana was acutely
aware that it was her own lack of diplomacy which had
started it.

"I'm Gaish of Two-Rivers Town arsenal. Say the prince
is a great hero, and take your treasonous slurs back, or 'tis
you who shall be slain!"

She lunged with her point at Jiana's chest, and the move
took the warrior by surprise. She had expected her to
swing, not lunge. Jiana barely parried the blow, then
withdrew a few steps.

"I withdraw my comments . . . Look, can't we just
agree to disagree—" Jiana gambled on a quick glance
around her, fearing other townspeople might join in the
fray. Only three people watched, and they seemed too
numb to do anything but cower.

Gaish launched a furious assault, feinting, striking, and
thrusting in a blur of steel, notwithstanding her wounds.
She was well-trained, fast and dextrous, but inexperienced.
Jiana, too, had trained for many years, but unlike Gaish,
she had defended her life and honor in scores of real
combats. She flowed back and to the side like a choppy
ocean wave, and Gaish's sword could not strike its target.

Finally, the young woman left herself off balance and
open, after a tricky strike from her left. Jiana lunged
forward, almost without thinking. She barely managed to
twist her blow in time, and only slugged Gaish with the
pommel, knocking a tooth out of her mouth. Gaish fell to
her knees, hand to her bloody mouth, but still the girl
cursed and swore, unwilling to quit.

Jiana backed away after the blow.

"There is no need to pursue this ridiculous duel any further," she gasped, but her words went unheard.

Gaish lunged forward in a thrust, catching Jiana by surprise with the same move that had begun the fight. Jiana stepped diagonally forward, aware she had been stabbed, and before she could stop herself she counterstruck.

Jiana backpedaled to disengage, and felt her wound carefully. It was neither deep nor wide, but she felt like a failed student. Had the strike been less tentative, Jiana could have died.

She looked up and snarled furiously at Gaish, but her anger died unvoiced in her throat. The young woman's face was white as she stared stupidly at the widening split in her tunic, through which a gaping wound was visible. Slowly, as if compelled, she touched the incision, gently opening it until the inside of her abdominal cavity could be seen. Her mouth was open, and she held her breath. She did not even seem to notice the blood flowing out of the wound, so spellbound was she. She sunk to her knees.

Jiana felt violently ill. She clamped her teeth together to avoid actually vomiting and showing her weakness. She staggered back to her horse and mounted shakily. She had not wanted this.

"Hold it together now," she said, "and call for a surgeon with a needle and thread. And, for the love of the Snake, just lie still and keep calm." Jiana turned about and rode away as fast as she could. She glanced back once—she could not help it. Gaish still had not moved or called out for help.

Jiana spurred her nameless, reluctant horse forward, through the fires, the ashes, the blood, and the smell of smoke and urine and death. She rode over the stone bridge, and across the smoldering fields, until the blackened town was far behind her, over a rise. Then she reined up. She sat high in the saddle, face up toward the clouds, until she had control over her stomach again.

Damn you . . . damn you, damn your bloody young idealism! A single tear rolled down Jiana's cheek, and it occurred to her that she did not know whether she meant Gaish or herself at Gaish's age. *Again, Ji, you bring only pain and death.*

"But I'm changing," she cried. "Look, have I felt this

way about a single death before? For the first time, it means something! What did it mean to Alanai?"

But like Alanai, whispered the tormentor, *you didn't stay to help rebuild either, did you?* The charge was unanswerable.

She paused, then forced herself to spit out the words: "Prince Alanai is a great hero. He really is." She imagined herself fighting by his side, facing terrible monsters and demons . . . on a desolate plain with not a town or a civilian in sight. After a time, she could stand herself again.

The clouds grew darker, boiling in from the sea, and a wind came up from the west. It was a chill wind that smelled of salt tears and soot—the King's Wind, the people had called it for generations. It was supposed to herald the king's return. Jiana rode into the King's Wind in silence.

A hero must kill; people must die. Alanai's a hero . . . a great hero.

"Heroes are people of action," she stated.

She forced the doubts from her mind and sought Alanai's tracks on the road. She kept an eye out for game, too; the squirrels had left a bitter taste in her mouth.

Chapter 2

Games of glory, games of dust, and what a little mouse told her

-1-

The sun arced across the sky.

The horse had evidently realized he was not going back to his comfortable stall in Bay Bay. It took only a little prodding for Jiana to keep him moving at a fairly normal horse-walk, but she was still losing ground to Alanai's party. Her best estimate placed her six hours behind, counting the morning's delay. Fortunately, there had been no rain, and their tracks indicated they still followed the Road of the Yellow Marshes.

"Damn," she said aloud, as her gloved hand brushed against her sword hilt. "Does that bitch Gaish haunt you now, Wave? Her face returns whenever I touch you." Jiana rode in silence, jumpy and nervous without a crowd of comrades around her. The stillness of the countryside kept her on edge.

The wind gusted cold as the sun sank low, and Jiana bound her cloak tightly around her body, shivering. The horse sped up. He was now indelibly dubbed "The Horse" in her mind.

45

"Aw, you cold, too, Horsey?" He snorted in answer, which she found amusing. But her subsequent questions met with silence, and she decided he did not really talk after all.

The last of the squirrel had disappeared in the morning, and it had put her stomach off food for most of the day. But as the sun set, she began to think about dinner, and worry about the lack of animal tracks or traces of game.

"People," she muttered. "There's so many people along the way . . ." She had passed a score of groups along the road, but they all went the opposite way, generally in a ripping hurry.

"You know, Horse, at your rate, I'll *never* catch up with Alanai. I've got to find a shortcut!"

It was easy to say. Studying the map, spread open across the horse's neck, she could see that the only bend in the Road of Yellow Marshes was when it detoured around a bog called the Suhuhu-Huisto Bayou—and Jiana worried endlessly about a piece of real estate which even the Ti-Ji Tul would not cross with a road.

"But that's got to be it. Everywhere else, the bastards gain on me, unless all their mounts break a leg simultaneously."

And how fast do you think you shall cross the bayou?

"Hm. As fast as my sweet little mount will carry. At least it's something to try!"

A faint memory nagged at her. The word for soul in the language of the First Ones was Suhuhon; huisto was a mystery, but the prefix hui- was sometimes translated as nihil-, "nothingness." The thought was disturbing enough that she forgot it, and decided instead to pitch camp.

The sun had just touched the tips of the mountains to her right when she turned the horse off the road into the crackly brush of the inappropriately named Yellow Marsh. She set up her bivouac, and then tramped out into the wilderness to catch dinner.

By the time the sun was long set and the great moon Fear had risen, Jiana finally conceded that there was no game to be found. She stumbled about in the bracken, just trying to find her own trail again, feeling miserable and incompetent.

Worthless. Can't even find your own tracks, O mighty huntress!

"I'm a warrior, not a bloody forester!" She drew Wave and mowed some brush with it, but the sword wobbled up and down, far from rigid. She felt stupid, and immediately put it away, sneaking a look over her shoulder to make sure no one was around to see. She pressed her lips together, and determinedly struck out in the direction she thought she had come.

The moons were nearly overhead before she finally made it back to her camp; half the hours of the night had passed. She stretched out as best as she could, and tried to sleep. This night, it was hunger that kept her awake. The nightfears, though returned, did not have a grip on her as they did the night before. There were no cries in the wind.

At sunup, though hungry and still exhausted, she forced herself to rise to avoid a repetition of the day before. There were no fish in the stream, no animals. There were not even any squirrels, which she would have gratefully devoured for breakfast. All she found were a few bitter plants she recognized, and some dubious fungus.

"Ah, well, by the Reign of the Reptile—caution won't catch the cock, uh, so to speak . . ." She stared at the wrinkled, parchmentlike mushroom in her palm, dithering. "Aw, you're just delaying, kid," she told herself.

She popped the flat, leathery thing in her mouth and forced herself to chew and swallow. Then she climbed aboard the horse and kicked him into a meander, guiding him back toward the road.

Within half a mile she felt queasy. After a mile she felt distinctly sick. Fewer than fifty paces later, she was kneeling at the side of the road, retching violently. Even after she lost what little she had eaten, she continued to heave for quite a while.

"Okay," she gasped. "So maybe that wasn't the best idea I've had . . ."

She walked unsteadily back to the horse, grabbed the saddlesack containing the fungus, and dumped it out on the scrubby bushes. Then, after a moment, she thought better of it and scooped it back into the sack.

Never know when a good poison might come in handy,
she thought. She laboriously climbed back aboard, and
continued along the road, hungrier than ever, and now
weak and dizzy as well.

The road began to slant up into the western mountains,
and as she urged her horse forward, she began to feel
scattered raindrops on her nose.

Jiana looked up, and for the first time, noticed the
clouds boiling in to cover the sky. The wind picked up,
and blew a healthy gust of rain into her face. *Bless you, o
Slimy One*, she thought. *You're such a comfort to Your
acolytes.* As if in answer, the rain poured down twice as
hard, soaking her instantly. Jiana slogged and cursed on
through the mud that once had been the King's Highway.
The tracks were obliterated, of course.

"Well, what the hell," she snorted. "At least I know
where we're going." The horse snorted as well.

Another day passed. Jiana, true to her purpose, grimly
struck out away from the road, across the greedy bayou.

The rain poured like ocean waves across the muddy,
sucking bog. The ground was chaos, covered with traps for
the unwary foot, holes to swallow Jiana into the bowels of
the earth if she did not keep both eyes and her nose wide
and wary.

Whatever she touched dripped and oozed; wherever
she looked she saw grey water—in the clouds or at her
feet, or dripping from a twisted, stunted half-tree. Salt
sweat dripped down her face, even in that downpour, and
she licked it off, for she had nothing else to eat.

The Suhuhu-Huisto Bayou allowed no rest, no dry place
to huddle with her horse and gear. There were not even
any real trees—only hideous, leafless things that pointed
in every direction but up.

Jiana struggled through a pool of clutching sand, feeling
gingerly ahead for each step and dragging her protesting
animal along behind. A slip in the beating rain, and Jiana
could sink into the bog without a trace, leaving none to
sing her song. But she worried more about the horse.

"Damn you worthless, motherless beast! Gonna trade
you for a bloody mule, first town we find!" But the anger
only covered real concern.

Then, as they left the sinkhole, he set his front legs and braced against her futile tugging. Jiana strained against him with brute strength. Without warning, he changed tactics and bolted forward, making her stagger backwards into a mud lake and lose her grip on the reins.

Jiana slowly stood and drew her blade, visions of blood and horsehair rolling before her eyes. But then a gust of wind and slate-grey rain tore away her violent thoughts like a swirling cloak dispersing a cloud. She shook her head, and slid Wave back into its sheath unused.

"Who knows if it's day or night? What's the difference under grey stone clouds raining rivers into lakes? Maybe I'm dead."

She sat on the ground, on a half-submerged tree stump, and sank her head into her hands. Her mind fell into greyness as opaque as the sky.

The sun rose again, brightening the forest lake for a few brief moments, before the boiling curds-and-whey clouds conquered the sky again. West, south—Jiana's sense of direction had sunk beneath the chaos of the bayou.

"But at least," she reasoned, "we have learned why the Ti-Ji Tul avoided it." She giggled without control for a few moments before fully waking.

The horse had found a few scraggly shoots to chew, and Jiana ate the last of her own supplies. She scavenged some of the shoots, wrestling the horse for them.

She chewed and forced them down, then began the long walk forward. It was the only direction of which she was sure.

At last her bucking, plunging horse slipped and fell a half-dozen feet into a gully the rain had carved. She gave up on the poor animal and turned it loose, taking the saddlesacks herself. It tried to follow her, then surrendered and leaned against the cliff.

Despite her harsh words, Jiana felt a lump in her throat as she turned her back on him and staggered on. No one had asked the horse if he wanted to go on a quest.

"Good luck," she said, "and I hope you somehow make it. Speak boldly to the Serpent and have a better life next time." She looked back once. It was huddled and shivering, futilely trying to keep dry.

Jiana still tasted salt, but not all of it was sweat; the tears only added to her blindness in the storm. She staggered on, hands spread before her, feeling for bushes and death-trees with fingers so numb and cold she only knew they had a grip when she could see it. Without the sun, the air had turned distinctly cold.

Don't cringe, she ordered herself.

The lack of food was telling, as she felt stupidly weak and even afraid. Her berries had rotted in the rainwater; the roots she dug up were inedible, except perhaps to a real bear. For a few short moments, she seriously considered eating the fungus, but it would have been surrender. She pushed the unnerving, alien thought from her mind.

At last, Jiana sank to her knees, and pounded her fist into the mud. *An empty cup*, she remembered. *Empty, empty, empty . . .*

She tilted back her head and let the water wash over her face, open to the sky. Salt sweat and tears were scrubbed away, and after three days, she allowed herself to slip the reigns of self-control. Jiana smiled in the wet, granite day, the accuser-tormenter dead within her for the first time in years.

"So this is death. I always wondered."

When she opened her eyes, she stood on her feet and strode like a warrior across the dead and crumbly ground. The rain had slowed to a faint drizzle, but even dry, the bayou shifted and sank beneath her steps.

"And when I die," she declaimed, her words hoarse and strange in her own ears. "If I die it'll be on my stupid feet."

Now the fog wrapped about her, as if the clouds had themselves fallen into the grabbing bog. Jiana tramped forward recklessly, and walked directly into a shifting, twisty deadfall of stunted trees. She pushed against it, and it felt treacherous, but she refused to believe that she had survived a dozen battlefields and a hundred midnight streets in her violent life, only to die in an avalanche of deadwood.

She grabbed a handful of branches, and pulled herself up into one of the trunks, even as the limbs groaned and cracked, and broke off suddenly. The wall was not high, but it stretched on for the longest distance, and the fog hid

everything from her sight. It was like crawling across a
lake of spears and swords, clutching at daggers for support. But at last she lunged for a branch and grabbed
nothing. Out of balance, Jiana toppled forward, and was
startled to land on fairly solid ground rather than a razor-
sharp stake.

She stood up; something called to her eyes in the distance.

The fog rose into the air, and a flash of light glimmered
ahead. Across a wind-whipped field of vines, a bright,
paper-covered lantern swayed and bobbed like a tide-
beacon in a harbor.

-2-

"In the name of nameless Tooqa, open your damn door!"
The blasphemy slid out of Jiana's mouth before she could
stop it. She fearfully glanced up at the lowering sky,
seeing the coils of the divine serpent in the clouds, hearing his hiss in the wailing wind.

She began to sag against the door, but with a wrench
she stood straight and warriorlike again. No one would see
her otherwise.

A faint scuffle from within pounded in her ears like a
battle drum. Her hand slipped, and the rough, splintery
wood of the door tore through her fingers like a spear from
the shock of a mounted charge. Every sense was taut,
resonant, brittle; and beneath her thin crust of consciousness was a river of molten shame. She had lost the road
and Alanai, and had no idea where she was, or how far
behind she would be. She barely remembered why she
chased him.

Jiana hardly noticed when the farmhouse door finally,
reluctantly opened to the dark and howling. Someone felt
pity for her, the dripping apparition on the doorstep;
someone showed more trust than Jiana could ever have
found in the city. She was hauled in and set before a fire.

A part of her, below awareness, noted every act of
kindness, and still watched animal-like for danger. But
consciously, Jiana's head swirled like the clouds in the

snake-eye of the outside storm, round and round and round and round and round—

For a brief moment, a vision loomed before her eyes: a young boy, leaning over her with concern. He had the eyes of an eagle, the horns of a buffalo, and the claws of a bear. But then he was only a frightened mouse, always running along the wall and never in the middle of the room.

What a peculiar thing for a young boy to do, she thought dreamily, slipping into sleep . . . round and round and round and round and round . . .

Jiana woke slowly in a modest parlor. It was draped with furs and flowers, strewn with grasses and cornsilks. She was rolled in a blanket herself. The room seemed strange and frightening, until she realized why: it was not a room or a barracks or an inn or a cell—it was a home. It was an alien concept, and it intimidated her.

She sat up before the dying fire, and felt a brief flash of anger that whoever had wrapped her had swaddled her arms inside, like a baby. Then she felt guilty for the ungrateful thought, and silly for her guilt.

An infinite regression of introspection, she thought. She shook her head and struggled free of the blankets.

Jiana stood unclothed before the fire. At once, she realized she felt good.

"I'll be squeezed," she whispered. "Didn't know I had it in me, did you?" The accuser stood mute.

She lolled before the hot, glowing logs for a few moments, letting the embers wash the coldness from her mind. But a sense of uneasiness crept across her flesh, as if she awaited something dreadful. She finally understood what she feared.

What if someone walked in and saw you like this? You're naked!

"Leave me alone!" she muttered, but she fumbled with the blanket anyway, trying to drape it about her. It was too short to cover everything.

"Damn you," she whispered. "Must you ruin *every* moment? The southers *always* run around naked—no one'll even notice me!" Yet even with the thought, Jiana wrapped herself so that only her legs from mid-thigh down were bare. She could feel her face flushing hot, no matter how foolish it was, and she had to force herself to stand up straight. Two years in Bay Bay had washed away very little of White Falls.

She surveyed the room, both to take her mind off her embarrassment and through simple habit as a soldier: three chairs, throwable and breakable; a rolled sleeping mat, in front of a curtained room, through which she could see children's toys and several messy piles of bedclothes. To the right of the curtain was a great-table, with a plate of some grey gravy-soup, some bread, and a pitcher of ale; then a kitchen, and behind it another curtain.

On a shelf behind the table was a folded pile of black cloth. She walked hurredly across the room and grabbed it; it was her clothes. She pulled them on, deliberately slowing her movements, trying to prove she was not really that bashful. She left her shirt untied to her waist, as usual.

So why, asked the childish voice in her stomach, *doesn't THAT bother you?*

"I don't know. It's different. Don't ask me why."

Hunger gnawed at her gut, though she could bear it better now in a warm, cozy room (*home,* she corrected). She eyed the plate of gravy glop, tightening her lips to avoid drooling.

"Now, I wonder," she mused, as loudly as a character in a miracle play. "I wonder if that food was set for me?" There was no reply. "Well, it must be, so I'm going to eat it! Hello?"

Jiana shrugged and sat at the table. She devoured the bread greedily, using it to sop up the gravy, uncaring whether that was the proper eating etiquette, or as rude as a Noondun nomad.

"The food's wonderful," she ventured. Still, no one popped in to respond. "Tastes like roast sea-goose? Boiled antelope?"

She wolfed the bread, uncaring for the gut ache that would surely follow such intemperance; that would be later.

After several minutes, she felt miffed at being ignored, and added, "'But maybe my hunger is more responsible for the flavor than the cooking." There was still no sign of life, and Jiana began to feel uneasy.

She swallowed a huge hunk of bread barely chewed. Common sense told her to eat more slowly, allowing time to reacquaint herself with food, but Jiana never allowed common sense to interfere with desire.

She gazed out the window, realizing it was silly to keep talking. The shutters were open, and light streamed through onto her plate. The wind still howled, and occasionally gusted through the window hole, blowing her raven-colored hair into her face. But the clouds had broken, as if, having steered her to this home, they had served their purpose and . . .

Hah! A silly view of the universe, ordered for your benefit!

At last she began to hear stirrings. In the distance, through the window, she heard the screams of children, cheerfully killing each other over some difference of opinion. Soon they ran into view, across the field. Each was clad only in the mud in which it had played.

"I am *not* in White Falls, New River," she insisted, drinking another flagon of the passable, bitter ale. "There is nothing *wrong* with my body—except for a little extra fat that everyone but courtesans has, maybe."

Then why did you never bathe with the other soldiers, in all of the armies in which you've served?

"Ah, self-preservation, O wormy one; nothing more." She worried a bit, then sat back, satisfied with the explanation.

The wooden door burst open, and a young boy tramped into the room. He was about fifteen.

"Oh! You're awakened—I—I was just—uh . . ." The boy stared at Jiana curiously; after a few seconds, his breathing became shallower. He shuffled his feet, then picked some of the rushes up from the floor. "I was just s'posed to clean out," he finished lamely, still looking at her.

"Come sit here, kid. Talk to me, please?"

He stared at her, and did not move, his pupils wide and his lips parted slightly. He had a very sensitive mouth.

"Do you have a name, sir?"

"Aye, mum," he whispered, and pressed his lips together.

They waited thus in silence for ten heartbeats, until he suddenly reddened and stammered, "Awn! I am Dida. Your clothes are . . . your clothes are . . . awn, you already have 'em. Sorrow, I wasn't here the food you were eating when."

Jiana tilted her head, trying to translate Dida's thick Souther accent. She had first come to the Floating City from the East, and had not been outside for the past two years. She had never heard Dida's dialect.

"Your face is flushed," she offered, just in case he had missed such an important fact. He flushed deeper, and she felt a pang of guilt; she had done that on purpose.

"Where your words are from? Just going my business about. If I be somehow offense-giving . . ."

"You sound like a peasant talking to a prince!" she laughed. "Look, I won't gut you, but I *don't* like being stared at." Even as she said it, she knew it was not entirely true. His eyes were wide, and a beautiful brown, vulnerable without demanding pity.

Stop it! He's half your age!

"Is not! I'm only twenty-eight."

"What'd you speak?"

"I—said I was twenty-eight. How old are you?"

Dida started to speak, then interrupted himself.

"I have seventeen years," he said firmly.

"I greet you, Dida of seventeen years. I'm Jiana of Bay Bay, recently." She extended her palm, and they touched fingers politely. Dida's hand trembled a bit, and his eyes kept straying to her loose shirt, open to her waist. She was going to lean farther back, to pull it closer to her chest; but somehow the signal crossed in her stomach, and instead, she leaned forward a bit. Her hand touched his a little longer than it should have; his fingers were so light and gentle.

"You come the Floating City from? Wow!"

"I've lived there a couple years. Ever been?"

"Well . . . *could've* gone, if truth I'd wanted to. But seen as many cities as I have—well, you know."

"Oh? How many cities have you seen?"

"I've been all the way the faire at Ox Crossing to!" he bragged. "I've seen Ti Lai, the border of Bay Bay lands!"

"Bay Bay lands? Oh, the principality. Gee, *I've* never been there. You're well-traveled for a farmer's son. No doubt your father is wealthy and kind."

"My Sir's a Gatherer. Didn't I speak that before?" Dida's gaze began to drift south, along her body, but he caught himself and fastened his eyes to her face. He seemed flustered. Oddly, Jiana's own mouth was a bit dry, despite the ale, and without thinking, she found herself wetting her lips.

"What's a gatherer?"

"You know nothing? The Family Gatherer calls all the free families the Assemblage to, and calls order. Haven't you heard this?"

Jiana shook her head, surprised she found the subject so fascinating, despite her usual impatience with local politics.

"He collects the parts—the parts of the crops—and disperses yan Assemblage scales the projects to."

"Disperses . . . what?"

"Yan scales what belong the whole Assemblage to. He disperses these monies the projects for, what benefits the whole groups of families for! Don't you underearth? You understand what I say?"

Jiana could see perfectly well where he stared. *Oh, Serpent's Lair—he's only a kid! Doesn't bother me too much. Besides, his bare legs were so smooth and dark. Where's the harm in a little peek?*

Whose, sneered the voice. *His, or yours?*

Lock it up!

"Dida, I understand you fine when you talk the tongue of the Water Kingdom. I 'underearth' you, or whatever you said, except when you use that funny accent." Reluctantly, he forced his gaze upwards again, trying to pretend it had been there all the time. He moved a little closer to the table, and crossed his legs in an odd fashion.

"I'm sorry. Everyone talks like that around here. Sir learned me to talk the city speech like, but sometimes I forget." Dida took a deep breath.

"Jiana, I think you're—I think truth you're pretty! Will you stay us with?"

Jiana opened her mouth to tell him about the quest, how she had to leave immediately to seek Alanai, who sought the World's Dream of O-onakai Tonoronakai. But the words would not come, and she hesitated. She tried to speak again, and discovered her right index finger tracing a line down the midpoint of her chest, between her breasts, as she looked into Dida's earth-brown eyes. She yanked her hand away and sat on it.

"I cannot st-stay long," she spat out at last. "I am on a— on a—" The word would not come. "I'm on a journey."

"Will you stay today?"

"I will stay today." She shook her head in wonderment.

Stay another day? He's ahead of you, dumble! He gains, hour by hour! What draws you here?

Well, snakehole, what's the use of questing if you can't learn about faraway people and strange, exotic lands?

Really! The exotic backwoods southers, a day's ride from the Floating City! I know why you're really staying.

"Lock it up!"

"Speak?"

"Nothing. I'm sorry. I was thinking out loud, a salty habit. What the hellmoon, sit and talk to me!"

They sat by the fire and discussed their lives, and it was not long before the shy Dida began to laugh and smile back. Soon his spirits buoyed, and his fifteen-year-oldness made Jiana feel young herself. She spoke nothing of philosophies, or portents, or predestinations, or dooms. To her amazement, she suddenly spilled her life to his ears, though they had only just met. It turned out that Jiana was responsible for Dida lazing about the house, instead of slaving away in the field: *somebody* had to keep an eye on her and the family possessions.

The two of them talked through the afternoon as if they were long-lost siblings, exchanging secrets of the world and dirty jokes. Jiana had heard all of Dida's, but she laughed anyway—somehow, they seemed funnier than before. Within an hour she had grown used to his souther dialect, and could only hear it if she strained. She even tried slipping into it herself, at times.

After the shadows had lengthened, and she and Dida had lit the paper-wrapped lamps; after the children had all trooped in from their labors and had refreshed the night-guardings at the windows and doors; when Dida's father would soon return from the field and his mother was about to come home from wherever she had been drinking, fighting, or dicing—only then did Dida mention the "too-wise woman" on top of the mountain.

"Too-wise woman? You mean a witch? Magick?" Fairy tales had been Jiana's favorite kind of story for as long as she could remember, especially since her days in the Flower Empire, where she had begun to learn the techniques of the spirit which the uncivilized people in the Known Lands of the west called "magick."

Dida nodded. "True as the songs of Corn Woman! I speak truth. I can't say anything about her now—Sir said he'd kill me if ever I spoke of her again!" He looked fearfully over his shoulder, as if he expected parental mayhem even as he spoke. From what he had told her of his father, Jiana thought the threat was credible.

"When, then?"

"Tomorrow, after chores."

Jiana felt like a little girl as she raced through supper. The gravy-soup was not half as good as she remembered from the night before, when her hunger seasoned it strongly, but she praised it anyway.

Dida's mother, Boolea, was a silent woman, who glared disapproval at Jiana all evening, even though the latter had buttoned up her shirt. Boolea looked older than her years, hard and bitter, and had a nasty scar on her face that reminded Jiana that the souther women were all fighters. *If they weren't so stupid and loutish, I could live here among them,* she thought. But it was ungracious, and she scolded herself for the thought.

His father lectured her all through the meal on kingdom and principality politics; as usual for such people, he knew nothing about it. Jiana nodded and agreed with whatever peculiar opinion he voiced, resenting the entire conversation. It was different when Dida did it.

At last supper ended, and she curled up for the night. Sleep seemed a thousand years away, and the morning an epoch at least. In the morning she would see Dida, and he had promised her the magickal tale.

She watched the souther world wind down, like the timepiece in Frothing Plaza, at the gaming-palace end of the Pier of Beginnings in the Floating City.

They blew out all but the guiding lantern, beat the children for good character, and left a plate of gravy out for the "Silent Walkers the Night Of—*who had better be strong-stomached*, Jiana thought, as her own began to voice an opinion of the food, *though perhaps it will be eaten by a dog*.

Unaware, she finally drifted into a dreaming sleep—*the too-wise woman! What a story it could be*.

-3-

In the morning, Boolea stripped and scrubbed the children, while the older ones washed themselves. Nothing would do for Dida but that he and Jiana should bathe together, of course.

Jiana had argued with herself all night, and had won. Only the faintest trace of modesty remained, associating disrobing with prebedding.

"It's a whole new world," she assured herself. "Everyone strips, nobody cares." But the voice responded, *I know why you're REALLY doing it!*

"Sorry, Voice. You don't disturb me anymore."

I should.

The problem was that Jiana's other midnight argument had been lost: she still felt for the boy what she knew she should not.

She felt outside herself, as if watching an etiquette drama: Dida insisting his interest in bathing with her was purely hygienic, and she feigning disinterest in his obvious excitement.

We erect a brave front, she thought. Dida had surely never been so clean, nor had Jiana when he had finished helping her.

"Nothing lustful about a backscrub!" he exclaimed. She smiled, glad it was a lie. Only when they were both shivering from the cold did they reluctantly pour out the water and dry themselves off.

Boolea made a surprise appearance and marched Dida off to his neglected chores, leaving Jiana to warm before the fire and seethe that she had been too immersed in bathing to remember to ask about the too-wise woman.

Hours passed. The sun climbed, and Dida's father Drulla came home for lunch. His importance as a Family Gatherer (Dida explained) allowed him to leave the midday heat, and work only mornings and late afternoons. Thus, though Dida too came in to eat, neither he nor Jiana mentioned magick, wisdom, or mountains. Jiana finally learned exactly where she was, and that the southers called the area New River Gathering.

"What gathering did you say?" she asked, astounded.

"New River," Dida responded. Jiana snorted, finding the coincidence humorous, in a surreal way.

"So what's a howler that about?" he demanded, annoyed at her mirth. She shook her head, and refused to explain.

Drulla entertained her with a diatribe against foreigners and immigrants. "Yan rootless, feckless—space for housing they demand! How thinkest they we'sh'll allow them to settle? An' always skittering like tiny lizards the hot rocks on, hither and back? Think we'sh'll lent them bastards yan valley, an' not caring the shed skin of a snake yan community for?"

"Yes, sir, I understand. I know what you mean. They certainly are bastards, ain't they? The nerve!" Jiana nodded earnestly. Guesting was a serious business, and Drulla had never done her any wrong.

She only understood half of what he said anyway; he too spoke the souther accent, and his was much worse than Dida's. She only noticed the boy's when he became agitated and excited. Mostly, she just murmured agreement.

"Wait a minute, what did you say? Sir?" Something had grabbed her attention. He looked at her like she was a dolt for asking a repeat.

"I spaked," he complained, stabbing his spoon at Jiana, "that aye, e'en to yan day, today, did come a packle of strangers yan Gathering to, questing an' storying all the farmers to! Questing an hundred things about, did I hear, an' seeking something a dream about!"

"Something about a dream?" She dared not call atten-

tion to herself by pumping him any further. But he was
not cooperative, and merely shook his head disgustedly.

The prince? Seen this very day in New River Gathering?
she thought. The gravy began to taste slightly more palat-
able. *I'll be treed. Maybe even an Eagle can be delayed by
a storm.*

She had stayed at the house one full day. There had
been no mention of payment, though in Bay Bay she
would have had to show two days' solvency to even get in
the door. What surprised her even more was that not once
had either Drulla or Boolea asked after her business,
though she tramped alone and foodless through a swallowing marsh, unlit by the spark of any gods of the city.

In fact, they had both carefully avoided such knowledge. She would have told if they had asked. The Gather-
ers were hospitable, but they knew she was not of their
world. And Jiana knew it, too. She had to leave.

Finally, after puttering about the house for an interminable period, Drulla left for the fields again. Dida's mother
growled at the younger kids to clear the table, then rode
out to drill her valley wardens, who were all women but
one, according to Dida.

Jiana's minimal store of patience was exhausted. She
loved a good story—more even than a quick victory or a
sensitive bedmate. Her vilest hate was waiting for them.

She said not a word as Dida led her to the barn; then
her curiosity burst.

"Stop sucking snake!" she said. "We're alone now, and
you'd bloody better well loosen that tongue of yours!"

*Strange choice of words. Which meaning did you have
in mind, Jiana, dear?*

"The too-wise. Tell me about her, sweet mouse." *And
you, you little shit—I know it's you, so just shut up!*

Dida grinned and leaned back against the damp, wooden
wall, pitching dried corn kernels across the barn to the
empty livestock stalls. With an effort of will, Jiana could
almost block out the horsey, piggy smell, but she still felt
the prick of every haystem like a needle.

Dida seemed complacent and well-settled, however. He
closed his eyes and began to talk. Jiana listened, and
watched the sunlight shine through the eaves, illuminating

tiny sparkles of dust in its path, and splashing silver through Dida's pale hair.

"It was a thousand years ago she moved in . . . wait, no, I think it was more like a hundred years. Anyways, even my grandsirs weren't born yet, and they're about as the stars in age, I think! We'd even never heard of Bay Bay yet, and my great-grandsir had only just invented fire, and not thought yet of writing—or so he tells.

"Once on a certain day, there were sky-flashes and thunderings. Snakes crawled out of their holes and slithered onto the roads, where the people ran over them with their carts. There were other portents, many and fell, but I don't remember them all. Grandsir might recall more than I do, for his own sir is the hero of the tale.

"Anyways, the people were fearing, for it was clearly signs of a war, or a famine, or an earthquake, else something else horrid, but none of us were very good portent-readers. Who could hone such a skill on the frontier, where everyone farmed and ranched? Thus, the great-grandsir chose to post bills in the cities, advertising for a magickal too-wise. Much money was offered."

"Wait a minute," said Jiana. "I thought you said you'd never even heard of Bay Bay back then!"

"Other cities, closer cities," said Dida impatiently.

"Closer than the Floating City? Where? And besides, you claim your great-grandfather hadn't even invented writing yet . . . how did he put up bills?"

"But that's I was *telling* you what!" said Dida, annoyed at her interruptions. "There wasn't any writing yet, and they put up bills written in pictures, of course!"

"But how do you spell 'too-wise' in picture-writing?" A smile almost betrayed Jiana, but she managed to keep a straight face.

"And slime it, Bay Din *is* closer than Bay Bay, the Gatherings to! *Anyways*," he continued, oblivious, "this woman shows up the doorstep on of the great-grandsir—he who was the very first Family Gatherer—and says 'Lo! I am one that can read yan signs.' "

"She said 'yan?' What a curious thing for a city woman to say."

"Well, she said 'Lo,' too, so curious I reckon she was!

Can I get back the story to now?" Jiana nodded, looking dour.

"She came, but then she laughed! She poked fun at all our oldest traditions. She put on airs and angered the wives, so they no longer rode the wards. Now they diced and only drank in the tavern, yacking each other about the Eagle bitch and complaining on their men.

"Great-grandsir Dudida, he they named me after, he saw she was a too-wise straight off; he pushed for her contracting, despite her disrespectful ways. 'We need her,' he said. 'And she be a city from, besides, and so should be excused, her conduct for.' And the others sighed, but had to agree.

"Great-grandsir Dudida called together the elders, and they all drew the contract up: she'd scry the signs, and then, as we say among the Southlanders, 'take the appropriate action.' It was a mistaken phrase. Among the Southlanders, nothing further need be said; our word is bond, for some have little else. Not every son's sir is a Family Gatherer."

"I doubt it not. Um, can I take your hand for a bit? I just want to—scry the lines in your palm. Honest."

Dida smiled, and made no objection. He continued his tale.

"For her return service, she was accorded fifty cows, or their equivalent in the market faire at Ox Crossing."

"This sounds like a contract dispute just waiting to happen," Jiana offered. "Who would decide what 'appropriate action' meant?"

"You think like a city-born. A Southlander would say, 'the action will be clear,' for who would contract to do a thing they didn't want?"

"Your experience with humanity is limited." An image sprang to Jiana's mind—a small village, ash-grey and smouldering . . . a young warrior woman, still believing in heroes and other fairy tales. *What contracts bind a prince to his people?* Jiana wondered. *Damn it, forget her! This is now, and she's either alive or dead.*

"Well, it wasn't too long then that the women came home from the lacquer tavern and read what the men had signed her. They had snakelings, did the wives! First-woman especially raved, and told the great-grandsir many terrible secrets about his wits.

" 'Addlepate!' she screamed. 'Dolt and dunce! Forgot you she cometh a city from? What honor hath they there? How thinkee thou such a one she is will honor yan words, 'appropriate action,' as one of the people?! 'Twill a chilly day be one the city from will show honor yan Southlanders to, thus when!' "

"What?! My head spins counting your damn prepositions!"

"And she knocked him across the room and into the gravy pot, spoiling his dinner and his jacket both! What did you say?"

Jiana was still counting on her fingers.

"Wait—think I got it. First-Woman—great-grandsir's wife?—said never trust a city-born. Did I get it?"

"Yes, yes! Those the city from work always the whim, never the will. The head the heart above—"

"But *I'm* the city from!" Jiana exploded. "I mean, I'm from the city!"

"And I'd give snake teeth to see the place! What's she like?"

"Oh, for—! Yesterday, you said you could have seen Bay Bay if you'd wanted to . . . quit shedding your skin and get back to your story! *Why* do you say the city-born always weasel out of their bargains?"

"But this is just what the too-wise did! Weaseled, indeed! For truly she scried, and saw she an invasion of foreigners, who would eat us like evil storks gobbling up baby frogs. Desperate for lives and freedom, we sued her fair nature for magickal orbs, or spells, or talismans— *something* to even the fight, and drive our foes before us like maddened cattle. We begged, and yet she insisted her only 'appropriate action,' under the circumstances, was to low-belly off back to her bloody city! 'Why, this be a war zone,' she cried. 'It'll be fearsome dangerous in a scant few days, and I've no death-desire!'

"Not all our pleading and appealing to her better nature convinced her to arm herself and join our fight, or even to stay and direct our own efforts. At last she spoke and allowed as how perhaps, just possibly, she *might* be tempted to stay . . . provided we agreed to another contract, for *twice* as many cows!"

"Twice as many!'"

"That's a hundred, you know," Dida added.

"I believe you're right."

"Much wailing and teeth-gnashing later, great-grandsir managed to persuade the Gathering Houses . . . cattles like that don't grow from the ground! At last the too-wise slithered back, towing her beeves, all oily grins and city smirks."

"Well," Jiana interjected again, "first blood teaches you to parry, as my master used to say. He loved saying things like that. The Scaly One alone knows what he meant."

"Yes, it's true . . . for *this* time, the sir of my grandsir had learned lessons. Her second contract he wrote himself, special for her. He invented writing for just that very purpose, he told me. He agreed and she accepted that the too-wise could not leave the Gatherings until after all the foreign bastards were driven away. Not before, or while they were leaving; but only *after* they had all gone. The too-wise took Dudida's whole herd and thought him a cluck, as did First Woman . . . loudly, too!

"Then the barbarians came, just as the too-wise had scried, unbathed and uncivilized, worshiping foul gods with hides and hooves. 'Twas a vicious, nasty war. Though we killed five each before falling—"

" 'We?' You look young for a thousand years old!"

"THOUGH WE KILLED FIVE EACH BEFORE FALLING," Dida continued, drowning Jiana out, "still their very numbers would soon have overwhelmed us, were it not for the too-wise woman! Her magick crackled and charged like rolling balls of lightning, flying across the field to bang like Jofana's hammers! She made the ground shake, and the heavens loose their urine—faces were seared by orbs of fire, men turned sudden berserk upon their comrades!

"She swept the enemy front to back, 'til finally they knew they were beaten, and ran faster than the gull dives, back their city to. We had won! But all knew those scaleless beast-men had vowed our destruction, the moment she left off protecting us."

Jiana said nothing, silent for once. She had done the same more than once, joining a fray to protect a "helpless" innocent. Now she worried what might have happened after she left.

Pass it, she ordered. *Don't brood on it!*

"And leaving us was just what intended she," Dida continued, relishing the tale of his namesake. "The moment the last barbarian brigand hied himself back across the border, vowing blood and destruction, the too-wise woman mounted her mule and rode for her city. But great-grandsir had learned lessons! No farther than the road she rode, but he and the young men reined her up and prevented her leaving.

" 'Unhand me!' she shouted, and rudely spat upon the ground, showing contempt for such a cluck. But great-grandsir said, 'What? Wilt lose thy contract out, so soon? 'Twas sworn all gods and goddesses, birds and beasts, and the Serpent 'round! There shall be wrath from all that crawl, swim, fly, and run if thou breakest *yan* oath!' The too-wise drew up, uneasy and fearing. She sleazy looked left and right, for indeed, not even she would wish the wrath of gods and beasts and snakes, you know?

" 'How be I word-broken?' she cried. 'So thou diest, but never did I contract but a single go at yan barbarians!' *Thus* did she pay back her allies, being from a city." This time, Jiana did not object.

"Great-grandsir pulled from his tunic the paper contract they had written, and he read her wherefore she could not leave, until after all the foreign bastards were driven away.

" 'How darest!' she shrieked, and made ready her last orb, which she had judiciously saved against emergency. 'Canst thou not see that they all be gone?' But Dudida drew himself up, and calmly pointed to the one foreign bastard still remaining in New River Gathering . . . the too-wise herself!"

Jiana slowly smiled. "That was mean . . . she'll be trapped forever!"

"Exactly. Herself can't leave until herself be already gone."

"I can see she's foreign. Is she a bastard—a bastardette—whatever you call it?"

"Show me the too-wise who is wise enough to know her own dam, letting be her sire! And *that's* why she's still up on top of the mountain, wailing and teeth-gnashing so that on clear nights, when the air is still and she can see the city lights far off, it sounds faintly on the wind, even out here. Listen, tonight, and surely you can hear her!"

"And the barbarians?"

"Never returned. They cower still, waiting for their chance."

Jiana looked at Dida, as the sun-stripes shone through the roof slats and illuminated his face. She could see the desire in his eyes, and in the way he leaned toward her, but fear would hold him back forever from simply telling her what he felt.

But what confused her was what she felt herself.

"Do you have a lover, Dida?"

For a long time he was silent; then he responded. "There is a daughter, of another Gatherer . . ." He thought, but then shook his head. "But no; she means nothing. None know I'm even alive."

"Oh, I'm sure you've bathed with dozens of beautiful maidens, scrubbing them cleaner than the finest prince of the Water Kingdom!"

"Never," he whispered. "You're the first ever, not counting my worthless sisters, or the Gatherings with a hundred old men and women scrubbing, too."

Jiana studied him objectively. He was very pretty—his lashes were long, and his many-colored hair was curly. She knew his long fingers would be gentle, and sensitive to her body. Except for his inexperience, he would undoubtedly be a wonderful bedmate.

But still she held back from her desire. It was not just his age, young as he was. She did care what people thought, and the teaching was deep within her that said it was evil and immoral. But that would not have stopped her alone, any more than the same sense had stopped her from thieving, though her feelings of guilt were strong.

"But what would happen to *you?*" she asked aloud, though softly. Dida cocked his head like a bird, not knowing what she meant. It was a characteristic expression of his; he often seemed to be hearing some song on the wind that no one else could detect.

"I worry," she continued. "What if you can't handle it? How serious should we be? But it's academic. I can't resist any longer." She closed her eyes, and in her mind imagined gently running her fingers through his hair. When she opened her eyes again, she saw it was not in her imagination.

With her bare foot she traced the outside hem of his breeks. Dida's face flushed, and he stared frozen-faced out the barn window, breathing shallowly. *I can't turn back,* she thought, as she let her fingers brush gently down his face. The commitment was a sudden, tremendous relief.

Jiana closed her eyes, and let her fingers see him. His cheeks were smooth, but his muscles hard under his jaw. His teeth were clenched—with fear or with need she could not say. She let her hand trail down his neck and chest to his stomach; it was not completely hard, for he had a thin layer of fat, like herself. It did not bother Jiana at all; in fact, it was a pleasure to stroke someone who was not hard-muscled and battle-scarred.

Dida trembled, wanting her, his fear alone the barrier between them. He started forward, but withdrew . . . Was it a game—a trick? Tentatively, he began to touch her. His trembling made his fingers so hesitant, the touch so light, that it sent shivers along Jiana's stomach.

Jiana let her hand continue down and press between his legs, both to raise his passion and to reassure.

It's not a trick; it's a new friendship game, she thought at him, hoping he heard.

Softly, with great patience, she smoothed and guided Dida's clumsy moves as he tried without experience to return her caresses. In their bath that morning, she had noticed he had very good hands, and as she expected, Dida had a great natural talent for lovemaking, lacking only the confidence of practice.

Their first embrace and kiss aroused her like very few had ever done before—more even than Dilai, master (he said) of every art of lust and love. Jiana pulled back in surprise. She had never felt such a sincerity of love touch her before! Dida's trust fired her brain. The feeling of corrupting his innocence was an aphrodisiac, infusing her with ecstasy, which anxiety only fanned.

She kissed his lips, his face. Her tongue tasted sweet salt on his neck, sweat of passion and of fear—what if Boolea came? what if *Drulla* came? *No, only me and Dida!* Jiana prayed.

Sitting in his lap, with her legs wrapped tightly around his waist and her body pressed close, she could feel his heart beating away like the hooves of a galloping horse, or the heart of a frightened mouse. She soothed him as she might a wild thing, and deftly pulled away his clothes. Her own breeks and leather followed, falling upon the hay. She began to play with her tongue. With some urging, Dida too experimented.

"Is that your first taste of love?" Jiana murmured dreamily.

"Yes," he gasped.

They were quickly warm and wet.

Now she found the animal smell arousing, and even the sharp stabs of the haystalks stretched her passion with tiny pricks of pain. She had learned much, growing up in her mother's house, and then still more from partners like Dilai. She held Dida captive, on the knife edge of release, for an hour. And then, when finally she felt he could stand no more before bursting, she pulled him on top of her and gently guided him in, letting him explode within her.

For a long time afterwards they lay together, kissing and playing with each other's hair.

"Hm," Jiana snorted. "I finally understand all those stories of farmer's daughters and their tinker lovers."

"What, Jiana, my love? What stories?"

"I'll tell you some later." She paused for a moment, studying him. "Sweet one," she said. "I must leave on the morrow. But I'll soon be back, if I'm still alive." She waited, but he said nothing.

"I'll miss you," she appended.

"But why?" He looked hurt, and she smiled at his tear-shining eyes and trembling lip.

"Why what? Why must I leave? Dida, you *know* I'm on a quest, even if the prince who leads it doesn't know about me yet. I have to follow them to Bay Din, and I have to rescue them from the clutches of whatever stupid mess they'll have started."

She paused again, and it suddenly occurred to her that she was hoping Dida would ask to come with her, even though it was impossible. Still, she wanted him to offer.

He stubbornly refused to take the hint.

"But why do you quest?" he asked

"Look, kid—"

"Don't call me kid—not after last hour."

"Hm, again. You're right. Look, Dida . . . life is small. You know little of my life, but I've done many things like this before." He looked questioningly at her, and her face flushed slightly.

"Well, yes, like *this*. But what I meant was that I've fought creatures that would make Alanai's hair straighten! And I've won and lost enough treasure to buy a ladyship and a nice manor house on the coast somewhere. But who the hell's ever heard of *me*? When I'm dead, who's going to remember my name? I want to live forever—on tongues, if not in time! I want immortality. Am I making sense?"

"But why will this quest give you that, if the others didn't?"

"Because a prince is leading it, Dida. Because Alanai isn't just a clown with a horse and a sword and a lot of nerve, but a member of the royal line. The bards will sing and the scribes will scribble, and in between them, they can't help but remember the prince's companions! I hope."

Dida said nothing.

"I leave at daybreak. I sure will miss you, love." But again he refused to understand her covert invitation. Was he really so dense?

Maybe he just doesn't want to come.

"You'll make it," said Dida. "You'll be immortal. I know as much."

"How?"

"I know everything. My father's a Gatherer, remember? I've read many books . . . I've even been to the faire at Ox Crossing!"

"I had forgotten. If I gain the treasure of the prince, I'll surely come back and gift you as a lord . . . Dida? Are you listening?"

He had a faraway look in his eyes, and did not seem to be paying the slightest attention to what she said.

"Hey, kid—I mean Dida . . . aren't you going to miss me, too? I mean, even a little?"

"What? Of course, I'll miss you a lot." He said it with no conviction, as though distracted by some idea.

Jiana pressed her lips together. *Damn him!* she thought. *Where did he get this power, to make me feel the pain of a jilted little girl?* She knew in her mind she had no right to feel so hurt, but that only made her anger grow. *I knew this would happen! The whole thing was a big mistake.*

"We'd better go in now," Jiana said, hearing a touch of bitterness in her voice. "Your mother will wonder what we're doing."

"Should we tell her?" asked Dida with a grin.

"Go ahead," she retorted. "*I* don't care."

"I can't. I mean, I guess it wouldn't be . . . I mean, she wouldn't—" Jiana felt a petty joy at his embarrassment. *You make me feel like a kid again,* she thought. *I hated being a kid.* They dressed in silence and returned to the house.

The next morning Dida was already out at his chores when Jiana awoke. She decided to leave anyway, but even so, she was hurt that he had not stayed until she woke, to say goodbye at least.

"Should have known better," she muttered, but no one asked her to elaborate.

Boolea wordlessly refused the promises of eventual payment that Jiana offered. The woman looked right through the warrior, and to Jiana it seemed she did not like what she saw. Boolea handed over some bread and cheese, and forced more of the gravy on her, in a bottle. Jiana put it all into her shoulder bag and trudged off along the road, moving southeast toward Bay Din.

She stopped at a fork, not knowing which way to go. "How the hell far behind them am I?" she asked, but no songs on the wind answered her.

To her left and in front of her rose the mountain that Dida—Dida!—had pointed out as the lair of the "too-wise." Jiana set out firmly to the right, having no desire whatsoever to meet the captive witch.

She stopped several times and cocked her head to listen, but she could never hear any wind whispers, hard as she tried.

Forget it, she thought. *Your stomach should have told you not to give in to your evil heart. Put it behind you and think to the future—forget him!* But every little mouse she saw reminded her.

Chapter 3

Food of the First Men;
Scenes Inside the Twig Castle

-1-

The road to the right was a deceit. It veered away and back, and Jiana soon found herself headed up the mountain of the too-wise anyway. Nor could she cut away—every trail, stream, and clearing that descended trickled to an ending against a solid wall of wood or rock. There was no other path, short of actually thrashing through the underbrush. She finally tried even that, but discovered the hard way the existence of a wide field of thornbushes hedging the side of the road.

"Damn you! Damn you all!" She hacked and slashed at the bushes, which died valiantly with hardly a complaint, inflicting many a dying strike upon her and her clothing. She emerged ultimately victorious, though her blade now dripped with a sticky goo that took the last of the gravy to clean away. It left a thin veneer of corrosion on Wave, which she would have to clean.

She grimly continued to march forward, and eventually the road joined what was obviously the other end of the

73

left fork. It was official: Jiana was headed irrevocably up the mountain of the too-wise woman.

Feet and heart aching, the warrior stopped for lunch under a withered clump of trees, and pulled out her notes to study them again.

Spontaneously, Jiana flipped the skin-paper over and began to write on the back. She drew two columns, and labeled them "do it" and "screw it." She began filling in the second column:

dangerous
burdensome
what if they suffer no catastrophe?
even so, what if I can't rescue?
if they do and I do what if A. doesn't want me anyways?

She squirmed a bit as she wrote the last line. After she had walked off the field at the battle of the Monks' Rebellion, she had fled the Flower Empire, west across the ocean to the Island of the Sun. There, she had been a professional duelist for cowards who had managed to offend warriors—a dubious and highly illegal profession. She fought for a year, until she got careless and caught.

Commonly, felons in the Sun Islands were allowed to commute their sentences from prison to the battlefield. She had carefully felt around her principles, and decided they were not as wounded as she had thought the year before, when last she had warred. So she had volunteered for spearswoman in the army of Holy Prince Hama-Okai of the Province of Great Smoking Mountain.

But the "eleven wise old men"—the Perfect Generals of the Sun—laughed at her application as if she had volunteered to fly like a bird or swim like a shark. She was remanded to a colony for the mad, from which she eventually escaped.

Neither your heroics nor your tactics impressed them in the Island of the Sun . . . who says they will impress Alanai?

"An uncomfortable precedent," she muttered.

For several long moments, she stared at the column headed "do it." She strained, but could not enunciate a single, clear, *sensible* reason to stick to her quest, to continue following the prince and his dreamers.

"Damn it," she muttered, as a drop of water fell on her nose. The weather had turned rotten again. Following a windless and warm morning, clouds had formed and light drizzle began.

The wind swirled the raindrops up under the leafless branches, and a big, fat blob of water plopped onto the parchment, smearing the ink. Jiana started to wipe it off, worried about the information on the other side, but she stopped with her hand poised just above the running ink. A single word graced the "do it" column—a word she did not remember having written.

foreverness

"Suck a snake," she exclaimed, and blotted the page carefully. She rolled the parchment up and stuffed in into her saddle sack, which she slung over her shoulder. Jiana stormed away into the rain.

Something moved behind her. She saw it in the corner of her eye, but it vanished when she turned around. She nervously fingered Wave, wondering whether to go back and investigate. *What's the difference, Ji?* she found herself thinking. *Whether friendly or unfriendly, it'll catch up sooner or later.* Not being anxious for an encounter, she decided to wait on the pleasure of whatever followed.

The road grew steeper, and the rain made it treacherous. It wound up into the hills now, bare trees giving way to scrubby bushes and eroded rocky ground. Twice she slipped and almost slid down a cliff of wet granite. In places, even the smallest path had washed away, and she had to leap across a deep cut, unable to clearly see the other side in the cloud-covered gloom.

Being watched . . . The feeling was unmistakable, a shivering under her ribs. Jiana closed her eyes and cleared her mind to pinpoint it, but the feeling came from all around—and she caught the faint stench of magick in the air.

She glanced nervously up the mountain. Could it be the brooding too-wise, spying her progress toward the witch's realm? The peak was above the clouds and out of view, but her imagination conjured up fell beasts and demons that swooped down suddenly from above and knocked her from the path, hurling her hundreds of feet to the ground. Still, she climbed in, there being no other choice of direction except a full retreat.

Retreat?

"No chance! Not after sweating my way this far up this damn hill!" She began to worry about whether the too-wise even wanted company. "It's this bloody road itself leading me to you," Jiana called aloud. "It's not my fault! I've no such aspirations." She trudged on, cursing a different god at every step.

Jiana rounded a bend and came suddenly upon a budding flower growing out of a dried deposit of dung. She stopped and stared at the bud, the only spot of color on the whole mountain, and wondered at its freshness when all around was filth and death. The sight echoed the state of her mind too well. She tore the flower from the ground and crumbled it in her leather-gauntleted hand, then threw it down the cliff.

The sickly sweet odor lingered on. "Damn you, Dida," she said.

At once her eyelids began to droop; the air was still and sodden . . . *quiet, warm, sleep*— Sweetness pervaded the air, and the magickal feeling grew strong, overpowering, but somehow stupefying.

"Think—I'll just—lie down—a minute . . ." Jiana collapsed slowly onto the ground, her mind becoming blank and cold, and without conscious control.

Slowly, the world slipped from her consciousness, and she lost all touch with what she had called reality. Whiteness pervaded her mind—fleeting doves in a snowy field. Ground, sky, air, clouds, mountain, all were gone, never had been. Even time disappeared. A whirlwind of sparkles invaded her vision, like gaudy stars fallen to earth, dancing about her head.

Suddenly, a wave of panic washed through her with a shock.

Fight! she thought. *Something attacking—fight it!*

The fear was more intense than she had ever felt, the

more so because of the utter lack of reference points she had to anchor herself to the world around her. It was the fear of a nightmare, and she could not control it as she could the fear before a battle. Panic surged again, and a quiet, rational voice intoned in her head. *This is Death*, it said. *This is Death, is Death, is Death.* Dream-despair followed the nightmare fear.

For a brief moment the whiteness and fear receded enough that a limited self-awareness returned to Jiana. She began to feel again—the touch of dirt beneath her hands, still on the ground, fading, fading, fading—

White terror flooded her again. *Death, Death, Death, Death, Death* . . . the word echoed around and around, as if in a tomb. The spark of Jiana-ness drifted upwards through the thousand and one forbidden crystal spheres of existence. She was lost.

Again the whiteness peaked and withdrew a bit. *Not all-powerful!* she exulted. Slowly, a dim, illusive scene flickered into existence—a memory of a room, a long time ago in the Flower Empire . . . a hundred people, disciples, chanting for days at a time . . . her soul flying out, out through the spheres, one by one . . .

Death, Death, Death . . .

You've been here before.

Death, Death . . .

"I have been here. And I have been *back*."

Control the breath. Remember that everything flows from the breath, stupid!

Again a slight recession, a fluttering awareness of her self and her world. She could feel her hands gripping the earth, hear the thunderings of the clouds, taste the mud in her mouth. Someone knelt over her, holding her.

She struggled to control her breathing, but her heart pounded so hard her chest began to ache. A pain lanced down her left arm and throbbed. *In—hold—out, slow—in—hold—out* . . .

The snow, the flashes, the sword-sparks at the edge of her vision began to fade. The memory returned—the memory of a chant, long ago in the Empire, when she had sent her soul too far from her body and gotten lost. Her master had led her back, painstakingly, for half a night, while she wandered the thousand and one realms and planes normally forbidden to the human mind in a white terror.

Now, you shan't be lost . . . even if you don't know the way back, I do! Here, I'll remind you.

Jiana remembered the way back. The breath was the key—the center for the soul, the anchor to the body. *Slowly . . . in—hold—out . . .* Jiana descended through the spheres, her mind held rigidly out of focus so as not to risk comprehending what she saw. Thus, she warded away the madness.

Each minute, the flickering touches of earthly reality grew stronger and she remained connected for longer and longer moments with the mundane world around her. The world focused and dimmed to its natural colors. It was like stepping into sunlight after crawling through a blackened cave. She felt someone over her, holding her.

"Jiana! Jiana, awake! I'm here, my love. I'm here for you. . ."

The weight of her body crushed down again on her soul, no longer free and wandering through the maddening spheres. The terror and sorrow was now all but gone, as she awoke from the magickal dream-attack. But a bit of unreality remained, and would, she knew, for a day at least. It had been thus before, after the chant.

At last, she was returned. She was back in her body, lying upon the ground, under a sky as black as an iron boot. Her heart had slowed, and the pain in her breast and arm was but a dull, aching memory. Her breath was slow again, but deep, as if after a long swim. Somehow, she knew that a long time had passed—but how much?

"Jiana, my life . . . are you alive? Are you here?"

"I'm here," she whispered, and forced open her eyes.

Dida kneeled above her, shivering, his face dirty with dried tearstreaks.

She wondered how he had found her. She was shaken that it was the voice of *the other* which had shown her back. And she burned to find out who had sent her there in the first place. But she asked only one question: "How l-long?"

"Half the night of," he whispered, and he held her while she slept.

-2-

"It was . . . a being. The white fear was part of a living creature—ah, hell with it. You wouldn't understand anyways."

Unlike you, who understand perfectly, mocked her inner voice.

"But you have to share your feelings with me! That's what—we're for. Is secreting any way to treat a husband?"

"Husband? Who are you marrying?" Jiana asked. Then a terrible thought occurred to her. "You *can't* mean—"

"But is that not what we intend?" Dida sounded completely disconcerted by her question. *You're going to hurt him,* she thought, *no matter what you say.*

"Best get it over with Dida. I love you—as a friend; maybe more, even. And you're great in the hay. But I *can't* bind myself to you forever."

"You mean you just used me, as a sport?"

Jiana sighed in exasperation. "Oh, yes, I need this. Look, how did you find me?"

"You mean when we . . . ?"

"No, I mean now! How did you come across me out here?"

Dida suddenly seemed uneasy, as if a memory had crossed his mind that distressed him.

"I—followed you from the house. I tracked you for miles! But you never saw me, did you? Then I . . ." He paused for a moment. "Then I found you here and—and woke you." There was something he was not telling her.

"But why didn't you tell me you were coming with me, damn you?"

"I wanted to surprise you!"

"Look, Dida, did you ever consider how *I* would feel, thinking you wouldn't even say goodbye?" He lowered his eyes, and again she thought he was holding something back from her.

She looked at him harshly. "What did you see? What did you leave out?" Dida looked stolidly toward his feet, his face as transparent as ever. "Did you truly come to my aid when you first saw me?"

"Oh, Jiana, forgive me! I couldn't move! It was like my feet had grown tree roots into the ground, and my body frozen as fast as an oak . . ." Dida's voice began to tremble. He stopped for a moment and took a deep breath, then continued.

"I saw the most horrible thing—a dark mist, like a black smoke . . ."

"Black? Not white?"

"It was wrapped around you like some horrible hand, squeezing, and you couldn't even cry out! You could only groan, like a sleeper unable to awake. I was afraid. I wanted to help—but I couldn't move!" Dida's face burned, and Jiana stroked his hair.

"You couldn't have done anything except get caught in it yourself, kid. You're only fifteen; there're just some things you don't know. I've been places, done things, seen sights—well, I've been a little farther than the faire at Ox Crossing, Dida. You're lucky it didn't sense you, or didn't want you."

The forest boy rose from the ground, controlled again. He reached out to gently stroke her cheek, and she let him, for he had stopped being a mouse for the moment.

"I'll marry you," he whispered. "We love each other. And I'm *seventeen*, besides."

Jiana answered angrily. "What love is it when you don't even think how I might feel before you trick me? Look, I'm sorry if you think our touching probed deeper than it apparently did. But I can't marry you. I reiterate: there're just some things you can't know at fifteen. And there're some things you can't do at twenty-eight."

"Why?" Dida trembled, and stuttered slightly. "You love me, I love you . . . what, is it our ages?"

"Obviously!"

"But *I* wouldn't mind—"

"Dida, I trust you to speak for yourself. I refer to me—I can't bind with someone half my age!"

"But you could *sleep* with someone half your age!"

"I am not twice your age! And anyway, maybe we

shouldn't have. Dida, I admit love is nice. But think: How could we live—by whose rules? Do you understand me?"

Dida glowered, and Jiana read naked anger in his face. *You're getting nought but what you deserve*, she thought to herself.

"We have to put this behind us," she said. "Things happen in their own times. If it happens again . . . I mean, it won't happen again, for a while—I mean never! Damn you, you've got me talking in circles!"

He looked at her, uncertain but hoping, but she stared him down with the intensity of her gaze.

"Walk with me," she snarled, and continued the long climb up the mountain of the too-wise. "That monster must have been conjured by the too-wise, I guess. That bitch is going to learn what it means to cross Jiana of Bay Bay!"

The detour to the too-wise seemed ordained, for at every hand they were forced farther up the mountain and prevented from descending. Trees had fallen across their path; rivers swollen from the rains defied crossing; even the goat trail they followed cooperated in the lure, for it was so steep that climbing down would have exhausted them long before they reached bottom, and night would strand them on the slope in the freezing winds. Their only path was up to the summit, and Jiana was so fearful they would not reach it while daylight lasted that she almost prayed.

Dida seemed unconcerned by encroaching night, though he was more subdued than he had been when they met. Jiana worried for both of them. *Why am I always worrying?* she wondered. *Even at Dida's age, I was never carefree or reckless, like a proper hero! Everything has to be debated, analyzed* . . . "Brooding is the curse of the brilliant," she said, but refused to explain the cryptic remark to Dida when he asked.

Dida climbed the trail, at times a vertical cliff, as well or better than she. Somehow, this too annoyed Jiana, who thought her warrior's experience should more than equal Dida's mountaineering skills.

They climbed through a flickering grey, enveloped in a thick, wet fog. As they climbed, it began to thin. Just as

Jiana wondered if it was actually a cloud, they broke
through into the waning sunlight, but the light was cold,
and the wind bit deep into her scrapes and bruises.

For a long time they struggled in silence. Then the goat
trail ended abruptly, beginning again fifteen feet up a
deep cut. The only method of continuing was to plant
their feet on one edge of the crack, grip the other with
their fingers, and struggle up a dangerous, fifteen-foot
layback to the upper trail.

Jiana felt an icy thrill of fear, as if a dead trool's finger
jabbed at her stomach. She buried the feeling in the
shame-pit of her mind, and recklessly threw herself at the
crack. Somehow, she made it safely, and helped Dida up,
wishing all the while she had remembered to bring a good
rope.

Afterwards, they stopped to rest at a ledge, and for the
first time, Jiana turned and looked down over the valley.

A great sea of white flowed from shore to shore, from
mountain to mountain. Jiana gazed across a vast expanse of
cloud far below, covering the entire valley like a shroud of
snow. There were frozen waves, with chops and crests.
The edges flowed down from the great surrounding mountain peaks, including their own, and looked for all the
world like great rivers of frozen whiteness emptying into
the cloud ocean, their currents so slow she could scarcely
see them move. But move they did, in the gusting wind.
And in the far west, the smokes of Bay Bay turned the
sunset light to fire, and it in turn made the cloud sea into
glowing lava.

Jiana drew a sudden breath; she had never seen the
clouds from above before.

"What does it mean?" Dida whispered, afraid to speak
aloud.

From a dark place in her mind came a haunting snatch
of poetry that seemed to fit. She could no more have
stopped herself from repeating it than she could have
stopped her heart.

> "For all the weary worlds wane,
> As Winter wends to fore;
> She falls unto the snowy lane,

To worship Winter's wond'rous pain,
To shout, to slay the living stain,
To die, to slam the door."

A shudder gripped her. For a moment she feared her mind might fly apart again—as it had once years before, when she was very, very young. In those long-ago days, a pudgy, fearful Jiana-child surrounded her life with terrible rituals, all designed to keep the madness at bay. Forgetting even the smallest of them would open a door, and her life would become, for a time, a grey, twilit wolf-hour, neither awake nor asleep, where phantom footsteps dogged her feet and demented dreams took life. White was always her enemy.

It was from the wolf-hour times that *the other* came.

"Did you write that?" Dida had to repeat himself before she heard.

"No," she said, and turned back to the mountain. It was true, in a sense; she was no longer that little girl. It was a time of her life she did not like to think about. At last, by ways she had blocked from her mind forever, she had conquered the beast that dwelled within her, gnawing at its bonds, ever hungry to escape and take control. But there was a price: poetic inspiration had withered in her stomach; never again would she feel the world flowing out of a quill.

"No, I didn't. The author was lost long ago. Sometimes, Dida, I wish we could bring her back."

"Okay. Let's make that our next adventure, Jiana of Bay Bay."

"Hah! Not for all the scales of the Snakelord Himself!"

The trail had disappeared, and the pair were forced to cliff-climb the final hundred feet. She took a rash leap at a hanging crag. Had she missed, she would have fallen down, down, a lifetime into the fluffy whiteness below, which masked the stone daggers of giants. *And was that to prove you really are reckless?* whispered the sibilance in her head. Conversation was effectively terminated; twilight was never more than a single misstep away.

The cliff was wickedly smooth, and Jiana's heart often fluttered wildly as her grip slipped. It sometimes seemed that blind luck alone kept her clinging to the rock face. She pressed against the stone, tasting it with each breath, scraping her bruised legs up and over rounded domes to hold on by friction alone.

Her arms ached, and she strained against the compulsion to look down, to see how high she was. She forced herself to think only one hand- and foothold away.

"Never let go," she said aloud, more to herself than Dida. "Never let go a limb unless all three others have a good grip." It was good advice, she realized. But in reality, embracing a cold, slippery, maliciously intelligent stone wall, with the sun nearly set and the icy air clutching at her like the claws of a demon-eagle, she was often forced to lunge for rocks and stretch dangerously for handholds, sometimes balancing for a sickening moment between the cliff and a wrenching death-plunge. But somehow, she climbed on, leading Dida.

"One time I slipped," he said, rambling. "Fell a hundred armlengths, scraping rock the whole way. We should have a rope, you know?"

Jiana scooped a handful of sand from a tiny ledge and threw it over her shoulder. "Here, make one," she said. He did not catch the reference.

They rested on the ledge; it was two-thirds of the way up.

After a few moments, he asked, "Jiana? Do you still love me?"

She closed her eyes. *Why does it have to be a game? Why can't it just BE?*

But she knew the fault was hers. Dida was as he was; he only acted his age, and reminded her of a dead time in her own past. It was she who ought to know better.

"Yes," she said, for simplicity, but her thoughts turned and ticked, round and round and round, like the plaza timepiece in the Floating City.

"Uh . . . Jiana, I wasn't able to get any food from home before I set out. Mother was in the cookroom."

Wordlessly, Jiana handed him some of her own supplies, wondering if that was what love was. On impulse, she showed him the fungus, as well, which she had saved in her saddlesack.

"How about this? Look familiar? I tried eating it and nearly died."

"You have to boil it first," he said. "Boil it until it turns black, then pound it into paste . . . it'll give you mystical visions, I hear."

"Haven't you tried it yourself?"

He looked at her strangely. "Of course not. Not until I'm twenty!" After a moment, he added, "I'm sorry, my love. I forgot you know nothing of the Gatherings." They turned back to the cliff and continued to climb.

At last, after another half hour of climbing, Jiana reached for the next handhold, and grabbed only empty air. She clutched wildly for a moment, feeling herself tumbling endlessly . . . but when she looked up, she saw that she had reached the top. She hauled herself up and over, every limb throbbing in agony. Then she reached over, and grabbed Dida by the scruff of his neck and hauled him up, too. They sat huddled together for warmth, panting and aching. The sun had set, and the moons had risen.

Suddenly, Dida gasped, silently touched her arm, and pointed. The dim, blue light revealed an ancient stone cairn, sloppily thatched over with twigs and hung with furs. There was but one path on the mountain peak, and it led to the door.

For several minutes, Jiana gazed at the forbidding hut, with its single, black, gaping maw of a window.

"It seems this song is already sung," she said. She rose unsteadily to her feet, strode to the door, and yanked it open. A sickly-sweet, syrupy blackness enveloped her.

-3-

Jiana blinked rapidly, trying to see in the darkness, but a heartbeat after walking into the hut, she was overwhelmed by an intense, honey-thick stench that flooded the air as thickly as locusts at harvest time in White Falls, New River. She tried to drag a sentence out, but made only a gurgle before collapsing, gagging and retching, to the floor.

"Shit!—snake!—slime!" she gasped. "You *live* in this?"

Jiana crawled to the door and flapped it back and forth, futilely trying to air out the converted cairn. In her agitation, she ripped the flimsy wooden flap off its hinges, and used it double-handed to beat away the noxious odor.

After several minutes, she could see and breathe a little. She was barely able to make out a tiny woman squatting in front of a green fire, trying to stir a cauldron whose contents had solidified into tar.

Jiana advanced on the woman. "You'd *better* pray! No one attacks Jiana of Bay Bay and leads a quiet life thereafter!"

The woman looked at Jiana and grinned toothlessly. "You be the one! You be the one!" she crackled, pointing a bony finger at the warrior maid.

"What?"

"I know her!" shouted Dida from the doorway. Jiana waved her hand in aggravation, shushing him.

"You were foretold—foretold, yes! You be the one!"

"Shut up! What the hell did you do to me back there on the mountain, hunh? Hey! Take your slimy hands off me!" The too-wise clutched and pawed at Jiana's arm, trying to drag her deeper into the cairnlike hut. It was nothing but a pile of stones, without mortar; and now that the sludge-smoke had cleared, the waning moonlight shone through the cracks, weakly illuminating the interior.

Jiana's head began to swim; the too-wise was probably burning something hallucinogenic.

"You be brought to this place of power—yes, power! You be brought here by Them What I Serve, to this place of power!"

Oh Snakelets. I need this. Yes, I'm certainly glad this is happening to me.

"Power. Right. Look—were you or were you not the one who sent that white-terror beast to attack me? Come on, be a man! Own up!"

"She's been in a thousand and another stories I've read," Dida whispered. "Don't trust her. She fly into a rage and gnash her teeth . . . 'eyes as big as saucers—as big as millstones!' "

"Shut up!" Jiana hissed. She drove her elbow backwards, but missed him somehow.

"Aye, power such as no one but me's ever seen before!"

Jiana looked around the room, slowly, her nose and stomach still turning.

Whatever being attacked you, she thought, *it CAN'T have come from this place! Let it slide. Change the subject.*

"Uh . . . don't you think this place is rather squalid? Do you serve the filth-god?" Dida pushed curiously past Jiana into the tiny room.

"Tread softly, Jiana, my love. There's great and powerful magick here. Excuse me, Mistress Too-Wise, but don't you have iron teeth?"

"Yer wanna see?" She peeled her lips up with her fingers, but the light was too dim to determine her dental material.

"Well, this 'great and powerful magick' sure ain't broom magick! Look." Jiana deftly plucked a stick from the roof thatching and wrote her name in the grimy soot on a wall-stone. "And I thought *I* kept an untidy house!" She turned suddenly to the diminutive too-wise, who twitched with some nameless palsy.

"What do you mean, I was the 'foretold' one? Foretold by what?" In answer, the woman gestured vaguely toward the jumbled pile of bottles, jugs, jars, and papers containing powders, potions, and essences unknown.

"Of course. All right, I'll try again. What do you mean, I was brought here?"

Dida mumbled behind her. She leaned over to listen, and he said "swollen rivers—fallen logs—'twould explain much, Jeelet."

"Dida, I have only one name: Jee-*ah*-nah. And rivers swell and trees fall of their own accord, too."

"But it fits that it should be so! From all the tales I've read and heard—"

"This is not a tale! And we're no storysingers, twisting the truth for a point of drama! Come on, kid. I'm *not* one of your story heroes. I wasn't 'brought' here, and there's no such thing as a place of power! Only beings can have powers." But Jiana glanced about nervously as she said this, a little uncertain of her certainty.

For several beats, the witch stared, vapid and irritating, into Jiana's face. Then she spoke: "I be called to show yer something—something special, yes? Then y'll watch . . .

and then y'll make Them stop *tarmentin' me!*" The last two
words rose to a piercing shriek, and Jiana cringed back
with her hands over her ears. The crone extended one
trembling hand, palm up, as if expecting something.

For a long moment, Jiana stared uncomprehendingly at
her. Did she want money? Then she felt a slight tug at her
sleeve; Dida whispered into her ear.

"You still have that fungus, my love, Jeelet? I mean,
Jiana?"

She angrily handed it over to the crone, who put it in a
bone bowl made from the upper plate of a human skull,
and began to pound it with an ancient, wooden pestle—
fump! fump! fump!

"I suppose you think I should have known that was what
she wanted all along, right?"

Don't be cross, scolded the unbidden voice. *You did
know, you know.*

After a while, the fumping noise took on a sinister
familiarity in Jiana's ears: the sound of a club beating a
broken, quivering, lifeless body, again and again and again.
The horrible image flashed before her eyes, given solidity
by the lingering, hallucinogenic fumes. It was a scene
from her own memory. As the too-wise continued pounding the fungus, Jiana began to even feel again the slime
and mud in her face, as she lay feigning death on a faraway
field. She felt the boneless slugs crawling over her body in
a feeding frenzy, felt the ripples of scum-water wash her
immobile face as the shambling, primitive half-men raged
among the corpses of the Honor Company of Tool in an
orgy of vengeance and larder-stocking. Tool had not subdued the South.

What? Wait, that never happened! Or did it? Or will it?

She shook her head, clearing her mind. *Maybe it's the
fungus spoors,* she thought. *They float through the air,
and I'm breathing them.* She knew that soon the witch
would hold out the pulpy mixture for Jiana to eat. Suddenly, she was very afraid.

The too-wise began to chant softly as she pounded, her
voice croaking with age and disease. Jiana tried not to hear
the woman's words, but somehow, the insistent chanting,
quiet though it was, intruded into her consciousness.

Every few moments she had to shake her head, as horrific visions driven by the ugly syllables and the floating spoors seized hold of her mind. Her stomach felt oddly hollow, as if she were falling endlessly . . . and somehow, no matter how she twisted her head, the witch's cairn was tilted on one end or another. Dida suddenly grabbed for her hand, and she held tight to him; she understood his fear. She managed to spit a few words out—or thought she did. She was not sure she actually spoke aloud, but believed she said, "Not you, kid—fungus. Will all come back to normal—all be all right, I promise."

Then at once, there it was—pulpy, bubbling in the bowl as if still horribly alive somehow—or was that just another effect of the spoors? Jiana slowly reached forth her hand and took the bone bowl, now glowing dully like fine alabaster.

From another sphere came a voice—Dida's—and Jiana's heart began to pound as she realized that, even without yet eating of the fungus, she was already lost in a lotus-world. *Where is he? Will he fall screaming to his knees, his mind shattered by the sudden disintegration of everything he believed solid and real?* But his voice was strong, if a bit shaky. It took her a few moments to understand his words, simple though they were.

"Give them to me, my love. I'm younger, stronger—take them for you, tell you what I see—" His ragged breath punctuated his offer, reminding her that brave he might be, but he had no frame of reference in which to fit such a wrenching experience. If he were to eat, to partake of the visions and voices without the training she had received, he might fly away, never to return.

She shook her head, forgetting he could not see, and squeezed both her hands tighter. One of them held his.

"No, kid—you're not even twenty yet, remember?"

Suddenly the white blob in her hand (which hand? the other held Dida's) swelled to consume her entire field of vision. She upended it over her open mouth, and allowed the tasteless, undulating mass to slide unchewed down her throat. Then she sat down, and the world exploded.

Slowly, everything about her began to rotate, stately and unhurried. But speed soon crept into its motion, and as the hut of the too-wise spun faster and faster, a sea of faces began to flood the tiny room. Jiana felt stretched, squeezed. She saw her entire past flowing behind her, as if in some other direction she had never looked before, it all still existed, was all still connected, like a twisty worm. More suggestive was the section squirming away ahead of her, but with a wrenching effort of will, she averted her gaze from the worm's head, where it ended—her own death?

Helplessly, she fell backwards along the worm's body, as if it were hanging head-to-top, and gravity pulled her down. She clawed at her life as it slipped backwards through her fingers. All around her the realness of the world in which she had lived became porous, ripping to let her through, and pulling apart in the process.

Her eyes, like birds, descended through the clouds toward the ground. At once she recognized the scene of desolation they beheld: it was the tiny hamlet, a day's ride out of Bay Bay City, which she had seen annihilated by the great battle between the prince and the alleged demons.

Jiana's gorge rose again in her throat as she gazed on what was clearly the prince's doing. Unlike the first time she had seen it, the blood and fire were still raging. She saw the pain and death as it occurred, not yet censored by time and ashes.

A woman screamed as her child was torn from her. It was rent asunder by unseen hands, and the still-twitching remains hurled back into its mother's arms before she, too, was similarly killed. A burning house fell, and those who might have escaped the crushing timbers were held rooted in place by visions of the dead and damned. On every hand, death seemed not enough to satiate these beings; in each case, a greater sacrifice was demanded.

Cruelty and bravery blurred together, and Jiana made no effort to keep track of them all, or even to see them as they happened, though she had no control over her eyes of flight. The scenes were enough to touch even Jiana's battle-hardened heart.

Nowhere was the prince to be seen. He was not yet there, and in backwards time that meant this scene occurred after he had left. He did not even know that it happened.

For some reason, an oblivious prince seemed worse to Jiana's mind than an uncaring prince. Rage flickered within her stomach.

Suddenly, as if aware of her distress, the dream-vision fled toward the skies and along the southern route Alanai had surely taken, or would take, far below. Jiana understood implicitly that they flew through time as they flew through the air.

Lives sundered. Armies fell, then victorious, marched. Castles crumbled, then built. The skies shredded like cheap lace curtains.

She walked a cold path, through piles of bodies heaped haphazardly, stacked together only enough to free a path through them for the horses. A war had been fought and lost—one she recognized. She wandered among the carnage (what was that vague memory that haunted her . . . a boy, a witch, a vile cancer of a prince?); she touched gently the lacquered bamboo armor, fingered the silks and favors, shied from the overhead spears with their cruel barbs for pulling men from the saddle. They had not pulled her down—had clutched but not caught her.

A petty warlord, rebelling against the Poppy Satrap. An out-of-favor son-in-law who had accumulated such as enormous gambling debt that his only recourse was a coup d'etat. A brilliant scholar; a terrible general. Jiana had never questioned the politics; the money and the joy of the sword were reason enough to fight.

She saw now, for the first time, what the scene must have looked like after she swept through with the Cavalry of the Yellow Reeds, her great war horse unseeing and unpausing as she trampled the broken men and scattered the living defenders many miles across the bleak countryside. She saw the dead, the maimed, the suffering ones crying for help, or at least a quick sword-thrust.

Jiana felt nothing, no sorrow or guilt. She knew the trick, to show her up to be no better than the Red Prince, Alanai of Bay Bay.

The hell with it! I know why I fought. No abstraction,

no principle, no transcendental purpose—I killed because it is my destiny to kill. It's who I am!

"You call yourself a warrior, murderess," clacked the bony jaw of a skeletal body, which lay slumped over a ruined war cart. It smelled of fresh death, and Jiana smiled as the odor touched a familiar memory.

"I am a killer. I am not a murderer. I don't kill for the joy of death, but the joy of the sword. I take joy only in a challenge offered, and accepted—not in arbitrary slaying." But who was talking? Who was this Jiana?

"So many dead. So much agony. What challenge was offered." It took her a moment to realize the last was a question, for the corpse's clicking teeth carried no inflection.

"I have fought where they fought, on my feet, against man and beast. I have fought foul odds. I've stood against magick and even against one they called a god. I know why I fight . . . and who I fight."

"How then do you condemn Prince Alanai?"

Jiana felt satisfaction; she had expected this question.

"Honor. Goodness. Piety. Faith. Tradition. He's a prince of abstractions, and all the ugly virtues. He's a palace prince, venturing forth only to stalk and slay in the name of purity and patriotism. He knows nothing of his world, and fights only to enforce his dreams."

"Yet you seek to join his quest?"

This was the harder question.

'I seek to—*travel* with his quest. My reasons are not Alanai's . . . they are mine, and not the world's. How can he think to speak for the world? Is my honest avarice and ambition more damning than his hypocritical, adolescent arrogance?"

"You speak from jealousy, Jiana, my slayer." The voice was hollow and, she suddenly realized, mocking in a toneless way.

"Well, what the hell am I arguing with you for? You're dead. I slew you, as you pointed out. If I feared you not when you were alive, what sleep will you lose me now?" She threw back her head and laughed, though it came out sounding forced, and strode across the field, further back into her life.

The sky turned iron, and the dried blood on the ground

blackened in the waning light. Soon, quicker than it should
have, her sun had set, and Jiana walked in darkness and
silence through the early parts of her life, the years of the
poetry, the solitude, and the terrible black torments of her
mind. Lady Death lay all around her, but Jiana was not
afraid. The Lady and the warrior were old drinking buddies.

She was moving to White Falls. Her Uncle Tonga was
hanged; her father's funeral was held in the rain. Much too
quickly, she flew toward what she did not want to see
again. Her father died when he accidentally fell on a sharp
knife. She felt the power of shame come upon her. She
had hissed the poem of death in his ear while he was
sleeping. What she feared loomed in the fast-approaching
horizon of the Past.

Then at last the Most Terrible Thing was upon her, long
before she was ready. Again, as in many a dream throughout this time, she felt his rough, dead hands on her,
holding her down, bruising her even after it was over. She
felt the sickness in her stomach, both physical and mental,
on this last night that He would come at her, the night He
finally came into her. She felt the ripping then as he
entered her—terrible pain, for she was utterly dry and
unaroused, held back by bonds of force and family.

Backwards through the night she flowed. He tore her
nightclothes off, spoke roughly to her of her duty to her
father, and reminded her of her mother's profession, that
she must follow. It was only after that that He entered her
room, which of course He had really done beforehand . . .
how else could her father talk to her?

But the worst was passed. Jiana gritted her teeth and
lived through the other five times, the earlier times He
had come. They were not as bad; He had only used His
finger. The ordeal was soon over. She had accepted the
Most Terrible Thing long before.

Much harder to take were the Songs. But Jiana just
closed her ears and her memory to them, and they grew
fainter as she grew too young to speak.

Through her entire life she fell, a blade's edge from
mindlessly screaming, grabbing at the pieces as they flew
unstoppably past her, until at last, with an agony of mental, emotional and physical compression, she squeezed

back between her mother's legs, up the birth canal, and back into the womb.

But the journey did not end there. Though her body soon disappeared from whence it had come, her soul traveled on—back, back. Soon the very cities began to unbuild, to be torn apart and hauled away by their citizens. It was as if it had all been an etiquette drama—"apologies, gentles, but the show is ended, and all the set is stricken!"

Then even the people dispersed, and wandered the plains—young, fiery, and dreaming of raid, not conquest. Twice more the cities rose—the Ti-Ji Tul, but then another after them! *Before them,* a voice corrected her, and after some searching she realized it was her own voice, and she was shocked to recognize the existence of an "I." Then they all were gone, and not long after that, even the tribes disintegrated into tiny enclaves of humans, living in caves and gathering food like monkeys, occasionally killing some beast.

Fear flooded through her spirit, but by sheer force of mind she quelled it. She knew she dare not let herself feel the terror that lurked just below the surface. To be lost now, so far before she or anyone like her would be born . . . ! *Courage,* she thought. *Feeling—reason—love.* The incantation was trivial, a child's rhyme from another life ago:

> Courage, feeling, reason, love,
> Terror from me shove,
> A shielding glove
> Above

Farther and farther back she fell, always but a breath away from a terrible mind-scream that would go on forever and forever, for there would be no return. If this world flew apart into nothingness, she had no golden rope to drag her back to her own. Even *the other* was silent.

Now the men were not even men anymore, but beasts themselves, and soon not even erect upon two legs. Back in the trees, tiny monkeys, then four-footed, giant-eyed starers. Then to the ground again, and quivering, darting rats.

Back and back. She no longer clawed at the world, grabbing as it fell past, for she kept pulling tiny pieces off like crumbling, rotted wooden walls. *And what horrible crimes are you committing against the yet unborn with your careless soul-fingers?*

Soon even the animals were gone. For a long, lazing moment, great dragons stalked the world. Then they did not.

Now the land was the demesne of the insects. They were monstrous in size, and dazzling in variety. Then they too were gone, and the land at last was silent. A great peace descended, as the trees reclaimed sole possession. Then, an even longer sigh for more primitive vegetation.

At last even the ferns retreated, and the slimy fungi, and then even the scrabbly algae ceased to cover the rocks, and the Earth was barren. It was only then that she saw the city.

At fist it seemed only a few more black rocks rising from the sea. But then she saw that they had been artfully erected, and she shuddered at the implications . . . how long had they lain thus? The lightless black stones stood in ruins, save for one tall, thin minaret, thrusting against the bright, starry sky. All else about the fallen menhirs was black void and chaos, no order or pattern to their placement. But the ugly, leering tower beckoned, and she knew it was there that she had journeyed, all these untold eons back through her own lifetime and that of the first sphere of the worlds.

She paused for a moment, for something tugged at the back of her mind. It was an image: a young boy, perhaps fifteen, seemed for a moment superimposed across the landscape, and the smell of sweet rot and filth obscured the sterility of the lifeless air. Words were spoken, in a language unknown and strange, and she suddenly trembled, as if shaken by an earthquake. But just as quickly the visions vanished. Once again she saw only the lone standing tower, unlighting the sky. She found herself in the court before the dark edifice.

She somehow passed through the gates, through the great, ebony doors, through the bare hall and the inner portals, and stood in the great Room of Kings, where the priests would lead the congregation during services to the Scaly One, were this any other castle . . . and if He had yet been hatched.

A blasphemous thought, she chastised her Self.

The room was tremendous, but its musty smell and brittleness bespoke decrepitude and collapse. Whatever lord it housed had let it all fall to decay. At once a young man, huge and muscular, sat in the lord's chair, though none was there before. He looked directly at Jiana and smiled with chilling effect.

"You seek the World's Dream," he said, smoothly guessing her very thoughts. "It will be yours, if you but follow me . . . now and forever."

She found she could talk, and had substance once more. *You live now only in his dream*, she thought.

"No, I don't seek the Dream. I'm just curious about the bloody thing, nothing more. Really! I think you want Prince Alanai. He—"

"Do not bandy words with me, mortal!"

"Uh, 'mortal'? Okay. Look, I'm really not involved in this. If you want the World's Dream, it's between you and the prince, right? After we find it, I'll be happy to watch you take it away from him . . ." Her words were light, but her stomach tightened. Who else but a god could live in the time before all things, and draw another back to meet him?

This bargain might be for your life, her inner voice told her.

The boy-god's smile died slowly into rage, and his golden hair squirmed and curled like a thousand worms suddenly writhing on his head. His skin roughened and puckered, and his knuckles, throat, and knees swelled like a victim of yellow-death.

"I DO NOT *WANT* ALANAI TO FIND IT!" he shrieked, losing all pretense of divine dignity. "He is a fool, and the fatherless offspring of a fool! He will listen to no reason, no bargains . . ." He suddenly became crafty again. "But *you*—you I know will not be so unreasonable. You will stay with me, and together—" the boy-monster-god smiled indulgently, and stretched forth his hand to pat Jiana on the head, a dozen paces away—"together we shall find the silly old thing."

Jiana's mouth was dry with fear, and she (*wake up! come back! Jiana, are you all right?*) cautiously queried, "And who is't I am to serve?"

"I am often called Toq," said the godlet, golden and sweet again. He reached out for her: "Come with me; come with Toq. Choose from any of my finest clothes, swords, meats, and meads. Choose one of my fine young boys—or girls?"

He gestured to the sides of the hall, and now there were many pretty boys and young girls, each clothed only in tiny gilt chains and jewels on their throats, though a second before, the hall had been empty, but for the warrior and Toq.

For a moment, Jiana was tempted by some of the males, but the meaning of their chains was all too obvious, and she felt her heart squirm up into her throat as she said firmly, "Sorry, Toq, but I serve only myself. I will not come with you."

For long moments silence reigned, as Toq passed through layers of emotion, from cocky arrogance to barely suppressed fury. The illusion of beauty fell from the slaves, and they were revealed in the hideous forms that were truly their own. Toq began pounding the arms of his throne in a tantrum, and Jiana felt the pit in her stomach grow deeper as she realized that emotionally, this God Before All Things was but a spoiled, prepubescent child.

"YOU, TOO?! YOU, TOO, WILL SPIT IN MY FACE?!" He leaped to his feet, waving his hands, and the hideous slaves were consumed by searing white fire. They screamed as the flesh charred from their bodies, and writhed in agony. Then they were gone, and Jiana felt a guilty surge of relief at not having to see their unnerving forms any longer. Toq was now bone white, and white had always been her enemy.

The warrior dropped back from the raised dais of the throne into a defensive stance, drew her sword from around her waist in a single snap, and raised it over her head, her hand level with her eyes and palm-inward. She noticed she trembled. *Calm, calm,* she thought. *Water flows softly over mossy stones; wind blows gently over snowy fields* . . . It was the first stanza of a chant to calm the mind, taught to her by her master.

As her fluttering heart slowed, and she smoothed some of the intensity from the scene, it faded, just slightly, as if ethereal.

Again, an insistent vision—the face of a young boy superimposed over the throne room, a look of concern (and love?). Somehow, she knew it was vitally important she remember who he was.

Toq rose from his throne and drew his hands together, as if gathering invisible strands of a web that had been spun from the air itself. His hands began to weave them rapidly while he mumbled. Jiana began to feel sluggish, as if a net of wind were being woven around her. She strained to remember the Name of the Face—Dogo? Doodah? Dimwit?

Toq suddenly caught at the magickal strands and yanked her off her feet. He began to reel her in, her arms pinioned, as a fisher would haul in his long-grass net with a catch of pinkfish and kraw.

It had a 'D'! She remembered the Name that went with the Face had a 'D'—two 'D's' . . . Dada—Doda—Didi . . . Dida!

"Dida!" she screamed as Toq hauled her, bumping up the steps, and again, "Dida, help me! Wake me!" as he grabbed at her tunic with hands now twisted and gnarled, stained sticky-white on the fingers.

The throne room, the black tower, the lightless, void ruins—even the barren rock world faded from her sight like a chalk drawing in the rain, all of the colors melting into one another and dimming. At the very last, Toq realized she had eluded him (for he was no fool, she knew), and he had time for one last promise before he, too, faded from her world: "we will meet once more . . . in my own mind, not yours!" Then he laughed—a short, ugly, suggestive laugh. And he was gone.

Jiana blinked, coughed, and found herself back in the renovated pile of stones that the too-wise woman of the mountain called home. Dida had the warrior by the shoulders and was shaking her, shouting, "Jiana! Wake up!" He slapped her face—not the first time, she realized by the numbness in her cheeks.

"All right, all right! I'm here! Lemme go!" She pushed him away and staggered back toward the door, tripping over the prostrate form of the too-wise, who was on the floor gibbering.

"I dunno! I dunno! I dunno!"

"Dida," Jiana asked, staring at the woman. "What the hell did you do to her?" He turned up his palms in ignorance.

"When your spirit flew from this place, hers did, too. Then just now she fell down and began to do what she does now, while you sweated and gasped. I *tried* to wake you—are you all right?"

Jiana nodded. She noticed, to her surprise, that she had drawn Wave. She sheathed it, unable to remember what she had meant to do with it. Would she have fought a god—fought Toq?

"How long, Dida? It seems an eternity."

"How long? Your eyes rolled up but a minute ago! And then just now, *she* fell over . . ."

"A minute? Well I suppose it balances out the last time, when it seemed like a moment, but half the night flew."

Dida bent over the too-wise and tried to shake her awake, too, but Jiana stopped him with a hand on his shoulder.

"Leave her. Let's make tracks. Perhaps she'll recover when we're gone, and the gods speak no longer through her."

"What if she doesn't?"

"Then there's nothing we can do anyways—I never chose to come to her, and surely none but she and the Slithering One chose her to be a too-wise in the first place. It's her problem, and we have our own."

Jiana felt in her purse, but found nothing. She broke a small, hammered-bronze bangle from her belt and threw it down near the whimpering woman. "Here—buy a bath," said Jiana. "Come on, Dida, we're going."

"Where to?"

"Bay Din," she said without hesitation. "I'm sure we'll pick up the prince's trail there." They left the hut and continued on down the other side of the mountain, breathing in great draughts of clean air with every step. The sobs of the too-wise soon faded into the murky black behind them.

-4-

Jiana and Dida followed the trail down the mountain, through the cloud-sea again. They struggled across a valley where the wind blew so angrily and close to the ground that mountain sheep fell over and hid behind boulders, where the two adventure-followers looked like scarebird rag merchants with their cloaks flapping behind them, dragging them back toward the too-wise mountain.

Nothing seemed to grow in the valley. "A sapling would surely be uprooted by yan wind before it gained a hold, and bushes stripped of their leaves before the sun could warm them," Dida explained unnecessarily. Jiana made appropriate polite noises.

"Look close to the ground," she suggested, and pointed to tiny green buds, a hundred to a hangnail, clinging to bare rocks and clustering in shallow basins. "Earth is modest. I've never seen a stretch larger than my hand without some growing gown covering her, except in the Tarn. The Ti-Ji Tul called Earth Tiki-Rika Riki, and in the Flower Empire she is Djino hi Jung Hwong, and both mean Green Embarrassed Mother."

Dida thought for a moment.

"I understand what they say, but why should She be embarrassed without a gown?"

"Kid—look, you have to realize South Bay Bay isn't everywhere, and southers aren't general models of the world. Oh, hellmoons, you'll see as we get away from here—but be cool! Don't light a pipe in a house of straw." She was mildly surprised that he understood the metaphor, and did not say "I don't smoke," or something equally silly.

Jiana told Dida of her visions, and of Toq. She told him of the black chaos, the ruins of a city that was ancient when the Green Mother stood bare and revealed, though none was there to see Her but Toq and his minions.

"But . . . is he really a god?"

She shrugged. "He can invade my mind, and seize control for a time, at least. What does the word matter? I wonder if the prince knows that Toq, too, searches for the World's Dream. They don't sound like allies."

"Will we find our answers in Bay Din?"

"We'll find the prince in Bay Din, or I'm a trool!"

"A trool?"

"Look, kid—I mean, Dida. The Ti-Ji Tul lost the bloody thing in the first place, check? Say 'check'."

"Check."

"The only city that still stands in all of the Water Kingdom that was built by the First Men is Bay Din, or Ruoy Uudn, if you like the old tongue, right?"

"Check."

"The Road of the Yellow Marshes, where I lost his trail, leads directly to Bay Din, right? The expedition that started this whole mess came from Bay Din."

"Check."

"You don't need to be a councilor to figure out there's some connection! Besides, I heard the prince say he was going there, to get some World's Dream commanding spell, or something."

"Check. But what if he's already been and gone?"

She sighed. "Look, *somebody* must have *some* sort of control over the World's Dream, or else one of these people and powers searching for it would have found it. Somebody's deliberately hiding it. If you had a World's Dream, would you want to just hand it off to some prince from the north—somebody you don't even like?"

"Check. I mean, no. But—what *is* the connection between Bay Din and the World's Dream?"

"Dida, if I knew that, Alanai would know it, too, and he'd have grabbed whatever or whomever he needed and cut out. We assume the connection is there, since he's going there. And we *have to* assume he hasn't yet found it, or else we're already sunk and we just give up. That's called argument by necessity."

"Okay, to Bay Din. Maybe we'll all meet and have an adventure!"

"By His Scaly Skulkiness, I hope so! I hope something'll happen to Alanai. I hope we'll arrive just in time to pull his rump from the roasting pit. I hope he'll find room for two more rogues to join his Dream-quest, okay, kid?"

Dida grinned and jogged on a little faster. Jiana matched his pace, cursing her years of lazy city living.

She found herself brooding again, and she realized that somehow, she felt none of the fever and excitement she saw in Dida's face. All she felt was an urgency she knew had more to do with her age than with the quest. She could not stop feeling that this might be her last chance to Do Something.

The warrior spoke nothing of her doubts. *Why let your Jiana-mood spoil it for the mouse?* she thought, and smiled wanly in response to his joy. Soon they cut in on the main road again, and Jiana was thankful that Dida finally ran out of fifteen-year-old breath and slowed down. Without him, she would never have found the road again; she had wandered miles away during the storm.

Despite the solitary nature of the ancient city's inhabitants, and despite their lack of interest in trade and entertainment, the Bay Din road was well-kept and easy, owing to the brisk pilgrim trade.

"In all regions of the Water Kingdom I've visited," Jiana explained, "the dominant religions like to trace their histories back to the time of the First People. Since Bay Din is the only city reputed to be that old—or almost that old— they all claim her as their Holy-of-holies."

Dida sniffed. "Do they think it'll make them any less of a fraud?"

"Hah! Even in the *true* religion—and we all know which religion *that* is, do we not? —the oldest Serpent Temple is to be found in Bay Din. Don't call a man a poisoner just because he serves you a spicy soup!"

"What?"

"Don't be so quick to judge the motives of others." She was glad for something to talk about that did not stir up the turmoil in her mind. "In the frozen northlands, your host puts a sword to your throat as you enter his house—

but he's only showing you he means not to kill you! I will admit, that's one I never got used to."

"Have you been *everywhere?*" asked Dida in wonderment.

"Well, I've never been to Tool, so the answer is no. Actually, I wasn't really up in the frozen northlands either, in a strict sense of 'been,' I've heard a hundred stories about them, though, from comrades who spent years there. That's almost like being there, isn't it?"

"I've never been anywhere."

"Nonsense. You've been to the faire at Ox Crossing! I never have. And your father is a Family Gatherer. I . . . don't even know who mine is." For Dida, the lie came harder to her than anyone else she had known, but she stubbornly stuck to it. *It's none of his scaleless business*, she thought angrily.

They walked in silence, looking at white butterflies and pale, scrubby trees, while Dida digested this piece of information. Suddenly, the day brightened considerably. Looking up, Jiana discovered the sun had finally broken through the clouds, for the first time since she had set out on her quest for the quest.

"An omen," she said. She did not believe in such things, but southers did.

They walked in the bright sunlight without talking for a while, then another cloud obscured the sun. The day alternated between bright and dim. Jiana found herself listening, as she had not done since she had studied sword in the Flower Empire far across the ocean. She heard the tiny clicks of crickets, the crackling of small animals and birds in the brittle bushes. A gentle breeze arose, and it sounded like the breath of a sleeping woman, as it blew through the bare branches of the ash-colored trees, along the now thickly wooded hillside. The footsteps of the old and the young scrunched loudly of the pebbly dirt of the holy road.

The breathing wind brought sudden and ever-changing scents to Jiana's nose: a vinegar smell from the sourpusses growing by the side of the road—exotic flowers she had forgotten after a year in the grey and brown of Bay Bay—even a whiff of mint from a far-off, invisible patch.

"Dida, I'm very glad I don't have a horse to plug up my

nose anymore. There's more magick in these dumb weeds and that chill breeze, and certainly in that faraway mint field, than in a thousand too-wise women and ten thousand hero-princes. And an even dozen World's Dreams."

"Well, it is nice, I guess."

"You're young; you have peculiar ideas of adventure. I admit you won't make a name for yourself smelling mint . . . but on such days as today, I regret the necessity of a name."

"You're old, you've ventured already! You've seen the world, and tested yourself, and challenged death and monsters. I've never done anything but visit the faire at Ox-Crossing!" Dida waved his hands about excitedly, assaulting mind-monsters and dueling ferocious figments. He hopped back and forth across the path, slaying all who came before him with grace and skill and daring dispatch.

"I have only twenty-eight years, and I've challenged far more than I've wanted already! I've tested death on eight battlefields, and won—though at times I was unsure until the morning light whether She had claimed me during the night or not. What have I gained?"

"You're a hero."

"Have you ever heard any sing of me? I own what you see, and my name is forgotten. My friends would face trools for me, or stab me in the kidney, depending on where the money was. And look—my left arm will never straighten fully again, as a souvenir of the Warlord Tanakusi Seshiyama, may his rotting corpse be comfortable enough to keep on sleeping. Had the bastard not broken his sword an hour before, and been reduced to a staff stolen from his dead brother, I would be armless. Were it not for my teacher, whose name I promised never to mention again, I would be dead regardless. He slew Tanakusi Seshiyama before the bloody general could cave in my skull."

"But you are still alive, and have known all these things of your life. That's got to be better than herding pigs and digging furrows in the ground!"

"I've dug many of those, too, though they were always eight feet long and six feet deep."

Dida stopped.

"Jiana, my love—let's make love again. Now, along the road, over the hill there, away from the travelers!"

"Hm . . . no. I don't feel like it. My mind is in too much turmoil."

"Oh, please! Please, just once more . . . no one will see us! There hasn't been a soul!"

"Dida, it has nothing to do with being seen. I've rutted in a room full of my comrades, with them wagering on how long it would take! But I just don't feel like love today. Accept it."

Jiana! I must have missed that day—or are you just lying again?

I just don't feel like it!

And it does have to do with being seen. You can't hide anything from me! Jiana pretended that she did not hear.

Dida dropped his eyes, and kicked a rock in the dirt.

"Okay. I understand. I know how you feel now."

For several moments she just stared at the back of his head, and tried to figure out how such a lovely day had just been spoiled. Then, she spun him around by his shoulder.

"Stop it. Right now. You want to be a warrior? A warrior never sulks."

"Not sulking. And I already am a warrior!"

"Think so? Why?"

"I can fight!" He whipped his long hunting knife from his belt in a smooth, well-practiced move and glared at Jiana, but she only laughed, mirthlessly.

"The soul of a warrior is not in her sword! Or *his* sword. It's in the stomach. You must *think* like a warrior to survive; swordplay is secondary. And rule one is that you can't pour ale from a teapot. Things are what they are, and you can't change them—not much, anyways."

Dida stared, open-mouthed, at her outburst. She continued: "So don't pout, or sulk, or stamp your little feet, because I won't stick around for it. Just be a man, and take what is offered!" He looked like he was considering what she said, so Jiana stopped talking and let Dida think.

"Then . . . why is Prince Alanai on a quest to—to give the world the dreams back that we haven't even missed?"

"Because Alanai is not a warrior. He thinks he is, but

I've met him. He was given a world, like we all were, and he wants a different one, so he goes on a quest for a dream."

Dida looked confused. "But so many bards and storytellers have passed the night under my father's roof, and all have sung tales of Prince Alanai! I thought that was why you sought to join with his quest for the World's Dream."

Jiana laughed. "And how many songs do you think they'd sing if he'd been birthed from a small-town whore, like I was, instead of from a princess-royal?" She shook her head, feeling frustrated at her inability to get the idea across.

"Listen. A warrior is like a bear; a prince is an eagle. The eagle can never be a part of the forest, can never live in it. Get it?"

"But your bear can't see the next hill over—can't see over the next hill, can he?" Jiana frowned, and mentally scored Dida a point.

"And anyways, what am I? I don't feel like a bear, and I sure don't fly like an eagle!"

"You're still a mouse. You live the world, but as yet you don't see past the ends of your whiskers. You still snuffle in the ground at your feet. Now don't be hurt."

"I'm not, because I understand nought of what you said. So why does the bear care what the eagle sees?"

"You understand more than you let on, Dida. I intend to join Alanai and his stupid quest for one reason alone: fame.

"Listen, I've adventured many a time before, faced and fought many demons and magickal monsters. I've hunted sacred birds in the steamy southern jungles, and stolen the jade eyes from a living idol-god across the sea. But who has heard of these deeds?

"If I travel with Alanai on this ridiculous crusade, though we do nothing but hassle a barbarian king or two, and kick the ass of some half-grown godling, then my name will still be sung from the frozen north all the way south to Tool!

" 'Jiana of Bay Bay,' they'll all cry . . . 'now *there's* a warrior all women can be proud of!' Gone will be the nickname 'Jiana the Whorechild.' People will even forget I came from White Falls, New River, which somehow seems to be a point of great amusement to lower forms of life, like captains and princes."

"I'm joining Alanai for *me*, and the rest of the bloody world can go hang itself!"

Jiana suddenly realized how ridiculous she looked, standing in the middle of the road screaming at Dida at the top of her voice. Without another word, she pushed past him and stomped on toward Bay Din. Dida followed several steps behind.

"All right, I just asked," he said.

Shortly after sunset, in the grey twilight that lingered long on the western coast before true dark, the two travelers reached the gates of the ancient city. They were shut tight, as against some terrible foe, without even a portal for the pilgrims. This, Jiana knew, was unprecedented in the recent history of Bay Din.

A great crowd of people was milling in the clearing, but staying far away from the gates. Many pointed in fear and agitation at the western horizon—toward the sea, if they could have seen it. Some prayed and begged forgiveness of sins before they died.

"Hail the gates!" Jiana cried. The sentries did not answer, though she knew they could see her clearly, since she could see them.

"Let us pass inside! We have traveled many days here from Bay Bay City! We want a room and some food, and we're solvent!" Again, the only answer was silence. She cautiously approached, keeping near enough to an outer grainery for reasonable cover, and keeping her hands in view.

A sudden glint in a loophole caught her eye, and Jiana leaped sideways, pulling Dida with her toward the stone wall of the building. An arrow thudded into the ground where they has just stood, burying itself a third of the length of its shaft in the spongy grass.

"SNAKE-SUCKER!" she yelled, making an obscene gesture at the sentry.

"What was *that* for?!" asked Dida.

"Uh, just a cruel soldier's joke, Don't worry about it."

"A warning," snorted a tall, fat man, standing up from behind a watering trough. " 'Keep away the keep!' They've closed the city and left their wretched peasants out to die." The man was dressed in the white robes of a priest, but he had no beard.

Jiana narrowed her eyes, and glared suspiciously at the giant. She was acutely aware that next to him, her own short stature resembled that of a dwarf.

"I'm Toldo Mondo, a former brother of the Fraternity of the Lidless Serpent—" He clasped his hands, and raised his eyes heavenwards, in the blasphemous mockery of reverence. "—whose Holy name shall not be spoken aloud by mere mortals and other worms . . . should any have some terrible, burning desire to hear it. Do you want to hear it?"

Jiana felt uneasy at the man's irreverence, and decided to set him in his place. But before she could think up a crushing retort, Dida spoke up.

"Do you know not who you speak to, Toldo Mundy? This is the famous hero, Jiana of Bay Bay, who has stolen the jade eyes from the Sacred Bird of the steamy jungles of the frozen north!"

Toldo Mundo scowled, and cleaned an ear out with his finger. "How's that?" he asked.

Dida appended, "At the moment, she quests after the well-known and justly renowned World's Dream of the First Men! Uh, I'm her squire, Dida. Also of Bay Bay."

"Mondo," the man corrected. "Toldo Mondo. Where-fore art thou famed, oh great and mighty Jiana? My poor province has never heard of your wonderful deeds, cultur-ally deprived as we are!"

Jiana finally found her tongue again, but decided to ignore the silly exchange with lofty indifference. "But why have those bastards locked everybody outside? What do they fear? Whose army comes? And why, by the Serpen-tine Slitherer?"

Toldo Mondo smiled cynically, and looked down at her from his great height.

"Very simple, heroic Jiana," he rumbled. "Before the sun rises tomorrow, Bay Din shall be wiped from the earth by a great army of rogues, thieves, cutthroats, and pirates, which is to say by all those Toradora devils whom the prince drove forth. And this is all because we have just been rescued from our terrible oppression by the wonderful Prince Alanai, may he live in great peace and prosperity in this city forever! Until the morn, of course."

"A *dozen* men conquered the whole scaley city?"

"Dozen? Three hundred, more like. Why do you say a dozen? His prowess is famed, but—"

"Picked up a few along the way," Jiana interrupted; "usual, I guess. I wonder how many will accompany him when he leaves?" She bit at a hangnail which had irked her for several days. Then she grinned. "Still—Alanai is trapped inside, with an army about to attack! Keep talking; this I want to hear!" Already she was churning daring rescue plans around in her stomach.

Toldo Mondo began to speak, in a tone of solemnity usually reserved for readings from the four sacred Books of the Serpent.

"Surely, there can be no greater joy for the common citizen, than to have the mighty of the realm take such a personal interest in his welfare . . ."

Chapter 4

Tunnels and Trollops

-1-

It was winter in the Water Kingdom. The air grew cold, damp, and dark quickly upon the setting of the sun.

Jiana cursed as her foot slid on a rock and she slipped. She grabbed a protruding brick with her leather-gauntleted hands, and saved herself from tumbling off the wall and down the cliff, into the city sewers below. It was a fortunate grab; creatures lived in the sewers that existed nowhere else in the world.

In the darkening sky, lurid red flickerings became steadily more visible, and Jiana could see the terrible extent of the firing of Bay Din.

"I've never before seen a city at war with itself," she shouted, the roaring of the falling water nearly drowning out her words. "Bay Din must be an inferno."

Toldo Mondo responded with melancholy, an emotion which seemed to be his natural state. His deep voice boomed from behind her, so loudly that she worried a sentry would overhear, even over the sound of the churning sewage.

"I have seen many things in this least of all worlds, young warrior. I have seen cities at war with themselves, and men at war with themselves, too. I don't know which struggle is the uglier, albeit one is more apparent to the untrained eye. Both tear and rip and destroy and ravage."

Jiana ignored the analogy; it made her uncomfortable. She believed she had finally conquered the remnants of The Other in her mind, and was prepared to give herself and Dida a chance. But a soul at war with itself was still a touchy subject.

"Where's this secret passage, Ji?" Dida asked. Jiana was glad to change the subject.

"A half mile distant, and fifty feet down. It's a way in that few would follow. I hope you have insensitive noses, both of you!"

"My dear," asked the priest. "I never did catch how it was you came to discover this hidden egress to the under-parts of Bay Din?"

"It connects with the prison."

"Ah. I am satisfied."

Jiana began to lower herself carefully down the tiny, chipped hand- and footholds in the stone wall, to where the natural cliff began. Here, along the east side of Bay Din, a chill wind from up-mountain swept down and across them as they descended. She started to help Dida, but he shrugged her off and made it down the holds himself. Toldo graciously accepted aid from both of them.

Every few minutes, a shift in the wind brought the cries of the people to Jiana's ears, and she saw again in her mind's eye the scene inside the keep—the scene so vividly described by Toldo Mondo, who had crouched inside a barrel and witnessed all.

Alanai was a brilliant tactician; no one could deny the fact. His brutal, unannounced attack upon the city had been devastating. He had struck and moved so quickly that the city guard thought his numbers were many times what they truly were. In panic and fear, hearing nothing from the palace, where Prince Am-Amorai III lay in a drunken stupor, the defenders broke and fled out the gates and portals to the surrounding hills. The bloodline of Bay Bay once more ruled the ancient city of Bay Din, fulfilling a longstanding vow of the family of Alanai: to extirpate the Toradora pretenders.

For three generations the family of Toradora had possessed the royal seat of Bay Din. Fifty-two years before, when Jiana's grandmother was a young woman in the trade in Runoville, Am-Amorai of the house of Toradora had seized the royal cushion from Al-Tanai the Languid, brother of the heir of Prince Alanai's great-uncle.

Al-Tanai had ruled Bay Din for fourteen years, since he had turned twelve. In those two weeks of years, he had written three books on exotic elixirs and the comestibles of ecstasy, and prosecuted one war to a lingering draw. He cared nothing for the disputes, grievances, terrors, duels, and tax burdens of his subjects, and none had been sorry to see his head gracing the gates of the city.

Am-Amorai was related by marriage to the royal line, but was not of the blood himself. He was, however, a fair man, and reasonably competent in running a city. The coup would have passed without condemnation but for two facts: first, Al-Tanai *was* the brother of the heir of the brother of the Prince of Bay Bay, after all; and worse, he owed the crown more money than his widow could subsequently raise. Therefore, the line declared jihad on the usurpers, the house of Toradora. It was purely a technicality, a device to save face. In three generations, the House of Water had taken no action save to condemn the tyrants in flowery terms every Harvest Week and during the Festival of the Rent Veil.

But Alanai, in his passionate devotion to the traditions of the Water Kingdom, had taken the vow to heart. Having seen his chance when he arrived, only one day ahead of Jiana and Dida, he could not resist the glory of holy conflict, of jihad. The despised Toradoras had been routed.

But the seizure had ignited a reign of terror throughout the town, according to Toldo. The priest had barely escaped himself before the gates were shut and the town quarantined.

"They had lived on the razor's edge for three generations, these citizens of a torn city. Some were loyal to the crown, still, though another man ruled much closer to their homes and shops. Others sided with the usurpers, and indeed, they seemed to have realism on their side. The two factions hated—but the hatreds were mere glowing embers, never allowed to erupt into conflagration! The two groups spoke rarely, socialized never. But they lived house by shop, attended guilds together, advised the Toradora both. They lived in a constant state of apprehension, as if besieged by invisible spirits of suspicion. But they lived."

Climbing down the cliff, carefully in the dark and windy night, Jiana suddenly smelled the stench she remembered so well, that told her they were close to the gap. She had lived with that odor for a month following her escape, years before; it simply would not wash out of her clothes. In the end, she had burned them and bought new pantaloons and a tunic, and could finally find drinking companions again. But the memory of the smell was indelible.

"Be very careful, Dida," she yelled. He leaned down and cupped a hand to his ear, and Jiana repeated the caution. "Touch nothing that flows or is shiny. And steer a wide berth around anything with more than four legs."

'More than four?" he asked.

"The rats have four legs; they're not too dangerous. At least they respond to the sword. You're not very attached to those clothes, are you?"

Slowly, feeling her way with her booted feet, Jiana eased past an obscuring clump of bushes into a thin, black crack in the side of the hill. The ground fell suddenly away before she was up to her waist, and she controlled her slide until she hung from the lip of the cave mouth. She could see nothing but blackness around her, and her feet dangled in the air. She could feel no ground or wall anywhere near. But the familiar stench was overwhelming; she knew she had found the right cave.

"Well, here—I hope—goes nothing." Jiana swallowed, and let go her hands. She dropped into nothingness.

She landed hard on a rock, and started to slip off, then dropped flat on her belly and clutched wildly at the smooth surface, finally bringing herself to a precarious stop. She crawled back to the top of the rock and waited for her eyes to adjust to the light. The roar of the fouled river brought to her mind the tumult of battle. Most sounds did.

The slaughter had begun soon after Alanai's initial attack, when the royalist citizens had perceived that the Toradora soldiers had fled. Then men turned upon their merchant neighbors, and women assaulted their homes. Shops were destroyed, stock was burned. A man protested and was gutted by his major competitor, who cried out that he did it in the prince's name—Alanai the Liberator! The butchery had begun.

The friends of the new regime soon realized they were not as outnumbered as they thought, and the city ran red with the fury of the battles. Hostilities that had been pent up for fifty-two years vented in a few moments of bestial wantonness, so much so that most of the citizenry fled in terror—"victors" and "vanquished" alike.

But those who remained staggered forth in a reverie of rape and robbery. Neither side was able to stop, and a mania of murder swept the stunned city in the wake of the conquest. Toldo climbed out of his barrel and fled, cursing himself as a coward as he did.

The Toradoras had fallen. Alanai was as yet barely in control of the keep. And enough people had fled that the pirates of Daburi Key surely knew the city was defenseless. Even now, they might well be landing on a beach to the west. It was they the soldiers feared, and it was against them that they had shut the gates.

"Jiana? My love?" The voice called from above, fighting the drone from the sewage waterfall, which flowed past Jiana's perch and tumbled down the distance the questors had just scaled.

"I'm here. It's okay. Go ahead and drop, Dida." He fell beside her and she caught him, preventing him from pitching head-foremost into the river of filth. Dida blinked rapidly, trying to see up through the crack in the ceiling.

"Now comes the hard part," he said, as Toldo Mondo's great bulk began to squeeze through the tiny hole. He said something, but neither Jiana nor Dida understood it. Then suddenly he dropped, too. He almost knocked them both off their eyrie, but they had a great motivation to remain dry, and they held their balance, steadying Toldo as well.

"Phew!" Dida gasped, as he discovered the stench. "How long do we have to smell this?"

Jiana smiled.

"Had you lived as long as I in Bay Bay, you'd welcome anything that so blatantly advertises its true nature."

"What?" Dida questioned.

"Never mind, kid."

"She refers to man's character," Toldo rumbled, "though I doubt she would describe it in such words."

"Oh, now I get it."

"I've traveled this world many times—far more than you, or even our doughty warrior here. Never yet have I met a seasoned traveler who has not known his own share of fiends in friends' clothing."

"So what the hell is that supposed to prove, priest?" Jiana snapped, annoyed by his cynicism. "I've known a dozen true comrades, too! You squint at the world like it's a print by a palsyed painter—but what have *you* ever done?"

"I only watch, and learn."

"Baug!" Jiana turned her back and stared out into the gloom. "We go upriver," she said, and began to trudge along the bank. She found her way by patches of green, phosphorus algae. In their glow, she and her two companions looked as pasty as corpses, and Jiana shivered in premonition. Soon her eyes adjusted to the dark.

For what seemed like miles they walked. Always the gurgling of the river guided them, even during intervals where the algae disappeared. After a time, Jiana ceased to notice the stench, and Dida ceased complaining about it. Toldo Mondo maintained a silence. Whether it was from scorn or simply having nothing to say, Jiana could not tell.

She stopped so suddenly that Dida bumped into her.

"Quiet!" she ordered. The three held their breath, and made not a sound. Jiana closed her eyes, though it made little difference in the almost tangible darkness, and stretched her hearing to its utmost limit.

She thought she heard a scraping rumble, as if something gigantic had brushed against a rock wall, but it was so faint she could not swear it had truly sounded.

"Did you hear that sound, either of you?" she whispered. Both of her companions shook their heads. Dida's eyes were wide, and the whites reflected sallowly in the dim phosphorescence.

"Sit. We'll rest." She lowered herself gingerly onto the craggy bank, and leaned her back against the wall of the tunnel. "I'll tell you what was told to me, many years ago when I—departed—from Bay Din through these very caverns. I don't know if this is true, or just a fishwoman's tale. But you ought to know, since you're here where *it* supposedly lives.

"In the days of the Ti-Ji Tul, there were many creatures walking and crawling the Earth who are no longer with us, thank the Scaled One. Most of these the First People subdued, or slew, and those to whom they could do neither they worshipped. But there were one or two beasts whose desires were so abhorrent or repulsive, and whose power was so great, that the First Ones could do nothing.

"The Ti-Ji Tul walked in fear of these—things. What else could they do? They ignored them, and for the most part, the creatures took no note of the human beings scuttling about on the surface of the world.

"So powerful were these damned things that they took to the under-parts of the kingdoms, for nowhere else could they feel at home."

"Rubbish!" interjected Toldo Mondo.

"Is not!" Dida responded.

"Superstitious rot! I've traveled all over this world, and been in each kingdom worth visiting. Never have I seen a single shred of good evidence for such creatures, beings, gods, damned things, or whatever you choose to title them."

"Down, boys," Jiana said. "I don't speak entirely from hearsay."

"Ghost tales of ignorant peasants, frightened by the opportunistic men of my former profession."

"Where exactly have you traveled, Toldo?"

"Where? Why, everywhere!"

"To the barbarous swamps of the south? The frozen northern wastelands? Have you ventured across the ocean to the Flower Empire, or the Island of the Sun, or any of the hundreds of petty kingdoms where the people have never seen a man or woman of my color? Have you ever even left the roads of your own Water Kingdom, and tramped the moors, the forests, the marshes, the fens, the plains, or the wild mountains? Have you stalked the underground, as have I, where dwell Those Who Have Never Known Daylight?"

"Well . . . I suppose there's traveling, and there's traveling."

"I have met things that would curl your cassock, and even one or two that might violate your vows."

"I am afraid that would be impossible, for surgical reasons."

"Well, I'm just saying, don't be so quick to mistake existence for experience. There is more to the world than can be known to we mere humans; perhaps only the Nameless Slithering One sees it all. Maybe not."

"But if *you're* telling me this, then to *me* it's only hearsay."

"All right, perhaps I'm just making all this up to scare you. Maybe I get off on fear. Or maybe . . ." She leaned close to Toldo and looked him crazily in the eye, a slight twitch in her lip. "Or maybe I'm *one of them*, and I'm trying to throw you off the trail now that I've got you down here in my element!"

"Jiana, don't talk so!"

"More rubbish. There is no great snake. I tell you, we call upon it only to impress, and to empower."

The warrior winced at the blasphemy, and silently prayed that the Great One would aim well and spare the bystanders when He blasted Toldo Mondo out of existence, or at least that He would delay the hellfire for a few years, as was common in such cases.

"I have seen creatures—monsters, Dida would call them," she said firmly. "I've fought them, and felt their teeth tear my flesh and bruise my ribs. And I've killed them, see?" Jiana turned the collar of her tunic and showed the former priest a long, razor-edge tooth. On one side, she had carved a scene of horrific violence, with herself fighting an indescribable beast.

Toldo Mondo took the tooth in his hand and squinted in

the dark. He ran his thumb over the cutting edge, but said nothing.

"But the creature that wanders these caverns, if the legends are true, is more fell than all of the others I've faced combined. I think it would kill us if we encountered it."

"Will we?" Dida asked.

"Who can say? Either or both of you can turn back here. You'll have only the stench of the sewer as punishment for your cowardice. All that I know of the thing that haunts these tunnels is that it's too big to fit through that hole there, and it's through there that we shall now go, into its demesne." By straining her eyes, Jiana could just barely make out the gaping blackness of the hole in the tunnel wall.

"Is—is there no other way, beloved?"

"It's through there that I came out, after escaping—after departing the prison beneath the palace. I know no other way. There is an iron grating farther up the river, which prevents entry by the sewer. I don't think the Toradoras know about this hole . . . I don't think anything human made it."

"Well, *I* won't desert you," said Dida, "though I like not this closed-in place, with the stone crushing all around us." His voice sounded hollow, and too quiet to echo.

"How about you, priest?"

"I am no priest, o boldness personified. And . . . I believe now that there are still a few things left to see in this least of all worlds which have not yet crossed my eye—perhaps. At the minimum, it is worth a crawl through a dusty hole to find out. I will always barter for wisdom, whatever the price."

"Then, let's go."

Hesitantly, Jiana crawled into the crack.

"It's okay, guys," she called back, "but it's a bit cramped. Toldo next—wait!—Dida, then Toldo. I want . . . the priest in back." She felt a twinge of guilt. What she really wanted was the boy where she could reach out and touch his hand when needed.

Dida whimpered something. Jiana turned back in surprise.

"What's wrong?"

"Oh, love . . . are we really going—into *there*?"

"Dida, it's the only way. Are you a mouse? Come on, warrior!" He pressed his lips together and crawled toward her hand. When she touched him, she felt him trembling.

"Don't fear. I came through here, remember?"

The tunnel smelled as fresh as flowers after the stench of sewage. Jiana could breathe again without gagging.

The ceiling of the passage sunk and sunk, until she was almost afraid it would narrow to a wedge and block them off. But she remembered her harrowing crawl from the prison, her heart pounding with fear, feeling the hot, fetid breath of *something* on her neck, and she knew the passage was passable. At last, they were scraping along with their bellies on the floor and their backs against the splintery ceiling. Jiana wondered how Toldo Mondo was managing with his prodigious girth.

Suddenly, she knew something was wrong. She crawled on a few more yards, then stopped. Dida was no longer behind her. She heard a faint cry from behind her.

"Jiana, help me—please help me . . ."

"Lady Jiana," called out Toldo, "I think you had better come back here. The boy . . . seems to have a problem." Jiana felt a chill in her stomach. Toldo sounded much too professionally casual.

"What's wrong?" She turned slowly around on her stomach, and inched her way back to where the two had stopped. She stretched out her hand and took Dida's; it was clammy and shaking. With her fingers she felt his pulse, and it was pounding wildly.

"I can't do it," he whispered miserably. "I can't do it—I just can't do it. All that weight—I can't breathe! I can't . . ."

"What? Oh, for Tooqa's sake! What next?"

As if in answer to her blasphemy, the ground began to shake and roll. Again she heard the scraping, grinding noise, only this time much closer. Dida continued to whimper.

"Oh gods, oh gods, oh please, let me out, oh please, take it away . . ."

"Too close," she whispered, trying to peer through the pitch blackness.

"Oh my lord," gasped Toldo Mondo. "Don't you hear it?"

Again the ground shook, and this time the scraping was closer yet, and accompanied by a slimy, sucking sound.

For a moment all were silent; even Dida stopped his whimpering. Then Jiana and Toldo began to babble simultaneously.

"I'm sorry," she cried. "I'm sorry, o Ineffable One, o Nameless Scaly One, o You Who Shall Not Be Named! I never meant—"

Toldo chanted something over and over in another language; it sounded like a penance. The fearful noise suddenly became much louder.

"Toldo! It's coming this way! Oh lordy, what'll we do? Crawl, damn you, crawl, crawl! And push the kid along— I'll grab his front and drag!"

"You fool! It's here! Don't you hear it? Am I the only one who hears it?!"

"Shut up and push, you fat tub of goat cheese!"

In a frenzy, they began to squirm away from the sound, dragging Dida, and Jiana discovered that the tiny crawlway was as wide as a king's hall, though the ceiling was but a foot and a half off the floor. Dida was no help; He was in shock, as if he'd been stabbed in a battle. He could only move his arms and legs in a feeble attempt at locomotion, praying to be "let out."

After a few moments, Jiana realized she was hopelessly lost. Had they kept going straight from the hole by the river, they would have found the next door. But they were moving to the right, and she did not know how far they had gone in the pitch black. In fact, she was not even sure which way they were currently pointing. The horrible noises had seemed to change direction, and they had concentrated on keeping them to their rear.

"Oh gods, I've done it now," she moaned. "We won't ever get out of here!" A sob from Dida caught at her heart, and she cursed herself for speaking aloud.

"We shall make it," retorted Toldo Mondo. "There must be *something* in this direction, if we go far enough!"

Soon, Jiana herself began to feel the oppression of millions of tons of rock pressing down on her. She had terrifying visions of being buried alive in the blackness by a sudden cave-in caused by the movements of whatever was behind them. With every beat of her heart it got closer, and the shaking grew worse. She could clearly hear a sound like a baby sucking on its fist.

"Jiana, go!" cried Toldo in a panic. "Crawl, go—faster, woman! It's here, it's—Jiana, I CAN SMELL IT!"

"How does it squeeze along, when even we barely fit?" she wondered aloud. *You're babbling, Ji . . . stop it!*

She surged and lunged forward, not letting go of Dida, though he was like a wet sack of cornmeal. And then, there was a rocky wall in front of her. There was nowhere left to crawl.

She pulled Dida to her. "I love you, kid," she whispered. "I love you. I love you. Believe it, okay?"

The stench of the creature was sickly-sweet, like a burnt apple or a rotting hibiscus. It made her gag.

"It's my fault," she whispered.

-2-

Fault, fault, fault, fault, fault . . . The word echoed about her mind like a shout in a well. *My fault!*

"Jiana, the boy—"

"Silence! I need quiet." Jiana closed her eyes, though the only difference in the blackness was psychological. She swallowed a hard lump in her throat, shoring up her shaky resolve. "I . . . have something to try."

On the mountain, before they met the too-wise, something had ripped her unwilling spirit from her body. Something white—a Haunt, a damned thing. But it had forcibly reminded her that she had learned a certain skill in the Flower Empire. It was evil, a sin against the Nameless Serpentine; worse, it was horrible and dangerous. The tormentor within constantly whispered, tempting her to push herself *outward*. She fought daily this urge toward ultimate arrogance.

But now, Jiana had no choice.

She recalled a faint, singsong round to her mind, and *fault fault fault* merged subtly into "death . . . death . . .

death," the song of the spook. But she had buried the fear, and it was a child's chant.

She allowed the word to spin within her stomach, as if borne on the spinning winds of her childhood home. She allowed her spirit to be caught up in the cyclone of the chant, and it suddenly burst its moorings to her body and rose up like yesterday's wash in the funnel of a tornado.

Higher and higher, with increasing trepidation, she sailed toward the outer crystal spheres, plying to the boundary of the star-sea, here-and-now world, freeing her soul from the anchor of a million million pounds of stone.

Jeweled sparkles began to plague her vision, and she worried she might lose her way—never to find her body again! Almost, she retreated.

Then suddenly, an image intruded into her thoughts—a real memory from many years earlier: Jiana, leading a platoon that was lost in a blizzard, after all of the other officers had died of wormfoot. Forward she staggered, a silver rope from the captain's chariot tied about her waist, a lifeline binding her to her men . . .

"A lifeline!" The thought was like black lightning, dimming to clarity the white-midnight sky. She visualized a slender, silver rope with rat-walls, stretching down from the great height of her spirit to her body, still barely visible far below, trapped in the cavern.

"Damn—simplicity itself . . . how else could the Masters find their own way?" Feeling elation at her discovery, Jiana raced up and up and crashed through the crystal ceiling with a sound like thunder in a china bell! Satisfied, she saw the lifeline trail below her, taut and stable.

The second sphere was all ice and jewels, diamond snows blowing in a freezing wind. A quicksilver river humped sluggishly through a vast plain, around rigidly geometric rocks of fractured gems. Golden clockwork fish swam slowly through the current as if they were automatoys for a spoiled Child God.

Jiana realized she was standing—in what seemed to be her own body—while the ground at her feet was littered with emeralds the size of artichokes, and rubies as big as the heart of a saint. The sand grains were flakes of gold, and even the trees grew jade leaves from the bark of some rich, brown glaze that was probably amber.

Lord of Scales, she thought, awe-struck at the stunning wealth it represented, could she but get it down to the first sphere, the sphere of human commerce. But something was wrong. She started at the jewels and tried to place what was missing. At last she realized—there was no sound, no smell, no taste of rain or dust or life in the air. All the senses that were left to her in this sphere were sight, to see the cold, lifeless gems, and touch, to feel the freezing wind against her face. It was a dead sphere.

I'll not find you here, monster, she thought. *You're too lifey.* She forced herself farther out against the universe.

Was that why they call the spheres crystal? she wondered. It was a transition thought, echoing hollowly between her ears as she flew toward the next level. *It's like falling backwards up a hole, past the floors of a topless tower!* Her fear controlled, she even began to enjoy the feeling. She burst without warning through another barrier, though this time the sound was that of a massive herbivore breaking wind.

Sphere Three was earthier; it was, in fact, made up of a vast plain of manure. There was no diminution of any of her senses, and she found it amusingly welcome, even as she gagged.

In the center of her field of view grew a single rose. Its stark solitude seized her attention and held it. Jiana began to wade through the offal toward the flower, but the moment the intention was firmly formed in her mind, she was there, and thus she learned another lesson about traveling the world-spheres.

"You," she said, addressing the rose, "remind me of something. Or someone. Can't remember, though." She gazed earnestly into the heart of the flower, trying to hold an open mind.

"Are you whom I seek? What is your shadow on the lowest sphere?"

The deeper she sought, the more complex grew the folds of its petals, until they began to resemble men's brains she had splattered on a battlefield. This brain, however, was intact and far more convoluted. As she leaned closer and closer, her breath began to stir the petals until the brain seemed to pulse and throb—though, of course, it was only an illusion.

Soon the scent began to overwhelm Jiana, and in her head words reverberated—words she did not think were her own.

"I am who I am who I am who I am who . . ."

"Are you whom I seek?"

"I am."

"Are you he who prowls the deep, beneath Bay Din?"

"Who I am. I am called Taku-Taku, the Beautiful-Deadly. But who am I? Why am I asking me?"

"I'm not you. I'm another. I am Jiana, the . . . Smart-Stupid."

"I am the Smart-Stupid. I am another."

"I'm not you. Please let us pass. We mean no harm to you, lord."

"I am . . . I am . . ."

I am Jianabel, silly, and I never died, said she.

"No!"

I killed you! In our fifteenth year I won . . . I slew you.

I never died, of course. But you know you have a clear choice now, precious pet. Do you ignore me, even after I've done so much to help you, and let your dumbo friends die . . . or do you open yourself up to me? I'm the one who made you, after all!

That is no choice. There would be nothing left of me.

Oh, don't be so dramatic. I wouldn't let anything happen to you, would I?

The jiananess inside of Jiana cried, knowing she had no choice. I AM WHO I AM WHO I AM . . .

Your choice.

"My choice."

"Who am I? Who is another?"

Desperately, she opened her mind to—

—a rhyme forced its bidden way through Jiana's head, a song from the long-ago time:

Sing a song of syrup,
Sing a lifeless horse,
A hangman lost his stirrup
To his terrible remorse.

* * *

Thirteen years of illusory control slipped from Jiana's grasp. The alien entity burt forth, unbound at last, free to sing again its joyous nursery songs of horror.

> Beautiful but deadly,
> Boundaries erased,
> Heavens in a medley
> But the syrup lost its taste!

Jiana-in-her-fifteenth-year whispered into Jiana's ear, and she knew the rose of the third sphere was, indeed, he whose shadow filled the cavern and pushed her and her friends to the end of their underground world. He meant no harm; he meant no benefit Taku-Taku simply did not care, and he would crush them as thoughtlessly as she had torn the black fungus from the tree trunk.

"I see you now," said Taku-Taku in her mind. "You are another. You are not me. I will use you for nourishment. I will consume you."

"No, you must not."

"Why must I not?"

"Because . . ." There Jiana stuck, being unable to think of a plausible reason for Taku-Taku not to eat her, Dida, and Toldo. In the Secret Place, the alien only laughed.

I've already told you everything you need. If you're still in the dark, you'll jolly well have to get your own candle!

The flower started vibrating violently, though there was no wind and Jiana's breath was light. She leaped back, abruptly breaking contact with the being that was both Beautiful and Deadly—both 'taku' in the language of the Ti-Ji Tul. In a second, the rose was shaking back and forth rapidly, as if in a terrible storm. She began to hear a scream, not in her mind but in her ears. It was so loud she had to clamp her forearms over her head in agony. Taku-Taku spoke aloud:

"AWAKENED! AWAKENED! SUMMONED, CALLED, INVOKED—AWAKE, AWAKE AGAIN! I AM WHO I AM. I ANSWER, I COME, AT LAST!" With the cry of a worldful of people being put to the torch, the flower tore itself from the ground, and pulled the sphere after it from the inside out. The ground gave way beneath Jiana's feet, and she plummeted as from a great height, the silver lifeline looping uselessly above her as she fell. She clawed madly at the air, as if she could stop her flight by grabbing the wind.

Directly in front of her a door seemed to open in the air. It kept pace with Jiana as she fell. She clutched at the door and pulled it open, dragging herself through by sheer strength of will. Looking back, there was only an unbuilt whiteness. The door had a cheesy-looking "D" painted on the outside.

She turned slowly about. Jiana was in a chaotic land, ever shifting and changing so that nothing seemed solid enough to be trusted while looking away. She knew it was a wounded land, and it seemed familiar, as if she had visited it before when it was happier and whole. The sky began with brown, then flashed hotly red. It shattered into a thousand confused shivers and became the white of fear, a color Jiana knew well. Half-seen shapes lumbered across the land, but only when her eyes were elsewhere. All was dark and uncertain.

Jiana took a step, and the world closed in on her from all directions, trying to crush her. She knew then where she was.

"Dida," she said, "let me go. You're trying to hold me, but you're crushing me!" A connection occurred to her. "You're crushing yourself, too. It isn't the mountain, it's your own death-grip of fear!" The pressure was a little relieved, and she found she could breathe again. The shapes in the corners of her eyes slowed and became bolder.

Some were fuzzy and existed in many forms. Jiana supposed these were potentia: hopes, plans, dreams, guesses about the future. The sharp, single ones were memories that had already been fixed in place and shape. Most of both were Jiana herself, but altered, resculpted. A few were Dida. She recognized also Toldo and the too-wise, and others she did not know. One memory was a woman—a girlfriend. She had three scenes, each sharp and distinct and quite erotic.

"You little bastard!" Jiana snarled. "You were no virgin

after all!" she smiled bloodlessly, remembering how easily she had been taken in by his innocence, his naive, bumbling "first time."

"Okay, kid. I understand." But she did not. "You really are fifteen. I remember how urgent it was to me when I was your age." But it had not been. "Dida, you have to loosen your hold; otherwise, we'll never get out of these catacombs alive. I can't carry you, kid. Help me!"

She found that if she concentrated, she could superimpose quietude on the landscape, though doing so drained her.

Slowly, the land began to calm. It stopped bucking and heaving, and the walls and sky receded. Until they did, Jiana had not realized how constricted she had felt.

Now that she and Dida's stomach could breathe again, the images of herself and of the rest of his life became more visible, but she carefully turned her eyes from them.

"I don't want to know, kid," she lied. "This is stuff that—that lovers shouldn't know about each other. It's all yours, Dida. You pri—" She cut the thought off, surprised at its unexpectedness and vehemence. It was time to leave.

Jiana was a little surprised to note that the silver cord had made it through the collapse of the third sphere. Carefully, hand over hand, she followed it down. As she did, it became darker and darker, until at last the light was completely gone, and she could find her way only by feeling the thin, sticky, gossamer strand through her calf-skin gloves.

Suddenly, there was a bump, and she knew she was back in her body.

"Dida," she demanded, "are you all right?" For a time he did not answer, but then he squeezed her hand. She realized only then that she was holding it.

"Jiana?" It was Toldo Mondo. "Have you returned? Jiana, you are a hero! The creature has vanished, crawled away without molesting us in any way. You did it."

"I did nothing. It was summoned."

"Summoned?"

"Invoked—whatever you say. I think . . . Toldo, I hope I'm wrong about this, but someone is trying to raise Taku-

Taku. Someone is using ancient rituals or somesuch to loose that thing upon the world—why, only the Nameless Slithering One knows. But I'm scared."

For a moment there was silence following her revelation. Then, when Toldo spoke, he was himself again.

"Oh, rubbish. There was some animal in the passage here, and it lost interest and wandered off. Let's not get carried away with ourselves, o glorious slayer of sundry monsters."

"What? All right, then have your own way of it! But let's get the hell out of here. Any ideas, o wise one?"

"Well . . . I must admit I do have one. We crawl directly away from the wall, and then follow our noses."

"Our noses? Forgive my density."

"I—well, I must admit that animal caught me by surprise, and . . . Well, not to mop around the spill, I seem to have lost a little control of my bladder when it began chasing us."

Jiana bit her lip, fighting an impulse to laugh out loud.

"Okay, that does make it a little easier, priest. Lead on—that is, if you can smell your own?"

In answer, Toldo Mondo slithered away on his belly. Dida, though he had not said a word, crawled weakly after him under his own power; Jiana brought up the rear. Soon she began to smell little bits of urine along the trail. At last, they came to the big puddle.

"This is where you screamed you could smell it—the nonexistent monster, I mean. Right?"

Toldo grunted affirmatively.

"Let me think . . . all right, we started veering to the right to escape. A hard right should put us back sort of pointing the way we were, right?"

"Check," Dida whispered. Jiana smiled.

"Let's be gone," she directed.

Again she led them. This time, she was not bothered at all by crawling through a thin crack with the rock ceiling scraping her back. Even Dida was able to keep going, though he was silent and subdued the whole time. At last, in the distance and slightly to her left, Jiana spied a dim red glow. It marked the tunnel to the dungeons, which she remembered was lit by an occasional torch. She made straight for it, and felt a wild surge of relief as the light increased and the ceiling retreated.

At last she stopped, and cautiously rose up onto her feet. She still had to crouch, but at least she could walk.

"C'mon kid," she urged. "Up on your own two feet. We're here." Dida needed no second invitation.

"W-where are we?" he stuttered.

"In prison," Jiana answered. "There's nothing between us and the main palace except three locked gates and a hundred guards."

"Gates?" cried Toldo Mondo. "A hundred soldiers?!"

Jiana strode purposefully up the slanting corridor. "It's a great feeling of freedom, isn't it?"

-3-

The slippery, upward-sloping corridor smelled of must and undisturbed decay, as if a thousand years had passed since the living had walked its length. Their eyes were well-adjusted to the dark, and the dim, red, leaping fire of the torchos cast enough light for Jiana to see every hole and crack in the ancient stonework. But phantom movements flitted through the dark places and in the corners of her eyes. The warrior nervously gripped the hilt of Wave and clenched her teeth until her jaw hurt.

In the tomblike silence, Toldo Mondo's steady bootsteps sounded as loud as a funeral drum. Dida's breathing rasped like that of a hanged man, and Jiana's own heart pounded like the gallop of a panicked horse. The stone walls magnified and echoed every noise. She heard tiny claw-clicks and scraping scales both before and behind the party. In the blood light, the three seemed as red as fire demons.

"I would that I had your knowledge of gods and demons and suchlike," Jiana whispered to Toldo.

"I would that I possessed your faith in them," he retorted.

Suddenly, Jiana stopped short.

"What's wrong, my love?" Dida whispered.

She gestured presentingly forward. Dimly ahead, they could just make out the first gate, wrought of iron, guarding the citizens who lived above from those who lurked below. They approached cautiously, and she could see the bars were cylindrical, nearly five inches in diameter. But the lock was delicately wrought.

"Lesson one," she enunciated, "in the fine art of walking through walls." Gently she touched a gloved finger to the black metal, with the barest brush. "Dida—see?"

The skin of her finger had frozen at the tip, gloved though it was, as if she had held it against a block of ice for an hour.

"Cold . . . cold as death. Damn, that's going to hurt later."

"Such a gate!" Dida exclaimed.

"Such a wolf to keep out," she said.

"The lock is so puny! Do we smash it?"

Jiana smiled. "Where's that great souther suspicion? Why bother with such a gate if a smashed twenty-serpent lock would open it? No, I'll wager smashing the lock would jam the gate—to protect against it being forced." She leaned close. "It should take little to pick it; the bastards meant it to keep out that Taku Taku thing, which probably isn't a locksmith. Strange—there's no rust or dust. Maybe it's been opened recently."

She removed a thread-thin wire from a pocket, and gently slid it down into the upper hole, where the U-bar entered the body of the lock.

"Just . . . feel for the catch . . . hah!" With a click, it popped open.

"Wow!" said Dida. "I wish I could do that!"

She shut it again with a quick squeeze, and without a word handed him the wire.

"Don't touch the bars, or you'll be sorry—unless you like frostbite."

Dida fished for a while, as Jiana encouraged, and made distracting suggestions. Toldo hummed impatiently and snapped his fingers at them.

"Get the hook over the catch that holds the bar. Pull sharply, it'll pop."

At last he succeeded, and exultantly pulled the sprung lock from the gate. She pushed it open with the pommel of Wave, and they passed carefully through.

"Leave it open?" suggested Dida.

"Are you joking?" She replaced the lock, and gently pushed. Tons of magicked metal swung shut again in silence, and the lock clasped tight once more.

"Nothing I said or did drove Taku away. If I knew the meaning of the words of . . . of a certain prophet, we might have had a weapon. But I'm not that smart, so we'll just have to wait." *Beautiful but Deadly, boundaries erased* . . .

They resumed their trek. At the edge of her hearing, the warrior began to hear faint cries. She stopped until she could identify the sound.

"Gods," she whispered, "it's the people—the citizens of Bay Din."

"The people?"

"We hear their death-lamentations, through the air vents." She drew the eyes of Toldo and Dida up toward the ceiling. Just below the molding was a series of coin-sized holes.

Standing still in the corridor, the sound was indeed that of a hundred thousand phantom screams, though fainter than crickets at night in Bay Bay City. She gestured the crew forward.

The tunnel widened suddenly. A *room?* Jiana thought. From the edge she looked about. It was half-hewn, half-bricked, and smelled as ancient as the dead stones of the mountain itself.

"Cross it," she ordered, terser than she intended. Something was askew.

As she passed through the midpoint of the room, a violent chill seized her for an instant. Jiana ignored it, and said nothing to the others. They passed on up the corridor.

Jiana came to the second gate.

It squatted like an ugly trool, blocking passage. The aged stones were shiny black in the firelight, and the metal bars reflected a lurid red glare, like the porticullis guarding the eyrie of the Firehawk, mythical enemy of the Serpent. The tunnel had gradually become smoothed and leveled, and resembled more a long, narrow hall in an ancient castle than a cave. It was wide—nearly seven paces—and the gate was solid stone save the middle five feet.

The stone was without crack or seam, and she wondered

for a moment whether it was carved of a single crystal, so brilliant a black did it shine. Almost, it seemed to make a face, with reflections in the stone becoming the features, and the bars the grinning, bloody teeth. It was an evil face, leering and mocking at her.

"Sneer away, wicked one," Jiana said. "I can break you, too, magick or no."

Jiana closed her eyes, and again pressed her mind upwards, but this time it was not even to the second sphere, just slightly out of her own. She sought the bright glare of magick.

I'm becoming addicted to this tool, she noted. The thought slid like an ice chip up her spine and down again.

Searching for the taint of magick was similar to being in a brightly lit house of mirrors: one had to step outside to find the holes in the wall through which the light escaped. Such "seeing" required no magick; anyone, even Dida, could have done it. But still, a premonitory shiver contracted her muscles: a feeling . . . a dreadful decision was about to be made."

As she had expected, the bars and the locks all glowed brightly, and so did a band along the walls and the ceiling.

For long moments she only stood and stared, shaking her head. Dida and Toldo stood behind her.

"Only the greatest lock-trip in the world could open *that*."

"Are we stuck?" Dida asked. His voice echoed hollowly from the stone, and Jiana needed no magick to know he was thinking of the long crawl back out through the low crack.

"Of course not. We have only to engage his services."

Though her back was turned, she was sure she could feel Toldo Mondo's eyebrows rising.

"And whom might he be?"

"I'm sure he'll come if we call." Jiana turned and strode briskly back to the cold and ancient room they had passed through. Dida and Toldo followed in her wake.

She hesitated at the entrance.

You can't go back. You can't forget again. You can't unknow what once you learned. . . . The voice sang round and round in her stomach, at once mocking and warning.

Many memories she had thought were dead and safely salted away in the smokehouse had fallen back into the fire of her thoughts—memories of what she had learned in the Flower Empire, of what she had discovered (what *Jianabel* had discovered!) all by herself years earlier.

Many talents; many a child's night haunts, terrors, and cantrips. Things she once could do, skills that had once fitted her lips and bowels the way the sword now fitted her leather-gloved fist.

"It will sicken me," she whispered, unconcerned that the words were incomprehensible to Dida and Toldo.

This is The Gate, the Titterer reminded her, unnecessarily; *this is where you watched Good Tobi die. Or will you crawl back out on your belly, prodding Dida ahead of you like a pig?*

The "serpent's-option" left her bitter.

"I have no choice," she spat. Jiana closed her eyes, hissing "quiet!" with an edge when Dida tried to speak. Deliberately—with full knowledge of the ancient pact with herself she was breaking, and of the black consequences—Jiana opened a door in her stomach to a particular, bloody room . . . a charnal house of steaming meat-memories that crawled and quivered with independent life. She could feel their hunger, even as she allowed them to hump and roll into her body.

Jiana remembered what she needed; and as she feared, she found the door would not latch tight again. But, Jiana remembered the *how*: she inhaled deeply; then, purely on her own, unaided and undriven by hallucinagens, she again shifted out of her carnal and corporeal Self and turned an astral gaze onto the floor.

A bright, burning, silver star illumined the room with an evil light. It was warped, bent in some invidious way so as to look twisted out of the plane of the rest of the room, even though it sat flat on the floor. The legs of the star wove under and around each other in a complicated, clinging, cobwebby way that could not be followed, tracing a delicate and spidery seven- or eight-pointed geometry.

Words written in dull blue spun around the legs, at times wrapping underneath like ribbons on a Serpentday

Pole. It was a language Jiana had seen before, but of which she was ignorant. A circle surrounded the entirety.

"A summoning room," she said.

But do you have the balls to do what you must?

Toldo wrinkled his nose. "More of this magick mumble-jumble?"

She turned and smiled at him. "Perhaps this will cure you of your easy blasphemies, priest, before the Lidless One decides to take offense . . . which I'm afraid He will do while Dida and I are lounging around in the firing line. Tobi was my friend."

"Who?" asked Dida.

"He and I broke out of this prison, years ago. He made it through that second gate—coming this way, of course. I don't know how. But then he died, a few steps later."

"Magick?" said Toldo, his lip curling slightly.

"I don't like that patronizing tone, mister. I've heard it too much from you. It was no disease that killed Tobi so suddenly."

Jiana stepped forward until she stood at the edge of the magickal circle. Then she allowed her spirit to fall back down into her body. At once, she felt a wash of weariness.

"This magick stuff wears you out. Toldo . . . in all your travels, observing other cultures and faiths, have you ever witnessed any rituals of summoning?"

He was a long time in answering.

"I have."

"Did you pay close attention—close enough to recall one now?"

"I did."

"Wait," interrupted Dida. "What does all this stuff have to do with the gate, Jianalette?" She grimaced at the name.

"I can't possibly open that thing," she explained, "without some help from the greatest lock-trip in the business. Lesson the Last in walking through walls: when all else fails, enlist the aid of He Who Owns the Key." She turned back to the magick circle. "It's a most powerful tool . . . *Didalette.*"

"And how, o great and unsung heroine, do you intend to elicit such cooperation?" said Toldo.

"Did you have a church, when you were a practicing priest of the true faith?"

"I did."

"What would you have done if another cleric had suddenly begun conducting a service from your dais?"

"I would have leaped up and punched him in the nose!"

"Right." She stepped into the circle. "Dictate to me that summoning spell, hm? Let's see who comes running up to punch me in the nose."

"I am loath to contribute to this magick nonsense."

"Well, our only other option is to go back and face Taku-Taku again."

"Or stay and starve," Dida added.

"Hmp. There is a spell I learned while traveling among the black-skinned leopard men of Khoor on missionary work. I told them how much superior our great and glorious and wonderful religion is—the worship of a giant, sleepless snake—not at all like the superstitious mumble-jumble *they* believe in."

Jiana looked nervously over her shoulder. "Stop it, will you? What if He's listening right now? We need the Nameless One's favor, not His fury!"

"Yes, yes. I'll translate. You do whatever you think magicians do, when they do it."

Jiana closed her eyes, and tried to shift again "above" the mundane sphere. Nothing happened. She strained, as against an invisible web, and finally, by brute force of will, she broke through. She could clearly see the bands of power again, but they wavered, like a heat-shimmy. She was trembling.

"I won't be able to do this again," the warrior whispered. "Hurry, Toldo Mondo."

As the priest spoke the words, Jiana repeated them as though actually addressing the entities involved. She visualized them performing the tasks described, directing their energies visually.

"O winged Queen, o godsister of the stars, o burrowing biting one—"

"Damn it, Toldo, the leopard men aren't that flowery are they?"

"I am merely improving the literacy of their mass."

"Toldo . . . this is *their* goddess, whoever She is. She won't respond unless we talk to her the way they do!"

Toldo Mondo was silent for several seconds.

"All right, Jiana; so be it. But remember: this was your choice . . .

"Flitting bitch-Queen, brother-loving sister to Star-King, to you, you burrowing, biting chigger! To Kiddikikitik bitch-Queen of Termites, bow heads, scrape ground, lay flat offering skulls to feed hungry hordes. Mistress come, burrow deep into the brains, wriggle, squirm, rut us and lay fat, white, twitching eggs inside our heads to grow and chew their way out! We adore you. We love you. Come, and come and come inside us!"

"A devil hell from!" cried Dida, but the other two ignored him.

"We remember you and your hordes and your terror, Mistress. We remember when not tree would grow nor longhouse would stand, because you hungered always and hollowed even the hardiest. We remember mountain caves that were your tracks, and wood like the shiny stone that was only your shit.

"But remember we too when Jabal the Twenty-Toothed built traps of your shit and the wings of your fallen sisters and trapped Kiddikikitik bitch-Queen of Termites for a thousand years and a day! And we remember mighty oaths sworn to the Servants of the Leopard and the tasters of Jabal's manhood, and we summon today our Mistress Queen and call on oaths that were old when the Forest was still a virgin!"

As Jiana repeated the words, she tried to summon up Kiddikikitik in her mind. At first she was luckless, but then suddenly a vision sprang into her stomach, a horror of white, pulpy body and tiny, ludicrous wings. As she watched, still repeating the words as they tumbled from an embarrassed Toldo, she realized that the hideous vision was not in her mind. It—She—actually hovered before Jiana above the mundane sphere. She was dim and shadowy, but recognizable. And what was hidden from view by incomplete materialization was repulsive in suggestion.

Straining her mind to its limit, Jiana rose to her feet and

touched the cool, leather hilt of her sword. It calmed her just enough to continue with confidence.

The bitch-Queen became steadily clearer and more real. She turned white, sightless eyes on the warrior, and her mandibles slowly opened and closed sideways, like an ant. Kiddikikitik did not much resemble a termite, not even one magnified a thousand times.

Jiana felt her stomach slowly rotate in her gut to an unnatural position. Instinctively, she drew Wave. She was only aware she had done so when she saw the blade already in her hand. Then, she did not know what she had intended to do with it.

"Favors we do you," continued Toldo Mondo, sounding terribly uncomfortable with the words. "Souls we give you, feed you, leave you, kill for you, as the Twenty-Toothed did say. Thus, you must return favors and loves, as the Twenty-Toothed did demand!"

Breathlessly, Jiana shouted the words, and with every syllable Kiddikikitik's image sharpened and enlivened before her. Soon all else faded from Jiana's eyes except for the pulpy white termite queen.

The warrior began to feel distinctly nauseated. Kiddikikitik squirmed forward, dragging her body along the ground with the noise of the booted foot pulling out of a pool of mud, though the corridor floor was dry. Jiana could not smell anything out of the ordinary. *Probably too mundane a plane for the divine scent to propagate,* she thought. She was deeply grateful for small favors.

A round, pulsing sphere at the insect's front—Kiddikikitik's head—rocked slowly left and right, and Jiana felt a disturbed certainty that it sought her.

Yet it was blind. Where eyes might have been on a crab or a fly, there was only the white smoothness of a burrowing thing. The Queen of Termites dragged Herself toward Jiana.

"No! Not me—not this way, fool goddess!"

Toldo Mondo stared at her. "What is happening? That is not part of the spell!"

"Toldo, damn you—what's the part about controlling Her?" Jiana began to edge around the circle. Kiddikikitik followed her, leg over leg over leg over leg. Her forelimbs clawed furrows in the stone floor, making a noise like "skrek! skrek!"

"Control," she said, her voice a bare whisper now. "Toldo, by the scaly lord, give me control!"

"You actually *see* it? The Termite Queen?"

"Toldo!"

"Ah, oh dear. I was never very good at thinking on my feet. Ah . . . wait. Here, this part comes a few stanzas later:

"We did his bidding, Twenty-Tooth's; killed and dedicated to you souls and blood and lives. Brains we ate, stomachs burned to you . . . debt you owe! Oops . . . Jiana, will it still work, even if you didn't do all that?"

"Well, something better work!"

Jiana repeated Toldo's cantrip and then she felt a questioning voice in her head. Though it did not come by way of her ears, she felt the sound of clicking mandibles in the words.

"SOULS? BLOOD? LIVES?"

"By the promises you swore to Jabal the Twenty-Toothed, you must serve!"

"JABAL? SERVE?"

"Yes! Serve, serve me! I control you now! Damnit, priest, give me more words!"

There was a pause, then the voice returned.

"BLOOD? BLOOD? BLOODLESS!" Jiana's throat constricted with fear. "SOULLESS!" it screamed at her, soundlessly. "LIFELESS! DEATHLESS! NO DEBT!" Jiana backed away from the circle as Kiddikikitik began to pull Herself forward again. When the Termite Queen began grinding Her shredding-legs together in front of Jiana, making the same "skrek-skrek" noise they had made on the floor, the warrior began to improvise wildly.

"Stop! Another step, thing, and I'll banish you to—to—to a limbo of eternal fire, your greatest enemy! Don't move, you!"

"FIRE," the insect repeated dully, and scrabbled forward out of the circle, toward Jiana.

Toldo screamed, and Dida gasped, "You see it, too?" Jiana yelled.

"We saw it come the circle from!" Dida shouted, falling back into the souther speech.

Jiana had crabbed three-quarters around the circle. Now she, Dida, and the Termite Queen formed a right triangle, and Jiana stole a quick glance at the boy. He was shaking like the last phase of the pox, but he had drawn his longknife, and she figured he had finally forgotten all about being so far underground. She looked back at Kiddikikitik and saw her own blade, which she had interposed between her and the creature. It was none too steady either, shaking like a leaf in a breeze.

"BLOOD," said Kiddikikitik, speaking still in Jiana's mind. "SOULS! BRAINS!"

"Take *my* blood!" screamed Dida, who apparently could hear as well as see Her.

"I'm sure She has every intention, kid. Right after mine."

Suddenly the creature shot forward with the speed of an arrow. Jiana barely threw herself to the side, covering with Wave. She rolled back to her feet, just as Kiddikikitik squirmed about at impossible speed and attacked again.

"*Run!*" Jiana cried.

"Never!" said Dida.

"Then fight!"

Kiddikikitik made another pass, and this time one of Her limbs rasped across Jiana's chest, slicing through her leather jerkin and tearing enough skin to make the warrior scream. But with a backhand swipe she managed to amputate a shredder and part of the queen's pulpy head.

Kiddikikitik spun as if nothing had happened. Jiana's chest dripped blood, and she clenched her teeth against the thought-numbing pain.

"Fight, Dida! Move!" she hissed. The boy stood frozen in indecision—unable to charge, unwilling to flee. Then he looked in her eyes, and something unstuck. He ran forward and stabbed at the thing with his knife.

Kiddikikitik flicked Dida away with one of Her rear legs. He fell, hurt, but this time he had no trouble leaping to his feet and renewing the attack.

"TOLDO!" Jiana called. The priest was nowhere to be seen, but there was no time to wonder where he had wandered off to. She dived right, snapping Wave like a whip and severing the Termite Queen's other front shredder. It was a mistake. Kiddikikitik twisted Her head and clamped her mandibles on Jiana's left arm.

Jiana screamed again—this time in both shock and pain. Behind the mandibles a mouth opened in the head, and a long, pink tubelike muscle reeled out. It made a sickening, gurgling noise, and probed for her flesh.

She stuck Wave in front of the tongue, flat side up. Her mind began to disassociate from her body, and she seemed to step back and watch herself from afar. She could feel the dreadful weight of the thing, crushing her; she felt the pressure of the mandibles on her arm.

So why hasn't She simply snipped your arm off? Surely no flesh could resist that! She saw Dida behind Kiddikikitik, hacking and slicing away with his hunting knife, and was grateful, in a wistful way. It would make no difference, in the end; she was already dead, and Dida would be, too, shortly.

But at least she had awakened him. He was no longer a boy playing at being a man. He would die fighting, clawing, forcing Death to work for every cup She took.

Dying was all so quiet! Jiana heard only silence.

Dida was knocked sprawling again, and Jiana saw another rip open in her own leg. The pain was sharp, and it confused her: *How can I hurt so if I'm dead?*

Then a sudden flare of brightness blinded her, and her nostrils filled with acrid smoke. Jiana choked and gagged, and realized she was still among the living.

Kiddikikitik was engulfed in flames!

With a surge of strength she would never have imagined, Jiana heaved the fiery, spasming thing off her and rolled away. Her hair crackled and stank, and she beat her head with her gauntleted hands until it stopped burning.

Jiana staggered up onto one knee. What was left of the goddess Kiddikikitik dragged Herself back into the circle, leaving a trail of bubbling goo where She had been. When She reached the center, she melted into a puddle, which continued to flicker and flame for a while.

Jiana shivered violently with a bad case of the shakes.

Toldo stood over her, still holding the torch he must have used on the Termite Queen.

"G-good think-think-think . . ." She stopped trying to talk and concentrated instead on her breathing—*in . . . hold . . . out; in . . . hold—hold—hold . . . out.* She rubbed her hands along the sides of her head. Much of the hair on her right side had burned away. Finally she began to calm.

"I know," she said. "I must look like shit."

Dida and Toldo both began to shout at once.

"My love! Are you—"

"Jiana—"

She held up her hand for silence.

"Yes. I'm fine. It was a brilliant tactic, priest. And Dida, you fought like a hero. Thank you, both."

"It was your idea, o unsung heroine. Remember? You said fire was the thing's greatest enemy."

"My mistake. I got confused, and misremembered. We always used fire to remove leeches and ticks from our skin in the Flower Empire. I don't have the slightest idea whether it works on termites!"

"Well, I must confess that at first I ran—halfway to the gate. Then . . . well, your insanities must be infectious, because I turned around and ran back. I grabbed a torch when I remembered what you had said, and stuck it into the thing's body. Ah, sorry I was so rough with you, Dida, but you were in the way."

Dida dismissesd the apology with a hand wave, still looking at Jiana.

"*I* still think you're beautiful," he declared. It was the perfect thing to say, and Jiana reached a hand up and touched his face.

"You've got weird taste," she said. "Hey, look!" She held out her left arm. "I just figured out why She didn't chew my arm off."

A thick, brass armlet she wore on her bicep was cracked and gouged.

"I guess Kiddikikitik got caught on this. Worth more than I thought—sure glad I gave a different bangle to the too-wise!" Dida still gazed worshipfully into her eyes.

"Oops," said Toldo.

"Oops, what?"

"Ah, you haven't got your nose bloodied yet, but I think they might be about to remedy that lack."

"What the hell are you babbling about? They, who?"

Toldo looked pointedly behind her, just as she felt a none-too-gentle tap on the back of her neck with a blade. She tilted her head back, slowly.

A group of eight men, armed with spears and swords, surrounded the party. They were led by an old man, who said, "The penalty for desecrating the altar of Taku-Taku is death by sacrifice. Now come along! Let's not make a big fuss."

He glowed a pretty shade of blue, and Jiana realized she was still shifted slightly out of the mundane sphere.

You're draining yourself, said the Other—whose identity, she reminded herself, she now knew: the unliving child that still dwelt within her. *If you don't drop down now you'll die, Dearest.* It sounded genuinely concerned. *When I die, you die,* she thought back.

Of course, silly! I'm only you.

Jiana turned back to her friends.

"I think we had better do what they say. Can you boys handle things for a while?"

They nodded, confused.

"Good. Goodnight." With a sudden, wrenching effort, she dragged her consciousness down to Earth again, and instantly collapsed into an exhausted sleep.

Chapter 5

Death white, touch beauty black; shadow show for a child

-1-

Little Jiana woke to the morning bells, standing at the window of her room. There was the temple, right across the way as it always had been.

Now there's a silly thought, she thought. *Where else should it have been?*

"And how did I get all the way over here? I must have been sleepstepping!"

She ran back to her bed and picked up her favorite dolly, Dida, and made ready to go downstairs.

"Shh! Quiet, Dida. We mustn't wake up Daddy." She stepped softly over the bloody, twisted body at the foot of her bed, and turned the latch to her room.

The night air was cold as she began to slide down the bannister to Earth.

"What a silly dream this is!" she cried. "Just a minute ago it was morning, and now it's dead night. I didn't know there was a bannister going all the way down from the Mountain to the ground!"

She had left Daddy up on top, of course. He was *much* too heavy to carry down now that he was dead.

"And besides," she told Dida, hugging him to her so he wouldn't be afraid of the long slide down, "even if I *were* strong enough, I should get blood all over my favorite nightclothes!"

Jianabel landed with a bump in her room.

"Why, how easy that is! Much better than the stairs." She set Dida upright on the pillow, leaning against the bedframe. "From now on, that's the *only* way I'll come down from the Mountain. Oh, dear . . . I wonder if Daddy's comfortable? The alter is so hard and cold!"

No matter how Jianabel squirmed and twisted, she could not get comfortable on the slab.

"But then, I'm not even sure it's an alter yet. Tell me, Krakshi," she asked her silent dolly, "does it become an alter as soon as I make it, or not 'til after it's used?" But the doll did not answer; he was becoming very tiresome that way.

Jianabel turned an ugly smile on the rag baby.

"You better *watch out*, Krakshi. Maybe after we take care of Daddy, you'll be next."

"I'm sorry, Jianabel," Krakshi said. He held his long, long rag arms out to her, and she picked him up and comforted him.

"I'm sorry, baby Krakshi. But you just have to learn. That's Daddy's trouble. He's so stu-u-upid!"

Jianabel looked up at the candle; it had burned to the second hour. It was time.

"Daddy," she called—softly. "Daddy, come up here. It's our time now, and we *mustn't* be late!"

The dead of the night began to creep in through the open window. Looking around, Jianabel could see horrid, ugly, squatting things in the black corners of the attic, Jianabel's Mountain. She smiled at one that had got too bold, showing it her teeth, which she had painstakingly filed to a point. With great reluctance, it slithered backwards into the darkness.

"I *could* break my circle," she said, "and let Her out to eat all of you!" She could feel the sudden terror in the things, the househaunts. It gave Jianabel a wonderful, tingly feeling to know she was the cause of such fear.

"Da-a-addy!" she called. She stamped her foot impatiently. Something stirred downstairs. *Thud. Thud.* It was her Daddy's footsteps, heavy as a horse—heavy as the dead. He was coming up the stairs.

He dragged something along behind him. She could hear it scraping along the ground—*skrek! skrek!*

He thumped up to the second floor, dragging his burden. He stumbled up to the third floor, and his burden grew heavier, the scraping deeper.

Thud. Thud. Thud. Thud. Skre-e—ek!

He began to climb the ladder up into the Mountain.

"I know it's very hard, Daddy. But you simply *must* do it! Your burden weighs you down, I know. Do you think we should help him, Krakshi?"

Again the doll did not answer.

"I wonder," she said softly, "if I haven't outgrown you, baby doll? It's happened before . . ." She grinned her filed teeth at Krakshi, and the doll trembled.

The attic door opened. Daddy stepped inside, in a deep, deep trance.

His arms dangled behind him. They were now three full strides long, and Jianabel could see them still growing, before her very eyes.

"Poor Daddy. You always did have your hands in everything, didn't you?" He looked pleadingly at her, his eyes the only thing about him that were still truly his. "Even in me. Even right inside of me. That was very naughty of you, Daddy . . . you should have *known* better than that!"

Jianabel hopped off the altar and pointed. Daddy plodded laboriously over to it, dragging his burden behind him.

On a whim, Jianabel turned suddenly back to her doll.

"I've made up my mind," she told him. "You're just too tiresome! You shall be next, Dida."

Nooooooooooooo—

—ooooooooo!

Jiana sat bolt upright, panicked, unable to remember where she was. Somebody came. It was Dida. He held her shoulders, calmed her. Her heart pounded like a hundred beating cavalry hooves.

"Just a dream," she said. "Just a dream—a stupid dream. It wasn't a memory. It didn't happen like that, it was like I remember. It was on my bed—he was doing it again! I only stabbed him, I never—I never—" She realized what she was saying, and where she was, and shut her mouth quickly.

"Jiana? My love, what was it?"

"I'm sorry, Dida. I didn't mean to wake you."

"We were not exactly sound asleep, good lady," Toldo rumbled. "In fact, I fear you woke only yourself. The boy and I were trying to figure a scheme out of this mess. Unsuccessfully."

"Jiana will get us out," Dida stated. "She's Jiana of Bay Bay, and she's stolen the jade eyes of . . . of . . . of whatever that statue was!"

"Right. Thanks. My game, hunh?" Neither one answered her. "All right. Fill me in on what's happened."

"They dragged us here," said Dida.

"That's it?"

"They tied us, and took us the gate back through."

"Dida, say that properly."

"They took us . . . back through the gate. I am sorry for my foolishness."

"No, it's okay. I just get tired of translating. So now we're . . . here. Where's here?"

Toldo took up the tale.

"If I remember correctly, after passing through the second gate—and you were right about the 'greatest lock-trip,' by the way. There is no way we could have broken that thing, for it was ten feet thick! After he opened it, Ata led us through a maze of twisty passages, all alike. We had good fortune, though; he did not blindfold us, and I remember the turns."

"Ata was the old man I saw in the summoning room?"

"Denzel Ata. But he does not decide the matters. Apparently there is a council, and a long tradition. I am positive that they do not represent the current de facto government of Bay Din."

"Most politicians do not politic from a hole."

"This is a dreary place. But are they Alanai supporters, which would imply he is not still sitting on the Juniper throne? Or do they follow the Toradoras? Royalists or loyalists?"

"Why do they have to be one of those two?" Dida asked. Both Jiana and Toldo turned to look at him.

"No. I don't suppose they do." Toldo did not sound pleased at Dida's contribution.

"Well, this stuff is important for planning purposes," Jiana said, smoothing the discussion, "but right now, we know first that they worship Taku-Taku; second, that Denzel Aka has access to more magick power than I, and—"

"Ata," Toldo corrected.

"And third, that Ata and his chums plan to sacrifice us. Do we know when?"

"Dawn," said both Toldo and Dida, simultaneously.

"Oh, that's a real help," Jiana snorted, looking through the bars to the torchlit hallway that was their only illumination.

She put her arm around Dida, and he leaned his head against her shoulder. Jiana laid her cheek on his matted hair and hunted for the alternative.

The air was hot and stifling, and full of smoke from the torches. Nothing except themselves stirred in the cell, and they moved as little as possible. There were not even any rats or cockroaches.

Jiana's hand began to throb. Finally, the frozen tip of her finger had thawed enough to regain feeling. She clenched her teeth against the pain and said nothing to the others.

But then she felt another hand, this one Dida's. He gently rubbed it over her leg, inching toward her lap. By twisting his head slightly, he was able to kiss her gently on her neck, and then run his tongue along it.

Jiana began to kiss back, and let her own hand—the uninjured one—press against his chest and slip under his tunic.

Something seemed familiar to her about the scene, but it was not from her own memory.

Dida's lips sought out the sensitive, front part of her throat, while his fingers gently separated her own shirt from her pantaloons and caressed her stomach, tracing a circle beneath her breasts.

Jiana looked over to Toldo. The fat priest had suddenly developed an amazing interest in a folded-paper book he had found in his robes, and he studied it intently, his back to the two of them.

But still, something nagged at her stomach. She had seen this exact scene before, with the tongue and the fingers and the head and the shoulder.

Then she rememberd, and she pulled away from Dida so fast that he fell over onto the ground. The scene was one of the sharpest from the chaotic dreamscape of Dida's mind, when she had entered it to calm him during their long crawl under the hulking mountain. It was a scene with one of his other girlfriends.

"Jianaling . . . what—?"

"Look, I'm just not in the mood right now, kid. Okay?"

"What do you mean not the mood in? You were just a few seconds ago!"

"Well, I'm not now!" She softened, and put her hand on his arm. "Look, probably later, okay, Dida? Just—not now. And not like that. Not like you did to—"

"Like what?" There was an ugly, belligerent tone to his voice, and he jerked his arm from under her hand.

"I don't like you like this, kid."

"Don't call me that!"

"I'm sorry, Dida. You've never sounded like this before."

"Go ahead—finish it!" He glared at her, his lower lip protruding slightly and trembling.

"What?" Jiana hoped that he would drop it, but she knew it would come out anyway.

"Finish what you were saying! You said 'not like you did to . . . '"

"I don't want to say. Let it lie." But he kept staring, accusing her with his eyes, and finally she began to feel anger herself. "All right, you want it, then? I was going to say, not like you did it to her!"

"To who?" Suddenly, his voice was small, unsure.

"Dida, damn you! I saw her in your mind—in the cave. I saw your memories of her—"

"Yan was not your business of!"

"It's my business that I was lied to!" The words lingered like an ugly smell: "lied to—lied to—lied to!"

Dida let his head fall into his arms and began to sniffle.

"Damn it, stop that! Stop manipulating me!"

He was silent for a minute then.

"I'm sorry. I didn't think. I didn't . . . I thought you would—you wanted to. I thought you might feel sorry for me and—"

A wave of anger crashed against her consciousness, and she rose up to her knees, her fists clenched.

"I DON'T CARE HOW MANY CHICKS YOU FUCKED! But you—you've been lying this whole damn time, and manipulating, and pulling my strings like I was a fucking marionette in a fucking—" Dida stared at her, white-faced with shock, but she could not stop herself.

"You like words like 'fucking'? Does it turn you on? You like having some older woman fucking you? You want to be fucked, hunh? Makes you feel grown up? Well here, fuck this!" With a strike almost to quick to follow, she slapped Dida across his face. He fell down, holding his cheek. She grabbed his pants and yanked them down around his ankles, and then fell heavily on top of him.

But it was not her. It was someone else, some other being, some other Jianabel. She knew it could not be herself, because she hovered over the scene, external to both bodies, watching in helpless shock. But who was on the inside?

Jiana forced her mouth against his, and shoved her tongue past his teeth. He could have stopped her by biting, but he did not. Tears ran down Dida's cheeks as someone pulled down someone's own pantaloons and began rhythmically and lovelessly bouncing on top of his pelvis.

Dida turned his face away from her, and he struggled against her hands pinioning his arms.

All of a sudden, Jiana fell inside herself again. A wave of nausea spread over her, like oil upon the ocean, and she rolled off and sat on the ground next to him. They quietly pulled up their pants, Dida trying to keep his tears quiet, Jiana wishing she had tears.

Toldo stood against the bars, gripping them with both

hands and hyperventilating. Jiana could smell his fear. Her senses heightened, and Dida's tears dropped like stones into water.

For the first time, she realized how much people could fear her.

"Dida. I'm sorry. I know that is not adequate, but—I've been strained."

"I understand. I'm okay." But his voice was cold.

Jiana leaned her head back. What had *happened?*

Wonderful, Jiana! mocked the little girl inside. *Next time, can we bite off his balls?*

Shut up . . . SHUT UP, SHUT UP, SHUT-UP!

With her eyes closed, she reached out and laid her hand on Dida's shoulder. He flinched, but let it stay there.

She moved closer, and kissed his shoulder softly.

"I'm sorry," Dida whispered, annoyingly.

"Don't apologize to me, damn you!"

She drew him to her tenderly—not forcing, only suggesting. They fell together easily, and lost themselves in each other for a time. Jiana forgot entirely about Toldo Mondo.

At last she felt it was over, and she could think again. A long time had passed.

"Jiana—m'lady hero, are you there?" It was the priest. "I realize this is an awkward time to ask, but have you thought of any plans yet? I mean, 'tis not too long until they come to . . . well, to do what they intend to do."

"Sing a song of syrup," she said, and opened her eyes.

"What?"

"I *do* have a plan, as a matter of fact. I didn't have to think of it—another person thought it up, a long time ago. Listen:

Sing a song of syrup,
Sing a lifeless horse,
A hangman lost his stirrup
To his terrible remorse.

Beautiful but deadly,
Boundaries erased,
Heavens in a medley,
And the syrup lost its taste."

* * *

"Ah, charming. So?"

"That's the first stanza, the riddle. It talks of Taku-Taku, the Beautiful/Deadly . . . once in a time, the author of the riddle knew He would have to be faced, and knew the weapon that would destroy Him. The second stanza is the answer."

Both Dida and Toldo leaned forward expectantly.

"But the trick," Jiana finished, "is in the remembering. And in the decrypting. Hush now, I must think. I need time."

Booted feet stomped up the hall, and a key ground in the ponderous lock. The wood creaked open, and a blast of cold air blew the little grey man into the cell.

"I don't suppose you coarser sorts realize your amazing luck," Ata said, jabbing at them with his little finger. "Normally, you would be just snuffed out of hand for your heinous crimes. Heh! But today, as it happens, is The Day. Instead, with profuse generosity, we have commuted your sentence to sacrifice—a great honor!"

"O rapture," Toldo yawned. Jiana smiled, without looking up from the floor. She did not need to look at Toldo to see his fear; certainly Ata could sense it just as easily. *A life as a butcher does not prepare one to play the steer.*

"After your miserable blood flows across the altar, the Great One, Taku-Taku, shall live again!" Carried away with the moment, he raised his eyes to the heavens, which lay somewhere beyond the ceiling.

Dida seized the moment to charge across the cell toward the magician, but he was anticipated. Ata stepped nimbly back, and two of his men filled the space of the doorway through which Dida was trying to run. The result was predictable.

The guard-types donned hoods, and gestured Toldo and Jiana out the door. Two other soldiers grabbed Dida's feet and dragged him along behind. They were pushed, dragged, and shoved into a great hall, still far underground. An assembled company of two hundred awaited them, all breathing as one organism.

* * *

Beautiful but deadly,
Boundaries erased . . .

Jiana tried to swallow, but her mouth was too dry.
You can't escape, Jianabel chuckled.
Of course I can! she retorted.
*You shan't. What's the difference whether you die or
someone else? They'll still let the monster loose, and THEN
what will be?*
Jiana could not answer; there was no argument. Even if
they had to resort to offing one of their own acolytes, the
fools would raise Taku-Taku, and the Beautiful/Deadly
would tear the world apart for the sheer joy, monotonously chanting I AM WHO I AM WHO I AM!

Boundaries erased . . .

Tentatively, Jiana probed upward, toward the top of the
first, mundane sphere. She had had somewhat of a rest
. . . It was useless. She could not break through, and she
fell back down with a thump. Her spirit-self had not even
enough energy to rise above her own head.
Hands shoved them within a circle, similar to the one at
the gate, but this one was painted on the ground and
visible to all.
"Lie down!" said a guard. When no one moved, he
slugged Toldo Mondo in his round belly, and the priest
collapsed beside Dida, who was just then beginning to
stir. Jiana quickly played the same suit.
"I never thought very well on my feet anyway," she
whispered to Toldo, trying to keep up his spirits. He still
gasped.
Ata entered, and began to chant, weaving a web of
words around them.
"The King of Naihared rode forth one day from the
ancient city of Ruoy Oudin, now called Bay Din. He rode
to the hunt, but soon became lost in an impenetrable
forest surrounding the city."
A strange, shivery feeling gripped Jiana, a feeling of
portent unjustified by the innocuous tale.
"The king rode with worry, seeking some familiar sign

or landmark, and at last, panic seized his heart. He galloped madly back toward his castle, trying to follow his own trail, but of a sudden, his stirrup broke beneath his foot, and in frantically reining in his horse, he caused it to stumble and shatter its leg. There was no choice but to slay the beloved beast, and tears marred the royal face."

You make a king a hangman, Jiana thought to the hidden Jianabel.

Aren't they all? O, but the first verse is the easy one! You simply must try harder!

—Sing a lifeless horse, a hangman lost his stirrup . . . You leave me only the riddle of the syrup . . . How does it come to lose its taste? What is it? The vicious little girl fell silent, but Jiana could feel her laughter.

"Weary wandered the king, his feet aching from the stones along the road. But the darkness grew deeper and blacker whichever way he turned, and soon he began to pray for but a little light."

Ata suddenly hurled a handful of presumably holy water into her face, which brough her back to present time with a jerk. At the same moment, the chamber suddenly flared with light as all two hundred witnesses pulled covers from their candles. To her dark-adapted eyes, they burned like a thousand suns.

"Then, of a sudden, he burst through the edge of the forest into a brilliantly sunlit land, and he knew he was in the southern kingdom of Door."

Between Bay Din and Door lie five hundred miles of wildlands! she protested.

Oh, it's just a silly metaphor for life, Ji. They've stumbled onto a secret, and they think no one else knows it.

I must know the second verse! Tell me now! It's no fair without knowing.

What's fair? But it IS less fun . . .

All at once it flew into her stomach, like a dove through an open window, flapping madly about the caves of her mind.

Dragon swallows syrup,
Sickly sweet inside;
Hangman, horse, and stirrup . . .
Who can say which died?

* * *

Dream the dream of ashes,
Dream another's dreams;
Dream the world unlatches,
For 'tis only what it seems.

A face frayed at the edges. It was Ata and his beard, and
he leaned over her like a chef examining the roast. He
brought an alabaster white coin down from the great height
of his arms and laid it gently upon her brow. One just like
it seemed embedded in his own skull, which now glowed
as blue as an azure summer sky. Jiana could no longer
understand his words, for he spoke an ancient tongue, but
the breathing of the witnesses began to sound like speech
to her ears; "Dreams to Dreams to Dreams," it seemed,
again and again, droning in the background.

They're playing pipes, she thought, but it was only their
spirit breath. The sound wrapped around her and pulled
serpent-tight.

Funny that I can see your aura, she thought at the
magician. *The coins must be a magick conduit, letting the
power flow from thee to me, to me, to me.*

And at once the alternative materialized in her stomach,
full-grown, like the Myrmidon of Taflaz from the fountain.

Jiana thrust out one tendril of her spirit in a strike as
quick as any she had ever seized with her sword. She
sparked through the coin conduit and into Ata's head, and
found herself in a vast, rolling ocean of magickal energy!

Ata's pupils shrank to peas, to pinpoints, to nothing—
but he had no time to react and close his mind, for without
pausing, Jiana hurled her Self upward, shattering the spheres
and playing out the lifecord behind her in great loops and
swirls. Far below she heard a scream.

Through the crystals, through the mud, she flew through
every sphere where Taku-Taku was but a shadow, seeking
the one which contained his entirety—something in-dwelling
told her it existed. At last, she impacted a clinging, rubbery sheet which did not want to give. She pressed and
pressed, and finally seeped through as water might pass a
porous wall.

She stood insectlike on the surface of a thick, sickly

pond. The air itself was ponderous and stifled her thinking. She felt on the verge of waking, at the edge of sleeping, where dreams are most demented and the shiveries lurk. Then she changed her focus (for He was everywhere here) and saw Him.

Taku-Taku grinned hungrily. His writhing, wormlike teeth filled the universe from the inside all the way to the outside, and His mindless roar rattled her mind:

I AM WHO I AM WHO I AM WHO I AM WHO I AM—!

-2-

Dream. The world. Unlatches. Dream the world unlatches, unlatches, unlatches . . .

Jiana wasted no time arguing with the idiot-savant, the beautiful-deadly—what was reason to I AM WHO I AM WHO I AM? Shaking, her spirit-self trembling like dust along a busy road, she threw her mind open—a bit! a motel—to the dreaded, hunched, gibbering, slavering Jianabel, the Horrid Little Girl.

Unlatches, dispatches, unmatches, detaches!

Detaches?

A balloon floated out of her mind and across the scrubbed wood of White Falls, up and up and out of her ken. And then it burst behind Jiana's eyes, and she saw the rhyme.

"Food," she whispered into the ear-things of Taku-Taku.

"FOOD?" it responded eagerly—it *sounded* eager.

"Food!" she confirmed, and seizing firm hold of its attention, she allowed her Self to sink back down and down through the molasses, the shadows, the manure, and the shimmerings. Oddly, Taku-Taku followed.

It's only the summonings—they've hungered it and drawn it forth from its own sphere, Jiana told her unbelieving self. *The stupid rhyme has nothing to do with it!*

Naughty Jiana! You know who's the real schemer, and who shall demand payback afterwards!

Jiana refused to think about it. Jianabel was dead. Jianabel floated belly-up like the shoretonies of Bay Bay.

Down and down did Jianabel draw Taku-Taku. For god though he was, at the heart he was only what he was, and what he was was hungry. They halted on the astral plane, the level just above the profane, and looked down on all that was below.

Jiana's corporeal body lay stretched upon the altar, limbs bound wrist to ankle and pulled needlessly tight. Ata stood over her, hand poised with an obsidian dagger over her heart, ready to release the life force which would feed Taku-Taku, and bind it tight. But connecting the two was a twisting, coiling serpent of raw crimson that lit the chamber. Its roots penetrated Ata's skull like a blood-tuber, sucking out the sorcerer's magickal essence to power Jiana's own journey, feeding her through the coin on her own forehead.

The old savant was a paper scroll, brittle and crumbly, his soul light entirely drained. Jiana burned with power.

Beyond, the apprentices stared, terror-rooted and no longer even breathing, it seemed. Toldo was caught red-handed in escape, but he moved so very, very slowly! Jiana understood then. Time itself had paused to await the manifestation of Taku-Taku.

And from the blackened corridor, from the cells, from the caverns, halfway already across the chamber, was that which had nearly crushed and rolled over the three before, in the crawling chamber. It was the shadow of Deathly Beauty.

Jianabel smiled sweetly, savoring the growing, ravenous hunger which began to fill the chamber, as Taku-Taku's complete self invaded. The shadow grew; more and more of the true being entered the lowest sphere. Nothing seemed to scare the girl—certainly not hunger. The Beautiful Death was only a mere godling, and stupid to boot . . . while Jianabel was the cleverest of them all!

Smirking with wicked malice, she pointed her soul like an arrow at the shadow of the god. "Food," she whispered.

"FOOD?" queried Taku-Taku. Then, without waiting for a reply, it fell ravenously upon the cave-lurker, the shadow . . . *upon its very own tail*, she cried. *Such a silly god!* And then, all the world inverted. All Jiana heard was a soft, anti-climactic:

phoooooomph!

The warrior woke quickly this time. Her hands and feet were still tied—Dida alive, Toldo nowhere to the eye . . .

"Dida," she called softly, fearing detection. "Dida, come help!"

He staggered up, facing the wrong way, and pulled out his knife. For a moment he acted blind and drunk. Then he shook his wits together, and ran to Jiana. He cut her loose, but his hands shook like an ancient beggar. She sat up, and saw Toldo Mondo on his knees on the ice-cold stone, white-faced and breathing fast.

"I . . . saw . . . I—I saw—"

"Get up, priest! Grab your nihilisms and stuff them in your robe. It's time to *move!*"

"The hooded ones!" Dida cried, his eyes clearing the last of the fog.

"LOOK! Look at them! Fear nothing, kid—we're freaking gods!"

The numbstruck students had all backed to the walls, their eyes stretched so wide they shone even in the uncertain light of the torches. A few had even dropped to their knees.

Jiana stood and gestured dramatically.

"Bless you all, peace and yatta-yatta. Now we must leave you—farewell!" Hands raised, she backed toward one of the doors, the one that looked well-lit, well-worn, and civilized. Dida and Toldo were out of her vision, but she hoped they would take the hint.

"*Stop!*" ordered a voice from behind her. It was a voice used to command tone, and instinctively Jiana froze, then turned, her eyebrows raised indignantly.

A man filled up the door arch, his head grazing the keystone and his girth quashing any thought of passage around the side. He wore a heavy brigandine, green-painted iron plates sewn into a boiled-leather coat, but his head was unarmored. In his right hand dangled what looked like an enormous meat tenderizer with a crowbar on the top. The gigantic dirk dangling from his belt set her to wondering if perhaps he had had an unfortunate battlefield injury.

She almost made a grab for Wave, but stifled the impulse before even moving. She could feel the sword there, still around her waist. Apparently, old Ata had thought it was merely a fancy belt. But sharp and fine though Wave was, it would never deflect the green man's mace even a finger's width from her head.

He must simply be prevented from swinging, whispered the ghost of her old master in her ear.

"Good even, mortal," she hailed, in a resonant contralto.

" 'Tis noon, witch," he answered.

"Not in *my* realm—Greenbelly." He frowned, thinking. Jiana had won the first round, and the green man chewed his mustache uncertainly.

"You have slain Lord Denzel," Greenbelly announced, surveying the room. He scowled at the cringing acolytes.

"He slew himself. He thwarted my will."

"He was weak. I am strong!"

"You, too, are a mortal. Denzel Ata summoned Taku-Taku to his aid, and I slew them both." Jiana knew it was a grievous error even as she said it. Greenbelly sneered with disbelief and annoyance and stepped into the room, brandishing his mound-pounder in one hairy ham-fist.

"You blaspheming witch! I'll crush your bones into flour and your blood into water, and bake you and eat you for biscuits!"

"*Stop!*" Jiana barked, imitating the man's command voice with consummate perfection. "Think you—what happens if you are wrong and I am right? Do you have the right to risk your men's last hope—to wit, yourself—in a useless attempt to die gloriously? Think! Think like a leader of men! Think what I could do for The Cause!"

Greenbelly hesitated, and Jiana could almost hear the gears going *dink! dink!* as they fell into place in his stomach.

"You know of The Cause?" he demanded.

"Why else would I have come? Freedom! Liberation! Justice! This shall be our battle yell, to drive the oppressor from the field!"

"FREEDOM! LIBERATION! JUSTICE!" echoed the hooded novitiates, right on cue, making the shouts reverberate throughout the whole hall.

"A well-trained lot," Toldo whispered. Then he loudly cleared his throat.

"Ah, permit me to amplify what Jiana, the Illuminated One, is saying. Long have her people languished in darkness, she laments; long, o! Too long have they been driven underground, hounded, tortured, raped, and stolen from! But at last the time has come . . . she scries a time for action, for blood, and for *vengeance!*"

"VENGEANCE!" bawled the true believers. Greenbelly began to drool eagerly. *Dink!*

"She, in her munificence, has decreed that *you*, my lord, shall be the scythe of her reaping, the spear of her hunting! You shall be the point of her arrow, the edge of her sword! Like the whirlwind, ye shall wreak havoc and destruction through the heart of the foe, terrorizing his armies, violating his women, despoiling his crops—yea, even slaughtering his flocks! And at your back, this army of thousands, thousands upon thousands, all falling dexter or flying sinister by the wave of your hand, rising like a flood and burning like a bolt of lightning! GREENBELLY! GREENBELLY! they will cry; Greenbelly will the enemy lament!" Toldo boldly surged forward and grabbed the giant by his shoulders.

"Man! Can you shoulder this great responsibility? Is your right arm strong enough, and your heart black enough? *Can you lead this great campaign?!*"

"YES!" he screamed, hurling off Toldo Mondo's hands like they were sticks of grasswood. "YES!" he cried again, pushing past the three and leaping to the floor, shaking his fists.

"SOUND THE CLAXON! DON YOUR ARMOR! TODAY IS THE DAY THE SERPENT SHALL PERISH!!"

"Now's our chance!" hissed Toldo, and he and Dida and Jiana sped for the door. But they arrived just in time to be bowled over by a great stream of iron men, armed all in green and eager to stand at their lord's back in his moment of glory.

Then a great, bronze bell began sounding and pounding, resounding, beating into Jiana's stomach with a round metal boom. Before they could make good their escape, the room filled from all doors to overflowing with men and swords and shields and helms, everyone bewildered and frightened by the great brass banging of the bell.

A ham hock gripped Jiana's shoulder mercilessly. A voice rumbled and drowned out even so monstrous an alarm.

"THIS IS THE AVATAR! FALL DOWN AND WORSHIP, YOU CRAVEN CURS, OR FEEL THE WRATH, THE FURY OF—OF LORD *GREENBELLY*!!"

Jiana stood quietly, wishing she had tried Wave after all. The giant seemed to like his new name.

"Freedom, liberation, justice!" the mob bleated, bounding and dancing around the trio in a mad frenzy. Dida shrank against Jiana, his breath coming raggedly and his skin cold. Toldo's eyes were as big as the two moons.

A wave of unreality washed through Jiana—the pounding of feet, the slapping of hands, the chants, the heat of a thousand bodies as the hall filled and filled and filled; the surge of flesh against leather against metal; the bulk of Greenbelly; and over all the skull-jolting BAWN BAWN of the claxon—*and where could such a monster be hung?* All these tore at Jiana's thoughts, and her stomach spun and twisted just as it had in the hut of the too-wise. With a silent scream of rage, her spirit was ripped from her body and flashed in an instant back along the same path it had followed two days and a thousand years ago. Back through her life, back through the ages of life on the world, back to—

At first they seemed like only a few black rocks rising from the sea. But then she saw that they had been artfully erected, and she shuddered, without any more knowledge of why than she had of where or how. How long had they lain thus?

The lightless black stones stood in ruins, save for one tall, thin minaret, thrusting against the starry-bright, primordial sky. All else about the fallen menhirs was black void and chaos, no order or pattern to their placement.

But the ugly, leering tower beckoned, and Jiana screamed with a horror that transcended death, of He that predated Those Who Walk Upright, Those With Fur, Those Who Swim, Those Which Reproduce, Those—

Alanamar. Tubyn. Destur the Destroying One. Nigthau Iman the Heavy-Lidded, and I.

Ar-Alaban, Ar-Flan of Two Divine Unions, the Sands of the Tarn, and I.

Tooqa, Serpent of the World, the Thousand-Eyed, the Seventy-Handed, Baak the Worldbreaker, and a thousand thousand thousand demons too foul to name, and too nameless to describe. And I!

These are they who seek the World's Dream in this moment.

"Toq. The sun-child."

"You remember me, sweetling Jiana?" The boy sat cross-legged on the dais, clad in a tunic of moonsparkle and a crown of sunfires. His smile cut through her like a knife. She felt a stirring of life inside her womb, though it was, for physical reasons, unlikely.

"I remember a beautiful angel, whose looking-glass reflected a bestial image. Is that a fair description of you?" For a moment Toq's face agitated, like a powder dissolving in water, but he regained control and smiled more achingly than ever.

"Of this illustrious list, which would you prefer to gain the Dream?"

"Perhaps none. Why not Jiana of Bay Bay?"

Toq's laughter was silver rain on a sharp, icy pond.

"What would *you* do with it? Try to bring some fallen warrior to life? You don't even know its powers!"

"What *are* its powers?"

"Find me that Dream. It is MINE!" For an instant, the world skewed violently, and Toq took another visage—a terror of writhing worms and open sores, a plague-corpse that walked and touched. In the wink of an eye, he was again the shining, good little boy.

A great green bulk superimposed the world. Toq, the throne, the tower, and the ruins melted and flowed, chalk drawings in rain, and became a chamber, a dance, and a gigantic green man.

"We march now to death, Jiana," he said with feverish jollity.

"What?" Jiana shook her head, confused by the sudden flicker in the worlds. Greenbelly took her arm and led her into a side room, away from the surging masses that jerked and spasmed inside the chamber, driving themselves into a battle frenzy with a war dance.

"We charge now, ahead! Death to the usurpers!"

"The Toradoras?" Toldo asked.

"The worshippers of snakes and eagles—Toradora and House Alanai both! For generations have we languished in darkness, as you know, o illuminated one. At least under Al-Tanai we could worship aloud! The vicious, slaughtering snake lovers made occasional raids, but for the most part left us alone. Al-Tanai's chancellor of the exchequer was a true believer and argued long in our defense."

"I take it Am-Amorai was not so cosmopolitan in his outlook," Toldo suggested. His only reply was a red-eyed scowl from Greenbelly.

"They are one of a kind. Birds are just lizards with wings and feathers, after all! They will pay, the tyrants. We still remember Uttich!"

"What happened in Uttich, o great chief?" It was Dida, on the prowl for a story.

"When Am-Amorai seized the throne, he generously allowed us three days to sell our possessions, pack, and leave Bay Din," the giant explained. He infused such venom in his words that Dida cringed back against Jiana.

"On the *second* day, his troops attacked our great temple, in Uttich Court, in the Slowburough at the north end of the city. It was our holiest shrine! He had it burned to the foundations. Those faithful who did not flee in terror were captured, locked in iron cages, and set to dangle along the Military Path, where they died by moments for four and twenty days! All but the young women, whom he . . . took."

"And did what?" breathed Dida. Jiana placed a warning hand on his shoulder, but Greenbelly only gritted his teeth.

"Those who survived often took their own lives." Through the door, Jiana could still hear the chanting in the main hall. It had taken on a new and ominous regularity, as if all the men had become one entity, chanting the name of power to invoke death. "After Uttich, the thought of flight or compromise was impossible. They will die. They must! If not by my hand, then by God's."

"Taku-Taku?" Toldo asked.

"Of course," Greenbelly said, looking at him in puzzlement. "Who else?" Jiana nervously cleared her throat, thinking of Taku-Taku feeding on himself, swallowing his own shadow, shrinking smaller and smaller, until . . .

"Well, are we going to do it," she asked, "or just talk about it?"

"We go. Death to snakes and eagles!" Jiana raised her fist in salute, but the moment Greenbelly's back was turned, she watched nervously over her shoulder for the heavenly bolt.

Surely the Nameless Serpentine knows we have to go along . . . Surely, but what if—? She put the thought from her mind; it was a useless speculation. She followed the green man out the door and back into bedlam.

Greenbelly raised his hands, and silence struck as hard as had the brass bell a moment before.

"We go!" was all he said. It was enough. The mad mob overflowed the great hall and burst up a corridor that led to the surface. Jiana, Dida, and Toldo followed, choiceless, buffeted.

"Alanai," she whispered, "this have you done. This is yours!" But no one heard except Jianabel, and she was biased.

-3-

Jiana discovered a new terror—the feeling of complete loss of control. The flooding crowd swept her along, at times lifting her clear of the ground and hurling her to the side. The crush of bodies and the animal screams from two thousand throats was unbearable, and she was pulled and dragged, cast forward and back, and nearly thrown under the pounding feet at times.

My ribs! My heart! I'll— The mocking voice favored her with only a lilt of laughter. Jiana's arms were pinned to her sides, and it took a great effort of will to double them up across her chest to hold the press of soldiers away. Toldo was gone from her sight. Rows away, she could see gentle, mouselike Dida crying out in fear and outrage. She could not reach him; he could not hear her. She could only endure.

Sudden screams—a great squeezing tighter than anything before it. Jiana found herself yelling, too, along with the crowd, raging at her helplessness. Something blocked the mob, and it compressed explosively, like an overinflated air bladder. Then suddenly, the pressure released, and they burst forth, streaming through the torn remnants of stone walls and iron bars—the third gate!

She stumbled over torn and pummeled bodies on the ground: city guards in mail armor, no protection against the stomp of four thousand hungry boots.

Light erupted—a cold wind of air, smoke—and they were outside!

She screamed inarticulately, seizing the green men ahead of her and throwing them aside like rats, swimming and clawing through the seething tide, until she could finally grip the hysterical Dida by an arm. Jiana dragged him sideways, and without warning, burst free of the pressing mob, which broke against the foundation at her back and washed around the two of them.

Dida moaned and collapsed into her arms. She held him for long moments, watching the waves of battle crest and break.

"A slaughter, a death just like the other one," Jiana said to no one. But after a few moments, she saw it was not. The battle raged beyond her position, and she could see most of the city was still intact.

No one walked but the warriors. The shops were closed, the citizens fled or hidden. Dida wiped his eyes, breathed deeply, and stepped away from her. He drew his hunting knife.

"Let's follow," he said, forcing the tremor out of his voice.

He set off, and after a pause, Jiana followed a half pace behind him.

"Prince, prince, who's got the prince?" she called out bitterly. Dida ignored her. "Dida—stop. Where are we going? We need to find Alanai. He's the whole reason we're here, remember?"

He stopped, rubbing his chin, unconsciously touching the wispy beginnings of a beard. Jiana turned slowly about, studying the ancient city.

Death lurked everywhere, but there was no death. Desertion overpopulated the streets. In all directions, the emptiness was grotesquely intensified by the circumstantial traces of population: the great boardinghouse, now all boarded and hollow; the wide streets and vast square, uncluttered by people, dogs, or carriages. In the distance were the songs of war—Jiana's theme—but the only visible signs were the smoke on the breeze and the occasional bloodstained roadmark.

Dida pulled his coarse brown cloak tightly about him, though the air was not cold. He looked to the left, toward the wall of the city, away from its heart.

"He is there," he whispered.

"He is? Did you see him? Is he still in Bay Din?" Dida bowed his head, and shook it imperceptibly.

"Damn," Jiana said, "What the hell. Let's collect Toldo and start trudging. I'm beginning to like that chubby creep."

"The only way out is . . . there, my love." Dida nodded toward the faraway tumult.

"Are you sure? How do you know? Did you see him?"

Dida shook his head impatiently.

"Then how can you be sure?" she demanded.

"Of course I'm sure! I've been yan faire at Ox Crossing to, ha' I not? I know everything."

Jiana looked questioningly at Dida.

"Well, us southers always know our way from here to yon. Trust me! This way." He led directly toward the red flicker, his hunting knife still clutched in his hand.

"I—" Jiana began, but *the other* interrupted her thoughts: *I should think you'd be very silly indeed, not to follow such certainty*. Jiana made a rude noise, and caught up to Dida.

A block later, they came upon a huge rain barrel.

"Do you suppose . . . ?" Jiana asked. She stepped up and knocked. After a moment, Toldo's bald pate and fat jowls poked up out of the top.

"Ahem, I figured it was likely to be you. You two."

"If you can fit back out through that hole, maybe you'd like to come with us?"

"Where are you going?"

"Over there. Somewhere where I can get killed with

greater ease and comfort. So where were you going in Bay Din?"

"To visit friends, in the temple here. I don't suppose there's much chance of seeing them now."

Jiana shook her head. "Not hardly."

"Well, then, I'm, ah, as you might say, at liberty. I should like to travel with you for a while, if I might. You seek . . . the Wish of the World, is it?"

"World's Dream," Dida corrected.

"We would be honored with your presence, o girthful one."

'Good. I really believe I can help you. You have some very interesting attributes that I would like to discuss with you. Lead on, o seeker."

"Lead on, Dida," she responded. They continued toward the flames.

Grey ash flurried like snow through the streets, and settled on everything horizontal. The city was a somber cinerarium, where the corpses marched heavily under their own power into the flames. Soon Jiana, Dida, and Toldo were as greyed as the broken cobblestones. The ash burned her eyes, but no tears fell.

"Out the front gate?" she asked, breaking the sepulchral quiet.

"I know not."

"Will we have to fight?" Toldo asked, fear singeing his voice.

"I know not," said Dida. "I only know we go this way."

Suddenly she heard muffled footsteps from around the corner of a building. She stopped, half-drawing Wave and holding out her hand to halt Toldo and Dida.

Around the corner careened a desperate soldier, not yet eighteen. His helm was gone, and blood clotted in his brown hair and mustache.

He skidded in the ash and fell to his knees, coughing violently. After a moment, a war hound pounded into view.

The second man was taller, better equipped, and seemed fresher. He looked scarred by a dozen campaigns.

"Traitor worm," he muttered, advancing on the boy,

whose back was yet turned. His knight's sword dragged in the street, the only sign of fatigue.

The boy sobbed, letting his face sink into his hands. *Kill me*, his body yielded. *I am defenseless.* Common courtesy dictated spitting, or a beating, but nothing more.

"You prince-worshippers wanted rebellion," the hound continued, enjoying the mouse-and-cat. "Your head shall now rebel from your neck!" He laughed at his own great wit.

Jiana's eyes narrowed. Dida stepped forward agressively, but she put the back of her hand into his chest, just hard enough to stop him.

"Crawl away," she advised the boy. "He and I will have words." She strode forward quickly until she stood between the killer and his victim. The visor of his helm was missing, and she looked him in his dead grey eyes.

"Boys or women, I don't care," he said. "Rebels die. With or without their swords."

She scanned him up and down. He wore a metal chestplate, helm, shoulder and knee plates, but the rest of him was armored by leather, or even thick cloth alone. He trotted forward, raising his sword cheerfully, apparently convinced she was unarmed.

"You're disgusting," Jiana said, and whipped Wave out of her belt sheath in a wide, low arc. The razor—thin blade sliced just under his left kneecap. As he collapsed to the ground gasping, holding his knee, she trotted around behind him and sliced away at his lower neck, which his helm did not protect.

His violent, seizure-like twitching told her she had severed his spinal cord. She watched for a moment, then suddenly turned on the young boy, who had watched it all.

"Run away!" Jiana screamed, and he staggered to his feet and fled.

Jiana wiped her sword and sheathed it. She gestured Dida on, and he quickly led them away from the still-twitching corpse.

Ahead there were many voices raised in unison, each in its own key. They chanted a word, over and over—a name: *ALANAI! ALANAI!* Dida led them through a dark alley, where even the ash from the dying city did not drift, so claustrophobic was it. Then they burst into a courtyard, which Jiana remembered had once been a beer- and wine-selling monastery, and discovered a jubilation.

At least a thousand men jammed the cobbles and the brick prayerways, she estimated. They danced on the tables and sang, and waved lit torches about like flamebird feathers at a midwinter festival. The heat was hellish, from the flames that licked unnoticed at the surrounding building, and from the massed human bodies leaping feverishly. The noise was a tumultuous roar, similar to a waterfall, in which individual voices were, for the most part, drowned.

ALANAI! ALANAI! ALANAI! ALANAI! Occasionally a cry of "liberator!" or "avenger!" prickled the texture of the chant. A dancing giant grabbed Jiana without warning and spun her into the center of a circle. He reeked of alcohol; all of the men staggered drunkenly.

"ALANAI! ALANAI!" they howled at her, playfully punching and pinching her. The blows became more pointed, more sexual. The cries changed.

"Take it off! Show us your tits! Take everything off! Show us! Show us!"

Hands began to clutch at her clothes, and with a snarl of rage she slapped them away. But the laughing, leering drunkards barely noticed her fists, and numbly reached back again and again.

Jiana began to feel real fear twist her gut. The circle closed tighter, and the men linked arms. They pushed their unshaven faces close into hers and wiggled their tongues horridly.

She saw an opening—fleeting, ephemeral! One of the men became dizzy and stumbled. Without a moment's hesitation, she broke for the spot. Hands clutched and her tunic tore, but she was through! She ran to a wall of the burning building like the Serpent Itself was coiling at her heels. Worming along the wall, she found her friends again.

The monastery was merrily in flames now, but in the anarchy of the jubilee, the mob did not notice.

"Quicktime!" she ordered, and Dida at once shot across the courtyard, right underneath a groaning and bulging adobe wall, hot to the touch. With many a nervous glance up, Jiana followed, Toldo clutching Wave's scabbard.

Just as they reached the opposite side, the wall they had just skirted suddenly collapsed inward, across the cobblestones. Hundreds of people never even saw their impending death. The screams of the injured were made all the more horrible by the fact that the rest of the people continued dancing and chanting, and even set up a rousing cheer at the tumbling horror of flame-orange and ember-red! Jiana turned her face away, but the vision—what she might have seen in the last seconds—burned her stomach like poison.

"People," Jiana mumbled, as they walked briskly and disconnectedly through the rambling streets of Bay Din. The faces of the citizens and soldiers knotted her stomach—they were so dead, so empty, whether chanting joyously, fleeing in terror, or numbly staring at the flames. Everywhere yellow, red, and green fires flickered, and dulling embers cast ash into the air. She choked on harsh smoke. What had once stood as beauty's sentinel against the black, scrubby plains of the southern Water Kingdom was fouled. Jiana ground her teeth, and mutely followed the unhesitating Dida.

A peculiar crash sounded behind her. She turned quickly, fearing attack, but it was only a pack of wild citizens, looting a very rich store—rich enough to have clear glass windows. Two of the men wore city constable uniforms.

Jiana turned back, and pushed Toldo along. The priest's footsteps were turning more and more reluctant. Dida suddenly lost his certainty, and began to look confused.

"I know the path lies this way, but . . ." He turned up his hands, helpless. "Which way? There's burning all around."

"I can see. It's too far to go back—we'd have to recross the sewer, and the next closest bridge is on the other side of the fighting. Wait—" Jiana chewed on her knuckle, remembering.

You're useless! You know that, Jiana, dear. How have you helped so far? All you've done is loose these nasty dogs on a bleeding city!

Useless? I killed a god!

The mocker laughed, loud inside Jiana's ears.
Who killed Taku-Taku? Are you the poet now?
"Enough!"
"What?" said both Toldo and Dida in unison.
"We go under. Again." Dida paled, but he did not shrink away. "This whole city is undermined with access tunnels—not as deep as before, Dida. Not deep at all. I once traveled with a thief, as a bodyguard, the last time I was here. Jobs for a warrior had run thin."
"As I recall," spoke Toldo softly, "you also spent time in prison."
She laughed. "What do warriors know of thievery? But I do remember the tunnels. Let's find one and get the hell off the street before the fires cut us off entirely!"
She led them in a dash to the nearest substantial building, which had once, so its sign proclaimed, been a gentleman's and lady's garment shop: "Thrifty, New-Fashioned, Successful." The owners had left the door locked and bolted. With scarcely a moment's thought, Jiana burst the screen, knocked loose the jagged splinters of wood, and climbed inside.
The interior of the shop was leaden and heavy. Smoke particles hung in the air like angry spirits, and her lungs and eyes burned. Through the grey, she saw bolts of cloth and finished tunics, cloaks, and kirtles.
She stepped gingerly across the room and wasted time fingering the fabric enviously.
"Cloth of gold, silk, and pressed organdy, velvet brocade. The bastards deserved to be burned to the roots, Dida. People starve in this town, and there's enough wealth here to feed the whole city."
"Feed it once, perhaps," Toldo wheezed, dragging his bulk through the Jiana-sized hole in the window. "Then after they've eaten it, the gold flows no more."
"Are you a closet usurer? Priest, do you now defend all those worms who were born kings, with no talent or labor of their own?"
" 'Tis like water, o mighty one. When it's all of one level, such as in a lake, it just sits stagnant and unmoving. But when some is raised high on a mountain, and the rest is in a valley, then it rushes from high to low, and back

again as rain, turning the wheels of civilization along the way."

Jiana dropped the fabric contemptuously and stalked behind the counter, then through the beaded doorway, trailed by her friends.

"Somewhere . . ." Jiana scanned the floor, then flung aside a throw rug with her boot. "Here. For loading stores of cloth when the streets are too crowded with potential customers and potential hijackers."

Flush with the floor was a trapdoor, fastened by a new bolt and a heavy lock.

"That looks bad, my heart," Dida said. "You can pick it, can't you?"

"Nope. Lesson four from the Jiana school of locktripping: a shield is only as strong as the strap which holds it on your arm."

Dida looked blankly at her, but this time paused and thought for a moment.

"Mean you . . . oh!" He bent and carefully began prying at the rivets which attached the bolt to the wood. He jammed his knife under the latch and yanked, but only managed to bend the edge of his blade.

"Right idea. Wrong strap. Hey, Toldo! How would you like to learn a new profession and become an expert locktrip?"

The fat priest ambled forward, rubbing his nose.

"Well . . . is it physically taxing?"

"Somewhat. Look, the lock is new; the latch is tightly riveted. But Bay Din has been here for a long time, and this is a very old building. I'll bet that door has been there for generations."

"So?" Toldo's voice rose defensively, and Jiana thought he might have put three and five together, and figured out her plan.

"So I want you to stand in the very middle and jump up and down until the door splinters."

"What!"

"It'll be easy! What could possibly go wrong?"

"I could possibly fall through the blasted thing and plummet a hundred feet to my death!"

"Oh, don't be a pussy. We'll all keep an ear cocked, and

when it starts to go we'll warn you and you can leap to safety."

Toldo drew himself up to his full height, a whole head and a half taller than Jiana, and folded his arms across his ample chest.

"I am *not* a leaping marmoset."

Jiana paced slowly across the trapdoor, stopping every step and stomping, listening for a duller resonance or a creak or groan.

"Here," she proclaimed, "is the weak spot. Now dance!"

Toldo Mondo snorted like a bison, and scraped his foot on the recently mopped tiles. But he finally stepped gingerly out onto the trap, with as much dignity as he could muster. He looked at her inquiringly.

Jiana pointed her finger at him, and then raised it to point at the ceiling, then down to the ground . . . repeatedly. The message was simple: up, down, up, down . . .

With a rumbling, bovine sigh, Toldo began to bounce his ponderous bulk into the air, and allow it to collapse back down onto the ancient wood—slowly at first, then accelerating the pace until he had attained a strong, steady rhythm.

Thud.

Thud.

Thud!

Jiana and Dida bent close, almost pressing their ears to the vibrating door. Toldo began to pant, sweat, and complain.

Thud! Thud! Thud! Thud!

The timbre of the sound suddenly widened, and a noteworthy crack developed in the wood. One more thud, and the wood had definitely split.

"THAT'S THE SPIRIT!" Jiana cried joyously, as Toldo crashed through the door and disappeared into the blackness below.

She and Dida leaned their heads into the chasm.

"Are you killed?" she inquired.

The priest's answer was muffled, but still Dida's ears reddened.

"We'll be down in a moment!" A ladder descended from

the hole to the ground below. The warrior pushed Dida at the top rungs, and then followed him down.

"I *could* have been killed!" Toldo bellowed at her.

"Nonsense. The tunnels are only a man's height below the shops. I found that out when we used them before." She looked both directions.

The light from the shop upstairs illuminated a long stretch of tunnel, and there were periodic vents for air and sunlight.

"My love! It's so long!" Dida was again nervous and breathing too fast, but he showed none of the pure terror that had consumed him in the caverns of Taku-Taku.

"Yes. Unlike the sewer route in and out of Bay Din, this underground is heavily trafficked; In fact, I'm sure there are armed men down here. We'll have to tread carefully. But we should be able to bypass most of the fighting, at least. Come." She led them down a passage in the same approximate direction that Dida had intuited while up on the surface. Toldo limped along behind, rubbing his shins and grumbling inarticulately.

The hall was long and wide, and reasonably clean. After a time, they came to a branching with eight different paths.

Toldo and Dida stared, astonished.

"I *told* you Bay Din has been here for a long time. Which way, kid?" Dida shrugged, then pointed down a dimly lit corridor.

"Come on, boys," Jiana said, and they trotted away.

A long time passed, during which the floor fell and rose, punctuated by occasional ceiling doors—presumably to other shops or to the streets. Suddenly, Jiana held up a hand to halt.

Ahead, she heard the faint noises of someone sobbing. The voice was high-pitched, like a woman. The warrior hesitated, but curiosity won out over prudence, and she walked forward, her two friends shuffling along in her wake. There was an alcove a few feet along, and she stuck her head around the corner.

A young boy, richly arrayed, sat on a stone bench with his head in his arms, letting tears and rage drip to the floor.

"Hey," said Jiana. "Hey, little boy . . . look, it's all right. What's wrong? Damn it, stop blubbering and answer me!" He looked up, surprised, and with a mighty effort of will stopped the tears.

"Nothing is wrong, fair one," he answered in very upper-class dialect. "I apologize for disturbing thee."

"Young boys don't often sob on stone benches in the underground without at least some sort of travail," Jiana pointed out reasonably. "So what's wrong?"

"Oh, what's it matter now?" he said, his voice quivering. "They're all dead, anyway. I'm dead, too, or soon will be!"

"Who's dead?"

"Everybody! Mother and Father, and Tandy and Tedi and Uncle Am-Amorai—"

"Am-Amorai! The prince?"

The boy stood as tall as he could and looked her in the eye, with a gravity chillingly beyond his years.

"I am now Prince Lyonalai. I am a Toradora. Thou mayest as well kill me now, and finish the job!"

Jiana shook her head. "I had nothing to do with it. It was Alanai, of Bay Bay."

Liar! Jianabel accused gleefully. She had returned from wherever it was she went at such times.

Only of omission! He would not understand the concept of joining with Alanai while deploring his actions.

Silly. Do you really think that is still your purpose? Jianabel faded in a mockery of laughter, and Jiana smiled to hide the conflict.

"I'm sure Alanai would not kill a little boy, your . . ."

"Highness. Why would he not? He slew my sister Tedi, who lacks a year of myself, while we were all forced to watch! First, he . . . he had her—" The prince abruptly closed his mouth, and refused to say any more.

Jiana stared in shock.

"I cannot believe Prince Alanai would do such a thing. He must be bewitched. Are you *sure* it was he?"

"Well, the coward did not have the nerve to face my family himself, nay! He left his minion behind, with the orders to—to do what he did. I only escaped by sheerest accident, in the confusion following my mother's honorable suicide from the Tower."

"A minion? Describe him, if you please. Highness."

Lyonalai thought hard; it was obvious the memory held great and recent pain.

"He wore grey and black, and he was a monster foul. He had the mark of the beast about him."

Jiana stretched her mind back to her encounter with Alanai, trying to remember everyone in the room. At once, a dread shuddered through her body, and she recalled Death, who wore black and grey and stalked the prince's right hand.

"Hraga si Traga," she whispered.

"I believe Alanai called him so."

"As surely as a hanged man dances. Black One, how could I have forgotten you? What did Toq say—that not all of those who sought the Dream were mortals? If ever a bogle assumed human form, the bastard Hraga would be his twin."

"He laughed as they pressed my father to death," Lyonalai whimpered. "And though he himself did not participate in what they did to Tedi, at his command, three of our own soldiers leapt to obey! They seemed to be not themselves— to act at his will as though they were puppets on a stick."

"And it seems," Jiana appended, "that he has gained at least Alanai's trust, if not his soul. Well, Little Prince, come with us. We'll take you out of Bay Din, and you can make your way to safety in another land. What do you say?"

He bowed his head.

"I care little for life now. But I thank thee for thy offer, and do accept."

She led him around to the group. Toldo seemed excited, and asked him questions about the rule of the Toradoras. Dida, however, glared hotly at the prince and said nothing. He only made sure he was always between Jiana and Lyonalai. Jiana tolerated this with amusement.

At last, after three hours of tramping the tunnels beneath Bay Din, and smelling the stale air, Jiana could no longer detect smoke or the faraway tumult of battle. She judged it might be safe to ascend.

Cautiously, she climbed a ladder and pushed on a trapdoor. This one was neither locked nor even latched, and it opened readily into an alley between a perfume brewer and an abattoir.

"Ooough!" gagged Jiana, pinching her nose. "We're surely on the Winding Path of the Odors, outside the main gate of Bay Din!"

"You can find our way from her, love?" Dida asked, choking on the stench of beauty and death. Jiana nodded, holding her breath.

She led them out onto the street, and then they cut at a run across to Bent Soldiers' Street.

"Ah, why would they dedicate a street to bent soldiers?"

"It's the *street* that's bent, priest—like your mind."

"I am not a priest," said Toldo a bit stiffly.

Again, Jiana began to hear wailing. But this time it was women, hundreds of them. The questers pushed through a doorframe into a public courtyard, and saw the women by the scores sitting on the ground under the Sorrowing Trees, tears rolling down their cheeks. All of the women had a vaguely eastern look, as if they were related to the people of the Flower Empire, and their weeping had a distinctly mechanical component, like the ticking of the clock in the square in Bay Bay.

Jiana watched for a moment, then stepped boldly up to the first lady she came to.

"Why do you weep so? Do you cry for Amamorai III and his brood?"

"NO!" hollered the woman, indignantly. "I cry for my husband, for he was taken by the Toradora ten years ago, and now that the dungeons have been emptied he is not to be found!"

"Where is he?"

"He is one of the disappeared," she said, lead weighting her speech. "We—my sisters and I—have wept here every week for a generation. We hope that someday a decent soul will take pity, and help us find our loved ones . . . or at least their remains."

"Sounds like a fruitless task. Who are the disappeared?"

"It was a specialty of Amamorai III. In the night, the soldiers would come, but they would be clothed in black, with no badges of office. In they would come, into our houses! They dragged my husband out, but would not tell me his crime. I have not seen him since, and the prince's ministers assured me His Highness had no hand in the incident."

"You don't buy it?"

"Who else would it be?" she answered bitterly. "My husband spoke often, publicly, about the excesses of the Toradora."

Prince Lyonalai spoke up for the first time since leaving the tunnel.

"How many have disappeared thus?"

"I don't know," she said. She turned to another weeping woman, and spoke rapidly with her in a foreign language. It sounded like a lower-class Bay Din dialect, which was said to be a corruption of the language of the Ti-Ji Tul themselves. Jiana did not speak it.

"She says more than two thousand," the woman continued, "but there are some boroughs of Bay Din she knows little about. Many could be missing from there unnoticed. And of course there's the ones with no one to weep for them. How many they are, none can say."

"My heart to you all," Jiana said, gripping Prince Lyonalai by the arm and dragging him away, "but we must leave. Wait—is Alanai still in the city? Is he leaving soon?" Again the woman consulted her friend, and translated the answer.

"The Prince of Water has already left yesterday, with nearly a hundred stout men of Bay Din, those who have always hated the usurpers."

Jiana clapped a hand over the indignant boy-prince's mouth before he could finish sputtering and spit out whatever he intended to say.

"I thank you all again, and wish for you happier days. Move out, men." She dragged the squirming prince away through the far arches, and onto the Straight Way of the Bookbinders. There were still no merchants on the streets. Bay Din was deserted and ghostly.

"Two things we need," she told Dida, "and here's one of them right now." Jiana ran into a shop across the street— Fregedata's Bindery—and forced open the door with her sword. Her memory from years before had not failed, and in a drawer behind the counter was a huge pile of maps. She leafed through until she found the large maps of the whole world—as much of it as the men of the Water Kingdom knew—and in particular one of the ones drawn by Onan Tondai's disciple, Atmag. She rolled it up and thrust it in her belt, then borrowed two copper serpents from Toldo and left them to pay for the map and the door.

"And the last thing we must get before leaving is food and horses. I know where they can be found, too." With another half hour zigging and swerving along the strange and woeful streets of Bay Din, they arrived at a stable. Unlike the previous establishments, the owner was indeed present and willing to haggle over the price. Jiana found it a welcome change, especially when it passed that the prince had plenty of money, and they could get whatever they coveted. At last, they rode out of Bay Din.

"A day. A full, whole, damn day," Jiana muttered. "We'll never make it up!"

"Well, why don't we think of our triumphs instead, my love?"

"What triumphs are those? I lost us in the caverns, nearly killed us among the fanatics, slew some dumb god, and then almost dropped a burning wall on us!"

"We're alive. We're unhurt. Not many from that place can say so."

Jiana turned in her saddle and looked back at Dida.

"You keep growing up like that, kid, and pretty soon we'll be the same age." She laughed, and they spurred their horses south along the Long Road of Kings, riding straight for the Valley at the Center of the World.

Chapter 6

Believing in tongues, or,
the Sword Cuts to all Directions but One

-1-

The four rode for a time, and for a time again, while grey waves of cloud fell crashing into the sky over their heads. Soon there was no sky left—just a dark and chill ceiling of iron. A dimness smothered the land.

There was no one else on the great road.

"The world must have escaped," Dida whispered. Jiana did not answer. Even a whisper echoed loud in her ears, and she looked fearfully back over her shoulder.

A long rumble of thunder drew across the land, as tight as a desert drum. There was no flash of lighting, nor any rain. The horses' hooves scrunched like brittle bones breaking, and Jiana's heart raced inexplicably.

"I don't like this place. Something's wrong. Prince, why have you said nothing since we left? What do you know?"

"O gentle lady, I am silent because I know where we ride."

"We ride through Caela, then through the wasted Tarn."

"We ride to Death."

Dida looked down into the dirt, and Jiana looked sharply at the prince. But it was Toldo who answered.

"Why don't you just be still about that Death rot, Your Highness? We have no need for your children's bogles and fishwives' ghosts."

Jiana's reply was barely audible.

"A ghost would be preferable to the creatures we might find in the Tarn."

"You have been there, good lady?"

Jiana nodded.

"Chasing scaleless demon-goats. For money!" She laughed, short and ugly. "I plead only youth, and pride. The Nameless Serpentine must love idiots; I skirted the edges, and maintained my sanity. Of course . . . the desert was in a quiet phase."

"I know only from the tongues of others," said Lyonalai, and he looked back as if he heard something behind them. Jiana followed his gaze, but there was nothing; it was only the wind, blowing from the Tarn.

"Rot," Toldo declared, as if passing judgment. But Jiana noticed that he, too, turned to peek, when he thought her eyes were diverted.

" 'Tis no superstition, goodman priest. The tarn is . . ." Prince Lyonalai struggled for a metaphor. "The Desert Tarn is a vertex, at which many of the spheres of the world intersect. On a diamond of the first water, if you continue each facet infinitely in all directions, they will meet and intersect in many places. Some points will be the intersection of many, many faces. The Tarn is like this, only the lines of intersection are—fuzzy."

"Do you mean, kid—Your Princeness—that you can cross from one to the other?"

"Yes, as can the rest."

"Of—?"

"The dwellers in the spheres. You were quite correct, beauteous lady." Dida stiffened noticeably at the prince's endearment. "But things have changed of late . . . Uncle Amamorai, before his—his death—"

Jiana rose in her saddle and turned back to stare at the prince.

"Exactly what has changed?"

"The tarn isn't boundaried anymore."

Toldo wrinkled his forehead.

"Do you mean no longer bounded?"

"Yes, that's the word."

"You mean those things can get out now?" Jiana felt fearful, senselessly . . . *do these clouds obscure my mind as well as the sky?*

There are some things, said Jianabel sweetly, a whisper in her mind, *that even I fear*. Jiana swallowed, not knowing whether the tormentor offered a genuine warning or merely played another complex, awful game.

"Nonsense!" Toldo Mondo retorted. "Superstitious mumble-jumble." But his voice quavered.

"It isn't, it has too, and you all jolly well better make up your minds to it," snapped the prince pettishly. "It's infected the Valley at the Center of the World. Can't you feel it? Don't you feel the fluxions?"

"I feel something," Dida admitted, pressing closer to Jiana. His grey stallion began nipping at the neck of Jiana's roan, who threw her head back and skittered to the side. Jiana wrestled her under control again, and glared at Dida as though it were his fault.

"What you feel is the fear of a child," Jiana growled. Dida did not answer, in words. His eyes spoke epics, and Jiana wondered what had possessed her to say it.

For a long while they plodded forward in silence broken only by the creak of leather harnesses and the crunch of hooves on gravel. Soon, the ceiling descended to shroud the air they breathed, and they rode through a thick and clinging fog.

"My uncle felt the change, of course," the prince appended suddenly, though he had last spoken a mile before. "He left Bay Din and traveled alone, without even the guards, into the Tarn. At least, that's what they all say."

Jiana allowed the silence to stretch, then cut it.

"And found . . . ?"

Prince Lyonalai shrugged, almost indistinguishable in the fog.

"He visited some sphere and cast some magicks, I suppose. What's the difference? He's dead!"

"Well, tell us about his adventures," Toldo prompted, trying to head off the boy's tears.

"I know not. I only know he returned with—something. This something had to do with the World's Dream, I'm sure of it!"

"You know of the Dream?" Jiana gasped.

Lyonalai looked at her as he might at a schoolchum who displayed an inexcusable ignorance.

"Of course. The Illuminated have *always* sought the World's Dream of the Breathable Thousand."

"Breathable Thousand?"

Prince Lyonalai began to recite in a scholar's singsong:

> In ancient days, in days of ancient years,
> When fathers' fathers never yet were born and
>   women all were virgins,
> When horses were as one with dogs in size,
> When giant lizards stalked the ground, and shook
>   the thunder tundra
> Under numbing strides . . .

Jiana began to swear softly, letting her head fall into her hands. Eventually, the prince worked his way to the good part.

> Then, did the thousand souls that danced beneath
>   the chopping waves
> Release as one the breath that were their Souls,
> And piping such a note,
> Did shape and curve, and elsewise form to be the
>   World Dream,
> As dreamt and prophecied, and scried and seen
>   by
> He Was He Who Holiest Was,
> The Long-Seeing Ar-Chakanai the Invisionless,
> Whose name is holy even unto this today.
> And in this Dream were formed
> All that sought was by the Light:
> All but good and vile,
> Life and death,
> Man and beast, woman and her mate, the water
>   and the fire;

> In the World's Dream were formed all that yet
>   had not become;
> All yet to be, that never was, that could not
>   happen or never would;
> For true, the Dream was never Truth,
> Nor False itself describe this breath.
>
> It was naught but the Choices, unvoiced, decided
>   not;
> It was the light which casts no shadow.

For several seconds, Jiana was silent. Then she snorted.

"Seem to be a bloody lot of World's Dreams going around these days," she grumbled. "Hey; you said your uncle returned from the Tarn with something related to the Dream . . . what did he bring?" Jiana bit her lip; a hint, however small or inconsequential to the prince, might tell her something about Alanai's control over the Dream.

Prince Lyonalai was quiet then, in his turn.

"I shan't tell you," he proclaimed at last.

"Why not?!"

"Well, how do *I* know what you're up to? Why are you following that horrid Prince Alanai, O beauty black?"

"Go ahead and tell him," Dida suddenly interjected, unctuous and oily. "Go ahead and tell him of your quest!"

"Quest?"

"Shut up, kid. Don't—"

"Aren't you going to tell Prince Lyona-lulu about your joining up with Alanai in his quest for the World's Dream?"

"DIDA!"

The prince reined in, looking wild-eyed at Jiana. Then, without another word, he spurred his horse and galloped madly off the road, into the watery bracken. In a moment, the swirling white had swallowed him like an ocean. Even the crack of his horse's hooves rebounded and reflected until they could not tell from what direction it came.

Jiana started to follow, but reined in sharply at the edge of the road.

Afraid, good old Jiana? Fearful of the white white white?

"I'm no tracker," she said aloud. "He's gone, and he'll have to stay gone, unless we stumble across him again later." She turned slowly in the saddle to glare balefully back at Dida, who sulked silently on his grey. "Whatever intelligence he might have told us is gone as well. Thank you, Dida. Jealousy is so romantic."

She kicked her horse into movement, a little harder than necessary.

You spread such light and cheer, wherever you go, Ji!

Shut up.

And you certainly know how to lead an expedition!

"SHUT UP!" Toldo and Dida stared, uncomprehending.

She cantered up the road, and Dida and Toldo spurred their mounts to catch up with her. Many miles passed in malevolent silence.

As the sun set, and the dead, white fog grew grey, they began to see a few houses along the road. Around every bend, the farms and houses grew denser. Atmag's map showed a river up ahead, and a ford. Apparently there was to be a town, as well. Jiana decided to press on through the darkness until they found it.

Shortly after sunset, partly into dusk, Jiana suddenly yanked her horse to a stop so quickly the others nearly bumped into her.

"Oh, dear," muttered Toldo, in a stage whisper.

Eight heavily armed men blocked the road, facing them.

"Who be ye?" snapped the leader.

"Jiana of Bay Bay," she answered promptly. "You?"

"Long Hyu Committee of the Holy Vehemence. Who'd-'you bow to?"

Jiana thought hard, but quickly enough that there was no perceptible pause.

"I bow only to God, of course." *If my luck holds . . .*

The man slowly shook his head.

"Not an answer. Afraid you'll be to come with us, Miss." Three more men rode out from behind some cover, surrounding the party. In the foggy gloom, they had been invisible.

"Where do we go?" Jiana asked, as a man seized their reins and led them away.

"Long Hyu. Believers' Hall. Grand Querier . . . be to be examined."

Jiana said nothing, but icy fingers caressed her spine.

The blackness of Long Hyu's road was complete. Faint, muffled illumination suggested thick draperies covering the windows of the houses, and there were no lanterns or torches lighting the square. Only the luminescent lichen cast a faint pallor below her feet.

Sounds were muffled as well, and their direction uncertain. When a leather harness creaked, Jiana could not even tell if it was her own or another's.

They dismounted and trekked through the scrub. Jiana stepped in a hole, and were it not for her stiff boots, she might have twisted her ankle. The followers of the Holy Vehemence nearly vanished before her again, as the fog pulled about her like a winding sheet.

She thought of making a break for it, trusting to the uncertain sights and sounds of the night to cover her path. But the thought of stumbling unknowing into a swamp or sinksand weighed heavily against the plan.

At once a building bulked before her eyes. It was impossible to gain any idea of its size or shape—all Jiana saw was a wall of dark wood, and an enormous door . . . open. It was not inviting.

She passed inside, and her booted feet echoed hollowly on the wooden floor. The fog swirled in with her, and settled to the floor in the warm room.

The darkness hinted at a vast expanse. The opposite walls were beyond the faint light from the outside. She strode forward, showing a fearlessness she did not feel. Others entered with her, and the great door shut behind them all, giving the room over to the black night.

A boy moved to her side—it was Dida. Suddenly, two torches flared on either side of her. For a moment, she caught a glimpse of a hooded figure with a candle. Then the bright flames tore away her night vision, and she was blind. After a moment, Toldo joined her in the light, and the party of three waited expectantly.

"Query away, o faceless ones," Jiana snarled.

"You be Jiana of Bay Bay?" called a voice from the front. Jiana drew a breath, nonplussed.

"I am."

"You have been named under a charge within the competence of the Holy Vehemence. Hod d'ye be to answer?"

'What's the charge? Who named me? None of you even know me!"

"We cannot divulge the exact nature of the charge. You shall be allowed up to eight friends to defend your character, and their lawyers."

"How the hell can I defend my character if I don't know how it's attacked? And I have only two friends—or three, if you count me as well."

"Do you refer to the two who stand before ye?" the voice asked. Jiana nodded. "Your friends stand to be named as well, so it were well other friends be chosen for your defense."

"But I don't know anyone in Long Hyu! What are the bloody charges?"

"A moment, m'lady," Toldo interjected. "I have had dealings with Church societies before. Wise ones, is it permitted to reveal what charges *are* within the competence of the tribunal?"

There was a long pause, during which Jiana could hear men whispering in the distance. She shielded her eyes against the glare of the torches, and could just make out a long table, behind which sat a number of hooded judges. As her eyes began to adjust once again to the gloom, she could make out a large, metallic circle hung on the table, reflecting the dancing torchlight dully.

She swallowed dryly. She could not see it, but Jiana was certain the circle bore the gilt likeness of a charcoal tong. It was the sigil of the Church of the Burning Ember, a young, "modern" religion that had been founded three hundred years before, in response to the excesses of the world's older religions—such as the worship of the Sublime Serpent. The Holy Vehemence must be a sect of the Church.

Jiana began to work her hand toward her jade necklace, which bore the likeness of the Nameless Serpentine. Then abruptly she dropped her hands and glared defiantly. Either they had already seen it in the bright torchlight, or they had missed it. In any case, she would not draw their attention to it.

"We have decided that is within your right," spoke a new voice, softer than the first. "Foremost, the judicial council of the Holy Vehemence tries those who reveal the evil secrets of the Ti-Ji Tul, those who practice or introduce heresy, those who fall from the faith and become heathens, those who commit perjury, those who practice witchcraft or magic or enter into any treaty with the Evil Serpent—" Dida gasped audibly, and Jiana ground her teeth in frustration at his blunder, "—and those who reveal the illuminations of the Society of the Holy Vehemence."

Swiftly, Toldo spoke up.

"We desire a few moments before the Wise, in which to confer and discuss the possible charges before us and our defense."

The first voice answered, "It is granted, but you shall not converse in a whisper, that the tribunal may better hear your character."

Toldo Mondo scratched the stubble on his chin.

"Well, it can't be the latter, for we don't *know* any illuminations of the Holy Vehemence. Neither can it be perjury, for we've appeared before no tribunals before now. Certainly, we should all be considered heathens . . . you worship the snake, and I am an atheist, while the boy is a peasant and therefore an avitiate. Yet, not one of us was ever of the faith of the Burners, so by definition, none of us could *fall* from the faith. Jiana?"

"I know nothing of philosophy or heresy," she added, "and I certainly made no treaties with the Serpent—or rather, he has made no treaties with me, much as I'm sure the god of these gentlemen has not condescended to visit them to share biscuits and tea. What's left? I'm no magician!" She glanced quickly at Dida, but this time he did not betray her.

"O glorious judges," he began, "Yan hero knowing not of any doings of the First Men, cannot be revealing what she'll know not!"

"Speak plainly, boy," snapped the second voice, a bit harder than it had spoken before.

"I'm sorry," Dida said. "I'm a souther, and it's effortful to speak in this dialect. I said, she knows nothing about the First Men. How could she reveal their secrets?"

"Perhaps she knew the secrets, but did not be to know whose they were."

"Your pardon, Wise ones . . . but then, where is her criminal intent?"

A third voice answered, from the far left end, and again Jiana strained to see the face that went with the voice.

"If the secrets be grim, then your negligence be to be such that the omission becomes commission, and intent is implied."

"Oh, hang the lot of you!" Jiana cried. "This is rampant silliness! I came here only—"

"We came only to apply for initiation into your glorious fraternity," Toldo interjected smoothly, without noticeable pause. "We stand Ignorant in the darkness, and desire to come by Wisdom into the light."

Jiana realized her mouth was hanging open, and she shut it with a pop. She forced herself to stare straight ahead, and not gape at the ex-priest in astonishment.

A chorus of groans echoed from the table, and she heard many papers being shuffled. At last, the second voice spoke, weary and frustrated.

"The matter of your guilt shall be tabled until after the conferring and possible initiation. Are ye ready to take ye the oath?"

"I am," said Toldo. Jiana and Dida repeated, "I am."

"Then ye shall be examined for brotherhood. Proceed." This last was directed at the others around the table, who immediately began a barrage of questions against the three.

Toldo took the lead in answering, and his hints were clear enough that Jiana could play along. Dida simply chose to act dumb, and his callow and bedraggled look helped to pull it off.

The doctrine questions were the easiest; the "correct" answer was always readily apparent. Jiana had the hardest time with the questions of ethics—who could know the taboos of the Holy Vehemence? But she forced herself to think like her old spinster aunt from White Falls, and the grimness seemed to pass muster.

Valuable practice for confronting Alanai on some future tomorrow, she told herself. In any case, it was fun.

Finally, after a forever of questions, the three were

ordered to kneel. An oaf walloped them on the head with a sack of coal, and they were illuminated. They repeated a dreadful oath, full of torments and agonies and taxes, and promised not to reveal anything about anything to anyone at any time.

"And now," said the owner of the first voice—Jiana could almost hear him rubbing his hands in glee—"the trial shall resume. But as you are now initiates into the illumined Order, and have ceded to us authority over your corporeal bodies as well as your souls, the punishment we may now consider is death!"

"Ah . . . just as a personal aside," the warrior interjected, "what was the maximum punishment we could have received *before* initiation?"

"Your souls could have been to be damned to the foul realm of the slithering one," intoned the first voice momentously, "and your hopes for future salvation might even have been forever closed!"

"Oh. Just checking." She swallowed, and the noise sounded unnaturally loud in the smoky auditorium.

"A moment, please," Toldo said, as unctuous as the Bay Bay livery master who had sold her Running Spots. "As initiates to the Light, we may now require to know whether he who has accused us is also an initiate."

Silence boomed.

"I suggest you reread the preamble to the bull of High Bishop Tauri XI, which allows for investiture of new orders to the Church."

Again, papers began to shuffle, and a whispered argument grew in intensity among the Wise Ones. At last they settled down, and a candle was lit behind a screen. It reflected off the pallid faces of the priests, and turned them into wrinkled corpses. The center-sitting inquisitor, clearly the ringleader, moved his lips as he pored through the manuscript—so much so that Jiana could almost read it with him.

"Hem, yes, it does appear that initiates have that privilege. I suppose." Number two cleared his throat, and continued. "The answer, I am constrained to say, is no. Your accuser, although an avid churchgoer, is not a member of the Order, as such . . ."

"And therefore, by the succeeding paragraph in the preamble . . ." Jiana glanced at Toldo Mondo. He had leaned his head back with his eyes closed, and placed one fat forefinger against his brow.

"Hem. Yes. That does indeed alter things. Doesn't it."

Toldo suddenly popped his head forward and his eyes open, and pantomimed scanning the room intently. In fact, he could see no more than Jiana could, which was virtually nothing.

"As I do not *see* said accuser in the room, and as his physical presence is required to bring the charges to our face, I move this entire trial be dismissed for lack of a charge."

The first voice began to chuckle. Jiana could almost smell the hate emanating from the second voice, which the shielded candle revealed to belong to an emaciated bald-head with a hawk beak (*the better to sneer at you*, whispered Jianabel in the warrior's stomach).

"Capital!" said number one. "I did so regret the necessity of this proceeding!"

The third priest had said little, and he struck Jiana as somewhat dim, and easily manipulated. Hawk-nose would be the one to watch.

He finally mastered himself enough to stage whisper to Number One.

"Before Your Grace falls overboard in your conviviality, there is still a matter at hand."

"Oh? I was hoping we had dispensed with everything. It's not taxes, is it?"

"No, Your Grace. Although we cannot try these . . . initiates, there have still been brought certain rumors against their characters."

His Grace seemed perplexed—at least, in the dim, flickering light, Jiana though she saw his brow wrinkle.

"I thought we weren't allowed to consider Traga's testimony."

Jiana's stomach gave a sudden lurch. Traga! Again?

"What a fool I am," she hissed to Dida. "Who else *could* it have been?" But still a white dread enshrouded her. *Why did he attack us? How did he know enough to influence the Holy Vehemence?*

How did he even know we were here?

And he had looked at her with eyes so dead . . . *Toq said there were others. Toq said they were not all mortals* . . .

"We may not consider our source as testimony—but we may certainly heed any rumors we hear, from anywhere. Perhaps our new servants ought to undertake a small quest, just to prove their loyalty and suitability."

"Hem. What did you have in mind, Frater Eilau?"

Eilau gasped. *Probably supposed to remain anonymous,* Jiana reasoned. But he recovered swiftly.

"I thought perhaps the coven . . ."

The ringleader frowned.

"A grave endeavor."

"Somebody must—we agreed."

"Yes, it must be done. All right, Brother, you may so assign."

"Of course, Your Grace." He turned to the three, grinning like the Treasurer Royal at harvest time. "There is a secret coven of snake-worshipers in Long Hyu—our own holy city!"

"Yes?" Jiana prompted.

"They must be infiltrated, and . . ."

"And?"

"Obliterated."

"Uck." Her stomach yawed again; she was becoming almost used to the feeling.

"By sunup twice hence. Now leave! And . . . do not try to exit Long Hyu without accomplishing your mission. Having taken the oath, you are bound to obey, else would be retroactive perjury. And we *will* hunt you down. You may, if you like, be to bet your life upon it."

Jiana bowed deeply.

"Before the sun shall spin twice more, there shall be no covert serpents in Long Hyu. Jiana's word upon it."

The doors opened, and they were ushered out into the clinging fog.

-2-

The bishops of the Holy Vehemence were not as insane as they had appeared at first. They were not pitting Jiana,

Dida, and Toldo against the entire serpent-worshiping coven.

The raid had long been planned, and they were only three of twelve. The leader of the expedition was a farmer, hardened by thirty years of stone-cropping and embittered by eight years of the Holy Vehemence. The coven was ensconced within a tiny village, downriver on the Hyu from Long Hyu, and economically subservient to its richer neighbor, the merchants of the Church.

For weeks, great calamities had befallen the land, and the church had pointed its gilded finger at the infidels. The earth had gasped and heaved; salt poisoned the rain that fell from the rumbling sky. The children were infected with the sleeping-worm, and cattle gave birth to three-headed calves. What else could it be but the coven?

"I have my suspicions," Jiana muttered to Dida, on an occasion when they were speaking.

"I'm sorry for my words this morning. Is it Alanai?"

"His quest. I don't know who's been invited, but Toq is not the only wraith or ghost involved. I know that, at least."

"Who is Hraga si Traga?"

The conversation ended there; it had for a night and a day now. How could she answer? He was a feeling of dread, a whiff from the grave. Hraga was the touch of a finger at midnight in your own empty room, a room gone suddenly strange. He was the winding sheet and the hunched and chuckling gnome, which became bedding and a chair by daylight.

Jiana could not answer the question to herself, even, let alone to the souther who still stirred her stomach with emotion under the anger and resentment.

And what of that other question, Ji?

Silence, little girl. I know you better now; I'll not listen!

And what of that souther, that mouse? He ventures frightfully far out into the room, now—does he frighten the fat bear back into her den?

Away! You're a horror. Awful suspicions are gnawing at me . . . just how much of a lie was the Most Horrible Time, the way I've always remembered it? Now, I can see an alter, an athame . . . Jiana rubbed her fists in her eyes. *I have this horrible feeling your father was—was—*

An ugly chuckle rolled around Jiana's stomach, from everywhere within her, to the core and out. Jianabel made her voice quite horrid.

My father. Was. YOUR father. Jiana, dear.

The warrior opened her eyes, and looked at Dida.

"I honestly don't know who Traga is, but he arouses such feelings in me that if I ever find him, I'll kill him without a crime—without even a reason."

"He must be such evilness of!"

She shook her head.

"I will do exactly what disgusts me in the Eagle prince. I'll gut Master Hraga si Traga because I judge him to be unfit to live. And I have no more authority than our heroic prince."

"Surely not less! You, too, are a hero."

"Yes. I know. It scares the hell out of me."

The preparations for the assault were simple, and for a while prevented her interminable internal analysis from eating away at her stomach like an ulcer. Goodman Rufes made the military decisions, and Jiana listened blankly when he explained them to the instruments of Vehemence. They were stupid ideas, but she did not care. She had no intention of actually engaging in the hostilities.

The pagans were rampant in Wolfton Along the Hyu, and Jiana had no doubt whatsoever it was a case of country against city, rather than wickedness against piety. *Maybe*, she thought, *I can crack a deal with the coven, squeal on the Vehemence? Tell the king? Play them off against each other?*

"The scheme," she confided to Toldo, "is to convince them we're striving mightily for the cause, while in fact we're hiding out eating bluebroos and crushing fleas between our fingernails. Whether they win or lose, we're off the hook, and can continue after the prince."

Toldo affected great shock.

"Schemes? Why, I thought most of your fighting was in the Flower Empire. Don't they have a tradition of chivalry, of face-to-face combat?"

"You'd be surprised. We used assassins, spies . . . even the nobles in the cavalry weren't adverse to a little night belly-crawling, in a good cause. Or for the hell of it, when we got bored with dueling."

"Wounds of the Lady! Can we not even depend on our legends and romances anymore?"

"What's the world coming to, eh?"

"Probably no good. But that's a tail of a different horse."

Toldo Mondo turned out to be a surprisingly good schemer, which Jiana cynically chalked up to his priestly experience.

Dida sulked. He and Jiana had quarreled again. On the surface, it was over heroes and how they slay their enemies. He had looked at her with judgment in his eyes, and Jiana had turned her back on him and stormed off. If anyone were to be allowed to judge her, it would be she herself. But another spoke up, out of turn but wounding with every word.

He loves you, dumble. You don't love him. You're hurting him every minute, and I think it's simply wonderful!

Jiana drifted outside of Rufes's stone house, into his corn field, where she could sit and wrap her arms around her knees, and let the rustling, yellow stalks hide her. In another day, Rufes would send his sons and his slaves out to cut down the empty stalks and . . . do something with them: make beds, feed them to farm animals, plough them under, press them into paper.

"What do I know of the world?" she demanded, aloud to the stars. "I think I'm so mature, so wise, so worldly. All I know is blood and steel, and the brotherhood of the battlefield! I can kill and burn and plunder, and raid and foray, and hold a line and retreat by sections. But I don't know what love is." The stars did not hear.

She felt a tear on her cheek—and then felt weak for crying—and then savagely berated herself for thinking emotions were weakness—and then wondered whether she was even a warrior, with a stomach full of such destructive introspection—and then worried that her heart had hardened into a seed and fallen out of her body during a battle one day—and then—and then—and then . . .

"What do I know from love? Who is more the child, me or Dida? What do I know of the world but cavalry flourishes and the standing sword manual? I don't even know what they do with cornstalks when they get the corn off!"

A steady stream of tears dripped down her face.

"At least I know I still have a heart," she whispered to the wind (which did not hear either). "The question is, who is it that has broken it? There are several likely suspects: Tawn, who drowned with his gold; Gaish, who fell with her town. The too-wise, whose mind fled south with her dream-voices. Dilai's father and our drunken duel, Lyonalai's father and his dream of power. Toldo's faith, Dida—Dida's respect for me, his innocence, his stupid love!"

She shook her head, brushing the prickly cornstalks, glad for the sharp pain when one stuck into her back as she lay down.

"Too many casualties. Toq. Alanai. Jianabel . . . myself." She was quiet for a long moment. "My father."

"Oh, hell," Jiana exclaimed, suddenly sitting up. "Who cares? My heart is nothing but another target for an enemy spear. Why should I need it? Why should I care for people killed by black demons and idiots crushed by a falling wall? Did I set the bricks ablaze? Hah!"

For a change, the accuser stood mute.

Jiana turned back, and with determination forgot the entire monolog. The assault was about to begin, and Dida was calling her back.

The greater moon rose just past full that night—bad timing. But shortly after sunset, it was hidden behind a thick ceiling of clouds. Dida and Rufes agreed it was a good sign, but Toldo laughed and said it was only a warm front. Jiana shrugged.

"Who cares? Let's move out while the damn sky's still overcast!"

At Jiana's suggestion, Dida had gotten himself chosen as a scout. It made sense, considering his woodsy background. He had insisted Jiana be his partner, and since Rufes had not been told anything about the Examination, he had no reason to say nay. Within moments, Jiana and Dida had pressed forward into the damp, rotting vegetation, and were instantly isolated from the world itself.

"I can track still," Dida bragged, loping a few yards

along and then turning back, like an eager hunting dog, "whatever the weather—my father's a gatherer! He taught me everything and all he knew!"

"Dida . . ." Jiana began, but her voice trailed off reluctantly.

"What?" She was silent a long time. "What's wrong, Jiana, love?"

Dida began to look scared, as if he suspected the tragedy that was about to occur. Jiana bit her lip, and her voice absolutely did not quaver.

"We're wrong," she whispered. "It's not working. There are too many problems."

"What problems? We can work them out!"

"It's not you, or me. It's just . . . we're not working together, kid. It's better we break if off now, and not let it grow into an ugly vine binding us together."

Dida's eyes began to get big and liquidy. There were no tears, yet even so, he had shrunk in a moment back into the frightened, snuffling mouse he was when she had first met him, a week and an age ago in the Suhuhu-Huisto Bayou.

"Damn your eyes, stop it! I won't take it—not from you or any other! Just look at us: how long have we known one another?"

"Forever."

"Seven days. Our love was birthed with a lie—"

"What lie?"

"—that you were a virgin, that you needed but an awakening, that I could mold—" She began to feel tears on her own cheeks. "Dida, honey. When, in either of our lives, would there be time for tenderness? Do you want a battle-bitch bear for a bride? Do you think I could live with a child who plays heroes and horrors? I can't!"

Without another word, Dida spun about and fled into the misty woods. For a moment, she stared dumbly after him; then she roused herself and plowed through the underbrush.

Jiana had never lived as a forester, had never tracked, but she had ridden with the greatest hounders of the mightiest empire in the known world, the Okotos of conquered Autikononi Province. Two of them rode at her side in the Cavalry of the Yellow Reeds, hounding down the enemies of the Poppy Satrap, and they had bantered casually between themselves about some of their tricks. Jiana strained to recall the lessons, cursing her arrogant disinterest in the monkey tricks of the noncommissioned officers.

At last she admitted the truth. She had lost him.

"Oh, you two tracking bastards," she hissed to her memories. "You never warned me the forest would be so dark!"

For a fruitless time, she cast about through the brush and the trees, stumbling into ditches and catching her tunic on tree branches. Then she sat down.

"Think, think—I've still got a mind beneath the brigandine. Well, there's really only one alternative. Dida will have to find himself. If I don't get back to the raid and fix things, I'll never sleep a full night again without night haunts and staring into the dark, hearing holy assassins at every window."

She looked at the sky. It was still overcast, and not a star or a moon could be seen. Likewise, the trees blocked the sight of the mountains, which she knew bordered the valley on the west.

Jiana shivered in the chilly night breeze, and concentrated on her senses. She heard the wind howl through the trees, like a mourning woman calling for her dead son. Listening carefully, behind it she could hear the lapping of water from some tiny forest stream. She smelled the crisp smell of the woods, bringing dying trees and decaying carrion to her nostrils. What did Toldo say the overcast was? A warm front?

It did not feel very warm to her. But he had said something else. He had said something about the wind. It usually changed when such a front passed, from blowing roughly out of the southeast to blowing from the southwest. The clouds preceded the change, he said, so the wind blew now from southeast to northwest.

She looked again at the sky—not directly overhead, but near the horizon. There, she could clearly see the tall trees silhouetted against the clouds. She watched carefully, turning back and forth, until she determined the direction in which the cloud bottoms moved the fastest.

From there, even Jiana's feeble store of woodcraft was enough to tell her which way ought to be west.

"When we fail to return," she said aloud, frightening away any ghosts or demons or jungle carnivores, "They'll surely just follow the Hyu to the village. I can't imagine Rufes showing more cunning than that."

She sighted westward, using the cloud movement as her guide, and picked out a particularly noteworthy tree. Then, fixing her eyes firmly upon it, she marched off across the spongy ground, trying not to lose sight even when she stumbled over roots or fell in holes.

An eternity passed, but at last she began to hear another water murmur, and this grew until suddenly, bursting through the foliage, she beheld the magnificent river Hyu, which translated to "spittle" in the tongue of the Ti-Ji Tul. It was fully wide enough to require a good, sturdy toss to get a stone to the opposite bank, and the color of a muddied swimming hole. But it stretched north and south a great-moon's journey, and was the center of civilization for the Middlins people—not quite in the Caela, not quite in the hills, but just middlin' between—along the entire length of the great central valley.

Trapping her thumb in her fist for luck, she turned left, hoping it was south, and began to pad along the crackly road.

After a while, the woods thinned out, and she sought for a sign that she had reached her destination.

It arrived in the form of an arrow, which thudded into the ground at her feet.

"Stand yer ground, if ye wants tae continue with life!" commanded a voice from the direction the tail of the arrow pointed.

Jiana froze, and carefully put her hands into the air. "What harm could you wish upon a poor, defenseless woman, o great warrior?"

He stepped out from behind a stand of weeds.

"I'd be wantin' nothing with such a one as ye describe . . . but with a minion of the foul order, the unholy vehemence—ah, now there be one I'd have business with!" He grinned evilly, and even in the darkness Jiana could see half of his teeth were missing. He wore animal skins and stank of blood and pungent herbs.

Jiana nodded wearily.

"I know. I must go to the council to be examined. Lead on, Master Elegance. This dream grows tiresome in repetition."

The peasant snorted and gestured, and Jiana tramped on ahead with her hands behind her head.

A grunt of strides brought her to a circle of eight elder tribesmen, smoking a strong-smelling herb and debating fate. A hot fire illuminated them all red and yellow, and turned them into bronze statues brought to life.

"Ye've come tae launch an attack!" accused one of them.

Jiana thought quickly.

"Not so, Grandfathers. I've come to *warn* of an attack. The Holy Vehemence plans to eliminate its enemies—those who worship the Nameless Serpentine—in a bold stroke. I hastened hither to ensure you were prepared to mount a resistance." She reached beneath her tunic and brought forth the serpent medallion she wore, the one she had prayed the Holy Vehemence did not find.

The elders studied it closely, and nodded to each other, seemingly convinced by such incontrovertible evidence.

"Wesh'll be ready. Wesh'll fight 'em in the fields, wesh'll fight 'em—"

"Have you thought of fighting them upriver?"

"Heh?" The oldest, hairiest, ugliest Middlin shifted his bulk, and demanded to know what Jiana meant.

"Instead of awaiting them here, where the battle might devastate your village, why not meet them en route?"

The council looked about confusedly. All around, in spite of the fact that it was the middle of the night, the Middlins people were throwing furs over their hut-houses, spreading flowers and malted barley along the ground, and trying on their frightful masks in preparation for some great ceremony. *The one where they're going to raise "the demon," I suppose,* Jiana thought to herself.

"But—yan festival!"

"Okay, so a few of your warriors have to miss the holiday this year. Won't you have one next year?"

"Aye . . . meseems it wouldna be too harsh tae go a year without communing."

"Be ye volunteering?" demanded a diminutive council

member in a shrill voice that reminded Jiana of a monkey—
an image aided by his scraggly beard and unkempt locks.
The councilor to whom he spoke was taller and darker,
and clearly stood out as a warrior.

"I be general of yan armies, so aye, I *do* be volunteering! You!" He jabbed his finger at Jiana. "Ye'll tell me
where they come, an' we'll meet an' butcher 'em in the
night!"

"I can do that. But I need someone, someone I believe
you have, or can find. There is one called Dida. Do you
know of him?"

The general stood.

"Aye. I know of him!" He drew his long knife and held
it in front of his face. "Hesh'll be well taken care of, before
the even's out!"

Jiana felt a hole open in her stomach. *Oops . . . now
what the hell has the kid done?* she wondered.

"I need him," she explained. "He is the only one who can
track point-to-point to intercept the raiders from Long Hyu."

The general slapped his chest.

"I be the best tracker in Wolfton Along the Hyu! I'sh'll
lead ye to yan spot!"

Jiana looked at him for a long moment.

"All right. I'll lead your army. You can put your trust in
me." She smiled innocently, like a newborn baby skeenik.
"And then, perhaps you'll grant me a minor boon." The
elder Middlin pagan grunted what might have been an
agreement. "Let's keep this simple, and not get lost in the
dark and mist. Just lead me up the Hyu, o valiant one."

The general of the Wolfton forces picked up his weapons and took a few practice swipes with his sword—apparently the only preparations he intended to take.

The raiders from Long Hyu were few in number, for
they intended to take the heathens by surprise. Jiana
made sure the Wolfton warriors outnumbered the Holy
Vehemence by two to one.

For half an hour they loped along the river, and at last
Jiana saw a spot that suited her.

"My lord—halt here, if it pleases you. Here you shall
await the infidels, and when they come along yonder trail,
we'll fall upon them like swarmflies upon the wheat!"

"And kill yan thieves and butchers where they stand!"

"Shoot 'em if they stand and cut 'em if they run! As for me, I must stay out of sight. *You* know what those butchers do to women. I'll hide up ahead and alert you when they come. Fare thee well, o my valiant officer!" Jiana bounded off into the swirling mist.

She jogged steadily along the river bank, gritting her teeth as her sides began to heave. It had been years since she had been in running shape. But resolve that had come with age drove her forward, compensating for ten years and more of comfort. It was not fear, or excitement, or the adventure of the hunt. She was a Hero. That was her job.

Several times, she caught her foot or her garments on a root or a branch, and was thrown sprawling onto the crispy ground. But each time she just stood up and ran on. Whenever her breath gave out, she slowed to a walk, still moving forward, until her heaving lungs had calmed enough for her to continue. Jiana could cover many miles that way, she knew. She had done it many times before.

Finally, after an undetermined but long time of dimmed consciousness, she crashed forward through some brush and was grabbed by a pair of burly yeomen farmers. For a time she just let them support her, as she gasped and panted. Then, she approached Goodman Rufes. She still breathed heavily, and tried to sound even more breathless.

"Sir—Captain—the infidels . . . Dida has been captured!"

"What happened to ye? How'd they spy your purpose? Where be they, in any wise?!" Rufes demanded. He sounded furious, and Jiana decided he had waited for her as long as his limited patience allowed, and then sent his raiders marching along the river. He had undoubtedly assumed that Jiana and Dida had skipped, leaving Toldo to his messy fate.

"Lost, somewhere in the woods—eluded them—sir. They've left their village utterly undefended. If we return quickly, we may yet save the day, alerted though they be!"

"But how did they signify your presence?"

"Sir, I know not. But it seemed . . . it seemed—" Jiana lowered her voice to a conspiratorial whisper, and looked back over her shoulder. "It seemed as if they *already knew* we were coming!"

"We have a spy!" shouted one of the men. There was a grumble of agreement.

Toldo crunched up. His hands were bound, but he looked no worse for it, otherwise.

"Oh, nonsense," he interjected. "There are plenty of other explanations."

"Like what?" demanded the man who had cried spy.

"Like, ah, like . . . well, perhaps the barbarians just plain out-thought us."

This was greeted by howls of derision.

"Well, heh, maybe the infidels received a divine revelation?"

This suggestion too was jeered down, and the raiders all began shouting at once about a spy.

"But I still do not ken how the wizards knew ye were there," said Rufes: like an interrupted grandfather, he returned endlessly to the same thought, unable to move beyond.

Jiana looked at him coldly.

"Well, however they knew, Good Rufes, God has illuminated our path: we must return to Wolfton Along the Hyu, and burn their village behind them! And we must free the valiant Dida, who festers in their unholy dungeon!" The men roared their approval, and Rufes, looking at the furies howling about him, was forced to agree.

"The river curves about in a great arc," Jiana said, "and the village is around the bend. Is there one among you who can navigate us straight through the woods in the night and mist, and intersect the waters again? We must make haste!" Two trappers stepped forward.

"Then onward!" she cried. "We'll fall upon them like swarmflies upon the wheat!"

"Aye. Shoot them if they stand and cut them if they run!" yelled Rufes. Like a stampede of cattle they smashed into the forest and bored straight ahead for Wolfton.

-3-

Goodman Rufes's trackers were good—as good as Dida. If Rufes had asked them, they could surely have led the raiders directly from Long Hyu to Wolfton. But Rufes had never thought to ask, and had ordered his troops to follow the circuitous river road instead. *Fortunately for me*, Jiana thought, *or I'd never have found him*.

Through the woods was about a third the distance, and this more than made up for having to pick their way through the tangled underbrush, especially as the band of twenty was small enough to follow the animal trails the huntsmen found. They reached Wolfton Along the Hyu while Fear was still a quarter of the sky above the horizon.

Rufes called his men into a huddle, and gave them their combat assignments:

"As I giveth the sign, we'sh'll all swarm down upon yan festival and butcher them!" He turned to Jiana. "You shall stay out of harm's way up here, Goody. Watch this tricksy, infidel priest."

She gazed earnestly into his eyes, batting her eyelashes. "I shall pray for you," she breathed huskily.

Rufes waved his arms about in a warlike gesture.

"ATTACK!" he bellowed. The men charged out of the treeline and fell upon the dancing and cavorting villagers.

For a time, Jiana watched. She saw the men beat women and youths, indiscriminate in their holy zest. The old men and children, and the few warriors left behind, fought a losing battle with the Vehemence, feebly resisting as the clerical soldiers smashed windows, overturned wagons and carts, tore open huts, and stole whatever objects of value they could find.

"I'll pray indeed," she said to herself, clenching her fists in fury at the pettiness of the raid. "I'll pray that I read you all well, you little men. Pray you bastards are just overgrown children playing at questing, pretending to be make-believe princes and fairy-tale heroes!"

It was smash and destroy. Some grabbed a torch, and a few huts were burned. There were beatings and lashings, and possibly an unpleasant rape scene somewhere out of sight of Jiana.

She wiped a tear of frustration from her eye. As punishment sorties went in this civilized land, only a day's journey from the Water Kingdom, Rufes's raid was extraordinarily mild.

"They got off light, Toldo." There was no answer, and she turned to find a face whitened by sickness, a mouth muted by horror.

"Toldo?" She drew her trophy knife and slit his bonds. His hands fell limply to his sides. He swallowed hard several times, then bit his knuckle, still ignoring her.

"What's your problem? You've seen fighting before—the battle of Bay Din!"

He shook his head.

"S-soldiers . . . soldiers!"

She turned back to the vision, smiling without humor.

"Welcome to reality. Your facade of worldliness has holes and cracks, it seems. Hard to believe you've never seen soldiers dust a town before."

"I've—I have been spared that privilege." Toldo's voice sounded weak and abrupt, as if he was holding his stomach down by main force.

"It's a lesson every warrior learns: sooner or later, warfare means assaulting unarmed civilians. It's—"

"Barbarism!"

"No, it's a job. Until you take the bloodshed to the streets, to the vassals and freemen and merchants and herders and councilors, it's just a bloody, awful game. It's nothing, because *we're* nothing, when you come down to it—soldiers, I mean. Who cares if a horse-archer in the Flower Empire or a master sergeant in the Water Kingdom gets spitted like a holiday boar? When the man behind the mercantile counter loses his arm or his head—then, it matters. Then begin the wails and the cries for peace. Only then will the people accept the costs of their security. They'll trade anything: gold, freedom, their daughters . . . just keep the arrows away from the innkeeper and the liveryman!"

"Your view of humanity is as foggy as this air, dark Jiana."

"I watch them through a red haze of blood, grey priest."

The raid suddenly turned ugly. A young man, little more than a child—about Dida's age, Jiana noted with a chill—ran out of a burning hut where he had hidden and clubbed one of Rufes's men from behind.

The man fell still, unconscious or dead. Rufes witnessed

the deed, and overran the boy, beating and kicking him. Soon he was joined by three more raiders, and before the eyes of the screaming women and the stunned children, who had danced and played with the boy during that day, the men stomped him to death.

The raid ended abruptly. Rufes stared down at the still, white form, and tried to master his emotions. The villages fell silent, and one by one, the raiders stopped and looked to their leader for a clue.

Jiana ordered, "Come, Toldo. Grit your teeth and follow." Then she strode purposefully toward the knot of people.

Rufes was unconsciously wiping the back of his pantaloons, as if embarrassed.

"Captain," Jiana began tentatively. "Perhaps they've had enough? I think they've seen truth tonight. Your charge is successfully completed." Rufes nodded, uncomprehendingly; he still stared at the corpse of the boy.

"I—have a son . . ." He looked at her as if seeking some sort of approbation or absolution. Then he shook his head and coughed, and turned away.

"Yes, the lesson be learned. No more shall they sin against the Church, upon the pact of the Holy Vehemence."

"Sir, earlier they captured my friend Dida. I must rescue him."

"What? Aye. Aye. We leave now."

"Sir?"

"What?"

"I must rescue Dida."

"Aye, of course. We shall leave upon yan moment. Fetch the boy; you have done your share."

She smiled. To Jiana's own ears, her voice was colored with mockery and hazed with a shimmer of hysteria, but no one else seemed to notice.

"Yes, I've done my share. Some of us found our calling early in life. Sir." She grabbed Toldo and spun him about, before Rufes could see her expression.

"Goody Jiana—you'll be coming back to yan council of the Vehemence, for by their own words they have yet business to transact with you."

"Yes, sir."

She scanned the frightened villagers until she found the familiar, hairy face.

"Where is Dida?" she demanded of the chief.

His eyes widened.

"*You!*" He said nothing further, eyeing the burly yeomen and their spears, but his face spoke *betrayer!*

"Where is Dida held?" she repeated.

His hands shaking with barely suppressed rage, he pointed at a hut that stood at waist level. It was all that had saved it, for the huts on either side had been fired.

Jiana wrapped her arms about her sides, and trod across the broken shards of pottery and shattered glass to the "dungeon." She noticed one of the huntsmen and another man sauntered along behind her, nonchalantly.

The door was tied intricately, but the leather thong yielded immediately to her knife. Dida was indeed inside, and at first he looked terribly disappointed.

"Oh, my love . . . they got you, too?" Then his eyes lowered, smoldering again. "I'm sorry, I forgot. You're not my love."

"Come, Dida. Let's get the hell out of here." At first he looked confused. Then the situation penetrated, and he crept gingerly out of the hutch. He said nothing else to her.

They returned to Rufes, and with a wave and no parting words he sent the army back along the way to Long Hyu. As Jiana had expected, they traveled the riverside road.

She watched carefully the terrain, and worked at her final plan. None of the three were under such scrutiny as they had been before the raid, and she could whisper freely to Toldo and Dida. In fact, quiet talk and silence seemed to dominate the entire company. One by one, the men all edged close and looked at their compatriot's body, then sidled away and returned to their musings.

"There will shortly be a battle," Jiana told her friends.

"Again?" demanded Toldo Mondo.

"When you hear the first sounds of fighting, both of you fade into the woods to the east, away from the Hyu. Listen for the wolf."

"But my dear—! The woods, at night . . . in the fog? How shall we find each other?"

"Listen for the wolf. And stay with Dida. If we separate, we journey east to the Caela Road. Dida? Did you hear?"

"Aye. East." It was the most she had gotten out of him since Wolfton. She jogged up to Rufes.

"Sir, I think there's something up ahead. Allow me to check it out before you continue."

"Aye, Goodwife. We shall pause to rest, but remain upon guard."

The company halted, and Jiana trotted on ahead.

She had remembered well. The warriors of Wolfton were still waiting, not far ahead. She burst in upon their ranks unseen until the last moment, and feigned a heavy breath and white fear.

"O, terror! O, catastrophe!"

"What?! What?!" howled the general.

"O, woe! We have been outmaneuvered!"

"What d'ye mean? Hast the devils sneaked aboot us?"

"Worse! They have bypassed this force and ravaged the town!"

His eyes widened in shock.

"Mean ye—"

"Aye . . . Wolfton Along the Hyu is utterly destroyed! Not a father, mother, or babe is left unslain!"

With a great cry of despair, the warriors of Wolfton arose and began to rush into the trees, back toward Wolfton by the shortest route.

"Brothers, brothers!" Jiana called. "I have escaped the wrath of the invaders, and I learned that even now *they march back to Long Hyu along this very road!*"

The men froze in their spots, and slowly turned to look at her, then at the general, who shook as with the chills.

"Back. Back abune the road, for yan way we'll meet and do 'em muckle harm!" Without another word spoken, they poured back onto the river road like waters overflowing the bank, and ran like the furies downstream. Jiana waited a moment to ensure they were truly committed; then she ran after them, at a more practical pace.

She slowed when she heard the screams of the wounded and the clash of metal on wooden clubs. She left the road, and cut southeast. As soon as she was far enough away from the sounds of souls being released to wander, she slowed to a walk and began howling like a wolf. It was a favorite call among the armed men of every army she had graced by her presence.

On the fifth howl, she was answered, and with a bit of casting about fell in with Dida and Toldo again.

"But," objected Toldo, "the Holy Vehemence—"

"—will think we died in the fight," the warrior answered. "I hope. East, Dida," she ordered. He led them through the woods, and they did not stop until they had reached the great Caela Road, leaving justice to work itself out along the river Hyu.

-4-

The days crept painfully past the sleepstepping trio on padded mouse feet. The sun rose, obscured by a frothing ceiling, and set the clouds churning like overboiling curds. Milky liquid fell occasionally; it was not rain, but something other and alien. It unsettled Jiana's stomach.

Whatever tracks had speckled the Caela Road had been washed away in the rains, but toward dusk of the first day of travel, in a natural shelter of overhanging Weeping Trees, Jiana found the same splay-foot horse track she had noted when Alanai left Bay Bay City. Dida declared it no older than a day.

She hungered to pull once again within sight of the prince.

"The farther ahead he slips," she confided to Toldo— Dida sulked still from the scene in the woods—"the further he falls back in my own life."

"It has been a long time since you have seen him. No mystery."

"But he's become such an elusive goal. Illusive, perhaps. Was he ever really there?"

"Are you in training for a career as a philosopher?"

"God-Snakes, no! But what I can't touch I can't believe. I'm a warrior. Even my philosophies are forged metal: look out for your buddies; if it lives, it can die; run from defeat but never from fear."

"And where in this sharp-edged philosophy is there

such a latitude for fretting, and analyzing, and debating life with yourself?"

Jiana leaped to her feet and stalked to the edge of the circle of firelight, staring out into the perpetual mist.

Is it that clear to all about me? You bitch, Jianabel— what have you done to unstick my soul?

"Don't run from me, Jiana," the little girl answered. "I won't hurt you. I only want to unlock you."

She stared silently at the world curtain for a moment.

"A strange thing to say," Toldo commented.

"What?"

"Unlock us from what?"

She felt an icy blade slide up from her mind to pierce her heart.

"Did I—speak aloud?" *No*, her own voice answered her. *It was another one. It was one you murdered, in the year that Dida was born—in the year the Jiana-now was born, as well. Are you so certain you have more years than he does?*

"One you murdered . . ." *Except, the dead do not always lie comfortably planted . . .*

No.

"No. I did not speak aloud. It was in your mind, Toldo." Jiana buried the incident in the back of her stomach, and hurried back to the fireside to continue her conversation, on a level too abstract to risk calling fourth a small, brown-haired girl who lurked beneath the damp and rotting ground beneath them—a girl whose teeth had all been painstakingly filed to a point; whose father had sacrificed so *much* to let her continue her studies . . .

Below their feet, the frothing clouds reflected in the pools of oily liquid that seeped up from the matted Caela floor.

Jiana shivered on the second day. "Someone speaks of me," she said. "Perhaps someone inhuman? A friend of Toq's?" Toldo opened his mouth to say he did not believe in signs, that it was only the chilled air, but he sat down again without speaking.

"What did Lyonalai say? That the Tarn is creeping north into the the Center of the World? Maybe also south into

Tool and west into Noon. What lies to the east of the Tarn?"

"The sun," Dida answered. The other two turned back toward him. It was the first he had spoken since the night of the raid.

He looked back at them.

"The sun lives behind the sands of the Tarn. That's why the desert is so hot and dry."

"Then I fear the sands have indeed blown east, and great dunes have piled over the sun and put her out. We've not seen her since we left your father's gathering."

"Warm front," Toldo muttered, insistently.

By midafternoon, the great Caela Road had narrowed to a deer path, and then disappeared entirely. The woods, however, grew to form a natural road that wound in every direction. Without conscious awareness of why they had done so, Jiana and her friends realized they had been walking for what seemed like a moon, with no clue as to where they were.

As the sky began to dim with the setting sun, even Dida admitted he was utterly lost. Nor could they backtrack, for whenever Jiana turned around, the party seemed to be at the edge of a clearing, with a solid line of trees behind them.

"Well, I think we should stop and sleep," Jiana said. "Morning might bring a fresh perspective." Since neither of the others had a better suggestion, they unrolled their mats and blankets and huddled together for warmth, of several kinds.

The third day dawned little brighter than the lightning-lighted night before. The road was the same, and there was nowhere else to go but the way of the trees.

Dida was the first to notice the insects had vanished, and the birds grown silent. Jiana began to parcel out smaller lots of the Holy Vehemence's food. Even so, there was only a day's worth left.

As their feet carried them farther, and farther behind the prince's mounted expedition, Jiana began to notice a putrefying odor that stirred terrifying memories within her. It grew more and more intense, until it nearly choked her with every breath.

But neither Dida nor Toldo could detect it at all. For a time she said nothing, afraid it was only her own conscience and the thick coating of crimes she had committed in her life. But at last she confessed to Dida and Toldo—more out of cowardice, she thought, than any chance they could help. She feared to carry the secret alone any longer.

Neither the priest nor the boy had any explanations.

"It must not be on this sphere, kid," she decided.

"Is it magick?" Dida's eyes grew wide at the thought.

"Call it whatever," she snapped. "This isn't like what a blasted too-wise would scry! I have no bubbling potions or noxious salves—I'm *actually* living in a different world from either of you two; or rather, with one foot in each. I *know* I have only to set my soul up just ever so slightly on its toes to look over the walls between the worlds, and see things that would drive me mad . . . things that might see me."

"This talent you seem to believe you possess—mightn't it be worth the risk to try it? I . . . well, I must admit it has been useful before. My dear, it we do not do something, we're going to die right here!"

Dida was looking at the sky.

"There's something terrible happening to us. Jiana, love—you've got to help!"

"You don't understand!" She ground the heels of her palms against her closed eyes, feeling cold spikes of fear thrusting up inside her. "I'm a bit player in a miracle show . . . the beings these on spheres are to me as I am to a bloodworm."

"You're a hero," Dida stated, simply. "It's just the same odds you always face."

"You *don't* understand. There is a part of me . . . that I think may be as strong as any of them. But once loosed—and in the battle, that could be my last resort—I don't think she would bury easily again in my stomach. I fear dissolution. I'm terrified I might become—"

Dida put his hand gently on her arm, urging her to continue by his touch.

"What I was. Who I was."

"I'll protect you," he whispered. Jiana chuckled. "No," he insisted. "Our love will hold your true self together!"

"That's exactly why I fear! If it was true I loved you, I'd risk it—I would call Jianabel forth in an instant! But I'm *not* sure of my feelings, and I'm afraid." She turned her back on her friends, and stared again into the dripping forest. "I've decided. This evening I'm going to do it. I'll force my mind upward and discover—whatever there is. I hope."

She sat down a distance from Dida and Toldo Mondo, and began to feel about for the energy in the air and under the earth, to store it up within her. She began to set her mind in order.

The sky darkened with a sigh of terrible pain, and Dida shivered suddenly as if a personal wind had knifed up inside his cloak. The chubby ex-priest rubbed his bristly chin vigorously, maintaining an air of normality at all costs. Taking a deep breath, Jiana pushed delicately upwards . . .

—Amapada of the Heaviness; Sleeping Tifniz; Alanamar; The Sands of the Tarn . . .

Jiana stood on the wet stones of Above, and the call rolled through her and about her. This time she remembered—she remembered the words of Toq of the Sun. She knew what they all sought.

Baak the Worldbreaker; Diasonous of Yellow Poison Waters; Paal; Tephas Longfinger; Tooqa, the Nameless Serpentine . . .

"No! Do not profane the true name with this gaudy company!"

"Oh, Jiana. Why, they're all the same next to me, silly!"

"Jianabel."

"Jianabel of Everysphere."

"Arrogance!"

"Don't you remember? *You* know who I am! And who you were."

"You'll be punished. You're an evil hallucination. You're nothing more than a disease of my own mind."

Jiana heard mocking laughter in her mind. The force of it pressed against her internal organs excruciatingly.

"What do you find so funny, you horrible little girl?" she managed to gasp.

"A disease of my mind! That's just what *I've* always said about the whole world!"

At first they seemed like only a few black rocks rising from the sea. But then, as she walked closer on her bridge of clouds, Jiana saw that they had been artfully erected—and she screamed . . .

Tagat. Tass and Tasstan. Toq, He That Predates All.

"Stuff it," Jiana snarled.

The corpulent mass on the massive couch slowly blinked fishbelly-white eyelids and yawned.

"Hardly . . . hardly an intelligent decision, thing," said Sleeping Tifniz. "The Order demands your service."

"Stuff it. I've had enough of clubs and societies and secret brotherhoods and orders and fraternities! Just leave me alone!"

"Ah, but you see, we . . ." The god's mouth stretched impossibly wide, and it shifted about on the divan, which creaked ominously. "We cannot 'leave you alone' under the present circumstances, as alone you would have no chance against the Fateful Prince."

"Alanai?"

"May he be cursed with insomnia. He wants a certain toy—little enough that he . . . that he would know what to do with it! And the . . . havoc he would cause . . ." This time when Sleeping Tifniz yawned, Jiana found her own mouth gaping along with its. "The havoc he would cause makes it impossible to . . . allow this acquisition. Thus, *you* shall be our . . . our agent in this affair."

"Bullshit."

Its toadlike eyes narrowed, and Jiana felt a sudden weariness dragging her down like heavy cement.

"Watch what you say, thing. You're nothing compared to me, and my . . . ahhhhhh . . . the brotherhood to which I belong."

From a huddled position on the floor, Jiana panted out her words, defiant but outwardly respectful.

"And who—who are these—brothers of yours, Lord?"

Sleeping Tifniz smiled, and its eyes slowly closed. For several minutes it slept thus, while Jiana labored with every breath. At last, after what seemed a timeless eternity, it awoke again and continued as if there had been no interruption.

"We are . . . simply the Order. Each is a being of power. Each . . . each is lord over a dominion of the thousand spheres. Between us, we rule over all that is, and all that was, and . . . and over all that will be." Sleeping Tifniz yawned again, and the great weight of weariness fell away from Jiana. She could stand again.

"Thank you, Sire. But, do you not know I am already recruited by the Order? I was approached by one called Toq, who was before all."

A long, slow silence dripped across the rushes covering the floor of Sleeping Tifniz's bedchamber. At first, Jiana thought the god had fallen asleep again. But it finally spoke.

"Well, there's a problem, thing. Toq's friends and the rest of us do not quite see . . . on a level about the World's Dream. I would prefer your loyalty was to . . . to the Order as a whole, rather . . . rather . . . rather than to any one member, such as Toq."

"So I should report directly to you, instead of directly to Toq?"

"Exactly! I'm glad you're able to understand, thing. It saves so much . . ." This time Sleeping Tifniz yawned for so long, Jiana thought it had fallen asleep with its mouth open. She had time for four yawns of her own before it finished. "So much persuasion."

Jiana bowed.

"I shall do right by the Order," the warrior said, "upon my word of honor."

For a moment, it looked sidelong at her. Then, evidently deciding she meant nothing deeper by the words, Sleeping Tifniz rolled over to expose to her its ponderous backside. Soon, loud snores shouted her dismissal from the presence.

Sinking back into the mundane sphere was the equivalent of letting out a great breath of spirit air. She fell back down to her knees with a thud.

"Jiana?" Toldo leaned forward, looking for sentience in her eyes. "Dida, wake up, boy! She's back."

"Wonderful," Dida said sullenly. He avoided her eyes.

"We are now under contract," she stated, "to the Order."

"The Order?"

"It's the Holy Vehemence, but with gods and demons as members. I believe this path is their doing, for they want to be sure Alanai does not pull too far ahead of us."

"They like us?"

"They fear Alanai. And another thing. They, too, are split into factions. Toq is the head of the others. Toldo, Dida . . . we'll continue tonight. I'm anxious to lay eyes again on our quarry."

"A shame this Order did not think to provide us with a few horses, instead of a road."

Through the frigid night they walked, Jiana and Toldo and sullen Dida. The warrior tried not to think of the persistent smell, and refused to focus on the distant sounds from the trees—sounds from no source on the lower sphere. Between midnight and daybreak, the road began to climb up a long hill. At last, they reached the crest, and Jiana called a halt. The weary party sat down to doze until dawn.

The sun rose. There were no clouds, nor any sign of a forest. Behind them, for as far as Jiana could see, there were only mountains and ravines—at least two weeks' worth of them, according to the map. The Order had indeed supplied a shortcut.

Ahead of them, the sun reflected white and blinding off the sand and salt. Yawning, she rose, and led the trio down into the desolate, baking Tarn.

Chapter 7

Sing a song of wishing, the trapping of the mouse

-1-

"No," mumbled Jiana. She bent again over Atmag's map, redrawing the lines, allowing for errors in the geographical features.

"NO!" Angrily, she threw the map down onto the sand and stomped on it with her boot.

"Ah—is something the matter?"

"The world! Look." She picked up the map again, and shook the Tarn off it. "Two days ago, at the mouth of the desert, we were here."

"How do you know?" Toldo scratched his thickening beard, and rubbed his belly. She wondered if he felt as hungry as she did, or if his girth gave him a margin of comfort.

"Here's Mount Aka Natu—here, where these concentric circles are drawn. Now look at the horizon." She pointed. In the distance, the great peak could be seen as a tiny nipple. "Two days ago it was south-southeast of us, and the oasis of the Waters of Dreaming Bay were west-southwest. I drew lines backwards from these two points

216

on the map, and they intersected here. Yesterday at noon, I did the same—and they gave me our position as two days' hard march from the first spot."

"So? We're making splendid time."

"Snakedroppings! I know fast marching, and we're not even going a third that speed through this damn sand. And look! Today, just now, I mark us *here*, a four-day march at right angles to our previous course, though I've steered us by the sun in the same direction since we first set boots in this bloody desert!" She let the map fall to the white, alkali sand and sat down, pulling up her knees to think.

"Well . . . maybe the map is wrong."

Jiana spat.

"Wouldn't matter. I *saw* that damn mountain, and the lake—and I can still see them now! Even if they weren't on the map, their relative positions and how they change would tell us how we've moved . . . and they tell us we've traveled hither and yonder—a week's worth of marching, in two days!"

"Maybe the sun's wrong." It was Dida. Lately, he had hardly spoken. *It's not just what's happened between us,* Jiana had been thinking. *It's being away from home, having the world turned inside about the outside, and seeing its guts for the first time.*

Dida's question had touched something lurking beneath the skin of Jiana's mind.

"The sun?"

"Maybe the mountain and the lake are moving. Don't you remember what that prince said, Jiana?"

"Alanai?"

"Lyon-whatever. He said the Tarn—the Tarn is the intra . . ." He gestured in annoyance, unable to recall the word.

"The Tarn is where all of the world-spheres intersect," Jiana said. "You can fade from one to the other here. Is that what you mean, kid?" Dida nodded.

"Well, now that you two mention it, I have been wondering about that myself," Toldo added. "It does sound rather queer, does it not? But Lyonalai seemed so *certain* . . ."

Jiana stood abruptly.

"We have some water. We can get by without food for a while. And, we have a mission to complete—a quest. Priest, would Alanai have crossed the desert?"

Toldo shook his head.

"Goodman Rufes said two armies were marching south to intercept Alanai, allies of the Toradoras of—who used to be of Bay Din. They know the prince headed for Door, since they know why he attacked Am-Amorai. Apparently, the prince of Bay Din made no secret of having found some great treasure, and of preparing to invade south to complete it."

"How did Rufes know all that?"

"He was present at a council of the Holy Vehemence when they discussed the news, and later when this Traga fellow persuaded the council to arrest you, and me and Dida. Rufes said Alanai was aware of the pursuit, and had already fought two great battles against wildly superior odds, winning each time and picking up many followers."

"How many?" She felt an uneasiness settle about her.

"Apparently, if this Hraga speaks the truth and if Rufes remembers correctly, Prince Alanai now boasts an army of two thousand men."

Jiana gasped, and stood up.

"Well," she mused, "it's not as if it's out of character for him. Did you ever hear the one about the prince and the grybbyn's daughter?"

"Hmp. I heard the tale about Alanai and the grybbyn, if that's what you reference. Many times, clothed in many different coats of detail."

"But the barracks-room rumors I heard suggested it was not quite the honorable, chivalrous, one-to-one battle that most of the tales claim. Then, as now, he gathered an enormous army about him to do the dirty work."

"He does seem to have a remarkable talent for attracting popular support. I suppose that does not make your plan any easier."

"I know." She sat down again, and picked up a handful of sand. "Surrounded by the two thousand, what hope is there he'll need rescuing, or that I could even affect a battle so large?" She let the salty dust trickle through her fingers, thinking of the sands of time running out for her own future.

"In fact," she added in a quiet voice, "I've begun to wonder whether I should join him or stop him."

"What?" cried Dida, leaping to his feet suddenly. Jiana and Toldo turned, startled. She had had no idea Dida had even been listening.

"What what?"

"Am I traveling a pair of cowards with?"

She eyed him frostily.

"Watch your tongue, boy."

"You're a hero! A hero must quest, or you're nothing but a fat bear with a sword! Are you running away from the quest, now?"

"No! I'm torn as to whether the world even needs any more heroes!"

"Well, I think . . ." Dida's face turned ugly, and his voice mean, "you're afraid! You're afraid because you can't compete with a great prince like Alanai!"

"I don't want to compete with him."

"He's the hero, not you! You're nothing—you're nothing but a lonely old woman who needs to think you're somebody, but you're not, and you can't even love anyone anymore!" Dida collapsed onto the sands, deflated like a ruptured waterbag. He did not weep or cry; he only sat and stared away from Jiana.

Strangely, his outburst hurt her very little. The pain was constant already, and the few more coals he had added did little to stoke her ache. Besides, the words burned too strongly with the truth to hurt like a cruelty would have. Toldo waited a few moments to see if she would respond. When it became obvious she was ignoring Dida, the priest continued, sounding somewhat abashed.

"Ah, hem. As I started to say, the two armies that pursue Prince Alanai will surely cut across to the coast, for they have much support from the mountain kingdoms in the West. Alanai will probably hug the east face of the mountains and cut around the Tarn, to border Noon, which is neutral and will shield him from the Toradora allies. But no one will enter this baking hell. Only a fool—" He stopped abruptly.

"Detouring along the mountains and through northern Noon will cost Alanai three days west, and six or seven days south. He might even sail to the Oort Isles, for a blessing by the Sisters of the Sacred Eagle . . . another three or four, depending on the winds. As for ourselves, if our luck is good, we can cut through the Tarn to South Noon in nine."

Toldo bit his lip, considering what she said, adding days on his knuckles.

"I am sorry, o cunning one. It seems a reasonable gamble, when you explain it."

"Sometimes it's a thin line between cunning and folly. Come on, let's get the hell out of this Hell."

"But which way?"

Jiana shrugged.

"You seem to know more about the situation here than I do. Which way?"

"Well . . ." Toldo looked first south, then shook his head and turned to the west—or what the sun said was west. Again he shook his head. Within moments, east and north had also been considered and discarded. He looked back to Jiana helplessly and turned up his palms.

"Ah, it seems there are good arguments for and against, whichever way I look."

"Well, having ruled out intelligence and wisdom, I say we try innocence."

The priest's eyes narrowed for a moment, then he and Jiana turned to look at Dida.

"Which way?" they both asked simultaneously.

Dida looked back at them, confused and frightened.

"But—I don't know which way to go!"

"Quick, Dida," Jiana urged. "Point us a direction!"

"I—"

"Move!!"

His arm snapped up, and he pointed far to the side of Aka Natu, in a direction nearly opposite to where Jiana would have chosen.

What the hell, she thought. *With all these gods and demons yanking our strings, we'll probably get somewhere, whichever way we go.* She waited for a moment, but

Jianabel remained silent. Like Dida, she seemed to have nothing to say for the time being.

"Dida's direction, march," the warrior ordered. Taking a last swig of water to hold her, she set out across the whiteness.

Heat shimmies danced on the waters of sand, and the sky swirled about their heads as they walked, as if they were flies clinging to a spinning ivory plate. The white dust rose and fell behind and around, rubbing raw every crack and joint it could find with its alkali fingers.

Jiana heard phantom trumpets in the distance. *A thousand bone soldiers battling for the same plot of emptiness*, she imagined. *A drowning pool of liquid rocks. Their own essence crumbled and decayed, and now became ghosts guarding nothingness.*

"I can see spheres and spheres," she remarked.

"It is not only your mystic eyes, o brooder. Even I see fading worlds and blurry cracks, where there should be nought but sand. I am humbled."

She looked to Dida, and he nodded, somehow aware that she had glanced at him, though he did not look once at her. He continued plodding relentlessly onward. Jiana could not say in what direction, for he seemed to turn and let his feet fall at random. There was no mark by which she could follow their track. Whenever she looked for the mountain, it had moved in a curious way, until at last, near sunset, it disappeared entirely. Dida seemed unaware and uncaring of their path.

Far ahead she heard the challenge of a battle horn—or almost heard, for it could have been nothing but her own heat-fever ringing in her ears. And was that an answering call, from behind?

"If all spheres intersect in this place," Toldo asked, "then can we truly be said to be in any particular one?"

"I guess not. Maybe we're nowhere at all."

"A disturbing thought. I think I would rather be in your serpent hell than in this—limbo."

"Priest, what is it that we fear so about nothingness and dissolution? I find I can contemplate a world in which my God is false, and another is true. Yet your world, with no God at all, profoundly disturbs me."

Toldo sighed, and Jiana realized she had struck close to the heart.

"If we are all there is to the world, and when we die there is no more, then what is the use of life at all? At least, that is the argument that I have heard, o fretful one."

"Some would say life was its own reason. But that's just semantics, and your point is taken."

"If it were possible for such a despair to overtake a man, a smart man, then he would see immediately that saying 'life is its own reason' does not answer the primal question: why not just end life, and embrace nothingness?"

"Such a despair is possible," Jiana offered. "I know for a fact."

"As do I. Have you ever considered dropping this quest now, and lying down in the sand for a million years?"

"We wouldn't lack for company" she said, kicking a rooster tail of sand into the air. "Legend says every grain in the sands of the Tarn is a soul that died unloving."

"What! There haven't been so many souls since the world was made!"

"Can I continue with my previous thoughts?"

"I've no strength to stop you."

"Every belief we claim," she explained, "every emotion, every institution, every work of art, is in some way just a denial of your root thesis, that beyond ourselves lies only nothingness."

"Do you say that despair has been the source of all that we call great in our race?"

"Not despair, which is a potent narcoleptic, but instead, the fear of and the flight from despair. Without the despair of aloneness and a hopeless end to life, there would be no life, and the nothingness would win. The existence of this fear of the void staves off the void."

"And thus fear, not love, is the noblest emotion?"

"Well—that's where my thoughts have led me."

Jiana laughed, pleased for the first time since the sunny afternoon in Dida's father's hayloft.

"And here I was, afraid my profession was a black one! Now I find out I should be a prince!"

Toldo nodded. "When you make war, you give your

enemies a reason to live—to fight against *you*. Alanai's problem now becomes obvious."

"Well, perhaps you should explain it to me. I may be the progenitor of the human race, but I still cannot follow the tangles of your argument, o weaver of thoughts."

"He has allowed this despair to overtake him, even as I have, and as you fear to do. He needs ever greater challenges and more terrible dangers to give him the will to live. He is weary with the world."

Jiana was silent for many, many steps. She tried to imagine the despair that might grow from the disillusionment of such a pure idealist as Alanai.

"Then," she asked, "is this entire quest nothing but an elaborate suicide attempt by the prince?"

"No, no. Compare it rather to a deep, deep trance under the influence of certain mushrooms or fungi—a visionquest. He's desperately seeking his lost innocence."

"Yes, I have some experience with such trances." She shuddered, and her stomach twisted again. For a moment, she could see a frightening image of—of some poor man, eyes vacant, approaching her, dragging his—dragging something from where his arms should have been . . . but then it was gone, like tears on the ocean.

"He is trying to find his soul. He looks everywhere for it, from high above the world with the eyes of an eagle. That's what his 'world's dream' really is, Jiana."

"And whole nations suffer and die, as he shovels among the flower beds for his own particular roots. And of course, he'll never find it, for he can't look inside himself, where his spirit really lives."

"More mysticism?"

"Not at all, Toldo Mondo. The reasons for your own life *must* be found within yourself. If you try to take mine, they'll only tell you why *I* must live."

Jiana halted abruptly and held out her hand.

"Wait . . ." Dida marched on for a few steps, then paused and looked back toward her. He seemed to wake up from a walking dream then, and looked about him, blinking and confused.

He looked frightened, and he scuffed quickly back to stand with Jiana and the priest. She could not fail to notice how uncertainly he ran across the sand now, compared with the mindless surety he had displayed since he had begun to lead them.

"Jiana—my love—what am I doing? How can I lead us? I know nothing about this place!"

"For a time," she said, "you were its master. But something lies in wait up ahead."

Toldo leaned close to speak in her ear. The rumble of his voice sounded like thunder tied tight.

"I can see nothing ahead. Is it an enemy or an ally?"

"In the Tarn? What do you think?"

"What—what do you see, love?"

"I only feel it. I've freed more souls from their bodies than I can remember. I know what one feels like when it brushes near!"

Jiana gripped an arm each of Toldo and Dida, and held them behind her as she stepped forward. She did not touch Wave. *Time aplenty if it's such a foe,* she thought.

The sun had sunk low in the sky, and the desert glowed red like drifting mounds of brimstone and blowing sparks of fire. Her eyes ached from the dryness of the salt sea beneath her, but she stared ahead, unblinking.

At last, in the blood of the sun, she saw a form in silhouette. It dragged closer and closer on legs that did not seem to take kindly to walking. Then, it came close enough to block the sun, and she could see its face.

It was a walking corpse.

Jiana gasped and retreated a step, then recovered.

"Stand!" she ordered. "I'll not shrink from a moldering body with the wanderlust!" There was no reaction.

"I don't fear you!" she cried, retreating watchfully. "I've fought pale, empty vampires in the snows of Tyu-o Tokai, and slain demon-goats in this very desert."

It seemed not to hear, but shambled toward her nonetheless.

"Stop! Halt!" She drew her blade, whirling it over her head and cracking it like a whip. Death approached undismayed.

With a battle yell to wake the dead, Jiana charged forward and whipped Wave in an arc that carried the rippling steel through the midsection of the zombie. The blade passed right through, and for a moment Jiana thought she had missed cleanly. Then she looked more closely, and saw thin, smoky wisps of ectoplasm stretching from Wave to the ghost. The streams slowly swirled about and drifted back toward their host, like drops of black ink in a glass of water.

It staggered toward her, and she stubbornly stood her ground, even when its form passed right through her own body. For a moment, as they occupied the same apparent space, she felt a hot flash. It was like standing too suddenly after sleeping all night and half the day, and she maintained her posture only by conscious control, for her sense of balance fled during that moment. Then the feeling was gone; the ghost had passed through her. Dida and Toldo stepped out of its way, but as it passed them, it turned to look at the boy, and stretched out its hand. It brushed him, ever so lightly on the forehead, then passed on, and vanished into the bright dusk.

Dida uttered a cry of despair, and sank to his knees in the sand.

"I've seen my own death," he whispered.

Toldo put his hand on the boy's shoulder, but he did not seem to feel it.

"I'm going to die before this quest ends."

She looked at him for a long time.

"Bullshit," she said. "No one knows when they'll die. Get up off your knees and lead us again." She added, when he had arisen, "I'll protect you, kid." But she knew he had spoken the truth, for she had felt it as well. She knew it as fully as she knew she was Jiana.

After a time, Dida began to look sheepish, sitting in the sand with Jiana and Toldo looking at him. He rose to his feet, still sniffing, and she saw his cheeks were wet. Without wiping them, he set off again through the sand.

As the sky grew black, and the sand grew sullen and brittle, they began to hear more cries, from the limbo over the horizon. Then the clash of a battle, the wailing of the women, the pounding of a thousand, thousand hooves echoed in the dust of the Tarn. Jiana could even feel the heat of flames, and once she tasted charred flesh on the wind. She remembered the smell from Bay Din.

Sometimes, as they walked through the hellish Tarn, she could even see the wars raging about them, far in the distance and indistinct against the starless sky.

"If this is truly an intersection of the worldspheres," she muttered, "then they must all be joined at the battlefields, like rivers joining at a lake."

"Perhaps such a mass sacrifice of lives is what brings about such an intersection. Maybe that's the true purpose of more than one petty war."

"Aren't priests supposed to comfort the spirit? Sometimes you make me loathe my brothers and sisters so, I would wish them away if I could!"

Toldo shrugged.

"It's one of many reasons why I am a priest no longer."

Now, every direction about them roared with the screams of the slain, and was fouled with the stench of fear and death. Yet somehow, Dida's instinctive path of innocence leapt from stone to stone of calm, without letting the tide of blood wash over them.

All through the night they walked. At times, the ambulating dead were so thick about them that Jiana imagined herself traversing a mad bazaar of the damned in Hell. They all trod stolidly past the party without a glance or a touch—except for the first one, for Dida. At times Jiana or one of the others could not step out of the way quickly enough, and had the unpleasant experience of being *passed*. But then the ghosts would continue about their violent business, and the party—save for the doomed Dida— continued unmolested.

At last, Jiana began to see a faint glow on the horizon.

Most likely another phantom fire, she thought, for she could have sworn that it was due north. But she kept hope nevertheless, and the glow grew brighter.

After a time a faint flash of green touched her, and then the brilliant edge of the sun showed above the horizon line.

Something loomed ahead of them. Dida stopped, and Jiana knew he would lead them no farther. Wherever they had arrived, it was their destination.

The three stood, staring at the mounds and humps. The sun inched its way up into the sky, and slowly the sands were illuminated. As the light spread, the ghosts of the past *or future?* retreated, though the Tarn still seemed an alien place.

Finally, the day grew bright enough for Jiana to see what lay ahead of them, where they had come—or what had brought them.

They stared across the seas of sand at an alabaster city, with a great, white tower the color of bleached bone rising up out of the Tarn like a skeletal finger pointing at the sun.

"I believe we are expected," Jiana said. She led them to the gates.

-2-

The bone and alabaster was *so* pretty and shining—it reminded Jianabel of the teeth pulled from a freshly killed sacrifice. She led her two new friends among the albino buildings and marble streets with a sure, lighthearted step.

To be sure, her friends were not exactly *bursting* with pleasure to see her. For some reason, they kept staring at her most annoyingly, as if she were a demon or a blackskin!

I must remember to teach them some manners, she noted to herself.

One of her friends was rather cute, in a primitive sort of way. He was young and strong, unlike the fat, old, bristly one. His spirit was meager—but then, he was only a man.

Why, I should be very surprised indeed if such a creature did not seem mean and pitiful to me.

All of the mortals are beneath you, whispered her spirit guide, Sibilant, *for you are above them.*

"Oh, Krakshi . . . that doesn't even *say* anything! If they're beneath me, of course I'm above them! But then, I'm also above so many, many others! Why, the absolute *nerve* of that silly, Sleeping Tifniz . . . he must not know who I am, or who that sissy Jiana really is." Sibilant slunk into the bottom of Jianabel's stomach, where he dwelt when she did not have her doll Krakshi along. He was cowed by his mistress; he feared her tantrums. "I wonder," she mused to him. "Does she even know, herself, what she is?"

"Jiana," bleated a strange voice. It was the young new friend. "You're scaring me. I don't like you like this!"

Jianabel looked him up and down and right and left. He was taller than she, and stronger, but it was merely the strength of an animal. He had none of the *real* strength, no more than a frightened mouse!

"Why don't we play the games I like," she suggested, reaching out and squeezing him just a *little* . . .

"NO!" Jiana dropped to her knees beside Dida, who still whimpered and held his head. She wiped away the liquid that oozed in tiny drops from his eyes and his ears, and held him against her breasts as she gently rocked him back and forth.

"Jiana—" began Toldo. "Is't . . . are you back again?"

"I am Jiana," she answered. "Jiana of Bay Bay. She took me over for a minute."

"Who? What has been happening?" Toldo worked his way down to his knees, and put an arm on her shoulder. Dida had grown quiet, and he seemed to pull away from her a little, so she let him go.

"I think the time has come for me to level with both of you. It's finally sunk into my stomach that your lives are endangered by her."

"By whom?"

"By Jianabel. By who I once was—by my mother."

"Your . . . mother?"

"In a metaphoric sense. She—thinks I don't know this. But I've only been hiding the fact from myself. It's never been wholly gone. Jiana does not exist."

For several moments of silence, Toldo Mondo and Dida stared, waiting. Finally, when she realized they were not going to ask the obvious, she continued.

"The person 'Jiana' was created by a little girl. Her name was Jianabel. It was after the Most Terrible Thing happened that some part of her—some tiny part that was still human enough to rebel against what the rest of her had become—killed her. Some part of her spirit killed itself, by burying Jianabel behind a mask . . . me."

Still, neither of her friends would speak. She took a deep breath and looked about at the whiteness of the city. It was not marked on Atmag's map, and she suspected that was because it did not exist in the worldsphere. Yet somehow, she knew the place.

"Jianabel was hideously powerful, with a matching intelligence. She was more than a sorcerer; she had learned how to simply alter the world. If there was something she wanted, or did not like, she merely willed it into or out of existence."

"So this 'Jianabel' must have believed she was a goddess . . . did she?" Jiana nodded glumly.

"Every day of my life, I have thanked the Nameless Serpentine that I can no longer remember my time as Jianabel. For this sphere—or perhaps all of the spheres— did not exist while she was here."

"I find this hard to believe. I clearly recall a whole life of experience before you were even born, Jiana."

"Which means exactly nothing, save that you were created with memories. You have philosophized yourself about this very point, haven't you?"

He snorted.

"Surely everyone has, warrior! This whole world could have been created a heartbeat ago, and your memories could be crafted as well! But it is an absurd statement, since there is no way to either prove or disprove it."

"There is a way. Whatever did it once can do it again." Jiana buried her face in her folded arms, feeling their disbelief like a physical tide, pulling on her.

"A part of Jianabel decided such a power was evil. I'm not debating the merits of the decision; that tiny piece of her had far more life than I have now. Nor do I know how a part can have an independent will. But it caught Jianabel by surprise, and created what I call me as an iron mask to imprison her. Jiana is far stupider, far weaker, and far more human than Jianabel.

"But Jiana is fairly normal. She grows old. And as the years passed, I naively supposed the horrid little girl was dead.

"It was wishful thinking. Jianabel was not truly evil, I guess. You can't apply such tiny labels to anything so immense. Is the world good or bad? Is sorrow evil; is love pious? The questions don't make sense, and they don't with Jianabel either, since she's so far beyond them. But she had a sense of humor. She enjoyed rearranging reality to suit her whims. The few things I can remember—from dreams, mostly—are enough to turn my stomach so badly I have to drink strong tea and ale until I'm numb, and I see the scenes no longer. She was especially fond of mixing things, like several different kind of animals, or of bringing cooked meat back to life, so that the leg of lamb squirmed and kicked in agony as you ate it."

"Was that Jianabel we saw?" Dida asked, unease weakening his voice.

"Jianabel did not die. She was buried, but she has finally succeeded in digging back to the surface. And she intends to take back her body."

"Poppydoddle!" Toldo exploded, unable to contain himself any longer. "Superstitious primitivism! You have a very tight personality, Jiana. you hold back too many of your feelings, and they've just started manifesting as an invented, childhood alter-being."

"And was it a childhood manifestation that nearly crushed Dida's skull a moment ago? Was it an invention that sucked the essence of Lord Ata dry to destroy a three thousand-year-old deity? Why the hell do you think so many gods and demons have been sniffing our trail and dogging our path? Because they sense Jianabel! They're drawn to her brilliance like moths to fire. This is no mad fantasy. If I were to open myself to her once—just once let down the wall—I could burn this entire world to the molten core. But I wouldn't be the same 'I'."

She fixed Toldo with her cold eyes, and she saw him shiver in spite of himself, for in that moment, she let just the faintest wisp of power brush across his life, past and future. A shock ran along his existence from womb to tomb, and he trembled as Jiana truly walked on his grave.

"I have only one power that she cannot fight; I have my life. Jianabel can't understand life, for she never lived— she only played. I truly *care* about the world—about all of the spheres! It's somehow held her back all these years. Maybe that part of her that created me also created a

world in which people care. I can hurt, and love, and
hate, and all that mushy stuff, and she can't."

She closed her eyes, and for the first time in fourteen
years brought forth the true memory of the Most Terrible
Thing.

"In that other world, I had a father who liked to, uh,
touch people. Women. He feared his daughter, but once
he made the mistake of touching her." She opened her
eyes, and looked directly at Dida. "She sacrificed him—to
Herself. But first she played with him, in ways that are
none of your business. Dida, Toldo . . . you have both
touched me more deeply than my father touched me then.
He only used his hand. Can you possibly imagine what
Jianabel would do to you?"

Jiana turned abruptly and began marching down the
street. She heard the two follow her. Somehow, she knew
that up ahead was an intersection, and she should turn
left.

"I refuse to allow that. I have something to live for now:
friends, a relationship—however bad at the moment—a
quest. I *refuse* to let a bloodthirsty little godlet get in my
way."

She walked on, head bowed, feeling the crush of a
thousand and one crystal spheres pressing heavily upon
her. Then, a hand touched her shoulder, and all of the
weight fell away. Toldo spoke, but she realized it was not
his hand. It was Dida, walking beside her.

"If the fact will please you, I will admit it. I find, against
all expectation, that I actually believe you. I don't know if
it matters."

"It matters. Thanks."

They trod the smooth, marble streets together, and
Dida's hand held her shoulder the entire way. That too
mattered.

Around a bend, and suddenly the great tower loomed
before them. Finally, Jiana understood why the deserted
town seemed so familiar to her—how she had known
which way to go at every turn.

"Dida," she hissed. "It's the city from my dream, in the
hutch of the too-wise. This is Toq's palace!" Now the
scenes crystallized. Although it was pale white where the

other had been char black, and still standing where the other had been devastated, it was clearly the same city. In the dream, the tower alone was not a ruin. Jiana suspected it had come first, and the town had sprung up later.

I wonder if what I saw was not at the beginning of the world, but at its end?

"We must climb the tower," she said. "Some stupid destiny awaits us at the top, and it would behoove us to at least find out what it is. Don't let Toq frighten you."

Without another word, she led them to the tower entrance, and across the main hall. It was hung with many gay pictures, but there was something odd and disturbing about them. She could find no particulars; the feeling was subliminal. In addition, the perspective of the hall itself was wrong, somehow. Jiana brushed it from her mind, and led her friends to the central stairs, which wound through the ceiling and far up out of sight.

She began to climb them, and Toldo came directly behind her. But as Dida tried to set foot on the steps, something seemed to stop him.

"No," he whispered. He tried again. This time his face whitened with fear and he staggered away in a panic. He looked up to her, a single tear wetting his cheek.

"My love, I . . . I don't know why, but I can't! I can't go the stairs up, not now or ever!"

She looked down at him, pity cheapening her heart.

"What the hell. You've done plenty. Wait for us—shouldn't be too long."

"I love you," he called.

"I love you, too," she lied. She turned back to the stairs, feeling like a prostitute. Toldo ascended wearily behind her, and in two spiral turns, the young boy was out of sight.

-3-

For a hundred revolutions, Jiana doggedly counted the number of times she and Toldo Mondo circumambulated the stairloops, but there were no marks, no clues as to when one loop ended and another began, and eventually she lost count.

She began to think the stairs had wound on forever, for far longer than the entire height of the tower. Then she lost all sense of direction, and became convinced the stairs were tilting alarmingly—that they were leading her down or sideways. Yet still her feet remained on the steps, and her body continued to lurch—forward? upward?—whichever direction the stairs led.

Then the stairs began to descend. There was no plateau or summit; she did not change direction. It was as if she had entered the illusory world of a Ritti Turika tapestry, where the stairs rose endlessly in a circle and met again their own bottom, and where yesterday's ceiling was tomorrow's wall.

"How long have we climbed?" gasped the priest.

"A moment. Forever. What difference does it make? We are not climbing a tower in the earthly sphere. Are you getting weary?"

"No. It frightens me; I am a fat old man. Yet I continue to climb, or descend, and follow the stairs unwinded."

Looking ahead of her, the stairs seemed to close off—not as if they wound around to the left or the right, or faded into the false convergence of perspective, but as if they actually contracted to a single point. Behind, it was the same. Toldo and Jiana climbed through a bubble in nothingness.

"Dida wouldn't have made it, faithless one."

"His claustrophobia."

"But he couldn't have known. What was it that stopped him?"

Toldo did not answer her, nor did he stop.

Forever and another day passed. Jiana grew suddenly afraid that if they did stop on the stairs, they would remain forever in limbo.

Around and around, and suddenly Jiana halted so quickly that Toldo ran into her.

"Move, hero! We daren't tarry here!"

He tried to push past her, then saw why she had stopped. A translucent door of quartz blocked the stairs.

"I think we're here, Toldo."

"Where? One of your crystal spheres?"

"I wouldn't be surprised. This looks very much like the

material that bounds our own sphere, from what I've seen."

"And beyond?"

Jiana reached out and pressed against it. It felt unexpectedly warm and moist. With some effort, her hand pushed through.

"I don't like it," she said. It made her uncomfortable, and she felt a wholly inappropriate sexual thrill through her body. She grew furious at being so manipulated, and forced her entire body through the warm wet white in a single move.

—alone; a gentle handtouch, fingerbrush; a caress
thrills the stomach the thighs the breasts the neck the face . . .
—waves from up-up-underneath the womb, spreading throughout her body
like amber
and honey
and molasses dripping up, touching thrilling tasting every bit of her—oh!

A gentle hand pressed firmly between her legs, the fingers
slipping so delicately into the moist crack, rising up like
moons and stars
wetting her belly with her own lubricating fluid—

No.

rigid unstoppable undeniable irresistible long thick hard
shaft driving driving driving—

No. I won't yield to your disgusting fantasies!

filling her up inside full filling her insides filling full—

*   *   *

I know you, Toq. Your illusions have no power
over me. Let me
pass; we must

—speak."

"You must have no soul, mortal." Toq faced her. He was
still the golden boy, this time with no hint of the hideous-
ness and the corruption behind the boy-mask. In his own
sphere, Toq was regal, even for a god.

"Whom have you brought to see me?"

"This is Toldo Mondo," Jiana said, bowing slightly and
extending her hand to indicate the priest.

"You're very round," Toq commented.

"My appetite for life is greater than my appetite for
faith."

Toq smiled, and Jiana felt a fearful premonition. Almost,
she looked over her shoulder for the lightning bolt she
expected momentarily from the Worldserpent.

"No, little Jiana; your fat friend has the right idea. I like
a mortal who wants nothing to do with gods and demons,
for rarely do we even notice your existence, as a rule.
Your snake totem has no power here; stop anticipating his
manifestations." He stepped down off his dais, his saffron
robes parting to reveal his golden, little-boy's body. Again
Jiana felt the sexual charge of the god leaping the distance
between them to enter her mind. She began to fantasize
about how erotic little boys were—their legs, their hands,
their soft, hairless bellies . . .

She shook her head, clearing the visions.

"Do you wonder why I have called you here?" Toq
breathed. Jiana's nipples pressed hard against her tunic,
and she stood very, very straight.

"I knew where I was. I sought you as much as you
sought me. I have news for you." She looked to Toldo. His
face was as red as any man's she had ever seen. One hand
clutched at his muslin robe as if he would tear it from
himself at any moment, while the other held the first in a
death-grip, its knuckles white and the hand shaking.

Dida.

"What news could you possibly have for me, little girl?"

"I am a woman. I am being pulled in two directions, like a rope between two asses. I don't like it. I don't want anything more to do with either one of you!"

"Two directions? What do you mean?" Toq's face began to darken until it was the color of the nighttime sea.

"I was visited a short time ago by Sleeping Tifniz. He mentioned you."

"AAAAAAAAAAAAAA!" Toq rose up into the air, growing until he was a thousand and one stories tall. He swept his fists back and about until his rage had battered apart the walls of his fortress. The great white stones exploded and flew apart as if they were shards from a potter's vase that had been dashed to the ground from atop the wheel.

"He insisted I join with him against you. Naturally, I agreed."

With a wrenching effort, the Golden Child regained his composure—at least, enough to articulate again.

"You—have done—what no other mortal has *ever* done! You have truly angered me! Oh, my love, now shall I notice you. Now shall I remember!"

"You remind me of a certain prince. Toq, what would anyone else have done? You said yourself, I'm a mortal. Should I tell a god to go piss up a vine?" Slowly, his anger began to abate as he ruminated about the circumstances.

"Actually, this works out quite well for me. Think what a potent weapon you could make, with heavy-lidded Tifniz believing you are his agent!"

"You didn't hear me, Toq. I resigned from service to you, or Sleepy, or the Order, or the Holy Vehemence, or to anything else that isn't Jiana Analena of Bay Bay!"

Toq smirked. "We shall talk of that momentarily. But I believe you have something else in your stomach."

Jiana nodded. "I came to you with more than this news. I came with a question."

"Allow me to anticipate, girlchild. You wish to know exactly what the World's Dream is. Your good fortune is momentous tonight! For it is for precisely this reason, to tell you this information, that I called to you in the first place!"

Toldo unexpectedly spoke up.

"So this World's Dream actually exists? This fairy-tale of Prince Alanai's?"

"Toldo! You would interrupt a god?" Toq seemed amused, not angry.

"Yes, o spherical inquisitor," he continued. "The World's Dream does, in fact, exist. But there has been a rather basic confusion as to its actual nature.

"My children, the story that Alanai has heard from his father, from his great-great-grandfather a hundred times over, is just a talespinner's fancy. The Dream is a hundred times simpler to comprehend, and at the same time, its power is incomprehensible."

"Toq," interrupted Jiana, emboldened by Toldo's example, "skip the platitudes, please. What does the damn thing do?"

He smiled mischievously.

"Anything."

"Anything? Any what thing?"

"Anything. No limitations. It allows its possessor a single free wish, once in the lifetime of a world."

Toldo exploded.

"A wishing coin! What utter nonsense! Bilge! A hundred children's tales—"

"It is real. Trust me, I'm a deity. I didn't say it gave a request, spoken aloud and always to the rue of the speaker. It grants the user's *wish*, whatever it might be. As to its power . . . I cannot be certain, but I believe this entire structure, the thousand and one crystal spheres—is but the nightmare of the last one to use the World's Dream."

"That's just plain *silly!*" cried Jianabel. Jiana listened in amazement as the words tumbled from her mouth. "I made these worlds! I made the spheres!"

"And who made you, o little dead girl? I, too, have existed since before this all—" he gestured to indicate Totality. "But we could have been created with such conflicting memories already in place. I must face the fact that a toy of infinite power cannot exist in a finite sequence of worlds, so it must exist outside of them, with only an eye or an ear pointed inward to see or hear the command to alter Everything. Look, old foe: if either you or I were the true progenitors, would our powers be so limited now?"

"Old foe?" Jiana said. "Did you know her—Jianabel?"

"I know *you*; you have not changed. You've just turned a blind eye to the greater part of yourself." Toq now stood on a level with Jiana. She could not remember when he had shrunk down, but he was no longer in the grip of his towering rage. She also noticed the walls of the tower were still intact. Perhaps it had all been an illusion.

"And I fear," continued the Sun Child, "that if you continue along this quest, your eyes will be opened. I will once again have a rival to my power in this system. But this I far prefer to what would happen if that madman, Alanai, were to gain the World's Dream."

Jiana fell silent, considering this image. The thought of a man so simplistic, so absolute, so sure of rightness gaining total power over the world raised such a spectre of fear within her that she began to feel sick. She bit her lip and tasted blood, and the bitterness restored her hold on herself.

"If I recovered the Dream," Toq continued, his voice a liquid summer breeze, "you know that I would use it far above your puny, earthy sphere. I hardly even notice that you exist. I am only drawn by the powers that have been unleashed across your world, and by the treasure they seek. Help me, Jiana my precious; help me, my love. Stop Alanai the mad! I think you may be the only one who can."

"I told you: I quit. Why can't you just strike him dead?"

"It violates the rules, and more than that I cannot say. This is why you may *not* resign."

Jiana stepped back, touching Wave involuntarily.

"You need my protection, sweetling. You are but one player in the game. Tifniz has his own player—he controls death."

"Hraga!" Jiana guessed.

"Once he was like you. He has become a shadow now, blotting out will and hope and endeavor. He belongs to that class of mortals, like yourself, whose destiny is more firmly fixed than that of the gods. He was old and crafty when your grandfather was young, and he wants you."

"Why does he even care? I've only met him once!"

"You two are connected; that much certainty I have.

You and he are intended to meet head-on like a flood against a mountain. I have no intention of getting in between you two."

"Thanks." Jiana envisioned herself in a long corridor. On every side, the doors slammed, leading her inexorably down and down, toward the one open door at the end . . .

"But I also shall ensure that Hraga's Hand will not interfere with the match, either."

"Ah, if I may interrupt this dialog for a practical question?" Jiana blinked away her dreams, and Toldo continued. "What exactly does this World's Dream look like?"

"Why should it have a physical form?" Jiana asked.

"But it does," said the god. "There is no reason why, but none why not, either. In this world, it bears the physical shape of a leaf."

"A leaf? Like falling off a tree at Autumn—that thing?" Toq nodded.

"What color?" demanded Toldo. Toq shrugged.

"I have never seen it."

"How does one use it?" asked Jiana.

"I've never used it. There is a rhyme that goes along with it . . . and the words themselves have potency. This is what kept your Toradoras in power in Bay Din so long, and their use is what first alerted me—and Alanai—that the Dream could be found. Listen, and you'll know everything that I know about it:

Dream another age.
Dream the dream of ashes,
Dream another's dreams;
The window world unlatches, crashes,
Tears apart its timesewn seams,
For he who holds the world within his hand,
Who crushes, casts it to the sand:

His heart an open page.
His heart an unbound page.

"Wonderful," Jiana growled. "Can we go now?" She was still annoyed at being so thoroughly manipulated.

"Leave. Do not let Alanai get it, whatever happens. Bring it to me."

"Ah, your pardon, Toq. But as your co-conspirators, can you give us something tangible to drive away Sleeping Tifniz and his minions?" Toldo sounded eminently practical again. "I fear he might not buy that argument about fate, regarding Jiana and Hraga, and that would not stop him from killing me and Dida, in any event."

"Hm. Here." Jiana found herself holding a snowflake in her hand. It was large enough to see, and showed no inclination to melt. "Break this in the presence of any unearthly being, while speaking the word 'debit'. It will banish the creature from the thousand and one spheres for a thousand and one years—myself excluded, of course, since I made it. And I won't allow it to be used on Sleeping Tifniz or Hraga si Traga, as that would violate the rules. Now go, and annoy me no more." He dismissed them a second time, but again Toldo interrupted.

"Horses, your godship. I grow tired of walking."

"They'll be waiting for you at the bottom of the tower! If you make me dismiss you a *third* time, I shall—"

Jiana turned quickly, grabbed Toldo's arm before he could speak again, and led him back through the door.

Again, she lost her time and balance sense as she descended the world-stairs, but familiarity had dulled the fear.

"Rules," she muttered. "Some stupid game. I should have guessed."

It seemed to take less time descending (if that was what they did), and then they were at the bottom. Jiana rounded the last turn, and stopped in surprise. Again, Toldo bumped into her; his bulk was harder to stop.

"Jiana," he asked, "where has the boy gone?"

"Look closely, my friend," she whispered. The floor was covered with muddy bootprints, which showed signs of a struggle.

"Oh, Lordy," said Jiana. She pointed at what she had just seen, leaning against the bottom step. It was Dida's hunting knife. He would never have left it behind unless forcibly dragged from the area. To him, it was the heart of

the warrior soul that he saw within him. There was dried
blood on the tip.

Jiana ran back through the hall and out onto the street.
She cast about on the ground, and found scores of hooftracks.
But at last in the chalky dust at the corner of the building,
she found one clear print: it was the splayfoot.

"Toldo! Alanai has taken Dida." From a deep inner
pocket in her tunic, under her brigantine, she drew forth
her old honor band. She carefully tied it about her head,
thus sinking under its oath. She could not deviate from his
trail now until he was rescued or revenged.

"Until now," she said, her voice dead, "I did not know
what he meant to me."

"Alanai? He's captured the boy?"

"I care nothing for Toq. Hraga is the devil, and all other
gods and demons just get in my way. Hraga will die for
this."

Jiana sought the horses Toq had promised, her thoughts
black and her vision red.

Between the parts . . .

"It was an admirable move," Toq admitted. To have said otherwise would have compromised his credibility. "But you have come perilously close to recruiting another player."

Tifniz's snores petered out, and he laboriously opened his eyes to narrow slits.

"I said nothing . . ." Toq waited silently while Tifniz yawned, and then yawned a second time for twice as long, ". . . nothing to turn the boy. My player and his pieces will do all—all the talking."

"I am referring to your conversation with Jiana Analena herself. That is unheard of!"

"Why can I not?" Tifniz smiled in an ingratiating, irritating manner.

"You harassed my player. And, you misrepresented the Order."

The sleeper's defense was unanswerable.

"So?" he asked.

Toq angrily turned his back and left the presence of Sleeping Tifniz. Where there were no referees, there were no rules.

The game continued inexorably. The World's Dream did not care about rules, their interpretations, and their violations.

Chapter 8

Tug the moons to tune the tides;
little mouse on a string

-1-

"HAH!" Jiana kicked her heels into her horse's red flanks, wishing for a pair of spurs. The horse apparently did not need them, for it bolted forward in a gallop that cut the wind across her face like a hurricane. She sneaked a look back at Toldo, and was shocked to see that he seemed perfectly at ease in the saddle. He caught up to her.

"I thought—" she yelled above the pounding hooves, which thudded in the sand as a normal horse's might on a wooden bridge, "I would've thought an indolent clergyman like you would be as clumsy on a horse as a sack of flour."

For a dozen booming strides he merely smirked.

"What the Eyrie do you think we do—" he retorted at last, "*walk* from place to place?"

Jiana almost laughed. It would have felt good, but it was inappropriate, somehow. She maintained a stubborn silence.

It had not escaped her notice that upon exiting the tower, they had found but two horses. *He knew, even*

244

while we bickered, that Dida was being stolen from me.
Jiana felt bitter and betrayed by her patron.

Miles fell past the pair like a river rushing backwards,
and Toq's horses neither tired nor turned aside. The one
Jiana rode followed Alanai's trail without any prompting
from her, and its brother never fell more than two steps
behind.

The warrior found ample time to study the sky, as the
ground rushed past too quickly to be observed. All of the
blueness had been bleached out, leaving only the pale
bones of the crystal shell behind. Notwithstanding the
heavy sun, a few clouds managed to form—thin, broken,
filmy veils that streamed for a short while and then
dissipated.

The air tasted salty, and carried a faint whiff of apprehension—less than an odor but more than a feeling. Jiana
had scented it before, in White Falls. Her mother's
bawdyhouse had been the front building of a double lot,
and the other was a house for those who were touched.

The scent of madness tinged the Tarn.

And something else. Once, when she brought her eyes
down to check that all of her gear was still intact, she saw a
bit of fluff on her tunic. Plucking it and studying it closely,
she realized it was the fluffy seed pod from an Old Man's
Beard bush.

Life! she marveled. *How the hell did you get out here to
hell?* A little piece inside of her felt good, and she brushed
the pod away. *Good luck. Root strongly—everything will
soon be shaking.* A bit of ice in her heart melted.

At last, after the giant, burning sun had set and Fear
had risen, the horses slowed and stopped as a single
creature. They allowed Jiana and Toldo to dismount.

As she climbed down, she became afraid that they would
bolt into the blowing sands the moment her feet left the
stirrups. But they merely stood and stared blankly at her.

The ground rocked up and back, and then rose to meet
her face. She thought of the terrible Things that haunted
the Tarn . . . during the run, she did not hear the phantom trumpets or the drums of war on the horizon, so loud
had been the beat of the horse's hooves. But now that they
were still, the lurid cries of the dying and the long-since

dead filled the air again as chillingly as they had the night before.

Spirits abroad to suck dry my soul! A funny trick of her mind made the phrase seem hauntingly familiar.

"Even Jianabel is too tired to mock me."

Toldo opened his mouth to speak, then seemed to change his mind. Then he did the same thing again.

"What?" she asked.

"Jiana—about your other . . . about Jianabel. There's something you must know. You won't want to believe it, but you must—it is the only way to exorcise her."

"Toldo, say it! Anything to get rid of her . . ." But just then, an irresistible wave of sudden fatigue and weariness lapped at her consciousness, and her eyelids drooped, as if by their own volition. She yawned.

It felt very much like the influence of Sleeping Tifniz. *No*, whispered a strange thought in her head. *That would violate the rules.*

Toldo hesitated.

"Ahem . . . perhaps I should tell you later. Yes, definitely."

"Promise?" she asked weakly, yawning again.

"I do," he swore.

Then Jiana felt herself adrift upon the lake of sleep.

The world in flames . . .

Mad armies of shopkeepers and candledippers—run to the left in a great frenzy! turn about halfway across and run to the new enemy on the right!

A crack appears in the earth. It swallows up a kingdom whole, and Alanai rides a screaming steed over a rainbow where once it stood. A thousand men are following him—but curiously, they are all facing about and running backwards . . .

"NO!" Jianabelana screams. "FOOLS! BLOCKHEADS! LOOK, EVERYBODY JUST *STOP*, DAMN YOU!" But, of course, it is one of *those* dreams, and her voice comes out softer than a shoretonie's midnight whisper.

("Jianabelana?" cries Jianabel, alarmed. "Who *is* that inside of *me?*" But Jiana looks within and laughs at the tormenter's astonishment. *It's like peeling an onion, little monster, is it not?*)

There is a terrible wrench in her gut, and the sound of a million wine goblets shattering above her head. Huge chunks of burning white crystal impact the ground, each killing hundreds of the men and women who scurry mindlessly about the field. The crystal sphere above has shattered! Soon another, then another, then another, then—

The sky is orange. The fields of the earth are all enflamed, and they reflect in the star-sphere that spins above Jiana's head. As far as Jiana can see marches a long line of the holy crusaders, from the ends unto the ends of the world. They are singing. They raise aloft an emblem, a design, a symbol of Good triumphant over Evil. They all wear hoods, into which no eyeholes have been cut. They, too, all march backwards.

(She feels him pressing against her young body. She is too little to prevent him, to afraid to cry out . . . She feels the Bad Snake—Daddy, stop! Why are you doing . . .)

"I hide my face from none," said Hraga, "and my name is open to all."

"I know you!" Jiana cried. Her father's rough hands held her tight—not like he sometimes did, when it was nice, but in a bad way. She had no name for it. Daddy was different some nights when Momma was away.

The grey man grinned all shark's teeth and rat's eyes, smelling of the crypt and rasping like a chilly wind across dry and ready bones.

"Come to me, my little Jiana of White Falls, New River. Come with your fat priest and your little brat alter ego. Come with your impotent magick and your limp-wrist, faggot sword . . . I am waiting!"

She spoke back, but a lump of coal grew in her stomach. Somehow, in a horrid way, she *knew* him. He terrified her; no one else ever had. No one except—

"Alanai will not tolerate one such as you. He fights for one ideal that he calls good against another that he terms evil. But you're Evil itself, in corporeal form! Even now, he's probably sneaking up on you, drawing his sword . . ."

"My, my; so little you understand! I've eaten Prince

Alanai, Jiana of White Falls, New River. I gobbled him up, and he's sleeping comfortably in my stomach now."

My stomach now.

My stomach now—

The flamehorses were still there when she awoke. They stood in the same positions as the night before, and still stared unblinking at Jiana.

After a few mouthfuls of the water from Long Hyu, she and Toldo remounted and continued their demonic ride.

Three days passed thus: Every day was spent in a furious chase, at a pace which would lather the sides of a mortal horse, but which left Toq's gifts unwinded and fresh; and each night, Jiana moaned and convulsed with foul dreams which clamped on her heart and left her limp and sweaty in the morning. Despite many drinks from her water sack—drinks which grew more frequent as the days ground by—it was always half empty.

"Another gift from Toq the munificent," she grumbled, letting the water pour down her throat, pretending it was something stronger. Toldo refused to answer her; they had not actually spoken since midafternoon of the second day. The sullen Tarn caught at their words and made them heavy, so they sank into the sands and were lost.

Probably me. Dida's gone. When Toldo opens his mouth, I shove my foot in it. Don't blame him a bit. But she did, and she began looking at him sidelong when she thought he was not aware, and at times when she knew he was.

He probably thinks I'm fat and ugly, with my burned hair and scarred face. Arrogant bastard.

While the sun crawled overhead, she could hear only the thud of the hellhorses' hooves, still making more noise than they should. At night, the warring nations of ghosts and ghouls made restful sleep impossible.

The dunes became higher and longer, and a few dead, withered bushes flashed by at the edge of her vision. At first, she did not know if they were real, or just blinkdreams to prick at her sanity. But they became common, then numerous, and then the ground sloped upward and became a plateau of scrub and thornleaf plants. Here, she remembered, was where the demongoats lived, but they avoided her and the horses of Toq.

The horses stopped early. For a long while, she tried to kick hers into motion. Then she realized they must belong to the Tarn.

"I suppose they've decided the desert is at an end," she said. It was her first civil words to her companion in two days and a night.

Tentatively, he responded.

"Perhaps we should dismount?"

She swung off the beast; Toldo did the same.

The horses stared into her eyes, mocking somehow. For a moment, she had the most peculiar feeling she was expanding. Then she realized the roans were shrinking.

Melting, as a matter of fact, she realized. Like lead in a hot crucible, they began to bubble at the feet and legs, then they slowly collapsed into a puddle of boiling flesh.

They began to scream. The sounds of their agony cut through Jiana like daggers, but a part of her seemed to feel a thrill of pleasure at the spectacle.

She wished she could lie to herself and say it was not her, it was Jianabel. But she knew better.

In a few moments, there was nothing left of the creatures. The last view Jiana had was of their eyes, still watching her . . . begging for some kind of succor.

Do you plead now? she asked. *Sorry. I just don't care. Give me Dida!*

They were gone.

Toldo Mondo scratched his bristly face.

"Well? What now, o love-forsaken hero?"

She shrugged.

"Now the satrapy of Noon. See the ocean, far off that way?" It was only the tiniest speck of black water, but she had seen many oceans, from too many shores. It was too big to be a lake. "Come on. Prince's probably just over the next ridge."

They began to walk toward the sea.

"I'm sorry," she said suddenly.

"I understand."

After another hour of walking, Jiana heard horses approaching. Looking about, she saw a convenient rock, and dragged Toldo behind it.

The horsemen galloped past. They wore robes and armor, and carried twelve-foot lances with streamers at the tip.

"Not good," she said when they had gone.

"Bandits?"

"Dressed like that, with a hundred copper serpents' worth of armor apiece? Hardly!" Jiana squinted back along the trail from which they had come. "Afraid we've jumped into some kind of war."

"A war!"

"And I can't think of a nicer prince it could happen to."

"Ah, what makes you think Alanai's at the center of this?"

She did not reply.

"Well," he answered himself. "Why not? The satrap is dominated by the emperor of Door, and he's related by three marriages to the Toradoras."

They emerged from behind the rock, and began to backtrack the riders.

"Well, here's your big chance, o red-eyed one."

"A time for sleep," Jiana said, "and a time to reap. Come, priestly one. Let's go mow some wheat," She set a pace her tubby partner was hard pressed to match.

-2-

Toldo Mondo lay on the ground where Jiana had hidden him. He, too, studied the scene far below them; anyone would have. But, while the emotions visible in his face were a mix of excitement and straightforward fear, Jiana felt only vindication and anticipation.

Well . . . all right. Maybe a little fear.

You can't very well lie to me, Ji! Jianabel objected. *I know what you're feeling. You're terrified!*

It was true, but it was a different kind of terrified. The troops below, six thousand strong, did not worry her.

I'm not afraid to die.

Shouldn't you be?

Should she be? Why, among so many other soldiers, were some unafraid, even when defeat seemed certain?

Four stark word-symbols had once been annotated to her file in the Flower Empire, where she had fought the longest and risen the highest. Four simple cross-and-box pictures: no apparent fear of death.

Was it a compliment, or a warning to other commanders?

"Are we—do we have to—" Toldo indicated the vast army with his hand and looked at her helplessly.

"Fight them? That would be pretty stupid. Even Alanai's going to have trouble facing six thousand! But we will have to cross through them . . ." Toldo gasped, and she turned to him in surprise. "I should think you'd welcome the chance to die, and finally find out, once and for all time—"

"Jiana. For a long time I have become convinced that . . . there is nothing after we die. I am afraid to cease to exist. I'm afraid."

The blasphemy was gargantuan, and shocked Jiana.

"Priest! I know you're not of my same piety. And I suppose a giant, intelligent snake is an image which hardly inspires deep faith in the Most High. But to believe in nothingness!"

Now Toldo half smiled.

"So you do have a fear. Throughout this quest I've thought it was an emotion alien to you."

"Hm. I'm afraid of a lot in the world—just ask Dida! But to believe in nothingness must be the greatest hell. Everything I fear—love, obscurity, performance anxiety—they're all just fancies of a mad child if our ending is so complete!"

The satrap's army spread out in all directions, without order. But it made hardly any difference, Jiana thought, since the concept of ordered warfare had not filtered across to this side of the ocean. No one here knew much about battle lines or reserves, or flanking, except on the most basic of levels. Even then, it was thought to apply only to cavalry-on-cavalry fighting. If anyone had suggested the strategy and tactics of sergeants be seriously studied by the prince-generals, the one offering such advice would find himself in more intimate proximity to the sergeants than desired. Jiana knew this from personal experience. It amazed her how little she cared for further discussions of strategy after two days spent marching.

"I don't see it that way," Toldo mused. "To me, since there is nothing after the final sigh, we ought to live in today. And to hell with next week."

In the gloom from the twilit sky, Jiana glanced back at the priest—ex-priest—and experienced a strange hallucination. For a moment, she was convinced she saw a huge, white buffalo lying in the cool dirt, hidden behind a bush, his shaggy head gazing out over his dominions with lordly detachment.

She blinked, and looked down at her folded arms. When she looked back, the vision persisted. Then, with a sudden shift of background and foreground, she saw Toldo again, his white robes bunched up around him, pressed down to be invisible from the valley below.

"A black bear and a white buffalo," she said, "lying in ambush to rescue a brown mouse from a golden eagle. Hell, we'd make a wonderful exhibit at the zoo." Her own words cut deep, and she was sorry she had said them. Toldo let them pass without comment. It was one reason she had begun to feel real affection for him. She would have called him brother if it would not have compromised her command.

When the sun neared the horizon, and the sky began to lose its glamour, Jiana stirred from her post behind a tall, thick weed, and motioned Toldo from his prone position.

"Time. Let's go tweak his beard."

Either some of the reports she had heard were exaggerated, or else Alanai had lost some men. But his force numbered no more than two hundred, against the Iron Satrap's six thousand. The Noondun riders had encircled Alanai's position, which, though well-positioned against a mountainside, would still surely be overrun within a single skirmish. Unless . . .

Jiana felt a queer jubilation as she and Toldo trekked down into the valley of impending slaughter. Everything had worked out exactly as she had planned, despite the fact that nothing had worked out even remotely as she had planned. She had not counted on love; she did not know the world would be so torn asunder; she had no inkling

the heavens would be so well represented on the World,
or that she would be impressed into service to so many
gods, men, and visions.

Yet, here was the prince. Surrounded by a ravenous
army of monstrous thirty-to-one proportions, he awaited
all-unknowing the hand of providence, otherwise named
Jiana-on-the-Spot.

"Mullanta, the Iron Satrap himself, has chosen to take
the field against so worthy a foe as Prince Alanai of the
Water Kingdom. See! Look there, his colors." At the
center of the narrowing circles of horse troops was an
enormous tent, with a fluttering banner depicting a band
of iron twisted into a knot, the ancient legend of the Noon
satrapy.

"So?"

"Mullanta, like all the Noondun buggers before him,
rules by the touch of divinity, guarded and maintained by
his college of shamans. There are no other formalities of
government—don't you see what I see?"

"I see an army of six thousand, who will slay us as a
snake slays a chuck!"

"Exactly! Cut the head from the serpent, leap back from
the convulsing body, and you've won! Look, all I have to
do is kill Mullanta, and his dynasty, his government, and
therefore, even his army, will crumble like a sand castle
dried in the sun!"

The priest's eyes grew wide, and his mouth opened
slightly.

"*Kill* Mullanta?"

Jiana grinned like a little girl, and pounded her balled
fist into her thigh in anticipation.

"Finally, a simple task of violence amidst all this abstraction! Something I can sink my fangs into."

"Toldo remembered to shut his mouth, then opened it
again to sputter.

"But—you'll be butchered! The six thousand—"

"A child's game. The real fight will be with his shamans.
Shaman? But I'm sure that bitch Jianabel won't let anything permanent happen to me."

"Jiana, dear . . . this is serious! This is real. You *must*
distinguish between reality and fantasy!" He grabbed her

arm—the one that beat her thigh—and dragged her to a stop.

"Darling warrior, until now, I've gone along with your fanciful dreams and curious visions of the world. But this I cannot allow! You're sick. I did not want to tell you these things . . . I don't know how you will take them. Remember what I started to say a few days ago, in the Tarn?"

"You said you'd tell me later. You promised."

"I'll tell you now. Jiana . . . Jianabel *is you*. She isn't some other, some little-child-turned-goddess that possesses you every now and so often. *You* are Jianabel."

"Well, I *was* her."

"No, that isn't it at all!" Toldo looked desperate to explain. Jiana took a deep breath, and braced herself to listen.

"You know I was a priest, and that I walked out on my calling. You never asked me what I did at the mission."

"I'm asking now."

"Jiana . . . I took care of people like you. People who had—lost themselves. Or lost a part of themselves. Jianabel is just your name for that part of you that terrifies you, the ugly part that you can't always control. Maybe you did something when you were a child—something so horrible you can't bear to think about it. Or else maybe you just kept thinking about doing something. I don't know. I never found out what causes such a multiple personality. It's why I left. I realized I cared more for my work than my faith, and I had to learn more about people. It's . . . forgive me, dear. It's why I initially chose to travel with you."

"Toldo, that's silly. I told you nothing of Jianabel until much later!"

"It was a breakthrough. I'll bet you've never told anyone else before that night."

Jiana nodded slowly; he had struck true.

"I didn't know what beasts lay hidden inside of you, but I knew the day I met you, outside the walls of Bay Din, that there was something repellent coiled up in your stomach like a thick, ugly worm—something you could not exorcise. Jiana—I felt a great hurt within you. I came with you because I wanted to help. I want to cure you."

An old, familiar, tormenting voice whispered within her ears.

Don't listen to the old fartbag, Ji. Do you truly think I'm not real? Then watch!

Jiana's hand suddenly shot forward and clutched Toldo Mondo by the throat. He grabbed her fingers, and as he tried unsuccessfully to pry them loose, his eyes began to grow big.

Jiana gasped. Her hand would not obey her! Her breath seemed to halt and draw raggedly in time with Toldo's. She gritted her teeth and determined to unwind her fingers from his windpipe.

"No! Damn you—Jianabel, NO!"

Toldo dropped to his knees, weakening. Jiana's heart pounded with white fear, more even than she had felt on the mountain of the too-wise, when the white cloud had enveloped her.

The Voice again. This time it boomed down from the heavens, and up from the cracks beneath her feet. All other sounds had ceased, save for the Voice, intoning monotonously:

—IS DEATH!—IS DEATH!—IS DEATH!—IS DEATH!

And finally, as though she had known it all along, the entire sentence padded out on hated cat-feet.

JIANA—IS—DEATH!

Agony exploded in her heart and along her left arm, the hand that held Toldo. The world dissolved into a white shadow—fleeting doves in a snowy field—frozen doves on the icy ground.

Toldo was dying. And with him, under the inexorable crush of Jianabel's iron-claw fingers, Jiana also died.

She had a single gambit left.

Though Jianabel's hand, the left hand, was out of control, far too strong to pry loose, the right hand still belonged to Jiana. It could reach her boot dagger.

"Ji—Jianabel," she gasped, dizzy from lack of breath. "Know this: if Toldo goes, so go I. And you—*are*—me." She pressed the dagger up against her own breast, just under her sternum, facing up. Just a quick thrust, a flick of her wrist, and it would be over. If Toldo was right, it would *all* be over.

Beast! You'll die!

"I don't care."

Who will rescue Dida? I promise to save your miserable little pet mouse, only let me have this wallowing buffalo! Dida will die if I die!

"I don't care. I'll be nothingness anyway."

YOU DON'T HONESTLY *BELIEVE* THAT—?

A second.

A heartbeat—an agony.

A timeless frozen moment, frozen dove, frozen icy ground . . .

The hand went limp. And the whiteness drifted away like windblown fog.

Jiana fell to her knees beside Toldo, stroking his forehead, talking to him, bringing him back like her Master had brought her back when her spirit had fled, so long ago. A long time later, he opened his eyes.

"Jiana," he whispered, his voice still hoarse. "O warrior bold. I knew you could defeat her."

"Well . . . I don't think I have. She's still within me—that part of me is still there, I ought to say. But I've driven it underground for a while. Toldo Mondo . . . is it really just *me?* What of Toq? He believes in her!"

"Perhaps I don't believe in Toq. I don't know what you mean by 'just' you. 'You' has an unbelievable amount of power, especially to you. The I-sense is at the core of who we are, and that's what has split within you. Because of some part of you you cannot accept, you've split your I into you and another. I'd guess . . . can you actually *feel* Jianabel inside you sometimes, like a hard, cold lump in the thinking part of your stomach?"

"Yes. It chills me. It's like I'd swallowed a living toad, and it still hopped and twitched inside my guts."

"That's something the others have all said—the other people I have known with your same sickness. Jiana, I know madness is a vile word. I don't like it, because it implies a kind of finality to your condition."

"I lived behind a madhouse when I was young," Jiana said, her voice quiet even in her own ears. "Jianabel loved it, and used to sneak in there all the time."

"You might have been trying to tell yourself something.

Or it might never have happened at all, really. You might not even have lived behind a madhouse, except in your own mind."

"The times when I was me, I was terrified of it. I was terrified of everything, actually—but that was before I was a warrior, you know."

She put her hand on Toldo's shoulders. They were surprisingly hard beneath her fingers.

"Toldo . . . I believe you. But this doesn't change things. Maybe it's part of this—sickness—you see in me. But I still can't live in obscurity! I've done a hundred things, any of which is the equal of this. Or at least the equal of what I thought this would be when I first started. But I have to finish it! The battle has to be joined. I have to try! I understand your fear: you believe in nothing; you told me so. So I guess you think everything—Toq, the World's Dream, the magick, the too-wise, the demons, the gods— you think they're all a part of my mad fancies.

"But it isn't so. I know I might not be the greatest witness now, since I've just admitted to being mad, and I can't think of any argument that doesn't depend on you trusting my perceptions of the world. Do you remember Taku-Taku? No, you remember only being frightened of something. Do you see the Tarn as just a desert, and the horses as just a good pair of mounts? What about Toq? You saw him yourself! Didn't you feel something about him— that he wasn't mortal? At least you must admit, Toldo . . . if all these dreams are madness, they're a madness shared by Alanai and Dida and the rest of the world."

"I admit many queer things have transpired. I don't claim understanding. But I've seen bizarre things everywhere I've gone. I've never seen this 'magick' that you say will carry you unseen through six thousand soldiers!"

"Toldo, being unseen is the easiest magick! I needn't be invisible. If they don't notice—if they don't observe me—I will pass unseen. I need only the power to deflect their gaze elsewhere. I might even be able to do it without magick . . . but probably not. Noon is a land of opportunity, and they're probably on their guard against somebody choosing Mullanta as his golden opportunity." She froze Toldo with a look of destiny on her face; it formed from the certainty in her stomach.

"Toldo, this must be done. Not only to save Dida, but for myself. I need to *be* someone more than I am. Maybe then I can shit Jianabel out once and for all time."

The priest's eyes fell.

"Go then," he said. "I've no hold over you."

"You have a great hold over me. I love you, my friend."

"You must do this alone."

"I know. I wouldn't allow you along anyways."

"Then go, a blinded hero! This deed of witless valor awaits naught but your old, familiar tread!"

Jiana turned and continued down the mount alone, lifting her hand in a farewell-til-we-rejoin. A tear streaked her cheek and made her itch.

She had almost reached the periphery of the satrap's lines when the battle began. At first it was only shouts, the clash and clang of spear on shield and sword on helm . . . sounds alone, for the front lines were far from Jiana. But she knew those sounds well enough to make a good estimate as to size and position.

Several hundreds were involved. This would be Alanai's entire army, and from his point of view not just a skirmish. It would have to be a full commitment, pass or crash. Jiana scrambled to the top of the hillock nearest her to see.

A sun rose from the midst of the melee—someone, prince or shaman, must be using magick of a high order. A burning ball floated high, illuminating the battlefield to twilight with a pale blue glow. In the glare, Jiana could see a wedge of men, overlapping their shields to form a wall. From their center a figure directed their battle. She could clearly see it was Alanai, despite the bluing. His armor reflected bright as only a prince's would, and his bearing and gestures shouted the House of the Eagle. Immediately, Jiana looked for the prince's beast, but Hraga si Traga was not in sight.

As Jiana watched, her mouth opened involuntarily. Alanai's men were seizing the field! She watched them cut their way through the numerically overwhelming Noondun with hardly a casualty, slicing toward a break in the mountains that could be easily defended, and could probably be sealed by a rockslide. Unless the Noondun knew hidden passes large enough for six thousand—passes not marked on Atmag's map—they would be half a day clearing the rocks away. By then, Alanai's lighter two hundred horsemen would be long fled—the bloody prince was going to win!

Worse: he would win without help from Jiana. She clamped her teeth down upon a leather-gauntleted finger to keep from screaming in frustration.

Then a miracle occurred. The warriors in the wedge, and those of the Noondun who were close, began to topple and sway, and Jiana realized the ground must be shaking with a fearsome earthquake. Man-sized mounds began to hump themselves up out of the earth, like sores or blisters. Then the mounds ruptured, and a score of squat, hideous earth-trools waded into the prince's lines.

From what she could see from a distance, striking the trools must have been like striking rock. The wedge began to crack and split. Then, in an instant, it had crumbled, and the men were abandoning fallen comrades to clump up around their Eagle, Prince Alanai. The trools pulled down the stragglers from behind and tore them asunder bare-handed. Alanai's men began to rout!

Then Alanai turned to his back, and Jiana at last saw Hraga si Traga.

The malignant figure lifted his hands in supplication, and at once a stinking, viscous rain began to fall. It drenched both armies, the trools, and Jiana as well. The rainwater was milky, if water it was, and it smelled like the hot springs in the caves near White Falls, New River.

A horrible thing happened. The trools, one and all, began to bloat and burst, and then to dissolve into twitching lumps of mud.

The stench of great magick permeated the air then, driving even the stink of the milky rain from Jiana's nostrils. The magnitude of the discharge was hard to believe. Even when she had bled the priest of Taku-Taku dry to kill his own god, she had never smelled such strong sorcery.

Without knowing how, Jiana understood what had happened. Something had been brought into the world that *did not belong*. Hraga had twisted the basic laws of the spheres with his magick.

Good Lord, Jiana thought, *but there'll be one hell of an accounting!* She looked fearfully skyward, but the Nameless Serpentine, the one true God, did not manifest his scaly self.

"You must have taken even Him by surprise," she said softly.

But by then Alanai's men had fallen back and regrouped, and the battle was stalemated again.

"A time to reap," she said.

-3-

Events required heavy thinking. Jiana sat down, and the gears in her stomach began to grind.

Magick, Magick, magick. Too much magick—too many gods and beasts and blood and hearts of black . . . The Unthinkable Questions dribbled through her mind: *Should I? Why? Is it worth the price?* . . . for Jiana feared the price of her involvement in this quest could be deeper than blood, more tangible than a hand or a head.

Something she had thought once nagged her. She pulled the leather pouch from her belt and fished around inside. Her fingers hooked a folded piece of parchment, crumbled by time and pocket treasures, smeared by tears and rain.

She stared at her notes of Alanai's conversation with Hraga si Traga for a long while, seeing nothing. Then she turned them over. On the back were two columns. 'Do It' and 'Screw It'. She read the single word under the do it column.

"Foreverness. Sounds like a Jianabel word. What did she—what did I really mean—immortal in song and tale? Or did I have a more literal meaning in mind?" The thought made her shudder. She had no trouble believing such a blasphemous ambition would come from Jianabel.

But Jianabel was *herself.* Jiana was quite certain of that now; Toldo's words rang as true as a crystal goblet. It was *Jiana* who wanted to be God.

"No, can't be sidetracked—I'm a warrior, damn it! Do it—don't dither about it!"

But the voice would not be stilled: *you* are Jianabel, it

insisted. She cannot save you. She does not exist, except as you exist. She has only the powers that you have.

Suddenly, Jiana clutched her belly as if in agony, but the moan that escaped her rose from the heart.

Voices:

Who shall we believe, Ji? A fat old atheist priest, or our own stomach? It was the Tormentor, but there were others:

"His Highness can't be blamed for war's destruction—"

"You'll be immortal—"

"'—brought here by Them What I Serve—"

"No!" Jiana shouted. "I make my own world! You taught me this, all of you!"

She clamped her gauntleted hands over her ears, but she could not block out the voices.

"Come with me. Come with Toq. Come . . ."

"—take it off!! Show us your—"

"Omission becomes commission. Intent is implied."

"SHUT UP!" Abruptly, the voices ceased, and for the moment, Jiana's turmoil subsided. She felt it still simmering, deep down in the pot, but she screwed the lid on tight and forgot it.

She rose to her feet.

"Time. Time to kill a shaman." She set off toward the lines of Mullanta, the Iron Satrap.

Calm. Calm. Let the stillness flow deep, as a bottomless lake in the middlelands, as the endless clouds piled above Bay Bay . . . It was easier and easier now for Jiana to put herself into a magickal trance. Her eyelids closed to slits, yet she began to see more than she would have at high noon in White Falls. Without conscious direction, her mind drifted upwards, as if on a tide—as if the moons had pulled her out of herself and into the limbo of the thousand and one crystal spheres.

Hide. Pass between, unremarked . . .

Jiana drew a cloak of the stars about her, and vanished into the river of spotted diamonds. Horrors lurked to the left and the right, but she stepped high and took the path between them. Once, void passed through her, and she felt as if she had stepped through the death of a world.

As she walked, she kept her mind unfocused—she looked and touched, but neither saw nor felt, and thus warded off the visions that might have driven her mad. But some shapes were safe to distinguish: the souls of several hundred mortal men.

As for the Noondun, they saw nothing when she drew near, but shivered and drew circles upon their breasts with closed fists anyway. To Jiana, their minds were turned inside to outside, and she could see as she passed that each had a premonition of the exact form of his own death.

A bright light shone ahead. It was not a light in the mundane sphere, though it might have corresponded to one. It was the fire of another soul such as hers, freed from the iron prison of the world and burning with power. The magickal stench, ever present, became overpowering.

"I have found you, shaman," she announced.

"I hid me not from your search, enemy," he answered. "Why do you hide from me?"

"Can't you see me?"

"I see nothing but the magical ocean, the stars, and yonder, the foul presence of Alanai and his dog."

"It may be the other way around, actually."

"But I cannot see *you*. I'd not hardly call that fairly done, would you?"

"Oh? And when did the Noondun learn honor?"

Jiana realized belatedly that she had stopped moving. He was trying to bind her with his words, and seek her out by her own.

"You use me the power well . . . but show yourself! Where's your own honor?"

Jiana did not answer this time. Instead, she began moving again, before the horrors could find her—before an ice-cold hand could grab her.

She strode vigorously toward the flame, but in her haste, she passed right through one of the satrap's men. His stomach became white with fear, and he flared like a beacon. He withdrew into himself, and Jiana knew she had slain his essence.

"Hah-nah!" cried the shaman.

His flame suddenly flared, as though he had been holding a curtain before him, and now had dropped it. He was much stronger than she had realized, far brighter than he had seemed! Jiana gasped, for his essence dimmed her own light to a candle flame by comparison.

He charged her, and it was due only to her fast warrior's reactions that she avoided his outstretched arms.

Jiana was afire! Flames burned into her soul, searing like sunfire. In a panic, she hardened the cloak that surrounded her into the image of a cold stone shell. Too late, she saw that she had become quite visible. The shaman's gambit had worked.

She could see him, too, now. He was at least as old as the mountains of the Sun Empire, and as fat as a market pig. His beard was blue, and it dangled from his jaw down to his knees like the moss from a hermit oak. The shaman cracked open his mouth to breathe, since his nose was smashed flat. She saw that his tongue was black and swollen, and it lolled uncontrollably in his mouth—stolen from a corpse that had been poisoned. Jiana became quite nauseated.

He struck, his hands reeling out impossibly far, hanging slack in the middle. His needle fingers pushed right through her stone shield, which had suddenly become as soft as butter, and grabbed her by the throat.

Again! she railed. *Again he bound me, with his image this time!*

Jiana tried to force her thumbs under the shaman's, but she could not budge them. Blackness flowed down from her throat to her stomach, and up to her eyes, though he had only held the grip for a moment. Life began to ebb.

Panic! Jiana forcibly calmed her mind, trying to think to remember. What was it Toq had given her—an amulet?

Break it . . . banish him from the thousand and one spheres for a thousand and one years! But she had to get to it, and the shaman had already nearly crushed the life from her body!

His long, long fingers squeezed her throat like a rubbery vise. Agony burned in her windpipe. Surely the shaman's fingers had met in the middle, with her throat in between!

Raggedly, she forced the last of her air up and through her larynx, and managed to croak a summons.

"Toq—help me—!"

Power surged at once along her right arm. As if by its own volition, it ripped open her pouch and seized the tiny snowflake. In fact, so eager was the amulet to be used, that it leaped into her hand itself.

Her fingers curled about the flake, and it flared in her palm like a miniature sun, bursting through the remains of her wall shadowing even the shaman's fires.

For an instant she paused, the word "debit" hovering on her tongue like a fly on a honeydrop, ready to burst forth any instant.

And the shaman suddenly recognized what she held. Maybe Toq had made more than one. Maybe they were a commonplace gift of the gods. In any event, he loosened his grip in shock, and skittered back a pace. He did not let her go entirely, and his arms stretched and thinned to the breaking point.

No one had ever accused Jiana of slowness of apprehension. With her free left hand, she grabbed the hilt of Wave and drew steel, as quick as a black bear drawing fish from a river. She twisted to the right and whipped the blade forward and around. It curled into a crescent and severed his arms at the wrists.

The shaman hopped backwards, screaming. Blood pumped out of his forearms, and with it spurted the fire of his soul. His disembodied hands scrambled and crawled about the ground like five-legged, headless spiders, still alive, but unable to see Jiana to attack her.

Jiana jammed the snowflake back into her pouch, and transferred Wave to her right hand. The shaman clumsily climbed to his feet, his light nearly as dim as Jiana's now.

"D-D-D-DIE!" he stuttered. He pointed his jerking stumps, and a spray of noxious fluid squirted out toward her.

Reflexively, Jiana snapped her blade directly forward, visualizing a shield wall. Wave stood rigid and unwavering.

The fluids broke against the shield and were deflected. Wherever the shaman's tainted blood touched ground, the rocky floor bubbled and sank, leaving steaming sink-holes.

That was the secret! She had tried to cloak herself, like a thief, but the warrior's way is different. A warrior triumphs by boldness and force of will; a warrior does not skulk the walls like a frightened mouse.

"I am Jiana, insect," she explained matter-of-factly. "I'm deeper than the world, harder than the gods themselves! Who the hell are you to get in my way?"

Jianabel smiled, the unshackled grin of a little child. "What need have I for that silly old snowflake? I shall banish you myself!"

The flow from the shaman's wrists tapered off to a trickle, and his fire dimmed to twilight. His eyes (she could see them now, and the rest of his face) grew wide as saucers, wide as millstones . . .

Jianabel saw Wave begin to stretch, just as the shaman's arms had done. It stretched and stretched, and she grinned wider. The tip pulled at her arm like a taut band of rubber and touched the shaman's chest.

He shrank from the touch, seeming to grow faint. He fell backwards again, his useless arms dangling at his sides. Helplessly, he screamed again as the steel burrowed into his chest like an animal, like Kiddikikitik the Termite Queen. It pushed through slowly, and Jianabel felt a joy surge through her at the shaman's anguish.

—and Jiana felt a brittle icicle of sorrow stab through her at the shaman's anguish.

Jianabel laughed. It was not the musical tinkle of an innocent child; it was short and hideous.

Jiana cried. Tears rolled from her eyes, as much for the stunted, dead thing within her as for the writhing remains on the end of her sword. "O Jianabel," she mourned, "are you going to haunt Wave, too, now? Will you join Gaish and Dilai's father and the rest of the blood-debt that drips continually from my sheath?"

The shaman was dead. Wave vibrated quietly.

A breath escaped his body. It was not the rapid, ragged sucking in and out she had heard many times before from the dying. Instead, it was a drawn-out exhalation. The mean and tiny spirit of the shaman vomited forth from his mouth and nostrils, and spilled down his chest to seep into the earth. She thought she heard a word as the last of it dribbled out, a name:

"Tiffffnnnizzzzz . . ."

But it could have been the wind through the tents and mountain passes.

Still dazed, Jiana watched herself stoop and pick from the ground two charred, spidery things, now stilled. A vague thought—that she would need proof of her deed—crossed her mind. She clutched both the shaman's hands in one of her own.

Jiana looked up, blinking away the salt tears from her eyes. She was at the center of a wide circle of terrified, staring Noondun riders. They divided their attention between her eyes, to see if she would attack, and her sword—as well they might, for the fluttering blade hanging from her hand dripped fire as a normal blade dripped blood. The fire had been drawn from the shaman's soul, and Wave quivered impatiently.

Looking right through the crowd (*am I still translated above this sphere, even yet?*) Jiana saw the beleaguered Prince Alanai's position. She fixed her eyes firmly on it, and strode forward, glancing neither right nor left. The circles and ranks of soldiers melted from her path, and none sought to tarry the whirlwind.

With every step, she felt as though she were sinking deeper and deeper into a bog.

I'm burned out, she told herself. *I'm dead. My magickal reservoir is bone-dry empty. It will be open hunting on Jiana Analena when I face Hraga.*

But there was nothing to be done; the time had come to meet again. She found she could not even bring herself to care who would emerge the victor.

"Destiny sucks," she muttered.

For an hour or more she walked through the clicking blackness, for the shaman had pitched his tent well behind the front lines. At last she reached the perimeter of the Noondun. The dead shaman's hands had grown colder and stiffer with every ring of the satrap's men that she passed. When she finally crossed the neutral ground and reached Alanai's territory, they were two lumps of frozen tar, whose coldness burned her flesh.

Alanai's men did not delay her either, though they did surround her and escort her toward the royal tent. Apparently, they had seen enough magick to be unimpressed, though Jiana reeked of sorcery.

An empty limbo loomed suddenly before her. Then she

saw it was Hraga si Traga in his robes, and her "honor guard" faded back into the night behind her.

"I expected you," he said.

"Yeah? So?"

"You fought the magus of the Iron Satrapy."

"I killed him. You couldn't have done better. You couldn't even have seriously annoyed him, because you're nothing, Hraga."

Hraga's grey and black robes seemed to absorb light. It was darker in his presence than under a clouded sky on a moonless midnight. Steeling herself, Jiana gazed directly into his face.

At first, a surge of panic threatened to overwhelm her. Then she realized, to her astonishment, that whatever his crimes and powers, Hraga si Traga was just a man. No more.

"I feel sympathy for you, oddly enough," she said. "You must be awful damned lonely, with that death act and all."

Hraga gritted his teeth, and his eyes narrowed in fury. Jiana stepped back quickly, regretting her words—regretting that she had told the truth, rather than using an artful diplomacy. But before she could even touch Wave, Hraga's seizure of hatred was smothered by his own will. He smiled like a skeenik, the double-bodied water serpent which was said to beguile its victims before consuming them, to lull them into passivity.

She and Hraga were alone. The others had all retreated, not wishing to linger long in the man's presence.

Alanai's camp was a cluster of small, one-and-two-person tents, where those not on guard duty could sleep for a few hours. The men were all haggard and drawn, as she had expected in an army under siege, repulsing attacks every day while trying to mount an offensive.

"Surely now you can break through," Jiana said. "With your own magick, you—"

"I have no magick!" Hraga exclaimed.

"What? But I saw you. I felt that crawling black rain! Whose work was that?"

Hraga spread his hands helplessly.

"I don't know whose, but surely not mine! I have no magick. It has never been necessary." He fixed her with his eyes, and she found she could not look away. "Maybe the Eagle was angry at Mullanta's blasphemy, raising such beasts from the earth. Maybe He sent the rain."

"Oh—of course," Jiana reasoned. "You don't have magick, so you—you couldn't have called it . . ." The candle of logic had a glowing corona of truth, but a warning flickered insistently in her stomach.

Hraga was looking at her left hand. The night was quite warm.

"What proofs did you bring," he asked, "of the magus's death?"

"I bring his cold hands, that called forth his blasphemies," she answered.

"And what will you do with them?"

"I'll give them to the prince. Then Alanai will know that his enemy is slain."

"Then will he reward you."

"Then will he reward me."

With the odor of hibiscus strong in her nostrils, she followed Hraga to the royal tent. The music was quite loud in her ears. Strange, that she did not remember hearing any music a moment ago, but she could not recall when it began. It seemed to have been playing for hours.

The tent was great, larger than the largest hall in the most profound palace of Bay Bay. It swayed up and down with the ocean swells.

A thousand warriors filled the hall. They feasted on boar and goose and squirrel *au brochette*. Trays heaped with shark steak and a flat, soggy fungus were danced around the hall by beautiful women and lovely boys, nude but for intricate red, blue, and yellow tattoos, tableaus of glory and ecstasy, battle and lovemaking.

The din of the warriors and the musicians lulled her, tired as she was after her battle with the—with the—

Something tugged impatiently on her left hand, on . . .

"No." She pulled the shaman's hands away from Hraga's cloying grasp.

"Pray, o Jiono of Bay Bay," he said, "come and dance with me! Didn't you say yourself how lonely I am? Come, be mine for a whirl about the floor!"

Some unsettling insect buzzed about her face, and she brushed it away with an angry, distracted gesture.

Distraction, Destruction—Hraga—the hands!

She yanked her left hand away, slapping Hraga si Traga's fingers from her trophy.

"It's this hall not a bit dingy and dusty?" she asked.

"No," he answered, "it is jeweled and gilt."

Looking about, she saw that it was. *How could I have missed such treasures?*

"Come," he whispered from inside her ear, "come dance with me."

Jiana was growing weary, so long had they spun about the dance floor. Or had they just started? She danced face to Hraga's face, hand to hand, but something was caught between her left hand and Hraga's right. Something bulky, something cold and hard.

"Something bad," Hraga thought. "Do you not let it come between us, Jiana, my love."

A bell rang. *Wake up! 'Tis the timepiece—*

"Gently . . . the music blows us like ships before the wind . . ."

—in Frothing Plaza, at the gaming-palace end—

"Softly . . . let yourself go to the music . . ."

—of the Pier—

"Silently . . . hear only the music; feel only the dance . . ."

—of Beginnings—

"Late! Tardy! Wake up, you stupid—"

—in the Floating City! Alanai! Dida! Hraga, the hands!

"—COW!"

Silence!

No music, no hall, no warriors or women or serving boys, nothing . . . no—

"No Hraga si Traga!!" Jiana cried. She stood alone in the bushes, far from the camp. The shaman's hands had vanished, along with Hraga.

The warrior turned and sprinted back to the camp, back to what was clearly Alanai's tent. Incautiously, avoiding the grasp of the prince's personal guards, she swept aside the tent flap. Then she froze, and beheld a curious scene.

"By all the angels!" exclaimed Prince Alanai, of the

House of the Eagle. "I knew you that if anyone could succeed, it would be you, Master Hraga!"

The beast bowed shallowly, from the waist, and held out a pair of charred lumps to the prince. Behind him, Jiana's mouth fell open. They were the hands of Mullanta's shaman!

"Here is the proof of the deed," Hraga continued. Though he gave no overt sign, Jiana knew that he was aware of her at the entrance.

"NO!" she bellowed.

"Sire!" pleaded the guard. "I couldn't stop her . . . she pushed her way through!"

Alanai looked up, startled. For a heartbeat, he stared at her in confusion. Then at once, memory flooded back, and he gasped.

"Jiono! Of White River! What dost thou here?" His face darkened. "Did we not say what would happen to thee should our paths cross again? Then so be it! Guards, seize the ragamuffin!"

They had already grabbed her before Alanai finished his sentence, and Jiana made no attempt to struggle.

"Wait—my lord! Allow me at least to speak!"

Alanai considered, then relented with a nod. He looked uncomfortable.

"Sire, this dog Hraga si Traga lies! It was I who slew the shaman, not he! I did it to free your august self, and your army, that you might continue your holy quest. I did it that you might see my worth, and allow me to join!"

The prince had begun to look dubious at the first words; by the time she finished, he was laughing.

"But my fine servant Hraga has proof! See, here, the very hands of the magus!"

"Aye. But it was *me* that chopped them off!"

Hraga chuckled indulgently, and shook his head. He looked at Jiana, then back at the prince, and rolled his eyes a tiny bit.

Damned effective, she thought bitterly. Such a little touch, and Alanai thinks I'm mad!

"Sire," he began with the air of a patient father, "allow me to recapitulate. I called upon the Holy Father, and cloaked myself in his darkness. Thus, Mullanta's devil saw me not. I stole upon him, guiding my steps by the brightness of his evil soul, which burned with sin."

"Lies!" cried Jiana again. "I was the one who did all that!"

"He felt the presence of his mortal enemy, one of the Eagle, and called upon me to reveal myself. I did, as befits honor . . ."

"Prince—he's cutting this tale up out of a whole hide!"

"—and the shaman attacked. Fear welled up within me at his fell powers. He stretched out his arms until they were as long as river snakes! And he burst through my armor of Holiness to strangle me, for I had dared to doubt the power of the Eagle!"

Jiana stood silent, shocked. *How did he know that!*

"But then I found my faith again, and a sphere of faith flared suddenly about me, severing the devil's arms at the wrists! My own hand I thrust forward, and the power of the Eagle did smite him where he stood. Life ebbed from the mage, and at the very end, he cried out the name of his patron as he died."

"What name was that?" whispered Alanai.

Before Hraga could answer, Jiana yelled out, "Tifniz! He called for Sleeping Tifniz, the Languid God!"

Hraga looked back sadly at Jiana.

"Yes. I'm sure you are quite familiar with the beast."

Alanai stroked his chin, thoughtfully.

"You are truly a hero of magnificent proportion, Master Hraga si Traga. I would say this deed ranks even higher in heroic vision than my slaying of Kagali, the father of grybbyns!" Hraga bowed, deeply this time. "And, I see your point about this girl. I think we had better take her with us, and help her back to the light."

Jiana turned her face toward the ground, to hide the rage that smoldered in her eyes, in the flare of her nostrils, in the curl of her lip. *I will bury you both,* she swore.

Again! Again they stole my glory, my victory!

The guards tied her well, and led her off to the prisoners' tent. Several Noon riders were being held there; Dida was not.

It was an anticlimax at dawn, when Alanai and his men

burst through the disorganized lines of the Noondun, who cringed before the horrific visions and magickal machinations of Hraga si Traga. Jiana had been wrong: it was not the divinity of the Iron Satrap that held the army to the lines, it was their sorcerer. With his death, they crumbled like a castle whose foundations had rotted.

The prince's army carried Jiana tied and blindfolded for three days of hard riding. Then the mighty company boarded a ship bound for the Oort Islands, home to the primal temple of House Eagle. Still, Jiana had not seen Dida. Her heart felt as cold and hard as the shaman's hands.

Chapter 9

Farewell to the Master

-1-

The essence of surviving interrogation and torture is to make them work, make them sweat.

Again, Hraga si Traga opened the door to Jiana's hold. This time he brought a set of razors. The stakes had been raised.

The angry creaks and groans of the ship as it sailed across the Channel of the Flying Fish covered her own screams and cries; she knew Alanai did not hear her. He would not have allowed it, if Hraga had not stopped the prince's ears with the music of a deep-draft transport crossing a very choppy sea—and perhaps with his own clouding powers.

Go ahead and scream. Let them know they're hurting me. Don't play hero, daring them to cut deeper. Make them work.

"Are you working for the Holy Vehemence?"

"I'm Jiana. I'm from Bay Bay, but I used to come from White Falls."

"How did you escape the querier?"

273

"My name is Jiana."

"Do you *like* being cut?" Hraga seemed entirely reasonable at times, in tone of voice if not in what was said. But Jiana knew it was his power, his essence. She shook her head in response to his question, but said nothing. The men cut her again—a long slice down the bottom of her forearm, just along the bone. It was agony, but she had been hurt worse before, in battles. Even so, she screamed uncontrollably, and tears rolled down her face.

Make them sweat. Eventually, they always get tired of hurting . . .

Hraga could last a good long time; he obviously had experience. Eventually, she would always answer. Anyone would have. Anything, to stop the pain.

No, I escaped the Vehemence. I'm not working for them.

I fled during a battle between them and the Serpent worshippers.

No, I don't love Dida.

After a couple of hours, she could not even tell what she said aloud and what was only in her mind. Everything had a dreamy, distant feel—everything except the pain.

Hraga finally left. He had tired at last. His men poured a putrid, magickal elixir over her, which healed the wounds without stopping the pain. Then they followed Hraga out.

Some more time passed. Jiana slept. Food appeared in the tiny hold, and the ship still rolled and groaned and sang. The Channel of the Flying Fish took only three days to cross . . . how could they have been at sea so many years? Or was it just the time sense?

The thick, oaken door was pulled open, and Hraga entered. This time he brought a brazier and coals.

He doused them with oil, lit them, and watched in silence as they burned to red and grey lumps. Then he picked up one coal with a pair of tongs and held it just above Jiana's eyes. She was tied to the deck, nude and shivering. She knew it was exactly the reaction they sought, but she could not help feeling ashamed and vulnerable. That, however, she did not show.

"With whom have you made alliance?" he asked.

Jiana looked unemotionally at him.

"My name is Jiana of Bay Bay. I once was from White Falls, New River." Hraga's face contorted with fury, and he pressed the coal against her face. Jiana screamed again.

Every session is a new beginning. Make them start breaking me anew each time. Eventually, they will tire of hurting me.

She kept track of things. It would keep her sane, she knew. She had talked extensively with former captives she had known in the various armies and commands in which she had served. Everyone did, to learn what to do if . . .

Find something for my mind. Have to use my stomach every chance I get, or become a beast without thought or will to escape. Eventually, they will get careless. Eventually, they will get tired.

She counted the meals, and divided by two. The number was unrealistic, so she tried dividing by three. This implied they had been at sea for four days, which was reasonable if a current had set them to drift off course, and the captain was backtracking to the Oort Islands. Then the meals began to come soon, then late, and she realized they knew she was counting them.

In her mind, she carefully stepped through each of the eighteen sword dances of the first set, the last three of which involved the snap thrust in which Wave should end perfectly straight and rigid. This, they could not take away from her. No matter how they hurt her, she was and would always be a warrior.

And she talked, of course.

(It was eight years before. A wide-eyed soldier boy asked his horse leader, Tij Teij, "How do you keep from talking, in case the enemy should take me hostage?"

"The truth is," said Tij Teij, "That no one ever does."

"But all the tales of the heroes—"

"—are all tales. Nothing more. You'll talk. Do not be surprised!"

Jiana, then only twenty winters, continued sharpening her broadsword, and listened.)

"Whom have you met?"

I have met with Toq. I have met with Sleeping Tifniz. I have met with death, who wears a robe of grey and black.

Don't be stupid. Don't be antagonize them. Make them sweat.

I have agreed to work with Toq.

I have allied with Tifniz.

I care nothing for either one.

I will ally with Alanai.

I did not ally with Toq.

No, I don't love Dida.

Yes, I love Dida. No, I do not love Dida. He's just a boy.

Jiana was alone. She slept. She composed a tale of her adventures thus far, and of what she anticipated for the future. She worried at her shackles.

Food arrived, and she ate. It would be the end of the fourth day.

Later, Hraga came again, and his men pulled the massive door to. He carried a handful of needles. The ship rolled only gently, and yawed not at all. Had they made harbor?

Hraga looked weary, and tired.

"What *exactly* did Toq say to you, the second time you spoke?"

Jiana closed her eyes.

"My name is Jiana. I'm from Bay Bay, but I used to be from White Falls, New River."

"DAMN YOU!" Hraga screamed, losing control for the first time. "Damn your eyes, you already TOLD me about that meeting!"

"My name is Jiana of Bay Bay."

"Just say you said it before."

"My name is Jiana."

"Say-you-said-it-before-and-I-won't-stick-you!" he yelled, all in one rushing breath. The strain was beginning to show, and Jiana knew she had beaten the mighty Hraga si Traga. Not even Hraga knew it yet. The realization made her chuckle as she looked up into his thwarted eyes.

"I said it before," she said, her voice agreeable and unconvincing.

Now HE'S stuck, she thought. *If he goes ahead and sticks me, I'll know he doesn't keep his bargains and I won't agree to anything again. If he had more time, he*

could go away now, play nice-guy, nasty-guy. But I think
we're ported, and Alanai won't be put off any longer.

Hraga turned to look at the door, then back at Jiana. He
fingered the needles, unable to decide what to do. Slowly,
he was beginning to understand that he had gotten virtually nothing out of Jiana that he could not have gotten
from other sources.

And most important: he did not break me. I know. He
knows, too, now. He has failed.

Hraga glared at her for a long time. Finally, he seemed
to decide on a course of action, but he looked resigned
rather than pleased, as if the decision had been thrust
upon him, and he had tried and failed to find a way around
it.

"Take her," he snarled. "I have a treat in store for you,
Jiono of White River. The prince has decreed that you are
to be taken to the Sisters of the Gilt Feather."

"What will they do?" Jiana asked. Weak and hoarse
though her voice was, the demanding tone of the question
deflated Hraga's bubble of dominance.

He grinned like a baboon, and stuck his face a finger's
width from hers, so his cold breath blew into her mouth
and nose. His teeth had nearly all rotted away, and the
odor of decay nearly gagged her.

"They'll heal you, Jiana, dear. They'll heal you."

The men unlocked her from the spar and dragged her
topside by the manacle chain. One of the guards gave her
a robe to wear. Then they brought her before Prince
Alanai.

"Sir Hraga has told me of some of your blasphemies,"
he said in his Severe Voice.

"I'm sure he has," Jiana answered, her breath a cat's
tongue that tore at her swollen throat. "Did you say 'Sir'
Hraga?"

"I know what I should do with you. I know the law."

"There is no law."

"But I simply cannot bring myself to kill you, or worse."

Jiana said nothing. *You've already done worse,* she
thought, *but I'd still rather be alive.*

"So I have decided, against the advice of others, to have
you committed to the care of the Sisters of the Gilt Feather.

Now—" he raised his hand to stifle objection, though Jiana had not tried to interrupt. "Now, I know you are not of my faith, and do not follow the Eagle's path. I know you worship the Inevitable Slithering One."

"*Ineffable . . . sire.*"

"But perhaps you do not know that the sisters are of mixed faith. You will find your own there. I shall allow you to keep your possessions, including your charm." For a moment, her heart leapt. Then she realized he could not know anything of the snowflake, and must be referring to her Serpent necklace.

"Any my sword?" she asked, keeping her voice neutral. Alanai shook his head.

So it's really gone, she thought. It was a strange thought: Wave had been a part of her for so long! Jiana numbered her years from the death, from the submersion of Jianabel. On that scale, Wave had been her long hand for more than half her life.

Strange that I don't feel what I thought I would. Has that part of me died as well? Did Hraga kill it? Another voice spoke in her head, an echo from another age: *the soul of a warrior is not in her sword . . . if the time comes, you must be prepared to cut off your hand to save your arm.* So many years after his death, her teacher still refused to die.

"Farewell, Jiono," said the prince, startling her from her reverie. "May your wounds be healed, and may you come in the end to accept your sex, and the glories that await you when you attain your full womanhood."

Jiana was pulled from the captain's stateroom and hustled out of Alanai's presence.

"Wait, please," she begged of the captain. It was the same man she had fought in the Dog's Tongue Tea Emporium. He looked suspicious, but held up his hand for the men to pause.

"May I be allowed to see Dida before I leave—if he is here?"

The man considered a long time, then shrugged.

"Get the kid," he ordered.

A long time passed, and finally Dida was led to her. He was not in chains, or bound; in fact, he was even armed.

Jiana looked back and forth in confusion between him and the prince's guards.

"Dida. Are you well?"

He nodded.

"Did they hurt you?"

"Jiana—" he took a deep breath. *Preparing to deliver a blow*, Jiana thought. "Jiana, the prince has invited me to join his quest."

She glared at him, trying to burn a hole through his heart with her eyes.

"You bastard," she said at last.

"What did you want me to do—wait forever for you? Follow forever the heroes behind? Damn yan green eyes and raven hair, I want to *be* a hero, not chase one!"

Every word was another nail, and Jiana could only stand silent and take them. It took all of her willpower not to actually cry.

"And what did you care me for anyways? You made *that* muckle plain!" He paused, then added quite deliberately, "I don't love you."

"I know," she said.

Dida's voice held a bitterness she had never heard from him before. It was hard and ugly. He opened his mouth, but had nothing more to say. He turned away and left her.

Jiana stood, and fought; her eyes remained dry. At last, when she was sure she was again in control, she turned to the captain and said, "Let's go. I'm ready."

They escorted her to the convent without incident. Once there, the sisters locked Jiana in a cell with three friends: a statue of the Nameless Serpentine, a padded stool, and the Book of the Scales. When the door closed, she was alone with herself, and she sobbed the sun down with no one to hear.

In the morning, a key turned in the lock, and the Lady High Sister of the Nameless Serpentine entered. A vermilion snake entwined her bodice, embroidered in green thread spun with silver. She was tall and powerful, and her face was as awesome and severe as a thunderhead. Jiana stood straight, afraid but proud.

The Lady High Sister extended her hand, fingers brought together to resemble the Crawling Dragon. Jiana closed her eyes and raised her head, allowing the fingers to touch her throat.

For the first time in many years, she felt compelled to seek forgiveness.

"Mother, I desire an intercession."

The Mother touched the snake to her own forehead, and sat down on the stool. Jiana kneeled on the floor beside her. The Lady High Sister held her hand alongside her face so she could not see Jiana.

"Mother . . . I'm lost. I have a sickness—I know that now. Prince Alanai sees it, and so does Father Toldo Mondo, a priest of the Serpentine." Again, Jiana felt the tears begin to roll down her cheeks. *Dear, dear. Twice in one day,* whispered her other self. *Maybe the prince was right, Ji! Maybe you should go home and get married, have a hundred little girls and boys, and scrub the floors and walls.*

"He knows of your sickness," said the Mother.

"No, you don't understand. I know it's evil—but I don't want to be healed."

The Sister dropped her hand and looked at Jiana in surprise. Then she caught herself, and quickly replaced her hand. She smelled of sandalwood incense.

"Maybe it is a disease," Jiana continued heatedly, "but damn you all, it's mine! If you cure me, heal me, who will I be? Not Jiana of Bay Bay! I don't want to lose *me*. Can't you understand that?"

"Why do you believe you cannot live in health, and still be Jiana?"

"Mother, forgive me, but I've seen what awaits the sane in this crazy world. I won't let you destroy me. I bow before His Scaly Majesty—but Mother, before I would banish the fires within me, I would overdose on the Sleeping Lotus."

"Good Lord!"

That's the spirit! cried the badness within her stomach.

"Mother, without it, I'm just another chubby, uneducated, lower-class woman with no more life than a beast!" Jiana leapt to her feet, startling the Lady High Sister, who toppled backwards off the stool and rose in a defensive posture.

"I know you cannot forgive me, and I know He can't accept me as I am. Oh, Mother, help me! Don't condemn me to hell, I beg you—but I have to do what I will do. Get out of my way."

"I can't let you leave, Jiana. You're sick! You don't know what you are saying, and I can't trust you to the unknown world. Don't you know what you've done?"

"Yes. I don't know what lies Hraga si Traga has told you, but I do know what I have done . . . and I have not done anything I cannot answer for, standing proudly on my feet like a warrior!" The words in the chamber echoed, and Jiana's heart began pounding.

The Mother looked at her with pain and sympathy.

"O sister, Jiana. I *know* what you're going through."

"You? How can a nun know what's inside of me?"

The Sister held her arms up, and her sleeves fell back to reveal a tattoo of a black fist. It was the sigil of the Sanchito Regular, a vicious mercenary army that had ruled much of the land south of Door by terror and valor, a quarter of a century before.

"Look at me. Look at me! I *know* you; I was once you. But I've found my peace, and I've accepted the Lord. I don't kill anymore, for it was never meant to be my world."

"Why, because you're a woman? Is that part of the hero's creed? Damn you all! Must that vision always be so divided? What killed you? What, specifically, burned you?"

"There were insults, taunts. I laughed at them, hurled them back. But the truth finally began to penetrate: what you do, what I used to do, is not a woman's world."

"They scared you away!"

The Mother looked at Jiana, and refused to take offense. Jiana felt cold, clammy sweat on her forehead. She felt feverish.

"It hurts, sister, I know. It's like pulling away armor after it's been beaten into your flesh. It tears and hurts, but when it's off, a great weight is lifted from your back. Jiana, hear me! Believe me."

Jiana shook her head.

"You sold yourself. You sold your dreams for his. Don't you see? He's consumed you, like a grybbyn. Mother, he's

a *Hero*—he swallows up freedom and shits out Truth!"
Jiana balled her fists, feeling the nails dig deep into her
palms. "Mother, I won't be swallowed. I can't—my fate is
to *slay* Truth, and neither you nor God can stop me!"

"Jiana . . . I must." The Lady High Sister's voice caught,
a sob of despair. For Jiana? For herself?

"Stand aside."

"Make me."

Without further warning, Jiana struck. The Sister caught
her blow on her open palm, and immediately dropped and
tried a sweep. Jiana was caught, but her weight was low,
and while it felt like her leg had been smashed with a
club, she did not lose her balance.

Jiana ducked even lower, and rammed her head into the
Sister's stomach. Her opponent grunted in pain, and tried
to grab Jiana around the waist, but the ebony-haired warrior's powerful legs drove them both forward, pushing the
taller woman's back against the stone wall of the cell.

Jiana drove her hand into the sister's ribs, again and
again. Something crashed against Jiana's skull; it felt like
two doubled fists. *Which will give way first?* she wondered, *my head or her ribs?* Again, the nun hit her, and
this time Jiana actually saw sunflashes behind her eyes,
and her ears rang as if she stood inside the great copper
bell in the Festive Round of Bay Bay.

But the repeated blows into the Sister's rib cage were
devastating; soon, the woman could not even draw a breath.
Jiana could neither see nor hear, and was only dimly
conscious of the damage she was inflicting.

All at once, the Mother went limp in Jiana's arms. She
threw the woman off, hurled her against the floor.

Her skull cracked against the stool with a short thud.
She rolled to her back, her eyes glazing, and lay still,
breath stopped.

Jiana's gorge rose as she saw what she had done. The
nun's lifeless eyes stared accusingly at her. Jiana staggered
to the farthest corner and heaved, again and again.

"Forgive me, Mother," she whispered, tasting the bitter
bile in her throat, but she knew the Serpent never could.
To slay the Lady High Sister of the Lord! There was no
greater crime.

My life can be measured in moments now, she thought dully.

For an eternity, Jiana stood trembling, looking at the body. She alternately clenched and loosened her fists as her heart raced at every tiny sound. At last she decided that no one had heard—*no one mortal,* she corrected herself.

"What the hell. I was getting tired of being pushed around anyways, by all of them. Even by You." Taking a deep breath and steeling herself against the blasphemy, she frisked the Lady High Sister and retrieved the key to the door. She opened it and fled, dizzy and sweating, out into the great courtyard.

-2-

Jiana sprinted across the open space, and the ground lurched beneath her feet. She lost her balance and rolled on the flagstones. She looked up wildly as clouds frothed across the darkening sky, and black rain began to pelt her.

Just then, a nun screamed. Looking back, Jiana saw her running out of the cell where the Lady High Sister's body lay. The nun was hysterical—but not so much that she failed to see Jiana scrambling back to her feet. She screamed and screamed and screamed, and it sounded like a great, burly pig squealing in terror to Jiana's ears. From everywhere, sisters began boiling out of their cells like angry ants from a kicked anthill.

Jiana ran again toward the wall, but another convulsion of the earth knocked her down. Again she rose, and again the world itself threw her.

"TOOQA, FORGIVE ME!" she pleaded, but still she jumped up and ran to the wall, already guessing His answer. Then she realized, on top of everything else, that she had just spoken His name aloud. The blasphemy only compounded her felony.

The wall was ten feet high, and to the nuns it surely seemed unscalable. But to Jiana it was a ladder to freedom and, perhaps, to life. She vaulted high, clawed madly, and caught the top. By kicking her feet sideways, she managed to swing high enough to hook her left elbow over. Then she could do the same with her right.

The world kicked her again, and this time the walls shook and crumbled. Great cracks opened in the courtyard.

Armed men began to pour into the garden, shouting in confusion. The nuns had finally roused the temple guard. Jiana shrugged her body up and over, and jumped clear to the other side.

A horrific roar sounded behind her. Despite her desperate flight, she could not help turning to watch. The great temple of Oort Aka Tajaka seemed to draw into itself, as if gathering strength. Then it expanded, a child's ball inflating, and collapsed back on itself. It left nothing but a tall pile of crumbled masonry, a chaos of stone, concrete, timber, and glass. The screams of the dead and wounded colored the air red. Jiana turned away and fled toward the bay.

The Nameless Serpentine was awake.

Thunder sounded from beneath her feet, and mountains cast themselves into her path. The geography of the Oort Islands twisted as the World Serpent coiled and thrashed under the Earth. It was here, Jiana had always been told, that He lived. Now He sought her in his fury.

Desecrated! Offended! Spit upon! Blasphemed!

Damn, damn, damn—if I'd tried, I couldn't have thought of a better way to kick Him!

Jiana—

"Please, Lord, I didn't mean—"

"STOP GROVELING AND LISTEN, STUPID!" Jianabel screamed through Jiana's mouth, verbally slapping her. "Don't you remember who makes the world, silly?"

Don't give me that line again! I know what you are— you're me, a part that grew in rather than up. No one makes the world.

"Don't we all make our own worlds? Listen, Ji . . . listen to me! All you have to do is make the world without that Slimy Serpent!"

Jiana ignored the little girl, and ran through the town of Bay Tajaka, joining the panicked herd of villagers fleeing the eruption of their island. The mass of their evacuation propelled her toward the bay and the water, as the two thousand four hundred citizens ran to their tiny fishing boats to flee the Pit of the Serpent and the Eyrie of the Eagle.

Jiana forced her way sideways, fighting and pushing through the mob. If she had still owned Wave, she would have severed arms and heads to smash through.

She punched a young netter in the jaw, knocking out a tooth, and after she tripped across his collapsing body, she saw the way before her clear! The shaking and lurching was constant now, and Jiana staggered across the beach as if she had swallowed a half dozen pots of strongtea. Ahead of her was a ship.

The ship was small—half the size of the one that had carried her and Alanai and poor Dida to the Oort Islands—but it was seaworthy. She would not drown like all of the fishers, who were even now putting out to sea in their rickety harbor skiffs, not yet aware that they were already dead. Jiana saw what the Nameless Serpentine did to solid land. Surely the seas were about to shake with typhoons and tidal waves!

The mud turned black under the tarry rain, and when the clouds blockaded out the last of the sky, the world was shrouded in sudden night. Only the running lights of the ship burned ahead, beacons that promised the slimmest chance of survival, but a chance all the same. It took Jiana three hundred agonized, slip-skewed strides to reach her.

She was astonished to see the boarding ramp still out. A frantic sailor stood at the end, and behind him a huge figure loomed.

"JIANA!" boomed the giant.

"Toldo!" Jiana vaulted up the ramp in two hops, and the sailor screamed at Toldo.

"NOW, you bastard?"

"Make it happen, Cap'n," Toldo answered cheerfully. The captain immediately ordered up-anchor, and cut the mooring lines himself. As he scurried out of sight to continue the launch, Jiana saw Frater Toldo Mondo replace a huge dagger in his rope belt.

"Hellmoons! Would you have used that thing?"

"Jiana—there was no way I would have let them leave without you. No matter what it took."

"But how the fuck did you know I'd come here?"

He gestured at the port. Other than their ship, drifting lazily away from the pier amidst the chaos and conflagration, the harbor was empty.

She looked back at Toldo and said, "What's that supposed to mean?"

"It isn't important," he said. "Later."

Jiana laid her hand on Toldo's arm; he felt warm.

"Father . . ."

"I haven't been called that in many years, o warrior accursed. I miss it."

"Toldo, you're the left hand of Hraga. You're his looking-glass twin—full where he's empty and warm when he's cold."

"You say strange things sometimes, Jiana. Who *is* this Hraga?"

"Alanai's dog. Or master, depending who asks."

"No . . . who is he to *you*, Jiana?"

"He's my—father." Toldo's eyes widened, and Jiana quickly amended. "Not physically, of course! But Hraga in my waking world is the same as my father in my dreams . . . and you know what Jianabel did—what *I* did to my father." She lowered her voice. "He seeks revenge."

"Revenge? How could he either know or care what happens in your dreams?"

A sudden thunderclap sounded above Jiana, and the water began to heave as badly as had the ground. At the same moment, the sails unshipped and caught the gale, sending the ship racing out of the circular bay and into the open seas, heaving and bucking like an unbroken sea colt dancing on the waves.

Jiana threw herself flat on the deck, and entwined her arms in the ratlines. Toldo began to slide as the ship stood up on her stern, but he grabbed a shroudline and clung as if his life depended upon it.

The salt waves washed violently over the deck, soaking Jiana and chilling her to the bone.

BOOM! DOOM! The sound beat her ears like a club, and she strained to see through the darkness. Then a hellish light flared for a long breath, in the direction of the island. The black became white, and she saw the moun-

tains torn asunder by sudden chasms, which spewed forth
lava to bury all traces of man. And then, as she watched,
the entire Oort Island slid slowly, majestically beneath the
ocean.

The waves crashed back to cover it, and it was gone.
The cataclysm left only a layer of foam and floating detritus
to mourn the passing of the great temple. As Bay Din had
been destroyed by fire, so Oort Aka Tajaka had been
swallowed whole by the sea.

The beginning and the end destroyed, she thought, *and
all because of a hero,* but Jiana was not sure if she meant
the mad prince, or she herself, who followed him.

Still, it seemed an excessive punishment for a single
murder!

The ship leaped a dozen feet into the air and crashed
back down again, as the waves from the sinking island
battered her. Jiana was almost washed overboard, but the
ropes were strong, designed to hold the weight of five or
ten men climbing them to the sails, and her arms and
hands were locked together around them. At times, she
was completely submerged, but each time, after an eternity, the waves would recede. The ship miraculously stayed
afloat.

The bow twisted left and right in the water, and once
even felt like it spun entirely about a circle. For the first
time in her life, Jiana felt violently seasick. Everywhere,
sailors staggered about the decks, trying to furl the sails
now that they had escaped the island, trying to lash up the
wheel, trying to lash themselves to anything solid. Men
screamed and threatened, and the captain could be heard
even over the booming of the waves against the hull.

Then suddenly, every voice was stilled. It was such a
startling effect that Jiana crawled up the ratlines to a
standing position to see what had happened.

A great mountain of water humped up, and a monstrous
shape emerged. It was the Nameless Serpentine Himself.

Jiana gasped. His body was as thick as the ship was
long. Each of the prismatic scales that covered His body
was as wide as a sail, and they all sparkled brilliantly with
a thousand rainbows apiece.

It was Tooqa's head that drew her stunned stare. Uncounted tiny eyes, each the size of a man's heart, speckled His head all about. Every one was yellow and lazy-lidded, a repellently reptilian orb . . . and yet Jiana experienced the queerest certainty that her God could see absolutely nothing.

Some of the eyes rolled up under their lids, uncontrolled and unattended. The rest wandered aimlessly, without a focus.

"The bastard's blind!" she exclaimed.

She heard Toldo's voice behind her.

"That would explain much . . ."

Tooqa turned at the noise of her shout.

"*SSSSSSHHHHHIANA!*" He hissed, His enormous serpent's tongue extending into the air to taste about for her scent. "*MURDERESSSSSS! SSSSSSHHHHHIANA MURDERESSSSSS!*"

"Oh perfect. I'm going to die. I'm having *so* much fun," Jiana whimpered to the priest.

"O wise one," yelled Toldo into her ear from behind, "I take it all back—everything I said about magick. Now make it go away!"

Still questing right and left for Jiana, the great head smashed itself into the ship, which instantly cracked and burst into shards. Jiana found herself ignominiously plopped into the freezing ocean, paddling and splashing and grabbing at every piece of wood flotsam that happened by. All about her in the oil-colored water she saw men doing the same, but she could not see Toldo.

Think, damn you! she urged herself. *Do something—be a bloody hero!*

Tooqa submerged again, sending a hillock of seawater out in an expanding circle to hurl the unlucky swimmers high into the air, and then drop them two stories back into the ocean. Everywhere, sailors and former passengers were in hysterics—screaming, praying, begging forgiveness for their sins.

Jiana clung to a piece of wood that she realized was a wooden leg, torn from its owner. Something that seemed to dwarf the world brushed against her feet, and she kicked it away in a panic.

"Toq, help me!" she bellowed. "Toq, do something!"

Tooqa, the only true God, the Nameless Serpentine, rose from the face of the deep directly in front of the warrior. He opened His mouth wider than all of the canyons in the White Petal Mountains. Jiana saw row upon row of triangular teeth, like a shark, except that each one was longer than she was tall.

"NO!" she screamed. "GO AWAY! GO AWAY!" And then she became aware that she had something in her hand.

It was a small, pointed, cold thing. She did not remember from where she had grabbed it.

Save us, Jiana, pleaded the Tormentor within her. *Jiana— help me!* Jianabel did not sound omnipotent; she sounded like a frightened little girl.

Jiana held Toq's snowflake aloft. "DEBIT!" she cried, in a sharp, clear voice, and crumbled it in her hand.

She heard a soft *foomp!* and found herself at the lip of an enormous crater of water. The waves crashed in upon the hollow, and Jiana tumbled in the foam, clutching the wooden leg to her breast as frantically as if it were her child.

She could not tell for certain, but it seemed a word hung upon the air, where He had been—a part of a word: "tttiffl—"

The winds ceased. The torrent of evil, black rain stopped, and the waters calmed. Jiana found herself adrift in a silent sea, gazing up at an azure sky and a baking sun.

It took an hour for her to paddle around and find enough wreckage to lash together into a makeshift raft, using the leather thongs from her leggings. She gathered as much of the debris from the ship as she could snare: rope and a barrel, a five foot swath of sail, and some extra wood in case the raft suffered a calamity.

When at last she had dragged together as much as seemed prudent, she balanced carefully on her feet, cupped her hands, and began to whoop and holler for Toldo Mondo.

She spied a figure in the distance, clinging to an armload of mast shards. She used a plank she had saved out for a paddle, and after several minutes of exertion, she rowed close enough to see that it was not Toldo. She paddled up to him anyway.

"Good morning, sir," she said. "Have you by chance seen a large, round man wearing the robes of a priest?"

The man did not answer, but grabbed instead for Jiana's raft. She frowned, thinking of her meager food resources, and when he began to climb aboard, she kicked him smartly in the temple. He sank back into the ocean, gagging as he breathed in some sea water.

"I suppose that means you won't tell me. Pity." She pushed him farther away with her oar.

"God's sake for!" the man gasped, coughing violently.

"It won't do any good. God's gone, vanished from the thousand and one spheres for a thousand and one years."

"Pray yer, let me climb yan raft aboard!"

"Are you a souther?" she asked in surprise. His accent seemed the same as Dida's father.

He sank beneath the waves, struggled up again, then seemed to give in to despair. He sank again, and nothing rose in his place but a few bubbles.

"Couldn't you even have waited for the third time?" Jiana called after him. Then she shrugged. "Surviving is work, friend. Only those who desperately *want* to survive are an asset."

She stood up carefully again, and continued scanning for Toldo.

Jiana paddled carefully through what she judged to be the center of the wreckage, where the biggest sections of the ship were still afloat. She steered well away from the other survivors, as soon as she had gotten close enough to verify that none of them was her friend. She ignored their cries and pleadings.

"I've heard far too many in my life, crying for help or a quick end," she told some of the men—those who did not beg her. "After a dozen wars and a hundred fields of honor, I no longer care. But I do wish I could help you without endangering myself."

One man did not accept this as an answer. When Jiana turned to row away, he cast off from his barrel and swam slowly but steadily toward her raft. She heard him when he was halfway across, and turned to watch him closely.

If he makes it, she thought, *I'll help him aboard. This one might have something to contribute.*

"Gracious lady," he gasped when he had finally crossed the choppy waters and latched hold of her raft, "may I permitted be to board?"

"Why should I allow you, when I left those others to die?"

"I have strength! Great terrors have I survived in life—always in the end I have come through! Please . . . I am boarding, easy, easy . . ." He began to draw himself out of the water, but lowered himself quickly again as Jiana raised high her oar.

"Why do you think I paddled right past all the rest?"

The man gestured vaguely with one hand.

"How do I know?" Food for one rather than two lasts longer! None does it matter, right is yours—I am boarding."

Something in his eyes . . .

"A real survivor, hm? And food for one lasts longer than for two. Sorry, friend, I don't think I trust your attitude." She swung the wooden oar with the suddenness of an axe, stunning the man. He grunted in pain, and then sank without a murmur beneath the surface.

Jiana realized she was panting with retroactive panic.

"He would have killed me!" she insisted defensively. "I saw it, right at the end."

Of course he would have, Jiana, darling. No need to fuss and carry on so for a nasty man who would have taken control!

She took a deep breath and paddled on. The second person she rowed near in her expanding spiral was Toldo Mondo. It took a monumental effort, but he managed to drag himself aboard the raft, with Jiana's help.

"The currents are with us, priest," she announced after he had dried himself off in the sun. "The sea is so cold because an icy current flows south from the frozen northlands, and skirts the coast. It flows into Diraul Harbor in Door, bringing every manner of detritus and debris to wash up along the beach there. We have only to sit and wait. And fish."

"Have you been there, to Door? Dida said you had not."

"Well . . . not been, exactly. I've stood amidships, soothing my frightened horse, as Queotzahan Tantatl set fire to great bowls filled with blasting powder and plugged with lead balls."

"Powder and balls? What are they for?"

"They're for raining lead boulders upon the towns along the coast . . . as a hypothetical case, along the coast of Door. The towns along Diraul Harbor, to take our example further."

Toldo scratched his head.

"Why did you have a horse on a boat?"

"Well, raining death and destruction on a town is rarely profitable, unless one then enters said town and plunders it. To that end, a company of horses on a ship can be quite effective."

"Ah . . . so you *have* been to Door, on a horse on a boat, to plunder the coast!"

"Hm. In theory. Really, our blasting bowl burst after three shots. Then the Dooran navy came out and chased us all the way back to Toztoq."

Late in the day, after much internal debate, Jiana finally said aloud, "I thank you, Toq. I owe you." She did not like the thought, but it would have been dishonorable to ignore the debt.

Many days passed on the raft, for the current did not carry them straight, the way the sailing vessel had come, but at a southerly angle. All of Jiana's trail gear had been stowed securely in her pouch and on belts, and with the exception of one of her sword gloves, it had all survived the storm and the shipwreck.

Since the water was so cold, the sea life was profuse. She wasted half of the last of her bread from the Caela Valley trying to catch fish with a hook before she thought of unbraiding the rope and typing it into a gill net to trail behind the raft.

Drinking water was a problem, until Jiana remembered what one of her first sergeants had said about boiling sea water. Toldo had a crystal that focused the sun's rays, and Jiana was able to get some of the wood that she had rescued to catch fire. They boiled the sea water in her empty canteen, with a tube made of a rolled piece of the sail to draw off the steam and her oilcloth wine sack floating in the ocean to condense it into fresh water.

Jiana and Toldo ate baked perch and razorfish, and debated philosophy and aesthetics, while the current drifted them ever closer to Door and the end of their quest.

"Toldo," she said on the second day, "how did you come to be in Bay Tajaka at that precise moment?"

"Because I followed you. I saw the battle between Alanai's men and the Iron Satrap—and I saw certain things I cannot now explain, save to say I'm sorry about what I said about magick. You were right. I have as much to learn about the world as do you."

"I wish you wouldn't give in like that. I need someone to argue with!"

"Then, the next day, I saw the prince's army carve its way through the Noondun, and I knew you had succeeded in killing Mullanta."

"I killed his shaman. Mullanta himself still lives, I suppose."

"Whatever. I confess I was taken aback when you left without waiting for me. I became worried that your plans for the prince had not gone well, so I followed you. When you reached the coast and took ship from Sig River Ford, the dockwallopers did not mind telling me where you sailed. So I bought passage to the Oort, and haunted the harbor waiting for you."

"But he had imprisoned me in a convent! I might not have escaped."

"I trusted in your potential to either escape, or to stir up so much trouble they threw you out. Either way, I had planned to slug you and cart you back to the mainland, if that was what it took. Jiana . . . they told me Dida had joined with the prince."

Jiana fell silent.

The days were an eternity of blue heat, and the nights were too-short respites in black, with brilliant diamonds above their heads. Jiana told her comrade all of the stories of the stars that she knew, about the Hunter and the Turtle, Dissipi the sun-bringer, and all eight tales of the Ti-Ji Tul's war with the Trool Kingdoms. She made up stories for those constellations which she thought had none.

On the fourth night, a howling storm lashed out at them, and Jiana and Toldo clung miserably to each other, shaking and terrified that the raft would break up, drowning them in the heaving sea. Jiana was certain the storm was a punishment for all of her sins: for killing God and the shipwrecked man, and for making up wicked lies about the heavens and the constellations. Toldo spent the entire monsoon apologizing over and over to her, and asking her every few moments if she was *sure* she did not know any hurricane magick.

They had tied themselves to the raft, and sometime in the middle of the night, during the worst of the storm, Jiana drifted off to sleep, exhausted.

When she woke the next morning, the clouds had gone and the sun was high. She untied herself from the raft and the priest, and stood up to look east, shading her eyes from the sun. She stared, and then bent down and splashed cold, salty ocean in her face.

When she looked again, it was still there. The coast of Door rose in the distance, like a tightly twisted scarf of dark blue silk.

-3-

Jiana stood on the dock of Tuk Diraul, wrapped in a borrowed cloak and staring blindly at the swarming city in the hills above her. Toldo Mondo hopped about, slapping himself to keep warm. The morning air was still nippy, and they both were wet.

Jiana itched in a dozen places from the patina of salt that coated her, but unlike Toldo, she had schooled herself to ignore such mundane distractions. He scratched energetically; Jiana stood still. She was aware that it fostered an attitude of disdain and aloofness, but at the moment, she simply did not care.

"How much money do you have, my friend?" she asked.

"After hiring a boat, and then bribing the cowardly captain to stay her in Tajaka Harbor until you arrived?"

"I shouldn't have asked." She opened her cloak, allowing the sun, which had wheezed out from behind the morning clouds, to warm her slightly. "Instead answer, how are we to raise enough money for horses and food?"

Toldo fingered his beard. It had grown just about long enough to stroke since she had met him.

"For that matter," she continued, in a bitchy mood, "which way should we go to find him?"

"Alanai?"

"Di— yes. Alanai."

"Jiana, have you ever spent time and money listening to the stirring adventures and rousing romances of a story teller?"

She scowled back at the priest for a moment, then abruptly caught his meaning.

"All right. Which one of us is going to tell stories?"

"Well, there are points to recommend us both. I would drag it out longer, giving the brutes a more polished tale of the banishing of the god and the submerging of the island. But you could give it the air of verisimilitude, being both a warrior and a wielder of magick . . . much as I hate to admit it."

"And I guess you'll be astonished when I admit that I *do* know what verisimilitude means."

"Reason would side with me being the story spinner," Toldo continued, "but there is another factor. A beautiful woman is more likely to get big tips from these men than a fat priest."

"Beautiful woman! Toldo, let's face reality here: a short, fat, black-haired, scruffy bear-bitch is hardly anyone's ideal of beauty, even in barbarous Door!"

Toldo bent over and strained to touch his knee, grunting with the effort. Then he hoisted himself upright again.

"Jiana, I don't know why you have this image of yourself. It's probably related to your generally dark outlook on the entire world, and to your delusion of possession, of a rotting interior, to which you attribute every black thought and deed."

He pushed his grinning face close to hers, and whispered in his most seductive voice. "But have you stood before a looking-plate recently? Have you seen yourself in a still pond? Where is this hideous monster Jiana lurking? I see only a hard, proud, better-than-average-looking warrior woman."

For a moment, Jiana was speechless. Then she put her

hand to her belly, and tried to grab a handful of excess weight, to prove her point. Her fingers slipped against hard muscle, unable to seize more than a quarter of a finger joint of fat. She felt her hips. Here, there was somewhat more padding, but not as much as she had imagined. Puzzling over how such a thing could have come about, she touched what other parts of her body that decency would allow in public. Everywhere else, her skin slid across muscle and bone.

"Make a muscle," Toldo exhorted. Jiana flexed her bicep, and Toldo clamped his huge hand as far around it as he could stretch. Nearly half of the circumference was bare. "Does *that* look like fat to you?"

Jiana looked with wonderment at her body, truly seeing it for the first time.

"Toldo—it *must* have all happened in the months I've been on this quest . . ."

"Claptrap. You've changed hardly at all since I've known you, and for the Serpent's sake, it's only been three weeks!"

"Three weeks!" Jiana exclaimed, incredulous.

"Twenty days ago we met outside the walls of Bay Din," Toldo insisted. "You've had no time to lose any serious weight . . . Jiana, this is *you*. You're no more fat that I am stupid. And as for short—certainly, compared to your usual companions, husky mercenary soldiers or royal guardsmen. But when was the last time another *woman* towered over you?"

Where did I get this idea that I was a fat, black bear? How did—a sudden suspicion pierced her stomach. Jianabel was strangely silent.

That was a low thrust, she thought bitterly. *To strike at my own image of myself!*

But to whom was she talking? Jiana fretfully remembered that *the other* was only herself apart.

Jiana became aware of how Toldo was looking at her.

"God's scales!" she marveled, incredulous. "You actually find me attractive, don't you?" *I thought only another soldier . . . Dida saw me only as a hero, and Tawn would have slept with anyone, male or female, save only they bought his teapots.*

"But why shouldn't you?"

"Jiana, if you were only to change your attitude toward people, and maybe to comb that rat's nest on your head every week or so, you surely could seduce any number of eager young men! Or women."

"Men, please."

"Just trying not to be prejudiced. So how about it? Are you ready to stop playing 'shambling bear', and take up 'beautiful war goddess' instead, for a little bit? For the rest of your life?"

Jiana took a deep breath, trying to center on her feelings about herself. So much kept changing! At last she found her resolve. She smiled, and her face felt as if it was cracking at the unfamiliar motion.

"The damned prince can wait a few hours—he and his pedigreed standards!" She spit on her leather gloves, and rubbed some of the dirt out of them. "And just as soon as we can sing up a few serpents, I'm going to see what I can look like if I really try."

"To that end," Toldo rumbled, digging into his belt pouch, "I *did* manage to save a few triplets, hiring a somewhat *leaky* boat . . ."

He handed her eight scalloped coins, putting the tiny things in the palm of her newly shined gauntlets. It was Dooran money from Kruz tik Tingle, the first that Jiana had ever seen. Such diminutive coins were rare and treasured in the Water Kingdom, but, presumably, common here in Door. She studied them with interest.

"Strange," she whispered, more to herself than to Toldo, "so small. Like shrunken seashells! Yet a handful can transmute a bear into a beauty. A trunkful up north could ransom a king, or finance a war. Here, it might possibly buy a small manor.

"Hell, I suppose reality's what we make it."

"Like magick," her friend declared.

She looked up, a sardonic smile from the old Jiana on her lips.

"Like life! Or love. Or anything else. The whole bloody world is just made up moment to moment, isn't it? A consentual canvas.

"So I'll consent to a bath and a hair-sculpting, and meet

you back at the Cold Waves of Ocean Lotus-house by noon, to tell tales for triplets."

"Ah . . ." Toldo looked confused. "Jiana, I've never had either opportunity or inclination to learn Dooran."

"You? The great white missionary?"

"There is nothing of interest here! Now, where is this Ocean Waves Lotus-house?"

"If it was a grybbyn," she answered, "it would bite you in the ass."

Toldo looked behind him.

"In *there?*" he asked, distaste showing on his face.

"That is what they look like. Noon, Priest." She held aloft the triplets in her fist, and strode off to find a barber and a tailor.

Two hours passed. Jiana hesitated at the door to the Cold Waves of Ocean, running her fingers over the sharp, spidery Dooran letters. The sun was as nearly overhead as it would get that day.

Well . . . is he going to like it? Or did I get silly?

"Come on, girl," she urged herself, "go on in! Snakes, he'll either like it or he won't." She turned once toward the door, then whirled halfway about to make a run for it. By sheer will she forced herself to brush aside the heavy tapestry and walk nonchalantly through.

She scanned the dark, cavernous interior, lit by thirty sputtering lamps and the flames from a dozen hookahs. She marked Toldo, and picked her way over the sprawled bodies to his table. The priest looked glazed and woozy from the lotus-vapors, but he managed to sober up with a swallow of ale. He looked her down and up, and smiled with addled approval at her clothes.

Jiana grinned back. The tailor had wanted far too much for the silk blouse, leather vest, and ruffled, ruby-colored collar and cuffs, all of which made her look more like a prince of the Eagle than an itinerant heroine, but his bargaining position had been severely weakened when she picked him up by crotch and collar, flipped him over onto his sewing table, and threatened to cut off his pride and joy and sew it to the end of his nose. Similarly, the cobbler had become considerably more generous when she had mentioned the possibility of nailing shoe leather to his forehead.

But she *had* allowed the barber to talk her into a more drastic alteration than she had originally planned.

"Toldo . . . I don't know how you're going to like the rest of where your money went. May as well get it over with." She reached up, and removed her new beaverskin Tastas hat.

Toldo's brows raised alarmingly, and for a moment he drew back.

Gone were the long, shaggy, raven locks. In fact, gone was nearly all of her hair. She had allowed the barber to shave her head bald, except for two narrow bands of midnight that flowed from the center of her forehead, straight back to join at the back of her head, and then to fall to a point midway between her shoulder blades. The strips were no more than a knuckle's width at their widest.

When the barber had wet her hair, and held it back against her head, Jiana had discovered that she had a very symmetrical face, with her eyes dead center between her chin and the top of her head. The barber had sworn it would look good, so Jiana told her to go ahead and shave it all off. She had left Jiana the stripes because she had thought the color of her hair was too beautiful to be lost.

And, after only a few moments of shock, Toldo leaned forward critically.

"Hm. On you, it looks okay. Good, even! Well . . . feel any different?"

Jiana nodded.

"I feel clean. I never felt this way before—not living with my mother the madam, or with Jianabel the monster, or with the grunts and jarheads in anybody's army. I'm *better* than those swine—I *should* look different."

"Apparently they think so, too," Toldo said, gesturing behind her. She turned around. Eight hopeful young men had gathered behind her. Three were rather well-dressed and perfumed.

Jiana smiled beguilingly.

"Have any of you gentlemen yet heard the true story of what happened to the Oort Islands last week, and what *really* became of the Nameless Serpentine?"

They all listened quietly, enraptured, as Jiana spun an imaginative version of the tale, as best as she could remember or make up.

When she finished, she waited politely, neither entreating nor demanding. Each of the young goodmen gave some, and the three of the upper class felt obliged to compete to see which could give the largest gratuity. She thanked them austerely and departed, leaving a trail of haunted looks and longing glances behind her.

Three more houses were equally profitable. She played to no bawdy tearooms. Each venue, at Toldo's suggestion, was somewhat expensive and very exclusive. And at each, she found a member willing to escort her inside.

She discovered an important lesson: the wealthy had the same tastes as the mean, but they were willing to pay more to satisfy them.

"Princes, beggars, priests, and thieves," Toldo enunciated, "they all laugh at foreigners, desire their neighbor's wife, and worship the great warriors. The Church learned that lesson an age and a half ago."

"Here," Jiana said. She gave him his eight triplets back. "Do we have enough for horses and food?"

"We shall. And for another map."

By nightfall, she and Toldo were drinking fast-ale in a private club, to which the priest had actually finagled a legitimate invitation.

"See?" he said, smugly draining half his bowl with a single swallow. "The golden boys all wish they were heroes."

"I had a peculiar thought, Toldo. So, I think, does Toq That Predates Everyone."

"So does Dida, and Alanai . . ."

"And Jiana of Wish Wish."

"Well, I don't."

"No? I don't notice you setting up shop here as a preacher."

"I obviously want to be a hero's companion. That's the coward's way of justifying herophobia."

"It's settled then. *Everyone* wants to be a hero, deep down. So what is this thing, a hero?"

"You don't know? Why ask me?"

"As an unbiased, impartial observer. Look, I know what

a hero isn't: he isn't an eagle flying high over the world, unable to see the grass and the trees and the groundstalkers below."

"Why not?"

"He's not a mouse, like Dida, full of naivete and a sucker for tales of valor and derring-do."

"He could be, could he not?"

"And he isn't like you, boy-o—so wise he sees equal merit in all points of view."

"So? Is he then so turned within himself that all the world disappears but he?"

"Well, damn it, at least he wouldn't muddy it up for the rest of us then!"

"Would he not? What if this quality itself, the inability to see anyone else as a real person, caused great hurt and confusion to someone . . . say, to a young boy who needs her, or loves her? Hypothetically speaking, of course."

Jiana stared down at the table, idly carving a serpentwine into the oak. She had no answer, and it annoyed her.

To escape Toldo's probing, she turned her attention to the other conversations in the club, trying to eavesdrop some word of where in Door the prince had lighted.

"— that the Prime Secretary intended to drive the—"

"—war is stepping lightly in ballroom swirls, while—"

"—inhospitable barbers are—"

"—able to requisition eighty wagons for wartime caravan—"

"—dancing. But does Alanai know?" Jiana craned her neck about violently, causing a stab of pain in her vertebrae, trying to find that last morsel of conversation again. Toldo started to say something else, but she waved him down, blocking out every noise in the club but that one, petulant, rich-little-kid whine that had mentioned the prince's name. She finally pieced it out again. It spoke, not the sing-sing of Door, but the cultured and chopped tongue of the Water Kingdom.

"I say, have you seen the rabble he's got with him? Positively plebeian! You'd think a knight or two, or a peer—not five hundred unshaven peasants!"

Five hundred? Jiana frowned in annoyance. The prince's ability to draw strength from the gullible disgusted her.

Then she remembered callow, naive Dida, and she burned inwardly.

"Rather . . . it's a pity to we of the Eagle that the chap didn't have an older brother."

"Do you think *any* of the Arturahoros family could rule? Let's be perfectly frank, old man. Who are the Arturahoros? Common merchants, that's who! Sons of a rich cobbler, who bought their way into the peerage a mere three centuries ago!"

"As anyone could see by the way he conducts the Naug Diraul campaign, brother. No honor, no gallantry . . . just throwing wave upon wave of howling sergeants at the gates of the city, battering them down with a ram made of human flesh. You know, old chap, peasants and freemen are people, too!"

"Well, let's not go too far."

Naug Diraul! Jiana wondered. *The City of Sickness— what's he doing there? And who would defend such a place, from Alanai or anyone? Who would care?*

Naug Diraul was a dead city. In ages past, a strange sickness had fallen upon the metropolis. It touched everyone alike: great or mean, strong or sickly, priest or murderer. Some accounts said the epidemic claimed as many as one out of every three citizens of the great city-state; no one knew for sure. In the early stages, when some still thought it could be weathered, Naug Diraul had shut fast her gates.

Later, when the horrible truth began to make its way about the land, the gates were forced by a company of missionaries from the Church of the Burning Embers (long before the sect of the Holy Vehemence had taken over the high offices of the Church). What they found, none shall ever know, for after seeing what lay behind the silent walls, they voluntarily joined in the quarantine and were never heard from again.

Three years passed, and a few people managed to escape. Each told a wild tale. Most were judged mad by the courts and tribunals of neighboring states, and they freely admitted it.

Madness, they said, had taken root in Naug Diraul. The lunacy was not induced by the disease—not directly. It was the madness of panic, of helplessness, of not knowing who would be the next to be struck down, or why . . . wife? father? daughter?

At some point, the citizenry crossed *en masse* over the line between the outlandish and the insane. Mad cures were tried—anything, shouted out by anyone in a crowd. The streets became a cacophony, from thousands pleading, praying, preaching, and prophecying; from a crowd that dashed madly from burning one house to urinating upon another; from an animalistic mob that gutted the Church and raped the nuns; from a pious flock that drank poison on the steps of the menstruating women's quarters; from twelve brothers who sacrificed children for a month-long nightmare, throwing them down the washerwomen's well.

Night became day, lit by hundreds of lanterns and torches as men and women ran amuck in the town streets, trying to slay an enemy they could neither see nor understand.

Finally, so the legend went, like an ancient water wheel set spinning too fast in a flood-swollen river, the city just flew apart. The beginning of the end was when nearly a fifth of the population threw themselves onto the huge bonfire that was incinerating the bodies for that week. It was a spontaneous mania, and soon thirty people a day were committing suicide by igniting themselves.

The rest of the population began to see witches under every hat, and many of these were summarily *thrown* upon the fire. An orgy of bloodletting ensued, until at last, some nameless cult, armed with oil and torches, fired the walls of Naug Diraul. Those of her population who still possessed a glimmer of sanity fled into the night, and the rest perished with the city.

That was the story of the city of Sickness, as Jiana had learned it in her grandmother's lap. The expression "as dead as the Naug" existed in every language Jiana had ever learned.

But now these Eagles were casually discussing the Naug as if it had sprung back to life again. Alanai had even laid it siege!

There was only one plausible explanation for both the city's rebirth, and the prince's siege.

"Toldo," Jiana whispered, "we have found what we sought. The prince is in Naug Diraul, and so is the World's Dream."

"And so, then, is Dida."

Jiana nodded, and closed her eyes.

"But which brought me here, Toldo? Was it glory, greed, or what a little mouse told me?" *None of them,* answered a voice in her stomach. *It was just garden-variety self-preservation.*

"Come on, Toldo," she said. "Let's get this thing over with. I want to go home." Toldo chugged his ale, and they rose up together to search out a stable and a cartographer.

Chapter 10

Leaves of glass:
King takes Queen,
but the Bishop is sacrificed;
Pawn advances to eighth heaven.

-1-

A ride to Naug Diraul took a full night and two parts of a day. Toldo was not used to such a sleepless run, but Jiana was awake and alert, if more than usually grim.

The empty countryside belied the gigantic battle in the City of Sickness. Jiana would have sworn the fields and roads would be clogged with soldiers and mercenaries, merchants, knights, squires, whores, and other such truck, all converging on the Naug to win their fortunes and die uselessly. But in fact, the five counties between the bay and the city were deserted.

"They fled," Jiana decided.

"Maybe they are already in Naug Diraul?"

"The old men and children would have been left, and they would be working these crops. Toldo, there's no one!" What intrigued her most was that all of the farm implements and wagons had been abandoned by the roadside, as if dropped.

Snakes, they must have run off in one hell of a hurry! But one other possibility occurred to her. *Maybe they were—taken?* She kept the thought to herself. She worried and fretted quite enough for both of them.

"Jiana . . . do you see? The livestock is all gone, too." She looked behind her, surprised.

"Damn. Why didn't I notice that?"

"Preoccupied."

Jiana shrugged, and spurred her new and unresponsive gelding without effect. There were no other tracks on the road besides their own, and there had been no rain. Jiana decided Toldo did not need to know that, either.

Through the chill of the night, they drove the horses as relentlessly as the beasts could stand. During the resting periods, when they slowed them to a walk and then stopped for a couple of hours, Jiana fumed and swore and used main force to stop herself from gobbling up the rest of their food supplies from her pack in nervous hunger. When the mounts could walk and then run again, she complained that they were too slow.

"Jiana! Any faster and these buggers will keel over."

She snarled in response, but reined in her horse. It had taken the bit in its mouth twice, and she wanted to maintain control.

Even with the delays, they reached Naug Diral by first light of the second day since she and Toldo had washed up on the shores of Bay Diraul.

Toward dawn, Jiana began to see a light in the east. She thought it was the sun until the sun actually rose, slightly to the right, and there were two separate glows. When they drew closer, she realized it was the burning of Naug Diraul.

The City of Sickness was much larger than Bay Din, and though it was in flames, torn by war and chaos, it was still mostly intact. Jiana found herself repulsed as she and Toldo approached the broken gates. It was the thickest fighting she had seen since the destruction of the White Hand rebellion, four years before. Yet, in unaffected parts of the city, the inhabitants still conducted normal business, as if unaware of the conflagration.

"By what's His scales, that Banished Serpent . . . Toldo, this place must boast a hundred thousand souls!"

"I would not be so certain that the numbers of souls and

bodies match, o weaponless one. Be careful, for us both, hm?"

Reminded of the loss of Wave, Jiana lapsed into sullen silence. She maintained her appearance, but inside, she cringed with apprehension. All would resolve here and now, in the Naug.

The battle had migrated far from the gates, and as the pair neared the granite walls, they finally began to see the crowds they had expected. Few were soldiers, however.

Jiana's double stripe of hair attracted considerable attention, but after glancing at her face, the lecherous looks turned to respectful bows, and the people hurried out of her way.

Then all at once, a young boy looking at her turned pale and screamed. A mob of twenty looked where he pointed, and bolted for cover.

Jiana whirled about and saw a giant shadow looming over Naug Diraul.

"Toldo," she whispered, after a moment's study. "Ah, buddy, I don't think there's anything *casting* that shadow. Maybe we'd better get the f—"

A clot of thick, opaque blackness hurled toward them. Jiana spurred her horse forward, and it chose to obey, charging forward into Toldo's bayard and bowling them both over. She felt the chill of death brush her shoulder. Jiana—

peace silent quiet flowing, gently, gently, sleep . . . eternal sleep—

—shuddered with violent repugnance.

"No! Goddamn . . . goddamn . . ." She scrambled for cover in a pile of masonry that had once, a sign proclaimed, been a bank. Jiana trembled with desire. It would be so *easy*, so restful . . .

Both horses screamed, and then were silent and still.

So, cutie, said the ugly part of her stomach, what once she had called Jianabel, *you are afraid of Mistress Death after all!*

"What scares me is how much I want her," she answered. Toldo looked strangely at her.

"Forget it, Priest. Look, let's get the kid and then just get the fuck out of here."

"But the quest! What about the World's Dream?"

"Let the hellmoons eat it, I don't care! It wasn't meant to be found, and it won't. And that rhyme of Toq's is stupid and meaningless!"

Toldo Mondo raised his head slowly, peeking over the edge of the rubble.

"Ah, well, I'm afraid that candle is already burned."

"Damn all of you pricks! You can't force me to play anymore!"

"Jiana, a week ago I would have agreed with you about grabbing Dida and leaving. But—too much has happened. I just have a terrible feeling that dream thing is *real*, o black-striped beauty, and that one of these buggers—Toq, or Alanai, or someone else—is going to find it whether it wants to be found or not.

"I know this is rather out of character, but . . ." He grimaced, as if tasting spoiled milk. "Jiana, let's stay and duke it out with them."

"Whom?"

"With all of them! Jiana, you're bigger than you think. Maybe you had it right when you said that as Jianabel, you made this whole world."

"Toldo!"

"Jiana, you killed your own God! Do you not understand what that means? Or have you been blocking it out?"

"No, it was Toq! It was *his* snowflake—"

"Balls. If he could have done it, he would have, long ago. He gave the blessed thing to you! Does that tell you nothing? He gave it to you, and you evicted your own Lord from the universe. How many could have done that? How many wish that they could?"

She and Toldo gingerly poked their heads out. The beasts were desiccated, nearly mummified.

Jiana stood up, and said, "That freaking shadow took our horses! I guess that tells us what happened to the people. Snakes, I don't seem to have much equestrian luck, do I?"

"The shadow was . . . Death Herself? Maybe you should have waited to use Toq's charm on Her."

"Maybe I should have used Toq's charm on Toq!"

"That's an interesting thought. He *said* it would not

work on him, but how do we know? What if the snowflake was just a focus? Maybe you would not even need it, if your mind could be totally convinced it had the power."

"Maybe the two moons will bump into each other. Come on, o tubby one. Let's find Dida and then decide what we're going to do."

For many hours they searched the city, asking after the boy or Alanai whenever they were in a populated part of Naug Diraul. They tried to skirt the rips and tears of the war itself.

Thousands of men raged through the City of Sickness, slaying and maiming, raping, looting, burning, and slaughtering animals. Some were so far lost to the battle madness that they tore into the bodies of their victims like wild animals, eating human flesh and swallowing blood as it spurted from fresh wounds.

The sickness is still here! It was here all along, just waiting for new carriers, new hosts to possess.

And what of me?

The thought made her heart pound. Would Jiana soon be blindly tearing at corpses, or killing Toldo—and Dida, if she found him?

Should she?

But then she recognized from whence the thought had come. Apparently, that part of her stomach that was black and cold was also a coward.

"I am who I am," she declared, and rationality allayed her fears.

Each time their search carried them into another combat zone, they saw a different war. There was only one other pocket of the Sickness. The rest were normal battles, but they were all different combatants.

By hugging the walls and crawling through burned-out or burning houses, Jiana and Toldo were able to avoid nearly all of the drunken, battle-raged, or frightened soldiers. Once, they had to lie hidden in a rat-infested cellar for what seemed to Jiana to be at least a dozen days, though the sun had not moved visibly. They shared the room with five dead men, who wore the ribbons of the Prime Secretary of Door. The warrior and the priest

crouched by a tiny window, looking out at the great crush
of men in the streets.

"Toldo, look! Those are Noondun—are they from the
Iron Satrap, or solos? And see—those are trogs from the
Southern Barbary. Who the hell is running this hell?"

"I know not," the priest sighed. "I've seen some of the
prince's men, but they were scattered, as if once the war
started, they no longer cared about alliances or the quest.
I think—"

A sudden light as bright as lightning at midnight blinded
Jiana, and the cellar leaped up and punched her on the
chin. Then it rocked to, from, and forth, and trembled
with a great shaking of the sod floor. A rumbling thunder
echoed in her ears and stomach.

She clawed her way back to the window, using the
ragged wall as a ladder to pull herself up to her feet again.

A smoking pit filled the street where the armies had
been. A pair of enormous columns rose up out of the
square, and it took her a moment to recognize them as two
legs of something that had six of them, and stood thirteen
manlengths tall.

"Ah . . . Toldo," she whispered, her voice sounding odd
and tinny after the explosion. "What sort of creature would
it be that's taller than the tallest building, has six legs, and
a million heads or so stuck all over its body?"

Toldo looked as if he had polished off more spoiled milk.

"Well, ahem. It sure sounds like one of the mythical
Fists of Destur, the Destroying God. From what I've heard."

"*One* of the fists?"

"From what I've heard."

"Toldo, how many of those things are there?"

"Well . . . three."

"Lovely! So it's Toq, and Tifniz, and Destur, and the
Nameless Snake alone knows who else—"

"No, He does not know. He's gone."

"And Alanai, and the Prime Sec, and the Satrap, and
surely every crusader and secret society north of the Tarn!
Priest, I think we have definitely found our World's Dream."

They waited another quarter hour until the Fist moved
on, and then crawled out, gingerly circumnavigated the
crater, and continued their search for Dida.

Jiana began to feel a sick certainty in her heart that he, too, was gone.

They had been sectioning the city, and finally they came to the inner wall, which divided the Old Naug from Naug Diraul, the outer city. The old town contained the government buildings, including the ancient seat of the Imperator, unused since Diraul had been an empire that stretched from the Tarn to the southern ice. The wall also enclosed the manors of the very rich, the finest private clubs and brothels, and the houses of the guild assemblies, which were the official residences and palaces that had stood empty since the Prime Secretariat moved to the coast.

It was there, amid the finery, that the fighting was fiercest.

Jiana and Toldo stepped high over intricate, erotic friezes of ebony, which once had graced entablatures high atop facades of pillared marble—now lying ignominiously on the ground, broken and trampled, their silver etchings pried out to be melted into ingots or coins. Brass demons, trolls, and grybbyns lay blind and burnt. No longer did they leer from cornices and copulas at the writhing, black couples, copulating in grace a thousand different ways. The demons' bloodstone eyes had been torn loose, and their highly aroused, carven members broken off for luck charms or dirty jokes.

"The ancient Dirauli prized lovemaking as high art," she told Toldo. "I've read that those who were very good were supported by rich benefactors, like painters or maskers are today. Snakes, what I could've taught Dida, with those sensitive hands of his, if he'd just been old enough to understand!"

"You do love him."

"You tell me."

They had to dive for cover then, as a surge of men and iron flooded the street, to destroy what little was left of the transcendent beauty of the Old Naug, and grind centuries of intricate and delicate care beneath a moment's ugly boot. They also killed each other.

Jiana could not help crying inside when they left; even the happy marble copulators were gone now. She led Toldo through a narrow alley, in which he nearly stuck.

They discovered a large courtyard. At the opposite end, a great building was guarded by twenty burly men. Each wore the eagle crest of Prince Alanai.

"Come on," Toldo said wearily. "Let's get this destiny nonsense over with and go home."

But Jiana hung back, still hidden by the corner of the alley.

"Toldo . . . maybe should just forget this whole thing."

"Again? Again you say that?"

"Look, this whole scheme is a stupid idea. How should I stop Dida from going on this bloody quest? What gives *me* that right?"

"Is that what you're wondering? Jiana, you have been propelled, knowingly or not, to a much sharper dilemma: did you have some sort of a goal, beyond a childish whim, in following this prince like a black-furred puppy, or have you just wasted three weeks of your life and mine, and nearly gotten us all killed a hundred times, and broken a boy's heart, just to be a spectator at the funeral of the world?"

"Leave me alone!" A crimson rage welled up within Jiana, a hatred of Toldo and Dida and Alanai and . . . *and what about yourself?*

"I can't leave you alone, dear. I told you why I came with you in the first place, after our first meeting in Bay Din. Well, you are not yet cured."

"Snakeshit! I'm not crazy anymore . . . I know that Jianabel is just a black part of me. I can work on suppressing her. She's dying all by herself! I can—"

"My God, Jiana. You still don't understand, do you? You can't just bury her, and she won't just die. She is you. She's a part of your mind that never grew up and accepted the world. She just kept squeezing harder and more morbid, like a rotting kunqut pit, fouling every stream of your life at its source. What in God's name have you done since you 'killed' your Jianabel, half a lifetime ago?"

"Done? I've stolen the jade eyes from the—"

"—from the sacred bird of the steaming jungles of the frozen north. Yes, I know. Dida told me. Your exploits make a grand telling to impressionable fifteen-year-olds. But what have you done of any *consequence?*"

"I . . ." Jiana stopped, trying to draw up the one incident in her life that would sum up her character and justify her existence. She closed and opened her mouth three times before she realized what she sought did not exist.

"Jiana, if you turn about now, after facing so much, and just go home . . . then you are no better than him, in there. Do you believe what Alanai is doing is wrong?" She nodded mutely. "Then what in your thousand and one globes are you going to do about it?"

She started to answer, but a gentle, reasoning voice spoke up inside her stomach.

Jiana, dear. You don't want us to die! I'm sure the fat priest believes what he's saying . . . but look around. What has he ever done in HIS life?

Yes, she thought. *What has he done? At least I've fought heroically! But you were the one who told me you could defeat anything, remember?*

Jianabel was silent for a long moment, and Jiana felt a cold fear emanating from that part of her mind. It was the fear of the coward.

You don't know, do you! she accused the Accuser. *You knew we would meet—but you don't know who will win at that meeting!*

"So that's why she was so brave," Jiana said aloud. "She knew this final confrontation was ordained, promised, fated—all that other stuff that says we have no free will."

"Who? Jianabel?"

"She knew I would eventually meet this Hraga si Traga— knew it before I did, in the rest of me. So she already knew the outcome of all the battles in between. That dirty, lying bitch."

"And now she wants to turn you around, and take you back home. Back to where Jianabel is queen, and Jiana tramps about fighting every war except the important ones, so wrapped up in herself that she cannot even see her way out of the forest."

Jiana rubbed her eyes. The day was too bright.

"No choice?"

"How can I tell you that? You could just walk away. Maybe you *like* living your life as twenty-two thousand separate day-tales."

Jiana leaned back against the cool plaster, closed her

eyes, and listened to the faint tumult on the wind. She thought of a lifetime of battles with never a war plan, each skirmish the end of today, the beginning of tomorrow.

Or, a direction . . .

"No choice, Toldo. Stay behind me."

She strode out from the cool, quiet alley into the courtyard, and marched up to the guards. Step, step, step. Her stomach shrank with fear, and she actually felt the physical presence of Jianabel for a moment, before she was forced out of her body for a time.

Even through the fear of death, Jiana felt the relief of a sick woman who finally vomits forth the poison that was killing her. She quickened her step, almost bouncing up to the guards, who, as soon as they saw Jiana, tackled her and pushed her against the wall of the inn.

They frisked her thoroughly, then twisted her arm behind her and led her into the august presence.

Alanai looked grave, as Jiana had expected. But there was something else about him that was different from their interview in the Dog's Tongue Tea Emporium: he looked emptied.

Hraga si Traga stood behind him, consciously trying to fade into the background. It was only with difficulty that she could see him. She could not tell whether he was using magick, or whether it was just in his nature to be the invisible one.

"I have waited for you, Jiono of White River. I hoped and prayed that you would not come, but I feared, even from the first time we met, that it would come to this in the end."

"I followed you, Princey. I saw some of the filth you left behind."

"What? How darest thou! The battles were hard fought, the victories glorious! Many fell demons were sent to waylay us, and armies raised up by foul magick from the halls of Limbo to stop us! But the righteous did prevail."

"Do you have it?"

Alanai's face lit up with a wicked giggle of triumph, and Jiana's eyes widened. This was not the same man who had begun the quest. This was not a sane prince.

"Yea, we have discovered the World's Dream itself! No

longer is it lost, or thought to be a legend. Now shall we give back to mankind all of the dreams they have lost . . ."

"They? Doesn't 'mankind' still include yourself? Well, Princeps, I'm sorry, but I'm not allowing you to do it. It just isn't worth the price."

"What? Thou makest even less sense than is usual for a woman! Dost thou not know what the World's Dream can *do*?"

"Yup. And I know who's out there trying to get it: besides you and Hraga there, hiding behind the throne, what about Toq? Tifniz? Mullanta, the southern armies of the Toradoras? How can I know which one of you bright boys is the *right* one to get the Dream? Well, hell. I won't believe any of you. I'll take the damn thing myself."

Alanai nodded. "It has come to the core: thy true motivations are revealed at last, before God and everyone! Thine ambition sickens us, woman." Alanai leaped up from where he sat, and drew his sword.

"Guards!" he cried. Instantly, eight men materialized from the alcoves.

Jiana looked about. The men were all familiar, from the Dog's Tongue Tea Emporium, three weeks before. But curiously, one was missing—the one she had respected the most.

"Sire, where is your former captain, he whom I fought before?" The men shuffled uncomfortably, and looked at the prince.

"We have discharged him," Alanai said. "He had overstepped his station, and had made unacceptable charges in our presence about our trusted advisor, Count Hraga."

"*Count* Hraga?"

The death-man himself stepped forward for the first time into the light. He looked smug, now that Jiana had been secured.

"I now have the honor," he boasted, "to hold the position of Captain of the Royal Guard."

He looked steadily at Alanai, and placed his hand familiarly on the prince's shoulder. *Like a puppeteer*, Jiana thought. Prince Alanai pointed an imperious finger at Jiana.

"Kill her," he said.

The guards were well-trained; they began to advance.

But they were also all born of the noble houses of the Water Kingdom, and had been raised in a fairyland of chivalry and manners. They stopped, and looked back questioningly at the prince.

"Sire," said a young boy, "are we to actually . . . kill this woman?" With a leap of her heart, Jiana recognized him. He was Driga Younger, son of Master Driga—the boy she had held hostage for her sword that same day in the Dog's Tongue Tea Emporium.

"Yes, damn you all!" screamed the prince, but it was Hraga's face that contorted in fury.

The guards looked to Jiana, then back at the prince. Then the eldest spoke, saying, "The Royal Guard does not slay unarmed women." He turned his back on Alanai, and after a moment, so did the other men.

Hraga balled his fists and worked them up and down in a tantrum at being thwarted. He danced around, his face beet red, and finally froze and pointed at Jiana.

"Then we'll kill you ourselves!" he screamed, forgetting in his rage to put the words in Alanai's mouth. The prince raised his sword and charged.

Jiana ducked his first blow, but the second came so fast it sliced deep into her shoulder, even as she rolled. The prince fought only with the skill of Hraga, so she could slip the blows relatively easily, but he fought with the strength of a demon.

She fell to her backside, and crab-crawled backward to avoid three ringing sword chops to the floor. Suddenly, a pair of hands grabbed her from behind, and a sword descended from the heavens to intercede between her and the prince. It was the old guard.

"A prince of Bay Bay," he enunciated in a cultured tone, "does not grub about on the floor after an unarmed girl. You will at least fight her fairly, weapon to weapon . . . Sire."

For the first and only time in her life, Jiana felt satisfied with the ancient traditions of chivalry.

-2-

It was Driga who had pulled her to her feet, and he gave her a slender javelin. It was a shrewd guess. She could never have effectively wielded the heavy swords the guards wore, and she needed the advantage in reach to make up for the lack in power.

Hraga laughed derisively, through Alanai's mouth.

"Go ahead!" sneered Alanai-Hraga. "It'll do you no good anyway, whorechild!"

Almost, Jiana lost control at the slur against her mother, but too much had happened since she had been so easily goaded in the first battle with Alanai. She held her temper, deciding instead to take the war inside Hraga's battlements.

She projected her mind out, just slightly above the mundane sphere. It was the easiest magickal skill she had, the same as she had done in the summoning room below Bay Din. She did not send her entire soul away. She sent just a tendril, a touch out to brush at Hraga's own stomach, and talk to him in the silence between the Worlds, in the dead emptiness of his own soul.

"I know you, death-man. I know what you are. You're nothing more than me."

"I am a god, Jiana!"

"You're not even a man. I shall kill you. You know that, but really, you've never even been alive."

Hraga laughed, with the sound of trapped bodies crackling in the flames of a burning house.

"Your magick is nothing! Do you know how old I am, Jiana? I was old before your mother the whore was born! I have had a century to perfect my abilities, and I've not frittered it away as you have on affectations like *love*, and *honor*." Hraga spoke the words as though they left a bad taste in his mouth. "You," he continued, Alanai edging slowly into strike range—Jiana expected an attack any moment—"you never even used your magick before this little jaunt of yours. Now who really do you think will DIE!"

The prince attacked, but Jiana had been waiting for the pause in Hraga's speech, and she was ready for the flurry of sword blows. They fell strangely, and Jiana suddenly recognized them as the third sword set of the Flower Empire style of dueling. Hraga probably thought them exotic and unanticipated.

She laughed back at him. But a curious buzzing, an air
of unreality had begun to grow in the back of her stomach.
She ignored it to favor the immediate fight.

"You dolt! I *taught* that cutting sequence in Bay Bay for
months! Did you think I'd be touched by it now?"

Jiana demonstrated a set of her own, one developed
uniquely by her second teacher. It was a flashy dance for a
leaf-bladed spear, where she thrust with both the pointy
end and the butt, and whirled the spear about her head by
the end. She finished in the Stinging Crab position, with
the javelin poised overhead, ready to strike downward.

Alanai, under Hraga's direction, had blocked the blows
well enough, but had been put off balance four times.
Hraga was not as good a warrior as he was a sorcerer. He
was not even as good a warrior as Alanai was alone. But
alone, he would not have fought Jiana.

Jiana knew Hraga would quickly tire, and shift the battle to pure sorcery.

"I need no sets to deal with such as you, bitch!" he
screamed in her mind. "I shall rain down burning pitch on
your head, and disease—"

The unease in Jiana's mind began to grow and expand,
until it matted out the present scene. She was trapped!
For a moment, she thought all had been a dream, that
instead, she had slipped and fallen through the ice, dragged
far along by the river current. She pounded uselessly at
the underside, her air giving out, the freezing cold eating
away into her bones . . .

But it was not Jiana's vision. She could taste the dream
as a stranger, not her own morbid imagination.

And abruptly, she realized it was Dida's. Dida was here!

A sudden thrust from Hraga-Alanai tore her mind back
to the here-and-now. Sensing her distance, he had finally
broken through her guard. Jiana felt the sickening pressure of a span of steel sliding softly into her belly.

She backed away, her entire midsection numb.

No—her stomach rebelled, *not now*—*not like this!* Her
hands shook, but with a sledgehammer effort she quelled
the tremor, and stood straight to face Alanai, contempt on
his face. The pain had not yet struck.

But then a dam burst inside her. She was unable to

check the flood of foreign emotions that filled her entirety from inside all the way to the outside.

Dida was in horror at something—fear, rage, guilt, lust . . . even the ultimate of self-loathing poured through Jiana. All the terrors of Dida's mind assailed Jiana—all the half-formed, misshapen monsters that had leered at her when she had calmed him in the caverns of Taku-Taku.

She sank to her knees, unable to overcome the joint assault of her terrible wound and the death of Dida's spirit. Dimly, she was aware that Alanai advanced upon her, sword raised, but all Jiana could feel was despair for Dida.

My lover, my child, my friend—what has happened? What have you done?

An ugly voice trespassed upon her mind. It was Hraga, pushing into her stomach, twisting the magickal knife in it to wring the last bits of anguish from her.

"I know what Dida has done!" he boasted. "And I'll never tell you. You're going to die here on these steps without ever knowing how your child fucking-partner has destroyed himself, you incestuous cunt!"

Gleefully, Hraga began thrusting himself against what remained of the walls of Jiana's mind. At first, she was unable to comprehend what he was doing. But as he began to break through, she understood sickly that Hraga was using his magick to try to rape Jiana's soul. He was thrusting the hard tendrils of himself through the wound in her belly into her stomach. He intended to violate her as much as inhumanly possible.

Jianabel arose at last. She had been quiescent ever since the docks of Tuk Diraul.

"Daddy," she called—softly. "Daddy, come inside here. It's our time now. And we *mustn't* be late!"

The pressures of Dida's guilt arose behind the walls, and Hraga thrust and tore before them. In the face of the rot from without and within, Jiana simply gave up. She simply dropped the walls and made ready to die. It was not as bad as she had always feared, really.

Hraga burst through the crumbling virginity of her Self— and then withdrew in confusion. The flood of emotion that had inundated Jiana through the bond of love which connected her to Dida now assailed Hraga, and he was unable to handle it. As he had said, he had never experienced such feeling before.

Hraga realized his mistake, and tried to bolt out of Jiana's stomach with the speed of a crossbow shot. But it was too late. The walls of her mind were gone, thrown aside at the end, and there was nothing to check the surge of Dida's feelings. Hraga writhed in agony, never before feeling any pain as great as the death of Innocence.

In a frenzy of chaos, he cast about for a piece of stability, a boulder in the flood with which he could grab and pull himself out of the waters.

He seized Jianabel, the only part of Jiana that he could still understand. He held onto the blackness, the evil, the hard, uncaring unconcern.

Jiana felt Jianabel smile. She felt the sharp, filed teeth sink deep into Hraga's heart, holding him tight. Jianabel laughed in Jiana's stomach, like a little girl again.

"Poor Daddy! You always *did* have your hands in everything, didn't you?"

And Jianabel died. Without a moment's hesitation, she did what Jiana could never have done: she slew herself, peacefully.

His anchor gone, Hraga si Traga was swept away by the waters, trapped below the ice, a stunned expression on his face. At the very end, Hraga screamed.

It was Alanai's scream that wrenched Jiana back into the present.

The prince stood frozen, his arm upraised in the moment of delivering her death-blow. Hraga himself stood white and palsied, his unseeing eyes rolled up into his head so that only the whites showed. Twice, his mouth opened and closed, dumbly.

Slowly, Jiana forced herself to stand. She withdrew entirely from the chaos in own mind. She thought no thoughts. Jiana pulled her Self forward as she had on the battlefield of the rebellion of the Monks of the Yellow Hand, unthinking, letting the tide of pain and fear and sorrow and despair flow through her without restraint, and without effect. She was as nearly dead in her mind, for that moment, as she was in her body.

Now, the pain of her wound began, but Jiana let that,

too, flow through her, as she had in the hold of the prince's ship, when Hraga had tortured her. She was a sieve, and none of the waters of the world could wash her from her stance.

Jiana turned on her back leg, stepped forward, and hurled her javelin into Hraga's chest.

In the last moment, somehow, Hraga tore himself back to the instant danger. Sensing the fatal blow, his iron will forced the body to react to the cast. But it was Alanai who brought his sword up in a block, not Hraga si Traga, even though the prince was on Jiana's other side.

Hraga's eyes rolled back down, and she felt him recede from her mind. He stared stupidly at the wooden shaft protruding from his belly. Then he looked up at her in shock, and spoke aloud.

"You'll—never find—" he whispered. Then he fell face forward. Jiana felt the life force that once had beat at her mind flicker and cease.

The eldest soldier stared at her.

"You killed the captain! Why did you do that?"

"My God of Serpents," she whispered, staring at Hraga's body, "it's so quick!" She could see the flesh hardening, just as the hand of the Noondun shaman had done.

Jiana sank slowly to her knees again. She felt a pair of massive hands grab her under her arms and lay her out on the floor. Toldo knelt over her, and began to bind up her belly-wound with some of her own bandages from her medicine bag, while the royal guards scuffled around her trying to decide what to do.

Something was missing . . . her heart seemed to skip a beat as she realized at once that Dida's voice was gone, leaving behind nothing but the rumble of distant ocean waves beating upon a beach. Jiana began to have a creepy feeling that something even worse than despair had happened to her love . . .

"My Lord!" cried Driga suddenly. He jumped over Jiana and rushed across the room. Turning her head to follow him, Jiana saw that Alanai, too, had collapsed. Two other guards belatedly joined Driga.

By the time they reached him, he had recovered. In the excitement, Jiana had completely forgotten about the prince.

"Your Highness. Welcome back."

"Welcome . . . back? Oh, 'tis you, Jiono! What do you do here?"

Driga asked, in confusion, "But . . . do you not remember the fight?"

"What fight?" Alanai asked, blankly, rising to his feet a bit unsteadily.

"I freed you," Jiana declared, hoarsely but triumphantly. She pointed at Hraga's withering corpse.

"She killed him!" the elder guard repeated incredulously. "She just threw her javelin and killed him!"

Alana stared at her in amazement. Then, his expression changed to sorrow and pity.

"I was afraid we would meet again," he said, trying for a tone of gentle authority. "And I feared as well that your madness would finally eat through all of the fine beauty I see in you."

Jiana shut her eyes, and sank back in disbelief.

"Oh, snakes. There's no end to it!"

Alanai continued, sadly.

"There is nothing to be done about poor Count Hraga. At one time, he must have been a fine and honorable man . . ."

"He was death," Jiana corrected.

"But I can and shall save you from the black, empty pit on whose edge you teeter."

"What do you mean?" She began to have a horrible suspicion. *Dida, Dida—my love, what have you done? Where have you gone?*

"Come with me," said Prince Alanai. "For I have finally succeeded in my quest. I have found the World's Dream at last."

"I know. You mentioned it."

"I have spent many years in contemplation of exactly what wording I shall use when I release the dreams of Mankind. But I would be less than a prince if I did not include your special case in the wish of my heart."

"Oh, no—" Jiana gasped. Gingerly, she sat up. Bound, the wound was not as bad as it had felt. Toldo was skilled in surgery, and she felt weak but alive.

"You mean you're going—" began Toldo.

"Jiono of White river . . . as I wish back the dreams of the world, I shall spend also a breath to cure your soul!"

He seized her by the wrist, and yanked her to her feet, ignoring Toldo's outraged cries. Pushing the priest to one side, Prince Alanai dragged Jiana out of the inn, surrounded by his men-at-arms.

His grip was iron, and Jiana wasted a long time, in her weakened condition, trying to pry his fingers loose, before she finally gave in. Alanai had spent a lifetime wielding a sword that weighed as much as her leg, beating on people and pells. His grip would not be broken, especially not when he was enmeshed in the grip of his own monomania.

"Your Majestyness," she gasped. "You've completely crossed over the line—you know that, don't you?" With every breath, Jiana felt another stab in her belly, but she talked on anyway, trying to prick the prince's armor of madness.

"Jiono, I am so glad that you could be with me to revel in this moment. The fulfillment of all the world's hopes and aspirations is at hand!"

"Alanai, look around you! See what your quest has bought: a mad, chaotic, anarchic, bloody free-for-all of butchery and betrayal! I . . . Prince, you're not listening! I can tell."

Alanai led Jiana and his men through the ruined streets, the broken dreams of the lovemakers of the Old Naug. Unseeing where his boots trod, he trampled artwork that had taken generations to carve.

He is a golden eagle, Jiana thought. *He only sees the far-away. And I'm still the black bear, looking within myself for the world.*

"Neither of us has it right, Prince—it's all a question of scale . . ."

"Jiono . . . we are here."

Jiana looked at Here. They stopped before a tiny house, indistinguishable from any of the other tiny, preserved houses of the Old Naug, except for the lack of ornamentation. It was a wood-frame cube with plaster walls and a domed roof, like a thousand other houses in ten thousand other cities in all the worlds on every sphere. Yet Jiana could feel *completion* emanating from the hovel. One or another way, she knew with a certainty that this House marked the End of the Quest.

-3-

"In the days of the First Men, the Ti-Ji Tul," intoned the prince, "O-onakai Tonaronakai drew all the World's Dreams to him, and fashioned them into one weird. But the Dream was lost. Do you know how?"

"I really don't care."

"Another man lived in those times."

"A lot of them." Jiana could think only of Dida, as she was dragged miserably along the boisterous street, and of what could have caused such an outpouring of guilt and fear.

"He, too, claimed great powers. But he was an evil, twisted man. His name was Ha-aka Taraka." A warning bell rang in Jiana's head. The coincidence was too ridiculous not to mean something.

"Was he by any chance related to—"

"He scried the great work of O-onakai Tonaronakai, and a vast envy filled his being. While the Master spent his energies drawing the dreams of the world unto him, Ha-aka Taraka studied instead how to steal the finished Dream itself, for he intended a great mischief upon the world!"

"Alanai, listen to me, please! It is a question of scale. It's all right to be a far-seer, but you have to be able to see the roses at your feet, too. And you don't need to kill a grybbyn or tumble the world rightside-down to be a hero!"

"The deed was done. O-onakai Tonaronakai was wearied to the bone after his mighty endeavor, and he fell into a deep and dreamless sleep. Ha-aka Taraka seized the opportunity, and cast his own greatest spell—he drew the World's Dream right out of the Master's house and into his own!"

"But I've been wrong, too!" Jiana insisted, unwilling to be drawn into the madness of Prince Alanai. "I admit it! I committed the worst form of narcissism, being turned so completely inward that I had actually created my own world—a world with a vicious, heartless little girl named

Jianabel. I looked only backwards, inside my own stomach. It's a question of scale!"

"But the effort proved too great for Ha-aka Taraka, and his life essence ebbed, just as the Dream materialized before him. His soul scattered, borne to the six vertices of the world by the Six Great Eagles of the Compass Rose! But he is not dead. He cannot die, as long as the Dream is here, to draw him."

Jiana stubbornly persisted in trying to break through and reach Alanai.

"Just as you must turn your gaze downward from the skies, so too I have to look out to the horizon once in a while. I have to have a goal, and you, Your Highness, must learn to live at least a little for today! How about . . . letting the Dream just stay where it is? Whatever the ultimate glory and hope it can give the world, it's just not worth the price. After all, to give the world *your* dreams, you must first take away their own."

"Ha-aka Taraka is doomed to return for all eternity to this world. He cannot take the Dream for himself, for he burned out his power to affect it those many centuries ago. But he can return and use his power over men to drive another hither, and subvert him to Ha-aka's own ends."

"Damn it, Alanai—Hraga si Traga was Ha-aka Taraka!"

"Yes, I know."

"Don't you—what do you mean you *know?*"

"I knew even before you killed him, but there was nothing I could do about it then. He had me. It is sad . . . once, he must have been honorable, but the Dream corrupted him. Strong as he was, he was too weak in character. I thank you for your brave and heroic deed, Jiono. It was by this bold and unselfish gesture that I realized you are still curable! As for now, ask of me any boon you wish; it shall be granted."

Jiana laughed.

"That's simple! Forget this phoney-baloncy quest, and leave the World's Dream where it's hid!"

"That I cannot do. First, because it would not stay hidden. You know as well as I the powers of Dark arrayed against me, all of them seeking nought but the Dream! And second, because I know you do not truly wish it. You know full well the world will be better off, once I get hold of the World's Dream and bring order and unity to the kingdoms."

"Then, I ask you to leave me out of your wish. Please?"

The prince shook his head, sadly.

"My heart is heavy that you should ask this, for it shows your sickness is still upon you. Who else but a madman would not wish to be cured of his insanity? This logic alone should convince you. Nay, ask of me something else, dear, beautiful Jiono."

Alana let go of her wrist, and she rubbed it with the other hand.

"Well . . . do you admit that it was I who slew the evil creature called Hraga si Traga?"

"How could I deny it?"

"Do you agree, then, that at least one woman can fight both a prince and a demon to a standstill?"

Alanai frowned and shuffled his feet, but again, he was forced to nod his head.

"Then this is my boon: give me back my goddamned sword!"

"Hm. Well. I do guess you have earned it. I do not have it anymore, but I will tell you who does. I gave it to brave Dida, the young lad we picked up in the City of Demons, in the evil Tarn Desert. He has a fighting heart, that one!"

"Dida, huh?" Jiana scratched her head. The hair was just beginning to grow back, and it itched. She wondered incongruously why Alanai had not made any mention of her grooming changes. Too polite, she decided.

"What on earth were you doing in Toq's city, anyways?" she demanded. "It doesn't even make sense! Why didn't you take the caravan route and circumnavigate the desert?"

"What caravan route?"

"The Monkey-Paw West Ocean caravan route! Which one did you think I meant?"

"I've never heard of it. I wish I had known; I would have."

"It's marked on the map!"

"Not on mine."

Jiana lurched away, furious. "You mean you took the same shortcut I did," she accused, "because you *didn't even know there was an easier route?* All that suffering in the desert, and I could have waltzed around the foothills and avoided the whole thing, including my bargain with Toq!"

Alanai looked heavenward again.

"We were drawn to the center of the cursed Tarn, and there we beheld a magnificent city where none had been before. We fought a great battle with an army of hellions, demons from the deepest pit. It was there that Count Hraga—or was he Sir Hraga then?—it was there that he raised up the shade of O-onakai Tonaronakai himself, who told us where to find the World's Dream, and what shape it took."

"Sorry I missed it. Toldo Mondo and I were enjoying a scintillating conversation with a god, over in the violent ward."

"Then, as we left victorious, I spied brave Dida on the road, beneath a wicked-looking tower. In response to my questions, he told us he was alone—that you, in your sickness, had abandoned him there. And though at first he insisted on waiting for you to return, out of loyalty, we rescued him anyway. After a time, he grew to appreciate his circumstances, and he has been a valued and valuable member of my expedition ever since."

"And he's got my sword, Wave." *And something dreadful has happened to him . . .*

"And he's got your sword. You can get it from him later, before we leave to return to the court. But first, we have more important things to attend. Behold! The World's Dream!"

Again, he seized her by the hand before she could leap away, and with his other ham fist he burst open the door to the hut.

The inside was disheveled and scattered, reminding Jiana at once of the twig house of the Too-Wise, far to the north in the land of the Southers. But an ancientness permeated the walls and floor. It was not as aged as Toq's city, but it seemed a fitting place for the Quest to End. Alanai, however, did not tarry inside.

Instead, he led her straight through, followed by his entourage, into the courtyard behind the house. In the courtyard was a tiny garden—just a few vegetables, a flowering bush, a tiny pedestal, and the most brilliant, sparkling, lively oak tree Jiana had ever seen.

The leaves were colored with the brilliance of autumn in White Falls, and the trunk was a deep, rich hue that was the essence of Earth and Wood. Yet the tree seemed sad somehow, as if it knew or could guess at the tragedies that awaited the fledgling races of Man.

On the marble pedestal sat a tiny, golden object. As the prince advanced breathlessly, towing Jiana along behind like an extra horse, they could see that it was a golden leaf.

Gently but inexorably, as if he was drawn by forces greater than any man, Prince Alanai of the Golden Eagle reached forth and plucked the leaf from the pedestal. Nothing happened—no portents sounded, and the earth did not open up. It was only after she suddenly let go her breath that Jiana realized she had been holding it, expecting something drastic.

"The . . . Dream," Alanai breathed, eyes as big as millstones. He let go of her wrist to reverently touch the leaf, and Jiana tried to rub the circulation back. Now both wrists were equally mashed.

It's wrong, a little voice told her. It was not the voice of the Tormentor; Jianabel was truly dead. It was a different part of her, the part that could look beneath the world. *He's got it all completely backwards!* She did not know what she meant by the thought.

Alanai's voice lit up with the fire of heaven, and Jiana's skin began to creep. She *knew* that look; she knew that lust for unclothed power. Alanai held the leaf aloft.

"And now for the moment!" he cried. Then he closed his eyes and silently moved his lips, as if praying.

Jiana moved a step away from him and nervously looked over her shoulder. She hoped she could see her "cure" coming before it arrived, before the prince's wish began to take effect. And she fervently prayed that he remembered all those gods and demons elsewhere in the city, who surely were now aware that the World's Dream was being used.

His lips stopped, and he stood frozen, his face contorting in what looked for all the world to Jiana like an orgasm. And he waited.

And waited.

And waited.

After several long moments had passed, he cautiously opened his eyes and looked around. Everything was as it had been: his men still grouped around him, gawking at the leaf and the tree and the pedestal; Jiana still crouched at his side, ready to bolt for the house if anything *did* happen; even the far-off screams and resounding clashings of metal on metal that was the war in the city still drifted past them now and again, when the wind was right. There was no change; the wish was a dud.

Alanai took a deep breath.

"That's something I wondered about, too," Jiana said. "How are you supposed to work that thing?"

The prince glared at her. He made as if to strike her, then deflated and backed away, letting his rage flow out of him.

"Thou art right, woman. We shall have to study on this a longer time. Come!" He bowed to Jiana. "We bid thee farewell, for we have much to ruminate, and only a little time. Fare thee fairly, Jiono. We shall hope to see thee when thou art well again."

Alanai turned abruptly and stalked off, back through the house, his retinue trailing obediently.

After a few moments, Jiana heard a crunch on the gravel behind her. She turned and saw Toldo, brushing the dirt off his white robes.

"I, ah, thought you might like some company. I see your royal host has deserted you."

"What was that rhyme Toq sang to us? Do you remember?"

"About the Dream? It was, um . . . 'Dream the dream of ashes/The window dream unlatches/Something-something crashes . . .' " He shrugged, and turned up his hands.

Jiana adamantly shook her head.

"Listen; it has to be perfect:

"Dream another age,
Dream the dream of ashes,

Dream another's dreams;
The window world unlatches, crashes,
Tears apart its timesewn seams,
For he who holds the world within his hand,
Who crushes, casts it to the sand:

His heart an open page.
His heart an unbound page."

"You have a good memory, o glorious bard."

"I have special reason to remember that song. I wrote a
version of it before I split myself into Jiana and Jianabel—
when I was whole but still insane. Toldo, that rhyme
doesn't make any sense if the World's Dream is a thick
piece of carved gold! Ashes? Who can burn gold? And I
don't think even burly Alanai can crumble that thing—it's
as big as my hand, and damned thick!"

"Jiana . . . do you think . . . ?"

She nodded triumphantly.

"As surely as eagles fly. The bastard got the wrong leaf!"

Both of them turned and stared at the oak. It rustled at
them, and seemed to cry out in despair and heartbreak, as
if it once had been free from the prison of the ground, and
had endured untold centuries now, bound to roots and soil
and mundane earth.

"It is one of those," Toldo whispered.

"As surely as snakes crawl." She approached the tree,
and gingerly began to pluck the leaves.

-4-

Jiana had no idea what the World's Dream would feel
like, of course, or whether it could be distinguished from a
normal, run-of-the-tree leaf, or even whether plucking it
from the tree would destroy it. The last possibility seemed
doubtful, though.

Of one thing she was certain: the Dream simply had to
be one of the leaves on the tree.

"Can you think of a better disguise?" she asked Toldo,
and he had no answer, for of course he could not.

"Why disguise it? Why hide it at all? Obviously, so that Alanai and people like Alanai couldn't find it." Again, Toldo said nothing. He plucked leaves, one by one, just as Jiana did.

"Jiana," he said at last. "Do you not think that pulling so many leaves will kill this ancient tree?"

"I hadn't thought about it much. Maybe it will. My heart says we'll find it soon, for as soon as the prince discovers he has the wrong toy, he'll be back. With heavy horses. I honest-to-God think I'm destined to find this baby before he does."

Jiana judged that nearly an hour had passed, and she and the priest had pulled a whole forest of leaves from the golden oak. She reached up to touch a particularly fine leaf. Just before her fingers brushed it, her entire body seemed to hesitate. She felt as if the world had taken in a deep breath and held it.

"Toldo . . ." she hissed. She closed her hands on the leaf, and twisted it gently from the bough. A shock of fulfillment flooded through her like the tide returning. A strange thought tickled: *I am finally complete*. She let herself slide down the trunk, oblivious to the bark that scraped like shapepaper, and held the leaf up into the light.

It was as red as the sunset on the ocean. It was as gold as the coinfish in the palace pond of the Cornsilk Caliph. It sparkled and shimmered like the sun shining through the misty rain in Dida's forest.

"Toldo—" Jiana moaned. She held the World's Dream of O-onakai Tonaronakai out at arm's length, and little shivers of golden fire-worms danced on its surface and crawled slowly up her arm.

Suddenly, Jiana's hand was afire, and she gasped and bit the knuckle of her other hand to keep from screaming. There was no pain, only a horrible anticipation, as if she were a beached whitefish, with a ravenous skeenik hovering over her.

"Toldo—it needs—to be consumed . . ."

The Dream grew large, and then larger. Then it filled her whole view, and all was lost except for the detailed lines of the leaf, ever finer, ever more intricate . . .

Toldo Mondo slapped her hard across the face, staggering her. Jiana shook her head, and dropped to one knee, her wound throbbing intently. She had pushed the pain into the background before Toldo's slap.

"I am sorry, Jiana. That thing was mesmerizing you somehow. You needed awakening. Are you all right?" He pulled her shirt up to inspect her bandage. More blood had soaked it, but not much more.

"Damn, you didn't have to knock my teeth out!" She glanced once at the Dream, then shuddered and stuffed it in her pouch, where everything else of hers ended up, sooner or later. "Thanks, I suppose."

"Well, at least you were right."

"About?"

"We did not have to kill this wonderful tree."

"Well, I wouldn't think we could! It's magickal."

"Oh, yes. I keep forgetting. Don't you think we had better . . . ?"

"Immediately. I have no desire to face Alanai and a hundred blades!" There was no back exit to the garden. In fact, Jiana wondered if it even existed from anywhere but the hut of Ha-aka Taraka. Nervously, she poked her head back into the hovel. Alanai had not yet realized his mistake and returned. She waved to Toldo, and within moments they had rushed back through the hut and out onto the street.

She led them around five corners at random, moving always away from the hut with its garden. Then at last, she allowed the puffing Toldo to slow down to a walk.

While they rested, she tried to push her mind out, seeking news of Dida. But the World's Dream weighed on her soul like an anchor, and prevented her from leaving her body.

"Where are we going with that thing?" he wheezed.

"A question in need of an answer. What do you *do* with an unbounded, absolutely free wish?"

"I wish we were home again."

"Fortunately, you're not holding the leaf. So, let's examine our options; in here, O spherical one." Jiana gestured to a tavern. Despite the war that had now burned or ravaged half the city, the Secretary's Golden Flow Tavern and Bath House was still open to business. "The kind of dive that would stay open throughout Armageddon," Jiana said.

Toldo wedged himself into one of the benches in the back, shrouded in darkness, since he did not illumine the lamp. Jiana stomped up to the bar and ordered two steins.

The shopman looked her up and down, his eyes lingering on her crest of raven-colored hair.

"No credit—Tooqa, what happened to *you?*"

"I've always wanted one," she said, slapping down a small coin of uncertain value. "You should see what I did to the rest of my hair." He looked at her in confusion for a moment. Then his eyebrows raised, but he refrained from asking if he could do so.

"Hey," she added as an afterthought. "If you had one wish, what would you wish for?"

He scratched his chin.

"I don't know, gorgeous. I'd wish for a night with you. No, wait! I'd wish for a really good supplier of strongtea across the ocean."

"Hm. Okay. It's all a matter of scale, I guess." She returned to Toldo's alcove with the ale.

"Toldo—something very bad has happened to Dida. I felt his mind cry out to me, while I fought with Hraga . . . we need to find him! Maybe I should use the Dream for that?"

"As I see it," he lectured, draining a third of the tankard, "we have three choices: figure out some useful, practical wish; make a frivolous wish, just to use the puppy up; or tuck it away and ride off to nowhere, and ditch it there. Maybe no one will ever find it."

"Use it, lose it, or waste it."

Toldo nodded.

"Well, there are problems with all three," she continued. "If we hide it, Alanai's sure to find it with his magick. If we waste it we'll wish we hadn't, and if we don't we'll wish we had . . . I don't have enough of a lawyer's mind to make a really good wish that won't sicken more than it cures."

"So wish for a pot of really *wonderful* strongtea."

"Strange you should say that . . ." Jiana finished off her ale, and leaned back, rubbing her eyes, behind which a headache pounded. "Oh, Dida, Dida ، . . what did you do?" She opened her eyes. "You left out one choice, chum. We could fob it off."

"Give it away?" he asked, incredulous.

"Sure. It's not my blasted responsibility! Why don't we give it to Toq?"

"He who predates all."

"I'm sure he'd love it. And I do owe him one: it was his charm that saved our asses in the Channel of Flying Fish."

Toldo frowned. He did not like being reminded of events that could not be fit into his skeptic's worldview.

"Yes. I suppose we do. Why not? Whatever He plans to do with the thing, I'm sure it will affect realms far above our own worries."

"I'd sure feel nervous monkeying around with this thing myself. Then it's settled! We keep our bargain with Toq, after all. Now please—let's find Dida, okay? He needs me."

She and Toldo clinked their steins, and he drank his own down to the lees. Then they scrambled out into the noontime streets of Naug Diraul, to search for Dida, and for Toq.

For Jiana, the City of Sickness had taken on an eerie surrealism. Great crowds surged about them, and the people cried and laughed and fought and killed indiscriminately. Once, an entire building collapsed beside them, and the flames that had eaten away at its intestines burst forth and set fire to a bank and an ancient mausoleum. Jiana and Toldo stared for a moment, then turned and marched on, stepping gingerly over the flaming debris that now littered the Street of Whispering Lovers.

A knot of struggling people grunted into view, popping out from an alley. Their arms were all locked. Half were pushing determinedly north, and the others were shoving just as stubbornly south. For a mad moment, Jiana thought they were playing some ball game. She and Toldo tried to pass south, then the south-going guards got the better, and the pair had to scurry around to the north.

They walked on, and finally passed out of the government district into a residential area. Here the houses were all multiply ravaged, as if six different armies had poured

across the town from all directions. Then they saw a house
that was utterly untouched. It was the O.K. Rabbit Co.,
and it stood next door to a church that was demolished.

Around another corner, and Jiana suddenly caught sight
of a familiar figure. It was the farmer Rufes, from the army
of the Holy Vehemence. She called out a subdued hello,
and he waved back before continuing his duel with a
horned, porcine fiend. She demanded to know if he had
seen Dida, but in that moment he died, and did not
answer her. Sadly, she and Toldo walked on, following no
path but Jiana's intuition.

"I feel all-powerful with this thing in my pocket bag,"
Jiana declared.

"Beware the wrath of wizards," Toldo replied. He would
have said more, but he did not.

"Where would a boy hang out during a war?"

Toldo shrugged. "I suggest we try the aleshops first,
since that is where he could expect to find *you*."

Jiana stopped. She found herself standing on the lawn of
a relatively unscorched hut, staring at the door. It sagged
off its hinges. For some reason, the door seemed to cry
out piteously to her.

"What is wrong, o transfixed one?" Toldo asked.

"I thought I heard something."

She stepped closer, right up to the opening, and listened. Inside, Jiana could hear the sound of whimpering.
It sounded like a young girl.

"I can't stand anymore," Jiana snarled. She pushed open
the door and walked in to see what was wrong.

The girl huddled in a corner of the family room, near a
cold fireplace. Her clothes had been torn from her, and
there were bruises on her arms. She held her arms across
her breasts, and seemed not to see Jiana. The warrior knew
at once what had happened to her.

"Honey," she said as gently as she could. She reached
out slowly and stroked the girl's hair. She looked about
seventeen.

"Honey, was it soldiers?"

The girl seemed to focus on Jiana's presence for the first
time, and the warrior was glad for her new clothes. They

made it much more obvious that she was a woman. The girl did not seem afraid.

"Was it soldiers?"

The girl looked Jiana in the eyes, and then turned and looked at the other side of the room. Jiana followed her gaze, and put her hand on her dagger.

"Are they still here?" She rose slowly, and walked through the far doorway, drawing the two-foot blade as she did.

The other room was almost black. The drapes were drawn. A boy sat against the wall, unseeing, his pants unbuttoned. It was Dida.

"Oh, no," Jiana moaned. "Oh, God, no!"

She went to him and held him, shook him, even slapped him. Nothing seemed to break through; he remained catatonic.

Jiana watched the girl across the house. Toldo had managed to gain her confidence, and was talking to her quietly. He motioned Jiana to him. She came, but kept an eye on the girl, ready to stop her if she should decide to attack Dida.

"What happened?" Jiana asked.

"Exactly what you think. Dida . . . well, Dida did what a million other soldiers before him have done. For the same reason."

"Battle-fury." Jiana realized her cheeks were wet. "Snakes and Spiders—I've seen too much of it, Toldo. In everyone—including myself. There's something about killing—about living for so many days in fear of sudden death. It lets loose the beast in us. I'm not exempt. I've killed when there was no need, fired houses, beat prisoners to death for useless, stupid pieces of information—!"

She stopped, her voice caught in her throat. Several unbidden sobs escaped before she could regain control. *But this was Dida!* railed someone inside her stomach; *this was an innocent.*

"Damn Alanai," she whimpered plaintively. "Damn him all the fucking way to whatever hell really awaits us! Damn me and you and everyone else that fucking turned Dida into—that made him—"

Jiana felt a horrible pressure in her throat, as if a great balloon had expanded inside her and threatened to explode and blow off her head. Tears flowed down her cheeks, but there was nothing she could do to stop it. At last, the pressure abated, and she could breathe and talk again.

"Well," Toldo began tentatively, "the girl is a victim, too."

"Oh, fuck her! She's nothing! Damn her, too, for being here when his heart shriveled!" Jiana glared in rage at the girl, no trace of pity in the warrior's heart—no sympathy; no compassion. "Girl, something lousy happened to you. But I just—don't—care. What died in Dida when he did it was worth ten thousand of you! Get out."

The girl looked at Jiana in shock and confusion, her face as tear-streaked as Jiana's, but she cried only for herself.

"I-I-I-I . . ." she stammered. Jiana cut her off by drawing her boot dagger.

"Be thankful I don't cut your throat," she quietly told the girl. Sobbing and sniveling, the girl jumped up in terror and ran out of the house.

"Jiana, this is her house!"

"I don't care."

"And she did not choose what Dida did. It was not her fault; she had nothing to do with it."

"I don't care anything about her. I care only for my love. I'm going into his mind again and bring him back." Toldo looked unconvinced. He stared at the broken door, through which the girl had run. Then he shrugged, and turned away to give her privacy.

Jiana laid Dida out, and pulled off her own cloak to roll and place under his head. His eyes were open, but glazed. They did not track as she waved her hand across his vision.

She kissed him gently on her brow, and talked to the Dida she used to know.

"I really do love you. I never could say that. But it just can't work. It's not just young marrying old . . . your innocence is lamp-oil, and my worldguilt is seawater. They'll never mix. I wish it could be otherwise." She brushed back his hair, tenderly. "I wish to Snake and Eagle it could be. I'm sorry this happened. I tried to keep you away from what war really means. I guess it didn't work."

Jiana closed her eyes, and laid her head on Dida's soft, warm belly, thinking of that magickal day in the hay, so many lives ago.

If you were older, a little smarter about the world, less of an innocent little boy, we might have had one hell of an affair. But then I wouldn't have felt as much love for you as I do. It's a lovely paradox.

She took a deep breath, calmed her mind, and let her spirit rise ever-so-slightly above the lowest sphere. She let it touch him, caress him, then softly flowed inside his stomach to his mind.

Once before she had sought him there, smoothed out the terrors and led him home. Once he had fled back into her. It was harder this time, but she remembered the way. This time, she willfully ignored all of his secrets, for they were nothing to her now.

Dida had hidden himself well. He had burrowed deep. He had surrounded himself with walls of stone and oak, covered the structure with a black lake of forgetfulness, and frozen the surface of the lake with icicles of pain and humiliation. Jiana found him by looking for the most defended and inaccessible corner of Dida's Self.

Patiently, she broke through the barriers, one by one, until at last even the stone walls of self-pity yielded to her insistent pounding, and she dragged Dida from the mudbath at the center.

His soul trembled. He was terrified of what he would remember, and of Jiana's judgment. She bore him back anyway.

"You're colder than dead right now. How could it get any worse?"

She brought him back, with love as her only digging tool.

Jiana awoke, and raised her head from Dida's warmth. He looked at her, intelligence in his eyes. When he spoke, his voice was weak and hesitant. All of the strength he had learned from her was gone; he was a frightened little boy again.

"Jiana . . . I—I don't think—I can live it with."

"Why not? I live with myself having done things I'm afraid even to remember."

"I can't! I remember—I can still feel my hands her body

on, lying her on, crushing her . . . sticking—pushing my—
thing—her inside—"

"So? Just live it down, like everyone else."

Dida wept, and shook his head.

"I can't."

She watched him for a long time, brutally repressing
her own urge to cry with him.

"Then don't."

"How?"

"Either live with it, or end it. But for the sake of the
Scaled One, be a man about it either way!" Jiana waited
until he looked up at her again. "I saved something for
you," she said.

She reached up under her new, soft, woven tunic and
unstrapped Dida's hunting knife, which he had left behind
when Alanai had seized him from Toq's village.

Dida looked at it.

"I would rather use this," he said, tapping something
that wrapped around his waist: it was Wave.

"No! Bullshit, my sword's haunted enough with all the
people I've killed. Use your own damn blade! I have
enough ghosts weighing me down already." Jiana reached
out and unsnapped the buckle. She pulled on it, and the
sword broke open and straightened. She buckled it around
her own waist, then handed Dida the hunting knife.

"Either do it, or stop talking about it," she ordered.

"I love you, Jiana. In spite everything of, there's still that."

"Come on, kid, say it right."

Dida looked up at her, grateful for being with her in the
end. Then, before Jiana could prepare herself, he inverted
the blade and thrust it up into his gut.

Jiana gasped, and turned her face away. *He actually did
it!* ran through and through her mind. Even though she
had halfway expected that he would, the reality was far
worse than she had envisioned.

It was a messy death. Dida must have faltered at the last
moment, and missed, for he screamed and kicked and
doubled over the wound. Jiana forced herself to turn back
to the spectacle, hoping she could help, but there was no
question that the blow was mortal, even if it took him
quite a while to die.

Even more strongly than on the long walk through the City of Sickness, Jiana felt an unreality about the scene. Dida tried feebly to crawl, to get away from the agony in his stomach. He left a trail of blood as wide as her hand. But it was not really *Dida* who was dying, and it was not *Dida's* blood that stained the wooden floor and felt tacky and sticky on her fingers. It was just a play. In a moment, Dida would pull out the fake knife and stand up, laughing at the joke.

The pressure exploded inside her throat again, and this time it forced her into a huddled ball on the floor, eyes screwed shut and her hands over her ears. But the ghastly nightmare held her *still*, as his leg kicked over to lie next to her, and she could feel the convulsions as he died. She threw up then, feeling as if she was vomiting forth all of the fullness he had given her while he lived, leaving her empty.

At last, Dida was still. Jiana counted three hundred heartbeats before she cautiously unrolled and dared to look at him.

Not all of the bodies she had seen prepared herself for this one. He seemed so stiff and waxen it was hard to believe he had ever really been alive. Crazy thoughts occurred to her: *maybe he was just an invention of Jianabel, to torment me. Maybe he's in heaven, looking down on the scene.*

Maybe I should join him in death.

But finally she just stood up. She felt queasy, and could not remember a killing making her feel that way. *Death has never touched me before. My God, I've even enjoyed it! Dida—*

Cautiously averting her eyes from the tiny lump on the floor, she walked around and around the room, trying to unwind the taut spring that strained inside her throat. Toldo was not in evidence. *I bet he couldn't take what just happened. I wish to hellmoons I had left with him.*

Then suddenly, Jiana stopped, and coldly evaluated what had been Dida.

"It's all a matter of scale," she said, caring only that Dida could no longer hear.

"I understand Alanai now, Little Mouse. I see what the

prince saw, and it's important. We need a big picture, a faraway vision. But we need me, too, because you have to stop and admire the lonely rose in a field of shit.

"Maybe we even need that windbag Toldo, and his knowledge of the past and the out-of-bounds.

"But hell, we need the innocent little mice, too! You're an essential weight on the scale, too!"

And she knew at once what to do. She ran to the fireplace. Embers still glowed from a fire of an hour before. She pulled some tinder from her pack, and threw it on the coals, blowing gently on it until it caught. Then she held a splinter in the flickering flames until it, too, burned.

She removed the World's Dream from her pouch. When she touched it with the burning stick, it flashed immediately and flared as bright as the sun in her palm.

Then she closed her eyes, gritted her teeth, and crumbled the ashes in her fist.

Jiana shook her head, and found herself sitting dazed on the floor. The heart of the world had skipped a beat. Outside, she could still hear the BOOM! DOOM! of the shockwave of what she had done, as it washed across the ocean of soldiers and their victims like a tidal flood. The tumult slowly died—or was it in her mind?—and more and more of the players became aware that the Dream had been used, that there was nothing left to fight over in the life of this world.

Even Jiana was not sure of the full extent of what she had wished for; she had not actually verbalized it. But she knew one part of it. She staggered back to her feet and ran into the other room, where she had left Dida.

He was sitting up. He was still stunned, and his breathing was ragged, but his great wound had sealed tighter than Jiana's own. He looked at her in confusion.

"Well," she said defensively, "it was *my* Dream, goddamn it! Who the hell's going to say I was wrong?" She sat down next to Dida and held him until Prince Alanai arrived.

-5-

Alanai stumbled in, accompanied by no one.

"Did your heroes desert?" Jiana asked. Alanai only stared. "How did you find us here, anyways?"

When the prince spoke, he sounded hoarse and sick.

"You *used* it!" he accused.

"That's right. It's gone forever to this world. But it was in a good cause."

Jiana gestured at Dida.

"I wished him back to life. I told you it was in a good cause."

Alanai stared at Dida, and then at Jiana.

"You used the World's Dream of O-onakai Tonaronakai for *that?*"

"Yup. Gone forever, now. Why don't you follow it? Your Highness."

Numbly, he shook his head, as if to negate by executive fiat the hard reality of a world without the Dream.

"DAMN YOU!" he screamed. Jiana was taken aback; she had never before heard Prince Alanai lose his temper. "Don't you understand what you've done? *Don't you understand what you COULD have done?*" His voice rose to a piercing falsetto as he ranted. "What *I* could have done? WE COULD HAVE BEEN GODS! I could have—"

He raised his sword, and staggered toward her like a trool, a thin line of spittle dribbling down his chin. He stood over her, arm and sword raised, trembling.

Jiana pushed Dida off her lap, and slowly stood up.

"I'm not afraid of you, Alanai—you or your whole idiot kingdom! I know I'm a true warrior. I held the world in my palm—literally!—and I put it down again. Can you say the same?"

She stared him down. His glance flickered and wavered, and then dropped. She knew it then—had guessed it all along: *the clowns in Tuk Diraul were right. You could never be a real prince. You have no balls, Alanai.* But it would have been a cruelty to tell him.

Alanai's arm dropped to his side of its own accord. He turned and shambled out of the house.

"Never to be seen again in the Water Kingdom," a voice rumbled behind her.

"Toldo. How do you know that?" She looked back at him.

The giant shrugged.

"Well, that's the way I'm going to tell it, when I spread the heroic tale of Jiana and the World's Dream across the thirteen great lands. To hell with Dida! I'll grant you your *real* wish. I'll make you a hero, o self-effacing one."

"Thanks," she admitted. "I would really like that."

Dida spoke from the floor. She kneeled down quickly: it was the first words he had spoken since he had died.

"I wouldn't've let him kill you," he said, his voice strained. "I first would've sent him to hell back—I mean, I first would have sent him back to hell!" Weakly, he sheathed his hunting knife. He must have drawn it while Jiana concentrated on the prince.

"Oh, Dida . . . that's the very *first* thing you should have learned! When to defend, and when to let an attack fail of itself."

"I don't really love you, my love. Not like that—you know?" He gestured helplessly, unable to articulate what he truly felt.

"I'm glad, and I'm sad, too. But you're right; you don't. It wouldn't have worked anyways, kid. A mouse is too small to satisfy a bear."

"A what?"

"Never mind."

"It's all right . . . you can explain it to me later. Check?"

"Check. We can stick together for a while, for a few turns of the moons, anyway. I don't think a repeat performance of the hayride is a good idea, though."

"No?" Dida seemed disappointed, but it was just an ordinary disappointment, not the tragedy it would have seemed in his first life.

"I'd rather remember perfection than try to top it."

"Aye, and aye," Dida drawled, pure Souther. "Yan thought do be one beauty of . . ." Jiana rolled her eyes.

"Um. I do not wish to interrupt this little tete-a-tete, but what about good old Toq? If that boob Alanai could find the epicenter of the Dream, I'd bet somebody's life that Toq can."

"That's a nasty concept. Look—he's already on top, right? So the Dream couldn't do too much for him. More than anything else, I would guess he didn't want anyone else to get his paws on it . . . especially not Alanai."

"So how should we explain this to him?"

"I'm sure you'll think of a way, o silver tongue."

"Me!"

"The civilized world's a little too hot for me and Dida right now—just look at all those armies out there! I'll see you around sometime."

"I—I can't—Jiana!"

But she and Dida were already up and out the door, loping along the broken streets, in the fading glow of the bursting Dream.

"Jiana!" Dida gasped. He still was not fully recovered, and seemed even more drawn and tired than was she. "Where the—the hell—do we go?"

"To the frozen jungles of the steamy South, of course! Maybe we can find some more jade eyes."

His heart an open page.
His heart an unbound page.

The Dream was done. The City of Sickness grew pale once more in the slanting rays of the afternoon sun.

-After the ending . . . -

Sleeping Tifniz and Toq faced each other warily. For once, Tifniz neither nodded nor yawned.

"Perhaps," Toq ventured, "my player served us both well. Who knows what might have happened had that unpredictable prince gotten hold of the World's Dream? Even you might have had trouble maintaining control!"

"You are at your divine least when you gloat, Toq. Will you take a new player for the next game?"

"I will stand on the winning player."

"Then let us start again at once! Who knows . . ." Here, Tifniz allowed his voice to coil about Toq like a serpent, "the next game might end with Jiana Analena deciding Toq's fate . . ."

They both chuckled, but Toq's laugh was rather hollow.

The game began anew.

Afterward

What feminists call patriarchy, and what I call the alpha-male behavior program, is based upon one particular neurological imprint: that men are *strong and dominant,* and women are *weak and submissive.* This image is imprinted upon the child toddler in the preverbal stage of growth, and it comes from a variety of sources, not the least of which are television, music, and the movies. As the child grows, the cultural programs of gender differentiation reinforce the imprint and bring about the "natural" segregation of the sexes into aggressive males and nurturing females.

In their dim, groping way, fathers and father figures (the alpha males of the record industry and of Hollywood) recognize that certain cultural images are dangerous, because they might lead to the *wrong imprint*—little boys and girls might imprint aggressive female or nurturing male. If that happened, then all of our centuries of sex-role programming will be as tears in the desert, because you *cannot program in contradiction to the imprint.* (This is why those who have imprinted an addictive personality can change addictions, or live with a craving, but cannot become non-adicts without a traumatic reimprinting.)

If boys and girls imprinted dominance or submission without regard to gender, then our whole sex-differentiated *weltansicht* would collapse under the unsupported weight of laws and traditions outside society's consensus; *our so-called sexist laws and customs would be no more enforceable than the drug laws are today.*

It is this which terrifies the "top dogs," more than any feelings of artistic admiration or greed can counteract; for they are winners under today's rules—and in the collapse of contemporary reality, things can only get worse for each of them.